When the Clouds Roll By

Other books by Myra Johnson

One Imperfect Christmas

Autumn Rains

Romance by the Book

Where the Dogwoods Bloom

Gateway Weddings (anthology of above 3)

A Horseman's Heart

A Horseman's Gift

A Horseman's Hope

When the Clouds Roll By

Myra Johnson

Abingdon fiction
a novel approach to faith

When the Clouds Roll By

Copyright © 2013 by Myra Johnson

ISBN: 978-14267-5356-5

Published by Abingdon Press, P.O. Box 801, Nashville, TN 37202
www.abingdonpress.com

Published in association with the Natasha Kern Literary Agency, Inc.

Scripture quotation in the Acknowledgments taken from the Holy
Bible, New International Version®, NIV®. Copyright © 1973, 1978,
1984, 2011 by Biblica, Inc.™ Used by permission of Zondervan. All
rights reserved worldwide. www.zondervan.com. The "NIV" and
"New International Version" are trademarks registered in the United
States Patent and Trademark Office by Biblica, Inc.™

Scripture quotation on page 59 taken from The Authorized (King
James) Version. Rights in the Authorized Version in the United
Kingdom are vested in the Crown. Reproduced by permission of the
Crown's patentee, Cambridge University Press.

Library of Congress Cataloging-in-Publication Data

Johnson, Myra.
  When the clouds roll by / Myra Johnson.
    pages cm. — (Till We Meet Again ; one)
  ISBN 978-1-4267-5356-5 (Book—Paperback / Trade Paperback) 1. Veterans—Fiction.
2. Triangles (Interpersonal relations)—Fiction. 3. Arkansas—Fiction. I. Title.
  PS3610.O3666W44 2013
  813'.6—dc23

                                                           2013015983

Printed in the United States of America

1 2 3 4 5 6 7 8 9 10 / 18 17 16 15 14 13

This story is dedicated to the memory of my mother. I'll always remember those long car trips to visit the grandparents, and all the old songs you sang to while away the miles. "Till We Meet Again" was my favorite.

Till We Meet Again

There's a song in the land of the lily,
Each sweetheart has heard with a sigh.
Over high garden walls this sweet echo falls
As a soldier boy whispers goodbye:

Smile the while you kiss me sad adieu
When the clouds roll by I'll come to you.
Then the skies will seem more blue,
Down in Lover's Lane, my dearie.

Wedding bells will ring so merrily
Ev'ry tear will be a memory.
So wait and pray each night for me
Till we meet again.

Tho' goodbye means the birth of a tear drop,
Hello means the birth of a smile.
And the smile will erase the tear blighting trace,
When we meet in the after awhile.

Smile the while you kiss me sad adieu
When the clouds roll by I'll come to you

Then the skies will seem more blue
Down in Lover's Lane, my dearie,

Wedding bells will ring so merrily
Ev'ry tear will be a memory
So wait and pray each night for me
Till we meet again.

Music by Richard A. Whiting, lyrics by Raymond B. Egan

Acknowledgments

Our family first vacationed in Hot Springs, Arkansas, in the mid-1980s, and the city remains one of our favorite getaways. Once a year, we enjoy a week of kicking back and relaxing in our lakeside timeshare condo (which we almost never trade for an alternate location!). We've ridden the Ducks, those amphibious landing crafts from World War II, and laughed while the drivers gave their version of Hot Springs history in touristy spiels laced with humor and the occasional grain of truth. We've walked Bathhouse Row and toured the Fordyce, restored to its original glory. We've visited the Alligator Farm, purchased bowls and vases from Dryden Pottery, sampled spring water at the Mountain Valley Water Company, hiked up Hot Springs Mountain all the way to the observation tower. And for years I told myself someday . . . someday I'd write a novel set in Hot Springs.

Well, here it is, truly a labor of love. My only regret is that it wasn't until 2010 that I discovered the Garland County Historical Society, a treasure trove of books, registries, documents, photographs, and myriad other memorabilia preserving the story of Hot Springs and the surrounding area.

Acknowledgments

I am immensely grateful to Liz Robbins, Mike Blythe, Orval Allbritton, Gail Ashbrook, Clyde Covington, and all the staff and volunteers at GCHS who assisted in my research. A special thanks to Mike for reading a draft of the manuscript and pointing out discrepancies. Although I strove for accuracy, in some instances the specific details were elusive; in others, I plead forgiveness for any errors or assumptions made for the sake of storytelling.

I must also thank my intrepid agent, Natasha Kern, for believing in this story and finding just the right home for it with Abingdon Press. Natasha, you are an encourager of the first magnitude! I treasure your wisdom, expertise, guidance, and friendship, and I bless the day you signed me as your client!

Ramona Richards, my editor at Abingdon Press, deserves thanks as well. I'm so grateful for the opportunity to benefit from your insight, knowledge, and experience.

And where would I be without my band of cohorts in Seekerville (www.seekerville.net)? Audra, Cara, Debby, Glynna, Janet, Julie, Mary, Missy, Pam, Ruthy, Sandra, and Tina—twelve of the finest Christian authors you'll find anywhere, not to mention the greatest friends ever! Thanks for your love and prayers, for bearing me up through disappointments and celebrating with me in times of joy. You're the best!

A special thanks to our church choir friend and antique car aficionado Steve Benson, who invited us and our grandsons to his warehouse for an up-close-and-personal look at his amazing collection. What fun to actually see and touch early-twentieth-century vehicles similar to what my characters would have driven!

To my beautiful daughters, Johanna and Julena, bless you for believing in your mom, because you have truly blessed me with your love and encouragement. I couldn't be prouder of my girls!

My husband, Jack, deserves the biggest thank-you of all. In the 30 years I've been pursuing a writing career, his support has never wavered. He never complained (much) during the lean years when postage expenses and conference costs far outweighed any income my writing generated. Now that he's semiretired, he has assumed many of the household duties, including laundry, cooking, and grocery shopping, so I can spend more time at the computer. He is also my first reader, my sounding board, my research assistant, my number one PR man, and absolutely my very best friend! I love you, sweetie!

Finally, dear readers, thank you for sharing this journey with me. I hope you enjoy *When the Clouds Roll By*.

Let the message of Christ dwell among you richly as you teach and admonish one another with all wisdom through psalms, hymns, and songs from the Spirit, singing to God with gratitude in your hearts.

—Colossians 3:16 (NIV)

1

Hot Springs, Arkansas
November 11, 1918

If perfection existed this side of heaven, Annemarie Kendall had just achieved it.

A thrill dancing up her spine, she rotated the tall, teardrop-shaped vase and examined it inch by beautiful inch. When she wasn't busy keeping books for the family pottery business or putting together Red Cross comfort kits for the boys serving in France, she found immense satisfaction in creating her own works of ceramic artistry.

Certainly not her father's preferred use of her time, as he'd told her often enough, but Annemarie aspired to more than utilitarian bowls, urns, and butter churns—the mainstay of Kendall Pottery. Someday . . . someday . . . visitors who came to Hot Springs for the baths would also take home a one-of-a-kind piece of her ceramic art as a lasting reminder of their stay in this scenic and charming city.

For the past few months, Annemarie had been experimenting with a crystalline glazing method, striving for the perfect blend of ingredients, timing, and technique. With this vase, she'd achieved her vision—a design reminiscent of a Ouachita mountain sunrise, the view she'd awakened to nearly every morning of her life here in Hot Springs.

Her smile widened, her cheeks warming with the glow of victory. Her ears hummed with imagined celebratory cheers—

Except the cheering wasn't coming from inside her head. Beyond the workroom walls, the sound grew louder, the eruption of excitement drawing Annemarie's attention from the vase she so tenderly cradled.

Suddenly the door from the adjoining factory slammed open.

The vase slammed against the stone floor.

"Annemarie!" Her father blew into the room like a late-season tornado. "Annie-girl, have you heard the news?"

A thousand shimmering shards scattered at her feet, Annemarie barely comprehended his words. She stood frozen and held her breath—along with the shriek that begged for release.

One . . . two . . . three . . . four . . .

With a stubborn lift of her shoulders, she turned to face her father. What news could possibly have Papa—and the entire factory, so it seemed—in such a state of jubilation?

Unless . . .

"It's over, Annie-girl! The war is over!" Papa lunged toward her, his work boots grinding the pottery fragments to powder. He scooped her into his beefy arms and twirled her around the shop.

"What? *What* did you say?" Annemarie's heart slammed against her breastbone. She pounded her fists upon her father's thick shoulders until he released her. "Papa, is it true?"

"You heard me, girl! Kaiser Wilhelm has abdicated. They've signed the armistice. Our boys will be home before you know it!"

Head spinning, Annemarie stumbled backward and braced herself against a worktable. Tears choked her. She pressed the back of her fist against her mouth. Dear God, so much suffering, so many lives lost. How she'd prayed for this day—the Great War over at last! "Oh, Papa. Praise God!"

"Praise Him indeed!" Papa enfolded her in his arms, with gentleness and care this time, and let her sob into his grimy muslin shirt that smelled of sweat and smoke and clay. "There, there, Annie-girl, you're not the only lass weeping tears of joy this day. The Lord willing, Gilbert could be home by Christmas!"

Annemarie straightened and sniffed away her tears. Finding a handkerchief in her apron pocket, she dabbed at her cheeks with a trembling hand. "I almost forgot. A letter came this morning. I haven't even had a chance to open it."

"A letter from your sweetheart and you *forgot?*" Papa clucked his tongue.

Her happy smile faded. It pained her to admit the letters she'd so looked forward to this past year now evoked more distress than delight. She wrung her hands and swallowed the bitter lump of guilt. "I . . . I was working at the wheel when Morris delivered the mail. He said there was a letter from Gilbert, but my hands were covered with clay, and . . ."

Papa's disgruntled sigh spoke louder than words. His gaze slid to the pottery fragments littering the floor before he skewered Annemarie with a disapproving glare. If Papa weren't so anxious to learn the latest word from Gilbert, she'd surely be in for yet another lecture concerning the "abominable waste of time and money" spent upon her "art."

He was right, though. She had no business concerning herself with anything so frivolous when brave soldiers lay wounded or dying on the Western Front. She prayed the Lord's forgiveness for her selfishness.

"Well, go on, now. Get the letter and let's hear what our Gilbert has to say." Papa pushed the factory door closed and then plopped onto a stool and propped one elbow on the worktable.

Her face burning with remorse, Annemarie tucked in her chin and strode through another door to the front office. Sorting through the mail on her cluttered desk, she retrieved Gilbert's letter and hurried back to the workroom, careful to sidestep the broken vase. She would not mourn over pottery shards, not when Gilbert—her dear Gilbert, the boy she'd loved since childhood—would soon be in her arms again.

Letter in hand, she scooted a stool close to her father's. She slid a stubby, clay-stained fingernail under the envelope flap and tugged out the single page. The thin, cream-colored sheet crackled beneath her fingers as she unfolded the letter. As usual, the censors had already done their damage. Though as an officer Gilbert was particularly careful to avoid specifics, smudged ink and the occasional blacked-out word interrupted his spidery scrawl.

Smoothing the wrinkled page, Annemarie cleared her throat. "Shall I read it aloud?"

"Oh, no, no." Papa chuckled and waved a hand. "I'm sure it's full of personal stuff between you and your sweetheart. Just tell me the important parts—how he's mending, when he expects to ship home."

Annemarie stifled another frisson of worry. Wanting to shield both her family and Gilbert's from further concern, she hadn't shared how utterly *impersonal* Gilbert's latest letters had become—a coolness that had nothing to do with concerns over censorship. The letters he'd written as a West Point cadet, and even during the early months of his deployment to France, had been filled with declarations of love, how he strove every day not only to honor his father's memory but also to do both Annemarie and his country proud. It wasn't long, however, before the tone of his letters had darkened. While she knew he did his best to protect her from the ugliness of war, clearly he had been changed by it.

Then in August, word had arrived that Gilbert had been wounded. An artillery explosion had taken his left leg and shattered his left arm from wrist to shoulder. He'd nearly lost an eye and for eight days had feared permanent deafness. His first letters after evacuation to a French field hospital, dictated to the chaplain on duty, were terse and factual, which she'd attributed to the fact that Gilbert chose not to share too personally through a stranger.

Yet when he'd recovered enough to take up pen and paper himself, Annemarie could no longer deny the truth that lay beneath his deceptively courteous words. Her dear Gilbert, once bold and ambitious, full of life and love and great plans for their future, now seemed dispirited, desolate, defeated. Annemarie couldn't begin to fathom the horrors he'd endured, but surely with time he would recover both physically and emotionally. She prayed night and day for his healing—as well as for the strength within herself to stand strong at Gilbert's side as the wife he would need in the months and years ahead.

Slowly, determinedly, Annemarie perused the letter, dated Sunday, October 6. "*Still in the hospital . . . constant headache but some vision returning to my left eye. . . . They say I'm one of the lucky ones—if you can call it that. So many wounded, so many dead and dying. More every day. Will this blasted war never end?*"

Annemarie's heart broke to realize Gilbert had penned these somber words only weeks before the armistice. With trembling fingers, she brushed away a tear. Her father reached across the space between them and patted her knee as she silently read on. "*Waiting for the next transport home—possibly December. Don't know where I'll end up yet. Probably a military hospital somewhere like _____.*"

The name was obliterated, but wherever it was, Annemarie would find a way to get there as soon as possible. She looked up with a hopeful smile. "He's getting better, Papa. He may be home next month! He says—"

The jangle of the telephone interrupted her. Papa hefted his bulk off the stool and hurried to the front office to answer. "Kendall Pottery Works, Joseph Kendall speaking."

Within seconds, Annemarie discerned the caller was Evelyn Ballard, Gilbert's mother, and it sounded as if she'd received a letter as well. Annemarie rushed into the office and hovered at her father's elbow, waiting to hear what news Mrs. Ballard's letter contained.

"Of course, we're as thrilled as you, Evelyn," Papa was saying. "What a homecoming that boy will have! Here, I'll let you speak directly with Annemarie."

A dark tress had worked loose from Annemarie's bun, and she tried in vain to tuck it back into place. The arrogant Evelyn Ballard, with all her wealth and sophistication, never failed to intimidate Annemarie. She could feel the woman's critical eye upon her even through the telephone line. Hesitantly, she accepted the earpiece from her father. "Good morning, Mrs. Ballard. It's wonderful news, isn't it?"

"Oh, my dear, it's simply the best! I've already made some calls, and thanks to my late husband's military connections, I've arranged for Gilbert to continue his recuperation at the Army and Navy Hospital right here in Hot Springs. We'll be able to visit him every day until he's discharged."

"Really? I'm so glad!" Annemarie drew her lower lip between her teeth. "How . . . how did he sound to you?"

Mrs. Ballard released a long and pain-filled sigh. "Oh, my dear, our poor lad has suffered so much. Of course, he is unhappy about his current state of disability and naturally concerned about the prospect of a lengthy recovery. But we cannot give up hope. We must encourage him in every way possible and keep him constantly in our prayers."

Fresh tears sprang into Annemarie's eyes. "Always."

"And once he's home and we set the wedding plans in motion, I'm sure it will lift his spirits even more."

Annemarie squeezed her eyes shut. "Perhaps we shouldn't rush him in that regard. He'll have so many adjustments to make."

"Yes, but keeping his mind occupied with happy anticipation of your nuptials will be the best medicine, I'm positive." Voices in the background drew Mrs. Ballard's attention for a moment. She came back on the line to say, "Sorry, I must ring off for now. But I'll have you and your mother over for luncheon soon, and we can start making plans!"

"Yes, well . . ." No use arguing with the woman—truly a force to be reckoned with. If Mrs. Ballard had been a general, the Allies would have won the war in a single day. Annemarie said good-bye and set the earpiece on the hook.

She pivoted toward the workroom, only to find her father had returned to the factory. Beyond the open door, she could hear his booming voice instructing the pottery workers to finish their current tasks and then take the rest of the day off in celebration of the armistice.

Annemarie's current task, unfortunately, was sweeping up the remnants of her shattered vase. She found a broom and dustpan and with each stroke sang a little song in her head: *My Gilbert is coming home soon!*

With a new lightness in her step, she made quick work of depositing the broken pottery in the waste bin.

Yes, perhaps it was time to put this dream to rest once and for all, because when Gilbert returned to Hot Springs, everything about her life was sure to change.

2

Aboard the U.S.S. Comfort
December 1918

*S*mooth seas today, praise God!

For the first time in days, Army Chaplain Samuel Vickary actually finished his breakfast without the urgent need to rush to the nearest head. He'd already "fed the fishes" too many times to count on this journey. The *U.S.S. Comfort,* formerly a passenger steamship, had been converted to a floating military hospital, and now ferried troops home from the war—a more blessed Christmas gift no one could ask for!

Teeth brushed, his uniform inspected, Bible in hand, Samuel prepared himself for a task that had grown even more draining to his spirit than those daily bouts of seasickness were to his body—morning rounds among the returning wounded. Once again he prayed for the Lord to give him words that would comfort and reassure, words to give strength and hope.

Words he prayed would find their way deep into his own wounded soul.

A refreshing breeze greeted him as he stepped out on deck. The ambulatory patients preferred the sea air over the medicinal smells of the wards, and who could blame them? Not to mention the smoke from their cigarettes dispelled much more quickly in the open air. While serving in the trenches, Samuel had been tempted many times to take up the tobacco habit but managed to resist. Tobacco might provide temporary relief from the stresses of war, but it too easily became a physical craving. Faith came hard enough these days, and Samuel intended to crave nothing more than his Lord and Savior.

He inhaled a bracing breath and tightened his grip on his Bible. Still getting his sea legs, he slid one hand along the rail as he walked. The deck beneath his feet rose and fell in a comforting rhythm, a certitude that somewhere ahead of them across the vast Atlantic, home and loved ones waited.

At least for some.

"Padre, will you pray with me?" A doughboy reclining on a deck chair reached a hand toward Samuel.

The thin, freckle-faced boy didn't look a day over seventeen. Samuel knelt beside him. "What's your name, son?"

"Private William Jeffries, sir. I survived Belleau Wood with nothin' worse than a bullet in my leg, but now they say I got somethin' called shell shock." The private couldn't seem to stop shivering, even beneath a wool blanket. "The things I saw, the nightmares—I can't sleep, can't hardly force myself to eat."

"I know, son. I know." Samuel knew all too well and briefly closed his eyes against the specters that still haunted him day and night, the doubts and questions that rose in his heart to battle with the remnants of his faith.

Private Jeffries fixed Samuel with a look of desperation. "Do ya think it'll ever go away? The fear, I mean? The shakes? The nightmares?"

"I doubt we'll ever forget what we saw over there." Samuel pressed the boy's hands between his own and squeezed hard. "But you must cling to the assurance that Jesus saw it too. Give it all to Him. Trust Him to carry you through the agony of remembering, just as He carried you through the battle."

The boy nodded, moisture rimming his reddened eyelids. "Thanks, Padre. I know you're right. And I do trust Jesus. It's just . . . so hard."

"This is why we need Jesus all the more." Samuel bowed his head over their clasped hands and lifted up Private William Jeffries to the Lord in prayer, while in his heart he prayed for all the other doughboys and marines and sailors and aviators, the doctors and nurses and Red Cross volunteers, the mothers and wives and sisters and children—

Dear Lord, he could pray night and day for the next century and never cover all the suffering and loss.

If he could only be certain God still listened.

If only he dared to hope heaven hadn't barred its doors against him for eternity.

With a parting word of peace to the young soldier, Samuel rose and wearily went on his way. One after another, he sat with the men, listening to their stories while silently reliving his own.

Desperate for a cup of coffee as the morning wore on, Samuel detoured to the mess. Attacks by U-boats during the war had severely handicapped supply lines, which meant what he'd find there would be little more than coffee-flavored water, but he'd need every last molecule of caffeine to get through the day. After filling a mug with the weak brew, he sank into the first empty chair, curled his hands around the warmth of the cup, and inhaled the aroma. Maybe he could extract some extra caffeine from the escaping steam.

Seconds later Dr. Donald Russ plopped into the seat across from him with his own steaming mug. "You look beat, Padre. It isn't even noon yet."

Samuel gave a sardonic laugh. "You look pretty tired yourself, Doc."

"After this bloody war we just fought, who wouldn't be exhausted?" The lean, stoop-shouldered man lowered his gaze. "And you know full well that for most of the men under my care, the toughest battle is still ahead of them."

Samuel nodded. He'd spent the last several weeks working alongside Dr. Russ in a French field hospital, so no explanations were necessary.

The doctor took a cautious sip of coffee and then narrowed his eyes at Samuel. "I can give you something if you need it for sleep."

"Thanks, but I'm managing." Wakefulness seemed almost preferable to the troubled dreams neither drugs nor Dr. Russ's compassionate concern could vanquish. Samuel ran a thumb along the ragged leather binding of his Bible. If only he could find the comfort there that he tried so hard to impart to others.

"Say, could you look in on one of my patients later?" The doctor massaged his temple with two fingers. "Turns out he's an officer from my home state of Arkansas—mending okay, but I worry about him."

"Certainly. What's his name?"

"First Lieutenant Gilbert Ballard. Wounded at the Marne River. Lost a leg, nearly lost an arm."

"Ballard, yes. I've tried to talk with him once or twice. He . . . wasn't too receptive to what I had to offer."

"Figures." The doctor offered Samuel a pleading smile. "Would you mind trying again? Seems like the closer we get to home, the more depressed he gets. Anyway, something tells me you two might be good for each other."

Samuel wondered at the doctor's remark. Did he suppose their wounded spirits might find some commonality—more so than with the myriad other traumatized soldiers Samuel dealt with day after miserable day? "All right, I'll do my best. Does he have family waiting for him?"

"His mother and a brother. His father died a hero in the Spanish-American War." Dr. Russ heaved a tired sigh. "You know exactly how it is—boys going off to war with visions of gallantry and a speedy victory, only to find themselves shot up and shell-shocked. Now they can't imagine how they'll ever return to their old lives."

Indeed. Samuel could barely remember what his life had been like before he enlisted and shipped over to France.

Truth be told, he didn't want to remember. At least in his role as chaplain he could focus on others' concerns instead of dwelling on his own. "Will he recover enough to work again, make a decent life for himself?"

"Physically, yes. He'll eventually get a prosthesis, learn how to compensate for the bad arm. But the trauma, the battle fatigue . . ." The doctor glanced up at Samuel and gave his head a helpless shake. "I wish I could help him—help *you* more than I have—but there's too much we still don't know about the human brain."

Samuel tilted his mug and stared into the murky depths. The Marne—he'd been there, too. They may have held off the Germans, but the cost in human lives was staggering. Then Saint Mihiel. The Meuse-Argonne. He could still smell the gunpowder, feel the mud of the trenches beneath his waterlogged boots, taste the stench of blood and fear and hopelessness.

"Sam? You sure you're okay?"

Samuel blinked several times. "I'll be happy to look in on Lieutenant Ballard. I'll let you know how it goes."

"Blast it all, I *don't* need your help!" Using his good arm, Gilbert Ballard gave the corpsman a shove and swung his right leg off the edge of the bed.

"Careful, sir, you'll—"

Gilbert's knee buckled the moment his bare foot hit the floor. With no left leg to break his fall, he tumbled forward into the corpsman's sturdy arms.

"I tried to tell you, sir." The corpsman lowered Gilbert into the waiting wheelchair.

Gilbert ground his teeth as he covered the remnants of his dignity with the blanket the corpsman offered. "Save your 'I told you so.' You made your point."

"Sir, I just meant to—"

"Go pester someone else, will you?" Gilbert tried to wheel the chair into the narrow aisle, but with his left arm still in a sling, the best he could do was turn in a drunken arc.

The corpsman took a step forward but froze in his tracks when Gilbert snarled a curse.

"Perhaps I can be of help?"

Gilbert swung his head around. A tall, sandy-haired man in a chaplain's uniform stood at the foot of the bed. At the sight of the tiny gold cross pinned to the chaplain's collar, something cracked inside Gilbert's heart. He sucked in a quavering breath. "Sorry, Padre, didn't see you standing there."

The chaplain nodded to the corpsman, who squeezed past the wheelchair and hurried on to assist another patient. "Lieutenant Ballard, right?"

Gilbert shrugged. "Says so on my chart. Some days I'm not so sure anymore."

The chaplain glanced away for a moment. "That's okay. There are days I'd just as soon forget who I am too."

"Is that allowed?" Gilbert lifted an eyebrow. "You being a man of the cloth and all."

A dark look clouded the chaplain's gray eyes, but he covered it with a lazy smile. "I'm Army Chaplain Samuel Vickary. I've stopped by before, but . . ."

A pang of remorse tightened Gilbert's throat. He gritted his teeth against the constant thrumming between his temples. "Sorry if I gave you the brush-off. This headache makes me half-crazy most of the time."

"Understandable." The chaplain nodded toward the wheelchair. "Looks like you were headed out for some air. Feel like some company?"

"Sure, why not?" Gilbert gave his useless left arm a disgusted shake. "Apparently I'm not getting anywhere under my own power."

He allowed the chaplain to wheel him onto the starboard deck and tried to ignore the stares of the men they passed along the way. Or maybe they weren't staring at him but into their own tortured souls.

The chaplain parked Gilbert next to the rail and pulled a deck chair alongside him. The ocean air tasted of brine, and the sunshine on his face felt good. He closed his eyes and drew a hand through his wind-tousled hair.

"I understand you're from Arkansas," the chaplain said.

"Hot Springs." It would only be polite to ask where the chaplain hailed from, but Gilbert let the impulse pass. Politeness didn't come easy these days.

"Bet your family can't wait to see you again."

"My mother will fuss over me. My brother will brag about me to all his friends." Gilbert snorted an ugly laugh. "The conquering hero home at last."

"It's no small thing, serving your country as you did. I'm sure they're proud. I'm sure your father would be proud, too."

Gilbert slanted the padre an accusing glare. "You've been talking to the doc."

Chaplain Vickary tilted his head and smiled. "It's true. Dr. Russ did ask me to visit with you. He mentioned your father also served in the army and lost his life in the Spanish-American War."

Gilbert glanced away. "At least he died a hero, not a cripple."

"Sometimes it takes more courage to go on living." The chaplain fell into silence for several long moments, his thumbs scraping the binding of his Bible so hard Gilbert wondered how he kept from wearing a hole straight through to the flimsy pages.

Finally the chaplain spoke again, his voice muted. "And do you have a wife or a sweetheart waiting for you back home?"

Gilbert's gut twisted as Annemarie's face danced across his mind's eye—raven curls that resisted every effort to restrain them, eyes as big and brown and luminous as a fawn's, lips so pink and ripe that he could taste their sweetness even in his dreams.

"Yes," he said on a pained breath. "I have a sweetheart. We're—we were planning to marry as soon as the war ended."

"That's terrific." The padre cleared his throat and sat forward. "What's her name? Do you have a photograph?"

"Annemarie. Her name's Annemarie Kendall." Gilbert reached into the breast pocket of his pajama top and slid out a worn, ragged-edged photo stained with flecks of Gilbert's own blood. Heart thudding, he stared into Annemarie's smiling eyes before passing the picture to the chaplain.

Chaplain Vickary smoothed the wrinkled photograph atop his Bible cover. "She's beautiful. You're a lucky man, Lieutenant."

"Yeah, I'm one lucky son of a gun."

Silence settled over them again, while the sound of waves crashing against the prow swallowed up the muted conversations going on nearby. Gilbert took one last look at Annemarie's faded portrait where it still lay upon the chaplain's Bible and then tore his gaze away. He knotted his right fist until it ached.

Pounding it against his thigh, he murmured, "How can I go home like this? *How?*"

The padre covered Gilbert's fist with his palm. "What are you afraid of, son?"

Son. The man couldn't be more than a couple of years older than Gilbert. But then the war had aged them all—the ones it hadn't killed, anyway—stolen their youth while turning thousands of them into little better than helpless infants.

"What am I afraid of?" Gilbert raised his eyes to meet the padre's. "Her pity."

3

Hot Springs, Arkansas

 nnemarie spread peach preserves across a bite-sized piece of a plump, golden roll. "These are delicious, Mrs. Ballard—so light and flaky."

"Marguerite's special recipe, dear. I'm sure she'd be delighted to share it with you."

Marguerite, the Ballards' longtime servant—of course. Gilbert's mother probably hadn't lifted a finger in her own kitchen in years. "I'll be sure to ask her before we leave." Not that it would help. Annemarie's own culinary skills left much to be desired.

The older woman chuckled. "And how many times must I ask you to call me *Mother* Ballard?"

"I suppose I'm still getting used to the idea." An uneasy shiver traveled Annemarie's spine, but she covered it with a smile. "I can hardly believe Gilbert is finally coming home."

She couldn't admit her deepest fears to her future mother-in-law—that there would be no wedding, that Gilbert's feelings toward her had cooled. Every time she reread his recent letters, the dearth of any words of affection, much less even the slightest reference to their future together, made her heart lurch.

Annemarie's mother cleared her throat softly. "Perhaps you'd pass me the preserves, dear?"

Annemarie looked up with a start and realized she'd been staring into space. "Sorry, Mama." She reached across the table with the crystal bowl of preserves, but the dish clipped her mother's water glass, toppling it and soaking the white damask tablecloth.

Annemarie jumped up with a gasp and mopped at the spill with her napkin. "How clumsy of me! Here, Mama, let me refill your glass."

"Don't trouble yourself, Annemarie." Mrs. Ballard caught her arm. "I'll ring for Marguerite."

"No, please. I insist." Hurrying to the kitchen with the empty glass, Annemarie collapsed against the counter and berated herself for acting like such a ninny.

She felt even sillier when Marguerite stepped through the back door with an empty dishpan. A gust of chilly December air nipped at Marguerite's skirt as she kicked the door closed with her heel. She cast a nervous smile toward the swinging door to the dining room. "Oh my, did Miz Ballard ring for me and I didn't hear?"

"Don't fret. I upset my mother's water glass and came looking for the pitcher." Annemarie spied it on the end of the counter and went to fill the glass.

Marguerite set the pan in the sink and wiped her slender, coffee-colored hands on a dishtowel. "You look a mite flushed, Miss Annie. You feeling okay?"

"Me? I'm fine." Annemarie gave a pained laugh and set down the glass and pitcher. "Well, maybe not so fine. Honestly, Marguerite, all this talk of Gilbert's homecoming and wedding plans—shouldn't we at least wait until he's home and has a chance to recover and get his bearings?"

A look of understanding narrowed the servant's soft brown eyes. "Getting cold feet, are we?" Marguerite pressed her cool palms against Annemarie's cheeks. "Why, honey-girl, you and Gilbert was destined to be together. I knew from the time you was both in diapers, and I was powdering your sweet little bottoms."

If Annemarie wasn't flushed before, she certainly was now. She rolled her eyes and drew Marguerite close for a hug before striding across the kitchen and sinking into a chair at the long oak table. "It isn't that I don't want to marry Gilbert. I love him as much as ever—more, if possible! It's just . . ." Her chest ached. She dropped her forehead into her hands. "I'm afraid he no longer wants to marry me."

It was the first time she'd voiced her fears aloud, and now, as the words echoed in the quiet kitchen, Annemarie knew what she had to do. She had to convince both her mother and Mrs. Ballard to postpone any further discussion of a wedding until she and Gilbert could talk face to face.

Marguerite settled into the chair next to Annemarie's. She eased Annemarie's hands away from her face and pressed them to her own bosom. "Now what would make you say such a thing, Miss Annie? You know Gilbert loves you with heart and soul, always has. Just 'cause he went off to war and got himself shot up don't mean he's changed his mind about marrying you. Yes, it'll be hard, him losing his leg and all, but you're both strong of character with a firm faith in Jesus. If that don't see you through, then—"

"Annemarie, dear? Did you find the—" Stepping into the kitchen, Mrs. Ballard gave a surprised sniff. "Is everything all right?"

Marguerite popped up from her chair. "Everything's just fine, Miz Ballard. We was just talking."

Annemarie rose with a shaky smile and went to retrieve her mother's glass. "My goodness, I completely lost track of what I came in here for. By now Mama will think I hiked all the way to the Mountain Valley Water Company and back."

"I should think so. I began to worry Marguerite's spicy rémoulade might have caused you dyspepsia."

"Absolutely not—it was delicious!" Annemarie sidled toward Mrs. Ballard. "Shall we go back in to lunch? I'm so sorry for the interruption."

"Very well." Mrs. Ballard cast Marguerite a disapproving glare. "You may serve dessert now, if you're finished monopolizing my guest."

Marguerite lowered her gaze and curtsied. "Sorry, ma'am. Be right in to clear the table and fetch dessert." She winked at Annemarie. "Bread pudding with lemon sauce, your favorite. I'll serve you an extra big portion."

Halfway through the door, Mrs. Ballard turned with an arched brow. "Not *too* large, Marguerite. Annemarie must watch her figure if she's going to fit into her mother's lovely lace wedding gown."

"Yes'm." Marguerite glanced at Annemarie and whistled out a breath. As soon as Mrs. Ballard left the room, she whispered, "Between you and me, girl, that is one bossy woman. If she didn't pay so well, I'd—"

Annemarie couldn't suppress a laugh. "I know, I know. You'd quit and go to work for Mr. Fordyce at his fancy new bathhouse." She gave her head a small shake and started through the door, then paused to smirk over her shoulder. "And make my dessert a triple-sized portion, with extra lemon sauce, if you please. I'm going to need the fortification."

"Padre! Ya gotta help me! I don't wanna die!"

"Hold on, son. Help's coming—just hold on. 'The Lord is my shepherd'—say it, son. Say it with me."

"I can't—it hurts! Oh, Jesus, it hurts so bad!"

Samuel awoke with a start, the smell of smoke and blood burning his nostrils. His gaze darted right, then left. Soldiers everywhere, a sea of army green. A constant clack-clack enveloped him, then a mournful whistle in the distance.

"Padre?" Someone was patting his arm. "Hey, it's okay. We're still on the train."

"The train . . ." He gave his eyes a violent rub and focused on the face of the soldier next to him. "Guess I dozed off. Where are we?"

"Somewhere between Richmond and Nashville." The soldier slanted his lips in a sympathetic smile. "I suppose it'll be awhile before we quit hearing the sounds of war in our sleep."

"Guess so." Samuel sat up a little straighter. He tugged at the collar of his uniform and tried to draw a full breath. His thumb scraped the tiny gold cross, and he clamped his jaws together with a shudder. *Where were You, God? Where were You in all this horror?*

As usual, he got no answer.

Yea, though I walk through the valley of the shadow of death . . .

He tried hard to believe the Scriptures, but sometimes—too often of late—they seemed like empty words. Empty promises for a world gone crazy.

He cleared his parched throat and stood, grabbing the seat back to steady himself. After finally growing accustomed to the ship's rise and fall, now he tottered to the lurch and sway of the train.

He edged up the corners of his mouth in a semblance of a smile and glanced at the soldier. "I'm going to find some water and then check on a friend. May I bring you anything?"

"Thanks, I'm fine. Gonna try and catch some shut-eye myself before the next stop." The doughboy scooted lower in the seat, tipped his hat to Samuel, and crossed his arms over his chest.

Samuel nodded and stepped into the aisle. As he started toward the rear of the car, the men he passed glanced up to offer smiles and handshakes. These were the lucky ones—the ones who'd survived—the ones released to go home while thousands more remained behind as part of the Army of Occupation. The journey had been a long one, and fatigue shown in their eyes, mixed with joy and relief . . . and no small amount of sadness for those who'd never see home again.

Making his way to the dining car, he found himself in another sea of bodies. Here the laughter and celebration rose to an ear-splitting cacophony. Civilians reveled with dough-boys, sailors, and marines, many still sporting bandages and crutches. Only a few wore the ubiquitous white gauze masks that supposedly protected against the Spanish influenza. Instead, they lifted glasses and beer steins high to toast the end of the Great War.

It struck Samuel as ironic that a microscopic organism could prove almost more deadly than the worst firepower the Germans had thrown at the Allies. Over the past several months, the disease had reached epidemic proportions, claiming thousands of lives at home and abroad, many of them soldiers who never even made it to the front.

As for Samuel, he was almost beyond caring about an enemy he couldn't even see. Death had stared him in the face too many times already. With a nod at a half-drunk sailor, he wedged himself up to the bar. "Just a glass of water, please."

"Sure thing, Chaplain." The bartender filled a glass and slid it across the counter. "Rowdy bunch we got here, eh? Guess they got plenty to celebrate."

Samuel thanked the man and downed the water in three quick gulps. By the time he wove through the jostling crowd to the next coach, his ears were ringing almost as badly as in the trenches amid the deafening explosions of grenades and artillery fire.

It was quieter in this car, more subdued. These men, still healing from massive war wounds, faced months of recuperation. Many had already departed the train in Washington, D.C., to be admitted to Walter Reed Hospital for further treatment. Others would continue their recovery either with loved ones or in a medical facility closer to home.

Samuel had barely stepped through the door before a soldier in the first row recognized his cross and insignia and stopped him to request a prayer. Samuel obliged—what else could he do? It was his job, after all. *Lord, give me strength.*

Another soldier, another prayer, and finally he reached the seat where Lieutenant Gilbert Ballard reclined. As Dr. Russ had predicted, they'd formed a bond of sorts while aboard the *U.S.S. Comfort*, and when Samuel learned the lieutenant was shipping home to the Army and Navy Hospital in Hot Springs, he decided maybe he'd like to go there, too. The thought of returning home to Fort Wayne held no appeal, nor did the idea of serving at one of the larger military hospitals, where ministering to hundreds of wartime wounded day after day would only extend his torment.

No, according to Gilbert, the much smaller facility at Hot Springs treated mainly older veterans for chronic conditions such as arthritis, rheumatism, gout, and various skin diseases and would receive few returning wounded from the Great War. To Samuel it sounded like the ideal situation—a chance, with God's help, to rest and heal and find his way again. At his first opportunity he'd put in a request for new orders, and his commanding officer had quickly agreed.

No doubt all it took was one look at Samuel's recent service record. He should probably thank God they had not stamped it UNFIT FOR DUTY.

Gilbert looked up with tired eyes. "You look worse than me, Padre. At least you've got two legs to stand on."

The train gave a sudden jerk, and Samuel had to grab for a handhold to stay upright. He forced a chuckle. "Not so sure my two legs are doing me much good at the moment." He lowered himself into the empty seat next to Gilbert. "How are you holding up, Gil? Much pain?"

"You mean besides this headache that won't quit?" Gilbert grimaced and rubbed his left thigh, now just a stump. "They said I could have phantom leg pain for a long time to come. Just this morning I tried to scratch an itch on the bottom of my foot, but my foot wasn't there."

Samuel couldn't even imagine. "Can I get you anything? Water? Something to eat?"

"I'm okay." Gilbert swiveled his head toward the window. He clenched and unclenched his right fist in rhythm with the clack of the train wheels.

They were in the mountains now, somewhere in Tennessee. "We should be in Little Rock by tomorrow, then on to Hot Springs. You'll be glad to be home, finally get some rest."

The lieutenant's lips flattened. "I wish they'd killed and buried me in France."

"You don't mean that."

"You bet I mean that."

The conversation was one they'd had a hundred times already, and Samuel struggled to come up with new arguments against Gil's defeatist attitude. His thoughts drifted to the tattered photograph of Gilbert's fiancée, the beautiful Annemarie. What Samuel wouldn't give to be going home to his sweetheart, to drown in her welcoming kisses, to fill his senses with the scent of her perfume and the feel of her glossy hair sliding through his fingers.

Helen, Helen . . . when I needed you most . . . why?

"You ever gonna tell me about her?"

Samuel pulled himself from his reverie. "I'm sorry?"

"The woman who broke your heart. Come on, Sam, tell me your sob story. Get my mind off my own."

Samuel gave a nervous laugh. "What makes you think I have a story to tell?"

"Because of the way you look at Annemarie's picture every time I pull it out. It's in your eyes, Padre. There for all the world to see." Gil nudged him with his elbow. "So who was she?"

A harsh breath raked through Samuel's lungs. He leaned forward and clasped his hands between his knees. "Her name was Helen. Helen Oakes. As pretty as your Annemarie but with bright golden hair and a sprinkle of freckles across her nose."

"So what happened?"

Helen's last letter was still tucked away in Samuel's kit bag. He should have burned it months ago, but instead he continued to torture himself by rereading it from time to time to see if by some crazy chance he'd misread the words that ended things between them.

He stared at the floorboards between his boots, remembering against his will. "We got engaged a few months after I finished seminary. We were planning to marry and move into the parsonage next door to the church where I'd already been called to pastor. But then America entered the war, and in my heart I knew God needed me serving at the front more than my congregation needed me in Fort Wayne."

Gilbert shifted to ease the pressure on his stump. "Can't say it was God's call, but the only thing I ever wanted to do with my life was to serve in the army and fight for my country." He tugged Annemarie's photograph from his pocket and stared in silence for so long, Samuel thought he'd drifted off.

Then Gilbert asked, "Did Helen say she'd wait for you?"

Samuel sat back and inhaled a tired breath. "She did, at first. But as the casualty lists grew, so did her fear. In her last letter, she apologized for being so weak, for doubting God's power to bring me home safely, but she couldn't live with the constant dread. She wrote she needed to get on with her life and find some peace."

"I'm sorry, Padre. That was cruel."

"She didn't mean to be. And I can't blame her. I remind myself how hard it's been for those waiting at home for their soldier's return, every day filled with the fear of bad news."

"Will you try to see her again, maybe patch things up?"

"Too late. My mother wrote a couple of months ago saying Helen had become engaged to a banker and is moving to Indianapolis." Just as well. Samuel had long since given up on the idea of returning to his pastorate or even attempting to resume his old life. He reached for the photo of Annemarie, drawn to it as always in ways he couldn't explain. "May I?"

Gilbert passed him the picture. "At least I know Annemarie is faithful." He leaned his head against the window, where snowflakes now collected in the corners. "But I'm going to do her a big favor once I get back to Hot Springs. She'll not be saddled with a cripple for a husband."

The finality in Gilbert's tone set off new warning bells in Samuel's brain. "What are you saying, Gil? What are you planning to do?"

"What I should have done a long time ago. Now leave me alone, Sam. I want to sleep."

Samuel had the sick feeling Gilbert was talking about a completely different kind of sleep, a sleep from which he'd never awaken. He wouldn't be the first soldier driven to suicide by the horrors of this wretched war. Father, help him find the strength to keep going. Give him the will to live.

He studied the girl in the portrait and realized with sudden certainty that if things were different—if he were coming home to a woman like Annemarie—he'd fight harder for her love than any doughboy ever fought on the Western Front.

4

"Wait, Mama, I can't find my other glove!" Annemarie tore through the assortment of scarves, mittens, and stocking caps in the base of the carved oak coat tree.

"You had them both this morning, dear. Now hurry or we'll be late!" Mama opened the front door, letting in a chilling gust. "Your father is already waiting in the drive with the motorcar."

Annemarie could smell the exhaust fumes from her father's Model T. He gave the horn an impatient tootle. Mama cast Annemarie a chiding glance and hurried down the front steps.

The horn screeched once more, and Annemarie banged down the lid on the coat tree bin. Glove or no glove, she must be on her way, or they'd never get to the station before Gilbert's train arrived. She dashed out the door, slamming it behind her. "I'm coming, Papa!"

Crawling into the rear seat behind her mother, Annemarie shivered and tucked her bare hand into the opposite coat sleeve. The depot wasn't far, just across town and down the hill to Elm and Market Streets—not nearly enough time to stop the ridiculous tremors that started the moment she went upstairs to change out of her paint-and-clay-stained smock.

After a hurry-up bath in tepid water, she'd ransacked her wardrobe for something presentable—something Gilbert's fussy, overbearing mother would approve of. She'd finally chosen her cobalt-blue wool suit with the shawl collar.

Mama swiveled to glance over her shoulder. "Goodness, Annemarie, I can hear your teeth chattering! You should have worn a warmer coat."

"This *is* my warmest coat." Annemarie hugged herself and clamped her teeth together to silence the noise.

"Well, we're almost there—watch the horse and buggy, Joseph!"

Papa braked and sounded the horn. "I'll mind my driving, Ida, and you mind our anxious daughter."

"I'm *not* anxious, Papa." Annemarie's mouth twisted. All right, she was *quite* anxious, truth be told. The thought that within the hour—perhaps in only minutes!—she'd see her beloved Gilbert again had her practically bursting out of her skin.

For days now she'd been imagining the moment, at least the way she hoped and prayed it would be. Their gazes would collide, a mile-wide grin spreading across Gilbert's face. Love would shine in his eyes, all thoughts of war forgotten. With one happy kiss she'd rekindle love and hope in her Gilbert's heart. He'd once again become the boy she remembered, the man she intended to spend the rest of her life loving and laughing with, growing into contented old age at his side.

They arrived at the depot, and Papa found a parking spot across the street. It was a gloomy day for a homecoming, a cold December wind blowing out of the north beneath lowering gray clouds and ice crystals nipping at bare cheeks and noses. Though when out and about they'd been wearing masks to protect against the Spanish influenza, recent news reports indicated the worst had passed. For this one special day, Mama had said it might be all right to leave the masks in their pockets.

Not to mention it would be hard to share a much anticipated welcome-home kiss through gauze.

Inside the Mediterranean-style building, Annemarie and her parents found Mrs. Ballard. She stood near a window with her son Thomas, Gilbert's younger brother and an assistant manager at the Arlington Hotel. A childhood bout with rheumatic fever had weakened Thomas's heart and kept him out of the war, and he hadn't been able to hide his envy of Gilbert. Would he feel any differently, Annemarie wondered, when he saw firsthand what the war had done to his brother?

Clothed in burgundy brocade and a luxurious fur stole, Mrs. Ballard looked as if she'd dressed for a night at the opera. A broad-brimmed, feather-trimmed hat was secured with a gossamer silk scarf tied beneath her chin. She rushed forward and extended a gloved hand to Annemarie. "I was beginning to fear you wouldn't arrive in time. The stationmaster says the train is not more than ten minutes away."

No sooner had she spoken than Annemarie caught the distant sound of the whistle. Its melancholy tone made her shiver anew. She hurried to the window and peered down the length of railroad tracks. "I hope he hasn't been traveling alone all this way. Will he go directly to the hospital, do you think?"

"It will be best to get him there straightaway and out of this frigid weather. I've already made sure an ambulance is waiting."

Of course. Mrs. Ballard always had everything under control.

"Besides," she went on, "we certainly don't want to risk Gilbert's being exposed to the influenza." She glanced around the station with a sniff. "I don't care what the papers say. People are still getting sick. You *have* been careful, haven't you, Annemarie?"

"Extremely." Although she could only imagine the exposure risk on a crowded train. Surely, Gilbert would have taken
precautions.

Beneath her feet, a rumbling vibration began. Annemarie
sucked in her breath and returned to the window. "The train—
it's here!"

The rumble deepened, setting Annemarie's insides aquiver
as the depot erupted into a flurry of excited activity. The big
black engine appeared through a cloud of steam, brakes squeal-
ing. Waiting family and friends burst through the doors and
waved frantically as the train slowed and finally stopped.

Stepping onto the platform, Annemarie scanned the passenger car windows for a glimpse of her sweetheart. An elderly
gentleman stepped off the train, his arms full of wrapped
Christmas gifts. His appearance brought a shout of joy from a
couple nearby with a young boy in tow.

Next came a soldier—Jack Trapp, the lad whose family lived
across the street from the Kendalls. My, how he'd grown up,
and praise God he'd come back alive and whole! Then, seeing only his mother and his fourteen-year-old sister there to
meet him—another sister still served in France with the Army
Signal Corps—Annemarie's heart clenched. Mr. Trapp had
passed away last summer, a terrible blow to the family, and
poor Jack must now shoulder responsibilities as the man of the
house.

Other travelers emerged, welcomed by friends and family,
but as each happy group departed, Annemarie's anxiety grew.
Where was Gilbert? The platform was nearly empty now.
Besides the Kendalls and Ballards, the only people still waiting
were a porter and two ambulance attendants from the Army
and Navy Hospital.

Finally, a soldier with a bandaged head limped down the steps
from the last car. He wore a vacant expression, as if he wasn't at

all certain he was supposed to be here. An attendant hurried over and asked his name, then wrapped a blanket around his shoulders and helped him into the back of the ambulance.

When two men in army green assisted an even more severely wounded soldier off the train, a coldness completely unrelated to the frigid December day crept through Annemarie's limbs. Until today, the war had been a distant thing. No newspaper article, no radio announcement, not even letters from the front could begin to convey the emptiness, the bewilderment, the stark disillusionment she saw in these men's eyes.

"Oh, Papa." The words were barely a whisper, a misty breath carried away by the wind. Annemarie hugged her father's arm and buried her face in his coat sleeve.

"I know, Annie-girl. Be strong now. Gilbert will need—" Papa gave her shoulder a firm pat. "Ah, look up and dry your tears. Here he comes!"

Annemarie pushed away from her father and choked out a sob, her gaze searching out her sweetheart. Someone was lowering an empty wheelchair to the platform. On the steps above, Gilbert leaned heavily upon a uniformed man who helped him descend on his one good leg.

"Gilbert! Oh, my son!" Mrs. Ballard dashed across the platform, the tails of her scarf flying like banners. She wrapped Gilbert in a desperate hug sure to crush the breath from his lungs.

By the time Annemarie regained her senses enough to set her feet into motion, she found Gilbert surrounded by his mother, brother, and now an ambulance attendant as his companion helped him into the wheelchair. Mrs. Ballard chattered like a mynah bird while tearfully fussing over her son. Thomas laughed through his own tears and gave his brother a hearty slap on the back.

The uniformed companion edged to one side, and as Annemarie drew near, she glimpsed the gold cross on his collar. He looked up at her with a sudden smile, then doffed his cap and stepped forward. "Annemarie. I'd know you anywhere."

Clear gray eyes met hers in a look both hesitant and compelling. Torn between urgency to make her way to Gilbert and curiosity about the intriguing stranger who somehow knew her name, she stammered a reply. "I'm—forgive me—he's—"

The fair-haired chaplain nodded and stepped out of her way. She hurried past, reaching Gilbert's side with barely time for a few words and a loving glance. Reaching around his mother's stout form, Gilbert found Annemarie's hand—her gloveless hand—and clutched it for a precious moment before Mrs. Ballard had the medics bustling him into the ambulance.

Disappointed, deflated, Annemarie felt the last remnants of hope slipping away. The reunion she'd dreamed about was over almost before it began.

"Chin up, dear." Mama wrapped an arm around Annemarie's shoulders. "Today a mother received her son back. Be thankful, and look forward to tomorrow. You and Gilbert will have the rest of your lives together."

If only, if only . . .

She held her bare hand against her cheek and thanked the Lord for missing gloves.

One glimpse of the real-life Annemarie and Samuel was smitten. Gilbert's fiancée was ever so much more beautiful in person than in the faded, crumpled photograph Gilbert kept close to his heart. Samuel had never seen such heavenly brown eyes, nor lips so full and inviting.

Get hold of yourself, man. She's spoken for.

He waited to be sure Gilbert was in the ambulance before collecting his baggage and deciding he'd better find a place to stay. Though the military hospital provided housing for doctors and certain other staff members, maintaining a certain distance between the professional and personal aspects of his new duty assignment seemed preferable. He left his things with the stationmaster, then set out to explore the city.

Gilbert's descriptions of forested mountains and burbling mineral springs had certainly whetted his interest in Hot Springs—not to mention the idea of settling amid new surroundings for a while. His mother back in Fort Wayne made no secret of her disappointment, but he wasn't ready to return there. Too many reminders of the life he'd left behind. If he'd known how the war would scar him, if he could have foreseen the nearly insurmountable challenges to his faith—

He paused on the sidewalk, fist clenched. *Lord, I'm striving with all of my being to remain faithful. Give me strength.*

As usual, the heavens remained silent, and Samuel could only walk on in the hope that the God he lived to serve hadn't completely forsaken him.

Except for the pines, nearly all the trees had shed their leaves for the winter. The landscape, while still wildly beautiful, now shivered under an iron-gray sky as Samuel marched up Central Avenue in search of accommodations. Bathhouse Row, they called it, this strip of health spas at the foot of a mountain. He read the names as he walked past—Lamar, Fordyce, Superior, among others—and wondered why so many so close together didn't drive each other out of business.

At the far end of the tree-lined promenade, he spied the Arlington Hotel and remembered Gilbert said his brother was a manager there. Considering how Gilbert had described the hotel, Samuel suspected the rates for a long-term stay would far exceed his chaplain's pay, but at least it was a place to start.

He marched up the front steps and entered an expansive and elegant lobby. Already Samuel felt out of his element. He clamped his sagging jaw and tried to look nonchalant while he got his bearings. An elderly couple in coats and mufflers nodded a greeting as they shuffled toward the exit. Excusing himself to move out of their way, Samuel backed into a glass curio cabinet.

The sound of rattling figurines shot panic through Samuel's chest. He whirled around and braced both hands on the cabinet until everything settled. Thank heavens nothing had broken. After a quick glance across the lobby confirmed his clumsiness had gone unnoticed, he pretended to admire the items gracing the shelves.

A moment later, he was no longer pretending. Behind the glass, a striking assortment of ceramic vases, bowls, plates, and platters were on display. *Original Pottery Designs by A. Kendall of Hot Springs, Arkansas*, read a small, handwritten sign on the middle shelf. Samuel looked closer to read the tiny price tags next to each item.

Or, more accurately, *hefty* prices printed on tiny tags.

"Interested in a gift for someone?"

Samuel glanced over his shoulder at a slender, dark-haired gentleman in a gray suit. He uttered a reluctant chuckle. "No, thanks. Just admiring the work."

"Well, you won't find anything finer—" The man moved into Samuel's line of vision, and his face spread into a sudden smile of recognition. "You're the soldier who was with my brother on the train."

Samuel studied the man's face. "And you're Gilbert's younger brother. He's told me a lot about you."

"Thomas Ballard, at your service." He gripped Samuel's hand and pumped it violently. "Guess we were too preoccupied at the depot for formal introductions. Then my mother took over and I decided to get out of the way."

Samuel had certainly taken note of the domineering Mrs. Ballard. No wonder Gilbert had so frequently voiced his misgivings about returning to such a smothering welcome. "It's a pleasure to finally meet you, Thomas. I'm Samuel Vickary. I got acquainted with your brother aboard the *Comfort* while we were shipping back to the States."

"Here, let's sit down and take a load off. You must be worn out after your long trip." Thomas ushered Samuel over to a brocade settee. From here they could look out over busy Central Avenue. "You're a chaplain, I see. In town for some R and R? Hot Springs is a great place to rest and rejuvenate."

"Actually, the Army and Navy Hospital is my new duty assignment, and I'm in need of some living quarters."

"Then look no further. You've come to the right place."

Again, Samuel let his gaze travel the expensively decorated lobby. He released a nervous chuckle. "I'm afraid even a night or two at the Arlington would obliterate my finances. Any chance you could point me toward a rooming house or a reasonably priced apartment?"

"Heavens no! Why, you'll stay with my mother and me, of course."

Samuel coughed his surprise.

"I'm serious. The house is huge, and it's just Mother, me, and a couple of live-in servants. You'd have an entire upstairs wing to yourself."

Wing? "Really, I couldn't impose. Besides, you don't even know me."

Thomas's expression sobered. "I saw you with my brother. I saw the genuine concern in your eyes. And even in those brief moments I could see how much he trusts and relies on you. That's enough for me. It'll be enough for my mother, too."

Samuel lifted his hands in a helpless gesture. "I don't know what to say."

"I'll give you a hint: *yes.*"

Still stunned, Samuel cracked a crooked grin. "All right, then, if you're sure your mother won't object."

"To my brother's new best friend who also happens to be a man of the cloth?" Thomas clapped Samuel on the shoulder. "Consider yourself part of the family."

"Thanks. I'm grateful beyond words." At worst, he'd try the arrangement for a week or two while determining whether he and the Ballards were compatible housemates. And he'd insist on paying a fair rate for room and board.

Then, as Thomas drove him back to the depot to collect his belongings, it occurred to him living at the Ballard home might mean he'd see more of Gilbert's fiancée.

Annemarie. Samuel's pulse quickened at the very thought of her.

He knotted his fists. What would it take for him to shake off such ridiculous notions? Gilbert's crisis of despair was only temporary, and any day now he'd come to his senses. In the meantime, Samuel had made it his sworn duty to make sure Gilbert found himself again and reclaimed the woman whose love had sustained him through the war.

At least one of them deserved a happy ending.

5

𝒢ilbert knew it would be like this, Mother hovering, Thomas pressing for details about the war. The only bright spot in this dreaded reunion was seeing his beloved Annemarie again. Dear God, she was even more beautiful than he remembered!

Dear God, give me the strength to give her up.

After days on the train, Gilbert was none too happy about the ambulance ride, three wounded veterans crowded into the back of the small vehicle. At least it was only a few blocks to the hospital.

At least it got him away from his doting mother.

For a while anyway. It didn't take long for her to find him once he'd been admitted. Her strident voice carried throughout the ward as she kept insisting her son simply must have a private room.

"There are no private rooms available, ma'am," a nurse patiently explained. "I assure you, your son will get the best of care right here on the ward."

"But he's an officer. Are you certain something can't be arranged—"

"Mother. Stop. Please." Gilbert sank deeper into his pillow and closed his eyes. Tired, so tired. If they'd just let him sleep . . .

"Gilbert?"

The soft, sweet voice ripped a hole in his heart. He slid open his eyes to find Annemarie at his bedside, the same unruly tress creeping across her right temple. At the depot he'd scarcely had two minutes to soak up her beauty, her longing gazes, the tender touch of her hand, until Mother insisted if he sat there a moment longer, he'd "catch his death."

Death. If the woman only knew how many times he'd faced death on the battlefield, how many times he still faced it in his own dark thoughts.

Annemarie stepped closer and ran a finger along his forehead, nudging aside a lock of hair. He hadn't had a haircut in weeks, hadn't shaved for at least two days. He'd seen the stunned look in her eyes when she first glimpsed him at the depot. Wounded, unkempt—how he must look to her! Heaven help him, this was *not* how he'd envisioned his homecoming . . . at least not before a whizzbang from a German 77mm field gun took his leg, tore his arm to shreds, and left him with the mother of all headaches.

Suppressing a groan, he edged higher in the bed and reached for Annemarie's hand. "What are you doing here? This is no place for you."

She glanced at their surroundings—rows of beds marching down each side of the ward, trays of medical supplies on steel carts, nurses moving quietly among the patients with cups of water, bowls of broth . . . hypodermics filled with morphine.

A physical craving curdled his belly. He tugged his hand free of Annemarie's and clenched a fist. How much longer before they'd bring him another injection?

Annemarie was speaking. He swallowed, his mouth tasting like cotton, and shifted his glance to her face. "What did you say?"

She gave a gentle laugh. "I just asked, if I shouldn't be here, then where should I be?" She bent over him, one arm encircling his head, her breath like gossamer against his cheek. A tear pooled in the corner of her eye. "Oh, Gilbert, I've missed you so much!"

"My, my, my!" His mother appeared at his left, hands clasped at her bosom. "How long I have waited to see the two of you together again. Gilbert, dear, I will leave you in Annemarie's care while I find your doctor to discuss your course of treatment. And see what can be done about a private room."

"Mother, I told you—"

"No arguments, my darling. Only the very best for my son the war hero." Dropping a kiss upon his forehead, she bustled out of the ward.

Before Gilbert could apologize to Annemarie for his mother's interruption—not to mention her usual high-handedness—a nurse approached. "Visiting hours are over. I must ask you to say your good-byes and let our patient have his rest."

Annemarie cast Gilbert another longing gaze as she stroked his forehead. "I'll come again tomorrow, as soon as I can break away from the factory."

This was his chance to tell her not to return, to never see him again. That's what he'd planned, anyway, all the way across the ocean, then the long train ride home. But she was so beautiful, so very beautiful. And when he looked into those wide brown eyes so filled with love, he could almost forget he'd come home half a man.

He'd never hold her in two strong arms again. He'd never stand beside her on two good legs. He'd never carry her over the threshold into their married life together.

At the far end of the ward, she turned with a smile and a cheery wave before slipping out through the swinging double door. He yearned to cry out, to beg her not to go. Though twenty other patients filled the ward, Gilbert had never felt so alone, not even when he lay blown to bits on a bloody field in France.

He clawed his good hand through the hair at his temple. A thousand cannons exploded inside his skull. "Nurse. Nurse!"

A flame-haired girl in a white apron hurried over. "Yes, Lieutenant?"

"The pain—I need my injection."

The nurse checked his chart and frowned. "I'm so sorry. It's too soon."

"There must be something—"

"Let me find a doctor."

He wanted to tell her to forget the doctor and fetch him a loaded pistol. He was ready to do anything if it would take away the pain.

Why couldn't You let me die on the battlefield, Lord?

Even a slow, painful death would have been so much easier than giving up the love of his life.

6

*H*appy endings. Was there any such thing?

Annemarie tossed the pulp magazine to the foot of her bed. The story she'd just read, a romantic adventure about long-lost lovers reuniting on a tropical island, left her teetering between scornful laughter and sentimental tears.

She normally didn't go in for such fluff, but sleep eluded her tonight. Ever since she left the hospital, worries over Gilbert had consumed her. As disconcerting as his most recent letters had been, seeing him today only heightened her sense that the war had stolen away the man she loved. This was not the same Gilbert who only a year ago, home on leave before shipping overseas with his division, had kissed her under the mistletoe and sworn his undying love.

Beneath the glow of the bedside lamp, she gazed into the fire-and-ice shimmer of her engagement ring, Gilbert's gift to her last Christmas. "Wait for me," he'd said. "Keep a light in the window and a prayer in your heart."

But today she'd seen no light of love in her Gilbert's eyes. When he looked at her at all, it seemed as if he looked right through her.

A rap sounded on her bedroom door before it creaked open. "Annemarie?"

"Come in, Mama. I'm awake."

Her mother tiptoed into the room, whisking the door closed behind her. Wrapped in a thick flannel robe, she motioned Annemarie over and crawled under the quilts next to her. She snuggled Annemarie beneath her arm. "An exciting day for you, wasn't it? And now you can't sleep. I don't blame you."

Mama smelled of lavender and talcum powder, her loose braid of coffee-colored hair showing glints of silver. Annemarie found the end of her own thick braid and twined it with her mother's, taking comfort in the satiny feel and the interplay of hues. "Is it wrong for me to be happy Papa didn't have to go to war?"

Mama looked surprised. "Of course not. Why would you say such a thing?"

"Only because so many others didn't have a choice." Annemarie sat up and hugged her knees beneath her chin. "I can't help thinking about our friends who are never coming home. Ollie Lang, Howard McNeil, Francis Ferguson, so many others. If I'd lost Papa, if I'd lost Gilbert—"

"You mustn't dwell on such thoughts. Just thank the Lord your papa was too old for the draft and our prayers brought Gilbert home alive."

"I do thank God, but—" How could she reconcile the seeming absurdity of believing their prayers had protected Gilbert when surely every parent, sister, wife, and child had prayed just as fervently for their own loved ones' safe return?

Tossing aside the covers, Annemarie scrambled to the other side of the bed and marched to the chair where she'd laid her robe.

"Come back to bed, Annie. I'll sit with you till you fall asleep."

"It's no use." Annemarie stuffed her arms into the sleeves of her robe and looped the belt at her waist, then pulled on a pair of warm wool socks. Finding her slippers under the edge of the bed, she slid them on and extended a hand to her mother. "Come on, I'll walk you back to your own room."

With a reluctant shiver, Mama crawled out from beneath the quilts. "And what exactly are you planning to do this time of night? It's nigh on one o'clock."

"The one thing I can always count on to take my mind off my worries." Annemarie hooked her arm around her mother's elbow and led her into the hall.

Two steps out the door, Mama jerked to a halt and pierced Annemarie with a sharp glare. "Annemarie Kendall, are you out of your mind? It'll be cold as the Arctic in the workshop. Your fingers will turn to icicles in that wet clay."

"I'll get the steam heat going. It'll warm up in no time." Annemarie tugged her mother along the hallway until they reached the door at the other end. She pulled her mother into a quick hug, stopping the protest she could see forming behind a fierce frown. "It's all right, Mama. I promise. I just need to work off some of this restlessness."

Mama shuddered out a resigned sigh and tweaked Annemarie's cheek. "So help me, daughter, I'd better find you under the covers and sound asleep when I go down to start breakfast in the morning."

Annemarie didn't dare reply, for fear she'd make a promise she couldn't keep.

An hour later, her sleeves rolled up and an oversized apron covering her from neck to ankles, she sat at the spinning potter's wheel. She worked more by feel than sight, the cold, wet clay oozing between her fingers like strands of silk. It had become an almost mystical process for her, a blending of faith and artistry, for while her brain hadn't yet decided the shape or function of her creation, eventually her heart would figure it out.

But now, O Jehovah, thou art our Father; we are the clay, and thou our potter; and we all are the work of thy hand.

What else could she believe, except that somehow her heavenly Father could yet shape the clay of her life—hers and Gilbert's—into something beautiful?

✐

"I'm so sorry, Miss Kendall, but Lieutenant Ballard has requested no visitors today."

Annemarie clamped her teeth together, one gloved fist resting atop the charge nurse's desk. "Please, I'm his fiancée. It's been three days now. Would you at least tell him I'm here?"

A regretful frown puckered the gray-haired nurse's lips. She came from behind her desk and led Annemarie over to the window, out of earshot of others on the floor. "I feel for you, truly I do, but the lieutenant wouldn't even see his own mother this morning. The only visitor he'll allow is the chaplain, and even that poor man gets tossed out on his keister when Lieutenant Ballard loses his temper."

Temper? In all the years Annemarie had known Gilbert, he'd never been considered a hothead. Forthright, opinionated at times, but always cool under pressure. The mark of a good officer, he'd once told her, a trait he was proud to say he'd inherited from his father.

Annemarie stared across the winter-brown expanse of lawn to the bustling traffic on Reserve Street. Christmas shoppers and the spa clientele were out in full force today, despite the threat of snow and lingering concern over the spread of influenza. What Annemarie wouldn't give for a glimmer of sunshine and blue skies!

The nurse laid a gentle hand on Annemarie's arm. "Would you like me to ring you up when Lieutenant Ballard is feeling more himself?"

"Thank you, I'd be very grateful." Though Annemarie wondered if Gilbert would ever truly be himself again. She cast a worried glance in the direction of the ward before hurrying downstairs.

She made it as far as the lobby before collapsing in tears onto the nearest bench.

"Miss Kendall?"

Startled, she fumbled through her handbag for a handkerchief and swiped at her drippy nose and eyes. "Oh, you're the nice chaplain, Gilbert's friend."

"Samuel Vickary. Though around here I answer to 'Padre.'" The trim, sandy-haired man nodded toward the empty space beside her. "May I?"

"Of course." Annemarie forced a shaky smile as he lowered himself onto the bench. "I'm normally not one to be so weepy. I must look a fright."

"Not at all. You look—" He coughed, or was it nervous laughter? When he spoke again, his voice had dropped to a raspy whisper. "You look fine, truly."

"I'm sorry not to have thanked you sooner for all you've done for Gilbert. I understand you're staying with the Ballards."

"They've been very kind to offer me rooms." Another self-conscious chuckle. "I'm not used to living in such finery, not to mention having servants at my beck and call. I telephoned my mother in Fort Wayne yesterday to give her my new address, and now she's worried I'll be spoiled beyond redemption."

Annemarie dried her eyes and tucked the handkerchief into her handbag. "After what you went through over in France, I'm sure you're quite deserving of a little pampering."

Neither of them spoke for several seconds. In the silence, Annemarie found her gaze drawn to the way his long, thin fingers splayed across his thighs. He tapped his index fingers in rhythm, *one, two . . . one, two, three*, and stared across the lobby.

Then they both spoke at once.

"Will you see—"

"I understand you're—"

Laughing behind her gloved hand, Annemarie tried again. "I was just going to ask if you'd see your family at Christmas."

"My mother is all I have left. She loves to travel and is already making plans to visit me here."

"How wonderful for you. I can't imagine how lonely it would be to spend the holidays in an unfamiliar city and so far from your loved ones." Hearing the words leave her mouth, she lowered her eyes in embarrassment. "But I suppose you already know exactly how it feels."

Chaplain Vickary sat back with a sigh. "At least I'm back on American soil. Far too many of our soldiers are still left in Europe."

"But praise God the fighting is over and they're only there to keep the peace." Annemarie shifted slightly and cast the chaplain a shy smile. "Your turn. What were you about to ask me?"

"I was just going to say I heard you work at a pottery factory. A family business, I understand?"

"Kendall Pottery Works. My grandfather established the business right after the Civil War."

"Kendall Pottery?" The chaplain narrowed one eye. "*You're* the 'A. Kendall' whose works are on display at the Arlington?"

Annemarie nodded, her cheeks warming. "Those are pieces I've made in my spare time. At the factory we make mainly serviceable items for everyday use."

"Well, I'm quite impressed. You have a real talent."

"Thank you." She pursed her lips and looked away, wishing her father would just once recognize the value of artistry. Surely there was more to life than plain beige bowls and urns. The world was bleak enough.

"Have you always lived in Hot Springs?"

Annemarie beamed. "All my life. I can't imagine a more beautiful place to grow up."

"It's quite a scenic locale, even judging from what little I've seen so far."

"Just wait until you see the mountains in springtime. When the sun rises big and bright and golden at the edge of the bluest sky you've ever seen, and the redbuds color the mountainsides in every shade of pink, and tiny new leaves of palest green pop out on every branch—why, words simply can't describe it!"

Chaplain Vickary grinned, his gray eyes snapping. "I think you just described it perfectly."

Annemarie's cheeks flamed again. "I suppose I did go on a bit, didn't I?" She shifted her gaze to the dreary landscape beyond the windows. "It's just this whole past year has seemed like one long, endless season of winter. I don't ever remember being so anxious for spring."

The sun chose that moment to pierce the clouds with one golden ray. Sucking in a breath, Annemarie rose and went to the window. One hand resting upon the glass, she angled her face to receive the sun's warmth.

"Spring will come again, you know." The chaplain stood at her left shoulder. "'Weeping may tarry for the night, But joy cometh in the morning.'"

"The thirtieth psalm—I know it well. 'Thou hast turned for me my mourning into dancing; Thou hast put off my sackcloth, and girded me with gladness.' I believe it as much as I ever did, but . . ." Annemarie released a shivery breath. "I'm afraid for Gilbert, so afraid for him."

"I've been worried, too." He seemed about to offer a comforting touch, but just as quickly withdrew his hand and lowered it to his side. He swiveled toward the window. "Looks like the clouds are lifting."

Annemarie tore her gaze away from his somber profile and glanced out at the brightening sky. "Perhaps a walk would do us both good. Chaplain Vickary, would you care for a personally guided tour of downtown Hot Springs?"

The chaplain cast her an uncertain glance. "Are you sure it would be proper?"

"To familiarize my fiancé's closest friend with his new surroundings? What could be considered improper about that?"

"Then I can't think of a more delightful way to spend an afternoon." The chaplain offered Annemarie his arm. "But only if you will also consider me a friend and call me Samuel."

"Samuel it is," she said, linking her arm through his. "But won't you need your overcoat?"

"Not if we stay on the sunny side of the street." He arched a brow and nodded toward the exit. "Shall we?"

Lightness rose in Annemarie's breast. She smiled up at the chaplain—no, at her new friend Samuel. "Let's!"

Gilbert sat in the dayroom, his wheelchair angled toward the window and a blanket over his legs—or what was left of them. A trio of aging veterans had invited him to join them in a game of dominoes, but he wasn't in the mood. His head throbbed. His left ear had started its incessant ringing again. He doubted he could focus well enough to count the pips on his tiles anyway.

He pressed his right palm into his forehead and rubbed furiously. Just one hour without pain was all he asked. Even ten minutes. *God, are You listening?*

Obviously not. God had already shown exactly how much concern He had for Gilbert. Let Samuel spout his biblical propaganda, say what he wanted about the Lord's protection. Gilbert knew otherwise. A loving God didn't save a man's life only to deprive him of the ability to earn an honest living, to be a good husband to the woman he loved.

He scraped his hand down his face and rested his stubbly chin in his palm. The sun had finally broken through the clouds and glinted off the roof of the New Imperial Bath House. On the pathway below he glimpsed a couple out for a walk. The man was tall, dressed in an olive-drab uniform. The woman on his arm wore a flat-brimmed hat that hid her features from Gilbert's view, but there was something familiar about her posture, her long, purposeful stride.

Annemarie.

Gilbert sat forward, his forearm braced hard against the arm of his wheelchair. He blinked several times in a hopeless attempt to clear his vision. But there was no mistaking it—*his* Annemarie, leaning on the arm of another man.

An explosion of rage ripped through his chest. "Who? *Who?*"

"Lieutenant Ballard?" One of those bothersome, hovering nurses came up beside him and rested a hand on the back of his chair. A round-faced redhead with a lilting Irish brogue, she didn't look old enough to be out of grammar school. "Sir, are you in pain?"

He bit down on the spate of curses burning the back of his throat. "I'm tired. Just take me back to the ward."

"Of course, sir." The nurse turned his chair and rolled him toward the corridor. "You know, sir, it might lift your spirits a wee bit if only you'd allow visitors. Your mother has telephoned countless times today already, and just awhile ago I saw the lovely Miss Kendall talking to the charge nurse."

Gilbert grabbed the right wheel and jerked the chair to a halt that spun the nurse off balance. She gave a yelp and righted herself, then planted her fists on her hips and pierced him with a chiding glare. "Lieutenant!"

The rage that had swept through him so completely now fell away like melting snow. He sagged and stared at the floor. "I'm sorry. It's just—my head—" A quavering breath edged past his lips. He felt his eyes welling up. Blast it all, had he no control over his own emotions anymore?

The nurse's gaze softened. "Now, think nothing of it, Lieutenant. We'll get you into bed and see what we can do to make you more comfortable." She nudged the chair around in the direction of the ward and started on their way. "Soon as you're settled, I'll hunt up Chaplain Vickary for you. The man does have a way about him."

"Yeah, get Sam. Maybe he can—"

Recognition slammed into Gilbert's gut with the force of a kick from an army mule.

Sam.

Sam with Annemarie. Arm in arm, like they'd known each other forever.

Like lovers.

The anger simmered again, but this time Gilbert clamped a firm lid on it. Hadn't he already vowed to give Annemarie up? Hadn't he promised himself he'd never be a burden for her, that he'd set her free to find a man who could love her as she deserved?

But Sam, Sam. *Why did it have to be you?*

7

*O*f all the women in the world, why did Samuel find himself falling for the one woman he could never have?

Of all the women in the world—the adoring French farm girls who'd beckoned him with flirtatious winks, the Red Cross nurses wearing compassionate smiles and crisp white uniforms, the sisters, daughters, and friends of friends who'd turned out at the docks and train stations to welcome the soldiers home . . .

Of all the women in the world, why did it have to be Annemarie?

Yesterday's stroll along the promenade, her delicate hand nestled in the crook of his elbow, almost made him forget about the war.

Almost made him forget his promise to do all he could to make sure Gilbert didn't give up on life or the woman he loved.

Gilbert had been in quite a state when Samuel returned to the hospital after his walk. The spunky little Irish nurse—Mary McClarney, if he remembered her name correctly—had stopped him in the corridor to express her concern.

"Something has him mighty riled up, Chaplain. It's understandable he's moody and depressed, but I've not seen him quite so angry—and over nothing he would admit to."

Samuel thanked her and went straight in to check on Gilbert.

And five minutes later found himself summarily dismissed. If he hadn't ducked at the crucial moment, he'd have been beaned by a flying water glass.

Maybe this morning things would be better.

Entering the ward, Samuel did a quick reconnaissance while sharing a prayer or word of peace with a few of the other patients along the way. He paused at the foot of Gilbert's bed and cast his friend a worried frown. Gilbert lay twisted in the bedcovers, his good arm cradling the injured arm. He appeared to be asleep, a good thing considering how frequently he complained of headache-induced insomnia.

Gilbert stirred, then cracked an eyelid. "Don't look at me like that."

"Like what?" Samuel stepped around to the side of the bed. "Like I'm checking to see what you have handy to throw at me?"

"All out of ammo. The nurses have disarmed me." Angling a glance toward his sling, Gilbert rolled his eyes at the irony of his remark. Then, using his right elbow, he pushed himself higher in the bed. "Buy you a cup of java if you'll help me with these confounded pillows."

Samuel made sure Gilbert had settled comfortably and then pulled over a chair. "How are you feeling? Is the headache abating at all?"

The tension lines around Gilbert's eyes and mouth answered for him. "I can't even bribe the nurses into slipping me some extra doses of morphine. And now they tell me I have to have more surgery."

"Your leg?"

"The surgeon says I'll never be able to use a prosthesis unless they fix it better." Gilbert's jaw hardened. He looked away. "I told him he could save himself the trouble and me the pain."

The cold ring of hopelessness had crept into Gilbert's tone again. Samuel braced his arms on his thighs. "You've got to stop talking like that, Gil. You have everything to live for— your family, Annemarie—"

Gilbert slammed his clenched fist on the mattress. "Don't you *dare* talk to me about Annemarie. Don't you—" His chest heaved, each breath grating like a rasp on green wood. His face blanched with the effort to control his fury.

Samuel straightened. No sense wasting the usual spiritual platitudes on Gilbert. He could do no more than let the outburst run its course. He looked past Gilbert to the next bed, where a nurse assisted a patient with exercises to restore flexibility to severely arthritic joints. Through it all, the veteran grinned and wisecracked with the nurse, though clearly the pain was excruciating.

Catching Samuel's eye, the patient nodded toward Gilbert and quirked his mouth in silent understanding. Returning the nod, Samuel planted his hands on his knees and started to rise. "I'll come back later, Gil, when you're—"

"Don't leave." With a hiccuping moan, Gilbert brought himself under control. "I'm sorry. I don't know what comes over me."

Easing back onto the chair, Samuel laced his fingers together. "I wish I knew how to help, but all I can give you are my prayers and my friendship. And my friendship won't do you much good if you keep running me off."

"I said I'm sorry." Gilbert slanted a glance toward the man in the next bed and chuckled softly. "You think he'd sell me a little of his optimism?"

"You'll have to find your own, I'm afraid."

"That's what I figured." Gilbert stretched a hand toward the nightstand. "In the drawer there—can you hand me the picture?"

Samuel pulled open the drawer. Lying atop a fresh pair of pajamas and Gilbert's shaving supplies was a sepia portrait of Annemarie. The oval frame appeared to be sterling silver, etched with tiny rosebuds and a trailing vine. Its weight surprised Samuel, and he feared if he didn't grip it firmly it would slip through his fingers.

The portrait must have been taken on a bright summer day. Annemarie sat beneath a spreading tree, a bouquet of daisies in her hand. Her soft, warm eyes seemed to smile at him, beckon him. He tried to swallow, but his mouth had gone dry.

Sensing Gilbert's silent scrutiny, he tore his gaze away from the portrait. "This is new." It was all he could think to say.

"My mother brought it. She's beautiful, isn't she?"

Samuel knew he wasn't talking about his mother. "She is. Very."

Gilbert reached for the portrait, and Samuel winced inwardly at how reluctant he was to hand it over. Resting it on his lap, Gilbert traced the outline of Annemarie's face with the side of his thumb. "You understand why I won't let her visit me?"

"Please, Gil, don't give up like this."

"I told you, I won't be a burden to her. She deserves better." Gilbert inhaled a breath that seemed to go on forever. He let it out just as slowly. Samuel had to strain to hear his next words. "Take her, Sam. Take her with my blessing."

"What?" Samuel stood abruptly, certain he must not have heard correctly.

The fine lines around Gilbert's mouth and eyes deepened, whether from pain or anger or grief, Samuel couldn't tell. "I said she's yours. Just be good to her."

Samuel palmed the back of his head. His gaze darted around the ward to see if anyone had overheard this insanity. Then he grabbed the lapels of Gil's pajamas and leaned over him until his face was inches away. "Listen to me, Gil. Annemarie loves you—*you!* You *will* fight for her. You will fight to *live.* Do you hear me?"

❧

"Mary McClarney! Are you eavesdropping again?"

Mary fumbled with the tray she carried, snagging a medicine vial a split-second before it careened over the edge. "I, uh—no, Mrs. Daley. I was just checking my supplies before I start rounds."

"Then you'd best get to it. We have a ward full of patients to attend to." Mrs. Daley's stern glare softened slightly, and she laid a hand on Mary's arm. "It doesn't do you or our patients one bit of good to get emotionally attached. Do your work and keep your distance. Take it from someone who knows." Giving her chin a firm jerk, Mrs. Daley marched off.

Aye, and no wonder the crusty old chief nurse remained a spinster. Besides, how could anyone who worked so closely with these poor servicemen *not* become emotionally attached? The stories they told—and even more to be pitied, the stories that never passed their lips! Had Mary been stationed at one of the larger hospitals like Walter Reed or Fort McHenry, she could only imagine how much worse she'd hear and see.

As it was, most of her patients were veterans suffering from rheumatism, arthritis, or other conditions unrelated to serving in the Great War. Only a few, mostly locals like the troubled Lieutenant Ballard, had been transferred to the Hot Springs hospital for treatment of their battle wounds. If Mary had been eavesdropping, it was only because she worried about the poor man.

Her greatest concern, however—in fact, the concern of everyone on staff—was the outbreak of Spanish influenza that had spread rapidly during the past few weeks. She thanked the Lord above that she hadn't been assigned to the isolation floor. Though the doctors and nurses took every possible precaution, Mary lived in fear of catching the disease herself, and even worse, spreading it to her poor sainted mother. Already suffering from chronic bronchitis, Mum would never survive this dreaded illness.

Donning her brightest smile, she set her tray upon a bedside table. "Good afternoon, Corporal Conroy. And how are those knees of yours feeling on this wintry day?"

The whiskered soldier sat up straighter and smoothed back his sparse gray hair. "One kiss from my angel in white, and I'll be dancing a jig down Central Avenue."

"Kisses, I have none, at least not for the likes of flirts like you." With a wink and a nod, Mary pushed up his pajama sleeve and swabbed his arm with alcohol, then reached for the syringe she'd filled with his medication.

Corporal Conroy winced as the needle pierced his skin. "Bet you'd have plenty of kisses for that pretty boy across the way."

Mary followed his gaze. Of course, he would be looking right at Lieutenant Ballard. Face tingling, she busied herself with the supplies on her tray. "Now, Corporal. I treat all my patients just the same. And that *doesn't* include kisses."

Still, her heart beat a little faster as she crossed to the lieutenant's bed. A handsomer soldier she'd never laid eyes upon. He had a dark, brooding look about him, a sadness in his soul that called out to some deep instinct within her. As he lay there dozing, she longed to touch the errant curl that barely hid the jagged scar above his left ear.

Enough of this nonsense, Mary McClarney. Giving herself a mental shake, she set down her tray and reached for the lieutenant's chart. It was time for another morphine injection, but she almost hated to rouse him when he finally seemed to be sleeping comfortably. Even so, better to stay ahead of the pain.

As she prepared the hypodermic, Lieutenant Ballard shifted. His back arched. His mouth twisted into a tortured frown. Eyes squeezed shut, he rocked his head from side to side, a mumbling stream of words pouring from his throat—something about rain and rifle fire and blood, so much blood.

He gave a hoarse cry and sat straight up. He flailed his arms as if warding off an unseen enemy.

"It's all right, Lieutenant. The war's over. You're safe now." Mary struggled to settle him before he threw himself onto the floor, only to have him turn his attack upon her. With a sharp blow to her jaw, he sent her reeling against the next bed. A thousand flickering fireflies filled her vision. Her cheek throbbed as though she'd plowed into a brick wall.

"Hey, get some help here!" someone yelled.

A flurry of bodies and voices surrounded the lieutenant. Mary tried to stand, but a wave of dizziness knocked her to her knees.

"Mary! Good heavens, child, are you all right?" Mrs. Daley crouched over her.

Mary rubbed her jaw and tried again to get her bearings. "Lieutenant Ballard—"

"The orderlies have him restrained. What happened?"

"Restrained?" Mary forced herself to stand. Leaning upon the chief nurse's arm, she watched as two orderlies struggled to hold down the lieutenant while another nurse injected him with a hypodermic. "Saints above, don't hurt him!"

"They're only sedating him. He is clearly out of control." Mrs. Daley seized the lieutenant's chart and dashed off some notes. To the orderlies she said, "I want this man under restraint until further notice."

Mary hovered at the lieutenant's bedside. "He was only having a bad dream. He didn't mean to hurt me."

Mrs. Daley seized Mary's wrists and forced her to turn away from the man now shivering under blankets in a drugged half-sleep, his torso, right arm, and right leg secured to the bed with strong strips of gauze. "Listen to me, young lady. You've no idea what a shell-shocked infantryman is capable of. You're to stay away from Lieutenant Ballard from now on. I'm ordering him moved to another ward until he can be transferred to a hospital with psychiatric facilities." Mrs. Daley harrumphed. "That's where they should have sent him in the first place."

"Yes, thank you, Mr. Jones. You have a merry Christmas, too." Annemarie disconnected the call and jotted a note on the order form. They'd be hard pressed to fulfill the request before the first of the year, what with several employees taking time off for Christmas, but Jones Restaurant Supply was one of their largest accounts, and Annemarie had no doubt her father would find a way. They couldn't afford for Mr. Jones to take his business to Ouachita Pottery, a much larger operation.

Which, naturally, meant even less time for Annemarie to spend on her own projects. Thanks to the display Thomas had arranged for her at the Arlington, she'd received several requests for her one-of-a-kind ceramics as Christmas gifts. At least most of the pieces had already been fired and glazed.

If only Papa could see the merit of artistry in ceramics. Ouachita Pottery already employed talented women to decorate their ceramic ware with artistic glazes and designs. Though the specialty items sold for a higher price, by their very nature they took more time and personnel to produce, and Papa was all about mass production and the bottom line.

The workroom door banged shut, and moments later Papa ambled into the front office. "Still at your desk, Annie-girl? It's after six o'clock. Your mother will have supper on the table soon."

"Mr. Jones called with a last-minute order." She handed the sheet to her father. While he looked it over, she tidied up her desk, then bolted the front door and shut off the steam heat.

"Hmm, looks doable—if Ben and Bryan are willing to put in some overtime."

Annemarie slipped on her coat, scarf, and gloves. "For a little extra income at Christmas, I'm sure they will be."

"Naturally." Papa set the order under a paperweight and retrieved his coat. He switched off the electric lights, and Annemarie followed him out the back door.

Crossing the alley behind the factory, they trudged up a long hill toward home, a brisk north wind whipping at their coat-tails. Papa held open the gate of their backyard picket fence, and Annemarie darted across the lawn and into the warmth of the kitchen.

"Just in time, you two." Mama ladled steaming mashed potatoes into a serving bowl. "Five minutes more and my gravy would have turned to glue."

Annemarie laughed as she slid her arms out of her coat sleeves. "You couldn't ruin gravy if you tried, Mama. Someday you'll have to teach me your secret."

Mama tweaked her cheek. "I've tried, dearest, I've tried. But a certain young lady seems to care not a whit for learning to cook."

"Well, she'd better learn mighty quick." Papa draped his coat on a hook by the back door. "Otherwise her husband-to-be will soon be thin as a broomstick."

At the mention of Gilbert, Annemarie turned away with a sniff. Late this afternoon she'd telephoned the hospital to ask about him, only to be told there'd been an "incident" and he was under sedation. Since she wasn't a family member, they wouldn't offer details. Thinking perhaps Chaplain Vickary would know more, she'd asked to speak with him but was told he was conferring with patients.

Annemarie couldn't shake her concern that "conferring with patients" meant one patient in particular.

The family sat down to supper, but Annemarie had lost her appetite. After forcing down as much as she could of her mother's savory pot roast and vegetables, she excused herself and carried her dishes to the sink. "Mama, would you mind if I went over to the Ballards' for a short visit?"

Mama reached for Annemarie's hand and gave it an understanding squeeze. "We're all concerned about Gilbert. Perhaps Evelyn has some news that will ease your mind."

"Let me drive you, darling." Papa eased back from the table and tossed his napkin next to his plate. "You don't need to be walking alone after dark, especially on a cold night like this."

While Papa went to bring the car around, Annemarie bundled up once more. Mama walked her to the front door and made sure her scarf was tucked snugly around her ears. "Tell Evelyn we're praying every day for her dear boy."

"I will, Mama." Annemarie tugged on her gloves, recalling that day at the depot. How she longed for the touch of Gilbert's strong, firm hand. How she hungered for a tender kiss from his sweet lips.

Mama used her thumb to brush away a tear that escaped the corner of Annemarie's eye. "Cling to your faith, my girl.

The Lord holds Gilbert firmly in His arms. You'll both come through this time of trial and be the stronger for it."

Offering a weak smile, Annemarie pulled her mother into a hug. "Faith is all I have right now. If only I could give some of it to Gilbert."

8

*A*nnemarie shivered on the Ballards' broad front porch as she waited for someone to answer the bell. A full moon crept slowly up from the east, casting silvery beams across the windows. Wood smoke and evergreens scented the crisp night air, reminding Annemarie that Christmas was only a few days away.

A shadowy form appeared on the other side of the beveled-glass door, and Marguerite peeked through the filmy curtain. The door swung open. "Get yourself in here, Miss Annie, before you turn into an icicle."

Annemarie bustled inside and greeted the servant with a grateful hug. "Is Mrs. Ballard in? I hope she won't mind my stopping by unannounced."

"Don't be silly. You know you're always welcome here." Marguerite helped Annemarie out of her coat and hung it in the entryway closet. "Everyone's in the parlor by the fireplace. Mrs. B's doing some sewing, and Thomas and that nice chaplain just started a game of cribbage. You go on in, and I'll fetch you a cup of hot cocoa to warm you up."

While Marguerite trotted off to the kitchen, Annemarie marched down the hall to the parlor. She gave a polite rap on the partially open door and peeked inside. "Mrs. Ballard?"

"Annemarie!" The plump woman tossed her handwork to the other end of the settee. "Come in, dear. I've just been sewing some buttons on pajamas for the Red Cross effort."

Both Thomas and Chaplain Vickary rose from their seats. The chaplain looked much different in civilian clothes, more relaxed and comfortable. Annemarie recognized the pale gray argyle sweater as one of Gilbert's, and it brought a pang of nostalgia to her throat.

She drew a quick breath and stepped into the room. "Please don't let me interrupt your game, gentlemen."

"Yes, boys, do continue." Mrs. Ballard patted the seat next to her. "Come and sit, my dear, and let's have a nice long chat."

Annemarie lowered herself onto the settee and picked up the pajama top Mrs. Ballard had been working on. The soft, blue-striped flannel smelled faintly of talcum powder. Nerves on edge, Annemarie decided busy hands might ease the tension. "Do you have another needle handy? I could help with these."

"That would be lovely." Rummaging through the cherry-wood sewing kit at her feet, Mrs. Ballard found a needle, thread, and packet of buttons. She handed Annemarie another set of pajamas from a stack on a nearby chair. Taking up her own work again, Mrs. Ballard released a noisy sigh. "I can guess why you're here. You must have heard about Gilbert's little setback."

From what Annemarie could gather, it wasn't a *little* setback by any means. She snipped off a length of thread and worked it through the eye of the needle. "I tried to visit him earlier today, but he still wouldn't see me."

"Small consolation, I'm sure, but he has refused my visits as well." Mrs. Ballard nodded toward the chaplain. "If not for

Samuel being such a good friend of Gilbert's, we'd know little more than what we can wheedle from those closed-mouth doctors and nurses."

Annemarie sensed more than saw the chaplain's sudden tensing. She glanced his way, and he offered a concerned half-smile.

Thomas tapped his cards on the edge of the table. "Your play, Sam."

"Right. Let's see. Here are fifteen for two, fifteen for four . . ." He ran his thumb along the side of a card and stared at his hand.

"You missed a run. That's three more points."

"So it is." Samuel moved his peg along the game board.

Annemarie stabbed the needle through the fabric and straight into her finger. She let out a startled gasp and inspected the injury. A single drop of blood appeared on her fingertip.

"Oh, dear, a war wound." Mrs. Ballard gave a humorless chuckle. "And in peace time, no less. Marguerite!"

Marguerite entered just then with a tray of hot drinks. Seeing Annemarie's bleeding finger, she placed the tray on the table in front of the settee and reached into her apron pocket. "Now where did I put my hanky?"

"Allow me." Samuel stood at Annemarie's side and tenderly wrapped her finger in his own pristine white handkerchief. "Better?"

Annemarie lifted her gaze to Samuel's and then quickly dropped it again, before those penetrating gray eyes read more into her expression than the gratitude she intended. "Obviously my domestic skills leave much to be desired."

"Which you more than make up for with your ceramic artistry."

Her cheeks flamed. "You're kind to say so, but there are times when practicality must take precedence over art."

Samuel slid his hands into his pants pockets. "If that's in a rule book somewhere, I've yet to come across it."

Mrs. Ballard waved her hand toward the cribbage table. "Did you finish playing your hand? Then pull a chair over, Samuel, and sit with us. You can explain much better than I what happened with Gilbert this afternoon. I know Annemarie is anxious to hear."

"Please, that's really why I came." Holding the handkerchief around her throbbing finger, Annemarie leaned forward. "They won't tell me anything because I'm not family, but I'm going absolutely crazy with not knowing."

Samuel's brows drew together. His lips flattened into a worried frown, and for a moment Annemarie feared he'd plead patient confidentiality or whatever you called it between a pastor and penitent. Then he gave a single nod. He drew his chair away from the game table and settled it near the end of the settee. Taking one of the steaming cups of cocoa, he sat back with a thoughtful sigh.

Mrs. Ballard handed a cup and saucer to Annemarie. "Now, Samuel, about Gilbert . . ."

About Gilbert.

True, Annemarie deserved to be told, but Samuel dreaded bringing more tears to those soulful brown eyes. He stalled for time by taking a couple of tentative sips from the hot drink—not as sweet as he usually liked his cocoa, nor as strong, what with the Ballard family still doing their part to conserve.

Thomas took a cup from the tray, then propped a hip on the arm of the settee next to his mother. "For pity's sake, the man's just returned from war. Gilbert's never had a violent streak, but after what he's been through, who wouldn't be a little unhinged? If you ask me, I'd say they went a little overboard with the whole straitjacket business."

Annemarie gave a stunned gasp. She turned an open-mouthed stare upon Samuel. "Straitjacket! What happened?"

"Thomas is exaggerating. It wasn't an actual straitjacket, but—" Samuel set down his cup and scoured his palms up and down his pant legs, as if he could wipe away the memory of this afternoon. "A nurse startled Gilbert out of a nightmare, and he hit her in the jaw. When they couldn't quiet him, they had no choice but to restrain him."

"That is utterly ridiculous." Annemarie's cocoa sloshed onto her saucer. "Gilbert would never hurt anyone—" She stopped herself with a hand to her mouth. Her eyes shut, and Samuel didn't have to guess what she was thinking. The war had turned them all into killers.

All of them, one way or another.

Samuel clamped down on the fragment of memory and stuffed it away in the darkest corner of his mind. He relieved Annemarie of her cocoa before she spilled anymore and used the handkerchief he'd given her to soak up the hot liquid filling the saucer.

Annemarie's face crumpled. She heaved a regretful moan. "Oh, dear, you'll never get the stains out of it now."

"Not to worry. It was an old one anyway." Samuel resisted the urge to take her hand and soothe away the anguish distorting that lovely face.

She straightened her spine, and while she fought for composure it seemed as if Samuel watched a different kind of war. Quiet, artistic, but such a strong, determined woman. He had no doubt she'd win this battle. She coughed softly. "The nurse—was she hurt badly?"

"She's fine, more surprised than anything." As tactfully as possible, Samuel tried to explain the reasons for keeping

Gilbert restrained and sedated. "It's as much for his own protection as for the hospital personnel. You've heard the term *shell shock*, I'm sure."

Mrs. Ballard gave a haughty sniff. "Call it what you may, my son is *not* insane. He needs tender attention, not to be treated like a rabid animal."

"They're doing all they can, I'm certain." Samuel's stomach knotted as he recalled the crazed look behind Gilbert's eyes this afternoon. "The problem is this hospital doesn't have the psychiatric resources of a military facility like Walter Reed or Fort McHenry, which is where many of the returning wounded are being sent."

Thomas stood and paced, his cup rattling against the saucer. "I'll fight them tooth and nail if they push the issue about transferring him to another hospital."

"Is that a possibility?" Again, Annemarie looked to Samuel.

He tried to reassure her with a smile. "I promise you, I intend to do everything in my power to make sure Gilbert can continue to be treated right here in Hot Springs." He went on to explain about the additional surgery Gilbert required. "It's all taking its toll—the pain, the fear of being permanently incapacitated. But as he begins to recover physically, I have every hope he'll find relief from the mental trauma as well."

"I pray you're right." Annemarie examined the pajama top in her lap. "I suppose they'll still be needing these, as long as there are wounded soldiers to care for." She drew a shaky breath and finished sewing on the button she'd started on earlier. "War is a wretched, evil thing."

Samuel couldn't agree more.

While the ladies returned to their handwork, Samuel took it upon himself to carry the tray of empty cocoa cups back to the kitchen. One dim light glowed over the sink, and a thin strip of amber shone beneath the door to the servants' quarters. As soundlessly as possible, he washed and dried each cup and saucer. As he placed them in the cupboard, it occurred to him how natural it felt, a normal, everyday chore that might be happening in any ordinary household anywhere in the world. As a boy he would help his mother clean up the kitchen after meals—and complain about it the entire time.

Washing dishes, sweeping floors, raking leaves, chopping wood.

Hot showers, hot meals, clean clothes, dry socks.

Soft mattresses, downy pillows, warm blankets, a fire in the hearth.

So much he'd taken for granted, until the war. Standing at the sink, he stared into his own face, reflected back by the darkness beyond the window. Where his eyes should be, he saw only black, hollow spheres, ghostlike, haunting.

Would he ever feel normal again?

❧

Annemarie folded the last pair of pajamas and rose to lay them on the chair with the others. "A productive evening's work. I'm glad I could help."

"I'm delighted you decided to visit." Mrs. Ballard packed up the needles, spools, and leftover buttons into her sewing box. "You know, dear, I still think we should be moving ahead with wedding plans. I realize it would be premature to set a date quite yet, but—"

"*Quite* premature." Annemarie stifled an angry rebuff, thankful she and Mrs. Ballard were alone in the parlor. She couldn't fathom how Gilbert's mother could still be so adamant about this. Was she completely oblivious to the long and difficult recovery that lay ahead for her son?

"I know it will take time." Mrs. Ballard crossed to Annemarie's side and rested a hand on her arm. "But Gilbert *will* get better. Once he has his surgery and can be up and around again, why, I just know he'll cheer up even faster with something to look forward to."

Annemarie glanced down at Mrs. Ballard's hand, where a bejeweled ring glittered beneath the lamplight and reminded her all over again of the differences in their stature. The Kendalls were a working-class family, while Mrs. Ballard, who could trace her ancestry back to Virginia plantation owners, had known nothing but wealth and ease.

It wasn't that Mrs. Ballard was incorrigibly snobbish—she'd welcomed Annemarie into her heart without reserve. No, the woman's greatest fault was an arrogant blind spot when any-one suggested a course of action other than her predetermined plans.

"Mrs. Ballard—"

"*Mother* Ballard."

Annemarie dipped her chin. "Not yet, Mrs. Ballard. And perhaps not ever." At the woman's surprised intake of breath, Annemarie faced her directly and clutched her hands. "Please understand. I love Gilbert with all my heart. But we must both accept the fact that the war has changed him, probably forever."

"Of course it has. I don't deny it. But don't you think—"

"What I think—what I *know*—is that Gilbert needs time to heal. He needs time to find himself, to figure out how to live his life again." Her voice shook. She drew her lower lip between her teeth. "And I have to be prepared for the possibility that I won't fit into his life anymore."

"That will never happen!" Mrs. Ballard pulled her into a fierce hug. "Gilbert needs you. He will always need you."

Annemarie returned the hug briefly, then freed herself and stepped back. She fumbled in her skirt pocket for a handkerchief, but finding none, she used the back of her hand to brush away the wetness on her cheeks. "As I told you, I will always love him. I will be there for him as long as he wants me. But I won't push him into marriage. Not now, not ever."

While Mrs. Ballard fluttered her hands and stammered, Annemarie strode into the hallway and retrieved her things from the coat closet. She met Mrs. Ballard in the parlor doorway, and her heart twisted at the look of utter confusion skewing the woman's features.

Mrs. Ballard stretched an arm toward Annemarie, her other hand clenched at her bosom. "Dear, dear, I've upset you. You mustn't go until we've come to an understanding about this."

"If you mean the wedding, there is nothing more to say." Annemarie softened her gaze into an apologetic smile as she pulled on her coat and gloves. She dropped a kiss upon Mrs. Ballard's powdered cheek. "Promise me you won't bring it up again—to me or to Gilbert. If the Lord wants us together, He will work things out in His own good time."

If . . . In Annemarie's mind that tiny word loomed like an insurmountable precipice.

She refused Mrs. Ballard's offer to let Thomas drive her home, claiming a brisk walk would help calm her thoughts and give her a little time alone with God.

Then she walked out the front door and straight into Samuel Vickary's arms.

9

The feel of Annemarie leaning against his chest, her gloved fingers digging into his biceps, disoriented Samuel for one glorious moment. He fumbled to regain his balance while making sure Annemarie had both feet solidly on the ground. "Steady, there. Are you all right?"

She laughed nervously and straightened, but her grip on Samuel's arms held firm. "My fault entirely. I wasn't watching where I was going."

He tried to breathe, but the cold night air froze in his lungs. Or was it the nearness of Annemarie Kendall? Clarity returning, he patted her elbows and gingerly stepped back as she lowered her arms. "Headed home already?" His voice sounded as creaky as the porch board beneath his feet. "Surely you're not walking?"

"It's not far." She smiled and adjusted her gloves. "And what are you doing outdoors without your coat again? Don't you feel the cold at all?"

"I'm from Indiana, remember? This is nothing compared to the winters we have up north." Grinning, he shoved his hands into his pants pockets. He'd never be cold again if he could spend the rest of his life basking in the warmth of Annemarie's gaze.

This was certainly not going to happen, at least not in the way he'd insanely begun to let himself imagine. Friends—that's all they'd ever be.

And a friend wouldn't allow a young lady to walk unescorted this time of night. "Let me see you home. After Marguerite's sumptuous cooking I could use the exercise."

She tightened her lips, sending a quick glance toward the parlor windows. "Well, I . . . "

How stupid of him. Naturally, Annemarie would be concerned about what Mrs. Ballard would think. Their being seen together along quiet streets after dark might be perceived much differently from two friends strolling the sidewalks of downtown Hot Springs in broad daylight.

"Forgive me. I was being presumptuous." Samuel reached for the doorknob. "At least let me ask Mrs. Ballard if her chauffeur can drive you."

"Nonsense. Zachary has probably already retired for the evening." Straightening, Annemarie firmed her smile. "I'd be grateful for your company, but only if you will go inside and fetch your overcoat. I won't be held responsible for your coming down with pneumonia."

"All right, all right." Barely able to conceal his pleasure, Samuel ducked through the front door and snatched his coat from the hall closet. Returning to the porch, he slid his arms into his coat sleeves and fastened two buttons. "Satisfied?"

Annemarie narrowed her eyes and tugged the collar up around his neck. "There, that's better." She marched down the porch steps and waited for Samuel to catch up. As they reached the street, she said, "Actually, I was hoping we'd have another chance to talk."

"Were you?" A spring returned to Samuel's steps. Keeping his eyes on the path before them, he asked, "Something in particular on your mind?"

"Gilbert, of course. It's hard to speak freely in front of Mrs. Ballard."

Samuel took Annemarie's arm as they crossed at the corner. How many times would he have to remind himself her heart belonged to Gil? "How can I help?"

Annemarie turned her face toward the shimmering moon and heaved a desperate sigh. "Gilbert's mother is utterly determined to go forward with wedding plans. I've tried to tell her we must wait until Gilbert says he's ready, but she won't listen."

Samuel murmured an acknowledgement but walked on in silence. His thoughts careened back to Gil's words this afternoon: *Take her, Sam. Take her with my blessing.* It was only the injuries talking, the fear and the pain. No man in his right mind would ever give up a woman like Annemarie.

"You do think I'm doing the right thing, don't you, Samuel?"

He looked up, startled. "The right thing?"

"Insisting we wait." A worried frown creased Annemarie's lips.

"Waiting is definitely wise at this point. Gilbert has a lot of healing yet to do." Even in the faint light of the moon, Samuel sensed more behind her questioning gaze—far more than a simple affirmation about the wisdom of delaying wedding plans. It was obvious she sought his assurance that she and Gilbert still had a future to look forward to.

They turned at the next corner and started slowly up a long hill, walking straight into the chilly north wind. Annemarie shivered and hunched her shoulders. "Happy as I am for Christmastime, I can hardly wait for spring!"

Winter, spring, summer, autumn—for Samuel the passing of seasons no longer seemed to matter. He sighed as dark memories crept in.

On his knees in a stubbly field, blood everywhere as he cradled a private's limp body and shouted curses at God . . .

Perhaps someday he'd shed his guilt and find the courage to hope again. Perhaps someday the words from Scripture he'd leaned upon all his life would flame anew in his spirit and bring back the joy he once felt doing the Lord's work, the joy he once felt in simply being alive.

For now, going through the motions would have to suffice. He'd have to rely on the *habit* of faithfulness, built upon years of prayer and study and service, while praying every day that God hadn't turned His back on him for eternity.

"But whosoever shall blaspheme against the Holy Spirit hath never forgiveness, but is guilty of an eternal sin."

"Sam?"

Her use of the shortened form of his name made his steps falter. She'd stopped beneath a streetlamp, its hazy glow haloing her dark hair.

"I'm worried about you, too, you know." She looked so solemn, schoolteacher-stern, her mouth twisted in an accusing scowl.

He tried to laugh, but it sounded weak and hollow in the night air, as if the sound had been swallowed up by the mountains reaching skyward around them.

"I'm serious. You may have survived the war without physical wounds, but you must have witnessed unspeakable horrors."

If she only knew. . . . "Don't be concerned about me. Gilbert is the one who needs you."

She reached for his hand and pressed it between her own. "You said we were friends, didn't you? So I just want you to know that if you ever need to talk, to unburden yourself about the war or—or just anything—well, if I can help in any way—"

He stared at their entwined hands and thought his heart would explode from his chest. With his last ounce of willpower he gave her fingers a gentle squeeze and then shoved his fists into his coat pockets. "Your friendship is all I need," he said, his voice scraping across paralyzed vocal cords. "Now I'd better see you on home before Mrs. Ballard realizes I'm missing and sends out a search party."

"She would, you know." A hearty laugh burst from Annemarie's throat. She linked her arm through Samuel's as they resumed their march up the hill.

And once he delivered her through her own front door and started on his way back to the Ballards', he realized he'd never been so loathe for an evening stroll to end.

✥

Mary McClarney tugged a wooly afghan from the back of the sofa and tucked it around her mother's legs. "Warm enough, Mum? Another cup of tea?"

"Stop fussing, daughter, and sit yourself down. You've been flitting about this house like a nervous bumblebee ever since you came home from work." Nell McClarney aimed an arthritic finger at the faded tweed chair nearby. "Now tell me what's got you in such a dither."

Mary crumpled into the chair. She knew better than to disobey a direct order from her mother. Mum may have weak lungs, but the same could not be said about her will.

Unfortunately, the chair placed the left side of Mary's face directly under the glow of Mum's reading lamp. So much for any hopes of keeping her mother from finding out about that little bit of unpleasantness at the hospital this afternoon.

Mum tossed the afghan aside and sat up. "Child! What's happened to your cheek?"

"Now don't get yourself in a state. It's just a wee bruise." Gingerly, Mary covered her swollen jaw with one hand.

"Wee! Why, it's nigh on covering half your face! Now tell me, did you fall? Did someone—"

"It was an accident," Mary blurted, wincing at the memory. "He didn't—I mean—"

Her mother gasped. "Someone *did* hurt you! Oh, Mary, not one of them soldiers?"

"No—yes—" Mary moaned her frustration as she rose to fetch her mother a cup of warm water to soothe a sudden coughing spasm. "See there what you've done. I told you, it's nothing to get worked up about."

Nell McClarney sipped the water and glared at her daughter until the spate of coughing subsided. "I don't know which upsets me more—your mottled face or the fact that you thought you could hide it from me."

"I'm sorry, Mum. I didn't want to worry you." Mary plopped into the chair and laced her fingers in her lap. "See, it's these poor, poor fellas coming home from France. This young lieutenant, he was having a bad dream, and no telling who he thought I was—probably a German with a machine gun aimed at his head—"

"So he *hit* you?" Mum started to cough again, and Mary shoved the glass of water into her hands.

"You can see I'm none the worse for it, except for a bit of a bruise, and I'll not say another word about it until you promise me you won't get so riled." Mary sat back and crossed her arms.

Drawing a steadying breath, Mum gave a reluctant nod. "I hope the lad had the decency to apologize, at least."

Mary glanced away, unable to wipe the image of the restrained and sedated Lieutenant Ballard from her mind.

Surely Mrs. Daley had overreacted. Men returning from the Great War should be regarded as heroes, not treated as raving lunatics destined to languish in asylums.

"Why, Mary McClarney, what do I see in those green eyes of yours?" Mum touched her hanky to the corner of her mouth and cleared her throat. "Would you be getting sweet on one of your patients?"

"Of course not! That wouldn't be the least bit professional, now, would it?" Mary pushed out her lower lip, feigning indignation. She'd never hear the end of it if Mum knew how close she'd come to the truth.

Besides, war wounds and shell shock aside, a fine man like Lieutenant Gilbert Ballard would never give an Irish immigrant working-class girl the time of day. No, he was meant for the likes of the beautiful Miss Kendall. The potter's daughter, though employed in her father's business, bore all the markings of a lady, from the cut of her clothes to the pride in her posture. Miss Kendall clearly was no stranger to the ways of Hot Springs society.

And if that weren't enough, she was an artist. Oh yes, Mary had heard talk of Annemarie Kendall's exquisite ceramic creations. Nurses on the ward said those one-of-a-kind vases and bowls on display at the Arlington fetched a pretty penny from wealthy tourists who came to town for the baths.

Mary looked down at her work-worn hands. Now if she had a fine pair of kid gloves such as Miss Kendall wore, perhaps no one would notice how frequent exposure to soap and water had left her skin so red and chapped. With a resigned sigh, she reached for the bottle of hand lotion on the end table and massaged a generous dollop into her palms and fingertips.

Someday . . . someday she'd own a pair of stylish kid gloves. Someday she'd dress in fashionable clothes and walk the promenade on the arm of a handsome beau.

Stifling a yawn, Annemarie refilled Papa's coffee cup and sat down to a steaming bowl of oatmeal.

Papa stirred cream into his coffee. "Up late again, were you, Annie-girl?"

"Just had a little trouble getting to sleep." With a dismissive smile, she sprinkled her oatmeal with a meager half-teaspoon of brown sugar and a handful of raisins. She'd rather not get into a discussion of last night's disturbing visit with Mrs. Ballard.

Much less the tentative friendship developing between her and Chaplain Samuel Vickary. Such a kind and likable fellow, though clearly those somber gray eyes cloaked an abundance of sorrow. And now, with both Gilbert and Samuel to fret over, Annemarie was at a loss as to how to help. While soldiers went through weeks and months of training for combat, while doctors and nurses studied wound care and surgery, who taught wives and mothers and fiancées and friends the skills they'd need to assuage a soldier's broken spirit?

Mama set a plate of toast in the center of the table and settled into her chair. "Joseph, dear, could I prevail upon you to do without Annemarie at the factory today?"

"I suppose, if you need her at home." Papa slathered blackberry jam across a piece of toast. "Things have slowed down quite a bit, what with Christmas right around the corner."

Annemarie spooned up a bite of oatmeal. "Papa's right. There's nothing much to do in the office but a little bookkeeping and some filing, and I can easily finish it another day." Although she'd intended to use the free time to glaze several of the ceramic pieces she'd recently fired. A tremor of guilt tickled the back of her neck, and she forced a compliant smile. "What do you have planned for today, Mama?"

"I was hoping to have the tree and decorations up by this weekend. Christmas is scarcely five days away, and I still have shopping and baking to do, and the choir concert rehearsal is tomorrow morning, and—"

"Now, Ida, don't work yourself into a tizzy." Papa patted her hand. "You do this every year, you know, and for all your fussing and fretting, Christmas manages to come just fine on its own."

Mama gave an embarrassed chuckle. "You know me too well, Joseph Kendall. But admit it. You love the trappings of the season as much as anyone."

"Speaking of shopping—" Annemarie finished the last bites of oatmeal and dabbed her mouth with the corner of her napkin. "I still have a few gifts to buy. Give me two hours, Mama, and I'll hurry right home to be at your beck and call the rest of the day."

"That would be lovely, dear-heart. While you're out, I'll get the lights and ornaments organized and plan our attack on the tree."

Papa laughed. "Ida, Ida! You make decorating sound more like a battle than preparing for Jesus' birth!"

Annemarie's breakfast sank cold and heavy in the pit of her stomach. She pushed her chair back and stood. "I think we've had quite enough talk of war for a long time to come."

Before her parents could respond with much more than sheepish smiles and understanding glances, she carried her bowl to the sink and strode out of the kitchen.

At the foot of the stairs she locked trembling fingers around the newel post and closed her eyes in prayer. *Dear Lord, help us. Help us all to heal from the wounds of war.*

10

Annemarie stepped inside the Arlington Hotel to find the lobby bustling with guest activity. Maneuvering between arriving and departing guests, she stepped to one end of the registration desk and signaled for the attention of a clerk. "Pardon me, but is Thomas Ballard available?"

"In his office, I believe." The thin-lipped desk clerk nodded toward a doorway before returning his attention to an elderly gentleman demanding to pay his bill so he could catch a train.

Tucking her gloves into her coat pocket, Annemarie started toward Thomas's office. She found the door standing ajar and peeked inside. "Good morning, Thomas. May I trouble you for a moment?"

"Annemarie! Come right in. I always have time for you." Thomas jumped up from behind his desk to clear a stack of papers off a chair. "Here, have a seat."

"I won't keep you. I just wondered . . ." She chewed her lip. Why did she always feel so awkward about asking if any of her ceramics had sold?

Thomas held up one finger. "I think I have what you came for right here." He rifled through his desk drawer, tossing aside pens and scraps of paper and rubber bands and all sorts of para-phernalia. Finally, from the back of the drawer, he retrieved a bulky envelope. With a triumphant grin he passed it across the desk to Annemarie. "I would have said something last night, but it was clear you had other things on your mind, and the next thing I knew, you'd gone home."

She offered a sad smile of understanding as she took the envelope. The weight of it stunned her. "This is all for me?"

"The hotel's percentage has already been deducted, and the rest is yours." Thomas came around and perched on the cor-ner of his desk. "Don't tell me you didn't notice on your way through the lobby. As of an hour ago, every last one of your ceramic pieces has sold."

Numb with disbelief, hands shaking, Annemarie folded back the envelope flap. Inside, a stack of crisp bills strained at the seams. She looked up at Thomas to see a smile splitting his face.

"We could have sold even more if we'd had the inventory. I took the liberty of accepting a couple of special orders from some big spenders who'll be back in town after the first of the year." Thomas swiveled to reach for a notepad near his tele-phone. He tore off the top two sheets and handed them to Annemarie. "Think you can handle these?"

She studied the descriptions. One requested a soup tureen with lid and four matching bowls. The other asked for a pair of oversized vases. Both specified her unique "Ouachita sun-rise" glaze. Hefting the envelope in one hand, the orders in the other, Annemarie laughed out loud. "This is . . . this is amazing!"

"Thought you might be pleased. I felt mighty lucky I set aside the pink and gold candy dish for Mother's Christmas gift before someone else snatched it up."

"Oh, Thomas, you didn't pay for it, did you?"

"Of course I did."

Annemarie started to count out the price she'd set for the candy dish. "I can't take your money, not after all you've done to put my work on display and handle the sales."

"Business is business. A craftsman—crafts*woman*—deserves to be paid for her work."

"I know, but you're—" She started to say, *you're practically family*, but considering how things stood between her and Gilbert, perhaps it would never be true. The elation she'd felt moments ago vanished like wood smoke in a gust of winter wind.

Before despair smothered the last remnants of her exhilaration, she tucked the money and pottery orders into her handbag and stood to give Thomas a grateful hug. "You are a dear, dear friend, and I can never thank you enough."

"No thanks necessary." A blush tingeing his cheeks, Thomas nudged her toward the door. "Now get out of here and go make some more pottery. The display case out front looks pretty stupid sitting there empty, and we sure don't want those Ouachita folks bringing in their wares to fill your space."

"I can have a few more pieces ready by next week." Annemarie patted her bulging handbag, tempted to rush straight to the factory and show Papa before she spent one cent of the money on Christmas gifts. Maybe at last he'd be convinced there was a viable market for ceramic artistry.

Halfway across the lobby, Annemarie skidded to a halt. A tall, blond man in a military overcoat stood before the empty display case and looked for all the world like a child who'd just found coal in his stocking on Christmas morning.

She edged closer. "Samuel?"

He started and swung around to face her, his boyish grin bringing a sparkle to his eyes. Then he seemed to catch himself, hemming and hawing and shuffling his feet. "I, uh, hoped to purchase one of your pieces as a gift for my mother. I see they're all gone."

"I just discovered that, myself. I hadn't taken time to stop in recently and had no idea they were selling so well." She glanced at the empty shelves and released a sigh. "Thomas said he meant to tell me last night, but . . ."

Samuel's smile brightened again. "You'll be glad to know Gilbert's a bit better this morning. I sat with him while he had breakfast."

Heart lifting, Annemarie pressed a hand to her chest. "Have they removed the restraints?"

"For now." Samuel's gaze skittered toward the floor for a brief moment. "He's still heavily medicated but lucid enough to realize what happened, and he's quite remorseful about hurting the young nurse."

Annemarie strode toward the front windows, her thoughts up the mountainside at the massive Swiss chalet–style hospital. "If only he'd allow me to visit."

Samuel came up beside her and hooked her arm through his. "Walk with me back to the hospital. Somehow, some way, I'll convince him to see you. It'll do you both good."

"I'm sorry, Lieutenant Ballard, but I cannot authorize an increase in your morphine dosage." The doctor pressed his lips together in a grim frown. "In all honesty we should be weaning you off the drug, but first we have get you through this next round of surgery."

Gilbert jammed his right fist into the mattress. A thousand curses exploded in his brain, but if he gave vent to them— or worse, flattened the stingy doctor's bulbous nose—a half-dozen orderlies would materialize out of the woodwork and strap Gilbert to the bed again. By sheer force of will, he held his tongue, instead drawing several deep, slow breaths until he sensed control returning. "When will you do the surgery?"

"No rush. I understand your family lives right here in Hot Springs. I can write you a pass to spend Christmas at home, and we'll do the surgery on . . ." The doctor consulted his notes, then looked up with a patronizing smile. "How's the twenty-seventh sound?"

"Fine, I guess." Gilbert ran his tongue across dry lips. "But I'd just as soon stay here over Christmas."

The doctor's eyebrows shot up. "Whatever for? Considering you're in tolerable health otherwise, I can't imagine anything more depressing."

Gilbert could. And did. His mother's fawning attention. Thomas's grating good nature.

Annemarie's pitying gaze.

Wetness slid down his left cheek, escaping from the eye that still occasionally blurred and watered. He swiped at his face with the back of his good hand and tried to keep his breathing steady, though his chest ached from the effort.

"Look, son," the doctor began in a condescending tone, "I've been a military surgeon for longer than you've been alive. War is hell, to quote the late General Sherman, and you've just lived through it. Now it's time to quit feeling sorry for yourself and start thanking the Lord above for what you *do* have instead of mourning what you don't."

With a final shake of his head, the doctor marched away.

Gilbert squeezed his eyes shut. *Curse this screaming headache!* "I am not a coward, not a coward, do you hear!"

"I hear." Samuel approached the bedside, a concerned smile turning up one corner of his mouth. "And so does half the city of Hot Springs by now. What was that all about?"

Embarrassment burned Gilbert's face. He glanced at the patients on either side of him, who quickly averted their stares. "He doesn't understand. If he'd spent even one day in a field hospital—"

Samuel slid his gaze to the man in the white coat examining a patient at the far end of the ward. "Did your *doctor* call you a coward?"

"Not in so many words." Locking his fingers around Samuel's wrist, Gilbert lowered his voice to a rasping whisper. "This isn't self-pity, Sam. It isn't cowardice or weakness. I led my platoon through some of the worst fighting along the Marne, and I never flinched, not once."

"Of course, you didn't." Samuel lowered himself into a chair.

"I just—" His stupid left eye started leaking again, and this time he couldn't restrain the muttered curse.

Samuel passed him a handkerchief. "Take it easy, Gil, and tell me what the doctor said."

Dabbing the corner of his eye, Gilbert heaved a frustrated groan. "He wanted to talk about my surgery. He won't do it until after Christmas."

"You sound disappointed. Weren't you just telling me yesterday he shouldn't waste his time?"

"Just shut up, will you?" Teeth clenched, Gilbert fought to keep from insulting his friend with an even stronger spate of expletives.

"I don't think you mean that, seeing as how I'm one of the scant few willing to put up with your guff." Samuel drew his chair closer and folded his arms along the edge of Gilbert's mattress. "So . . . this is all because your doctor gave you a surgery date?"

Gilbert rubbed his mangled left arm. Sometimes it burned like the stabs of a thousand needles. "He's giving me a pass to spend Christmas at home."

"I see." Samuel's expression said just the opposite.

"I can't do it, Sam. You know why, and it has nothing to do with being a coward."

"No, but I do think you're afraid of something—and not just your mother's hovering or your brother's admiration." Samuel sat back and crossed his arms. "I think it's because you know you couldn't avoid seeing Annemarie."

The mere mention of her name shot waves of agony through Gilbert's chest. He let Samuel's words hang in the air while a nurse stopped at the foot of the bed to check his chart. Not the young redhead this time—he hadn't seen her since yesterday's fiasco—but a wizened hag who looked ancient enough to have served in the Civil War. She made a *tsk-tsk* sound, tapped a pen against her yellowed teeth, and moved on.

Apparently he'd have to wait awhile longer for his next pain injection.

"Gil?"

"*What?*" As soon as the snappish word left his lips, he wanted to snatch it back.

Samuel filled a glass from the water pitcher on the bedside stand and offered it to Gilbert. He took several swallows, relishing the coolness sliding down his throat. Small comfort, but he'd have to take it where he could find it. Memories gnawed at him—craving even a small sip of water as he drifted in and out of consciousness in an artillery-scalded crater, his mouth tasting like the dirt that half-buried him, his own blood staining the ground.

When his hand started to tremble, he thrust the glass at Samuel before he dropped it. His left ear throbbed in time with his pulsing heart. Any moment now, the top of his skull would rip away. *Dear God in heaven, help me!*

"Take it easy, Gil. Take it easy." A cool hand eased Gilbert's tangle of hair off his forehead. A soft chuckle sounded next to his good ear. "Remind me to make an appointment for you with the hospital barber. You're long overdue for a haircut."

The friendly chiding helped Gilbert refocus. Shallow breaths gradually deepened. The black mists retreated. "Guess if I'm going home for Christmas, I should at least look presentable, huh?"

"That would be a start." Relief flickered behind Samuel's eyes. "You don't need me to tell you how blessed you are to have so many people who care about you. Let them love you, Gil. That's all they want to do."

"I'm not sure I can bear up under such love."

"You can, Gil. God will give you the strength if you ask Him." Samuel cleared his throat and sat forward. "In fact, someone who loves you more than life itself is waiting right now to see you."

Gilbert's stomach convulsed. "No. Tell her—"

A vision in forest green plaid moved into his line of sight, and his words froze on his lips.

"Tell me yourself, Gilbert Ballard."

Annemarie! Heaven help him, she was beautiful. While Gilbert floundered for words, fumbled through his muddled brain for some logical argument to send her away again, Samuel rose and offered her his chair.

She sat primly, hands folded in her lap, and pierced him with a determined glare. "But it'll do you no good, because nothing short of a stampede of wild mustangs will budge me from this spot. And even then, I'd wrap my arms around you and hold on tight to save us both."

Gilbert shifted his gaze to Samuel. He tried to voice a plea for help—for understanding—but Samuel's position remained all too clear.

"I'll check in on you later, Gil." Sam winked. "Enjoy your visitor."

She could see it in his eyes, in the way his mouth twitched, in the curling of his fingers around the bedcovers. He didn't want her here and would send her away in a flash if she didn't hold her ground.

"I mean it, Gilbert. I'm staying." Catching Samuel's reassuring smile as he left the ward, Annemarie allowed his confidence to infuse her. Gilbert must be made to believe she'd never turn away from him. She would wait as long as it took for his body to heal and his spirit to find wholeness once more.

When she reached for his hand, he pulled it away and knotted his fist. "Don't, Annemarie. I'm sorry for how I've treated you since I came home, but I—I've changed. I'm not the same man who proposed to you last Christmas."

"Of course you are, Gilbert, in every way that matters." She ached to hold him, comfort him, make him believe in her love. But part of her knew he spoke the truth. This was not the Gilbert she remembered, and the sight of him fighting for control—for his dignity—nearly ripped her heart from her chest.

Again she reached for his hand, this time gripping his fist between both palms and refusing to let him pull it free. She could see she'd have to be strong for both of them and swallowed the anxious tears threatening to escape. "I'm not asking for anything more than to stay by your side through this ordeal. The past is behind us, and the future is in God's hands. All that matters right now is that you are getting the very best care and taking all the time you need to get well."

Gilbert's chin lifted imperceptibly. The cords of his neck tightened. Dark, brooding eyes met hers, drifted away, then snapped back with a fierce calm that nearly stopped her heart. A slow smile spread his lips. "I'm glad you feel that way, Annemarie. Your . . . friendship . . . it means the world."

She faltered, tried to draw air into lungs that seemed to have forgotten their purpose. "Friendship?"

"How long have we known each other? Twenty years, if it's a day." He closed his eyes for a moment, the corners crinkling as if he winced from pain. A strained laugh tore from his throat. "Remember in grade school how they used to tease us? Everyone just assumed we'd get married someday."

Annemarie forced a titter. "I remember." *Dear God, he's breaking it off!*

"And we played right along, didn't we?" Gilbert eased his hand from her grip and gently tucked her fingers into his palm. "It's all right, Annemarie. I won't hold you to promises made in haste. We both went a little crazy last year. But don't blame yourself. Lots of couples jumped into engagements—even foolish marriages—when Wilson declared war and started sending troops off to France."

She stared at their entwined hands, her engagement ring mocking her. A single tear slipped down her cheek, fell to her lap, stained her skirt a darker shade of green. "Foolishness. It would seem so, wouldn't it, when so many of those men were destined never to return?"

"It's good we waited, didn't rush into anything permanent." His firm nod belied the merest tremor in his voice. He barely concealed it with another of his rakish grins.

Why don't I believe you, Gilbert Ballard? And why, after months of anticipating this moment, was she so unwilling to accept the bald truth, that his feelings for her had dimmed during the time they'd been apart? As if the horrors of war weren't enough, a year was a long time for sweethearts to be separated.

She slid her hands into her lap. Her spine ached with the effort to hold her body erect, when all she wanted to do was crumble at Gilbert's bedside and plead with him to say he loved her, would always love her, and that their future wasn't disintegrating before her eyes. With shaking fingers she tugged off her engagement ring and thrust it into Gilbert's hand. "This was your grandmother's. You'll want to keep it for—for—"

A sob began deep within her chest. She pressed a fist against her lips to hold it in, but it escaped as a burst of near hysterical laughter. She popped up from the chair. "Oh my, I must go. Mama's waiting for me so we can decorate the tree, and I still have shopping to do, and—"

Please, Lord, tell me this isn't happening. Let me wake up and find this has all been a horrid nightmare!

But the stoic set of Gilbert's mouth, the coolness in his hooded hazel eyes, told her it was all real. "Good-bye, Annemarie. Thanks for understanding."

"Yes. Good-bye." She prayed she'd make it past the door before she fell apart completely.

11

$\mathcal{G}$ilbert Ballard, have you completely lost your mind?" Half an hour, forty-five minutes at most—that's all the time Samuel had taken to look in on a couple of patients after leaving Annemarie alone with Gilbert.

Apparently, it was plenty of time for Gilbert to make the biggest mistake of his life. Annemarie's visit was supposed to change everything, make Gilbert see how stupidly selfish he was being in pushing her away.

Everything had changed, all right, and not the way Samuel had hoped. By the time he returned to the ward, Annemarie had gone. A nurse said she'd flown by so fast she'd forgotten the coat she'd left on a waiting-area chair.

Gilbert tugged the blanket up around his chest and rolled away, his eyes glazing in the dazed look another dose of morphine always brought. "Lea' me alone. Wanna sleep."

Clawing the hair at his temple, Samuel wished he could give himself permission to use a few of the swear words in Gilbert's repertoire. "You're a blasted fool, that's what you are. How could you do this to her? How could you do this to *yourself*?"

Staring at Gilbert's back, he fingered the tiny gold cross pinned to his collar. Fat lot of good he was at this chaplaincy business. He'd managed to ensure not one but two broken hearts this Christmas, because judging from Gilbert's blubbery, drug-induced snores, the idiot had just cried himself to sleep.

No, the only idiot in this room was Samuel. He should have known Gilbert was still too weak, too fragile to think and act rationally. The best he could hope for now was with the passage of time Gilbert would come to regret his decision and realize how much he loved and needed Annemarie, how much she loved and needed him.

Well, there was nothing more to be done here, at least until Gilbert's drugs wore off and Samuel could try again to talk some sense into him. In the meantime, the least Samuel could do was apologize to Annemarie and try to assuage her broken heart. He shoved through the doors at the end of the ward, retrieved Annemarie's coat, and raced downstairs. Seeing no sign of her in the lobby, he hurried out the main doors and down to the promenade.

The clang of a streetcar along Central Avenue drew his attention. He reached the curb in time to see a woman in forest green climb aboard just before the streetcar lurched forward.

Out of breath, furious with both himself and Gilbert, Samuel heaved a despairing sigh. How could he be so utterly stupid?

The answer stabbed him like a bayonet. Because keeping Gilbert and Annemarie together was the only way Samuel could keep his own heart intact.

He hugged the folds of Annemarie's wool coat to his chest. A delicate scent lingered, a poignant mixture of roses and mothballs. Barely a week had passed since he'd first met Annemarie, and yet he felt as if he'd known her a lifetime. She was everything Gilbert had described and so much more—beauty, grace, intelligence, artistry. She deserved better than this, better than Gilbert's rejection, better than Samuel's ineptitude.

He must find her at once and somehow make amends.

✿

Mary McClarney peeled off her mask and gown and stuffed them into a hamper. Of all the duties Mrs. Daley could have reassigned her to, why did it have to be tending Spanish flu patients in the isolation ward?

Punishment, no doubt. Mary's just reward for letting herself get too emotionally attached to a patient.

As if Lieutenant Ballard even knew her name—much less, cared.

She went to the sink and scrubbed her hands, using a stiff brush to scour nail beds, knuckles, and every crack and crevice where invisible influenza germs might hide. Even though deterrents and home remedies remained unproven, Mary had faithfully tried anything that sounded the least bit likely to ensure staying healthy herself and prevent the spread of this vicious disease to her mother. Camphor balls, doses of turpentine-laced sugar, onions by the bushel cooked into every recipe imaginable.

She had to laugh. She must reek to high heaven. Was it any wonder she'd yet to find a beau?

Another nurse barged into the dressing area, ripped off her mask, and flung it into the hamper. Bursting into tears, she sank onto a bench and covered her face with her hands. "Such a horrid, vile, merciless disease! I can't do this anymore!"

Mary's first impulse was to rush to the poor girl's side and comfort her. Even more important, to get her out of her contaminated gown and over to the sink for a thorough hand-washing.

But common sense prevailed, and Mary held her ground on the far side of the room.

"There now—Lois, isn't it? It's hard, I know, but have a care for your own health, or you'll be no good to anyone. Wash up real good now, and let's go have a cup of tea. We could both use a few minutes away from the ward."

Lois lowered her hands and gaped at them as if seeing them for the first time. "Oh my. Oh my!" She leapt to her feet and yanked off her gown, then staggered to the sink and scrubbed her hands furiously, then leaned over to wash her face with equal vigor. "I can't get sick, I can't!"

"Aye, so we must take every precaution." Mary handed the girl a clean towel. "How long have you been assigned to this ward?"

"Two weeks, five days, and"—Lois patted droplets from her cheeks and chin before checking the watch pinned to her smock—"three hours, twenty-four minutes."

Mary's eyes widened. "Indeed?"

"Today's your first day, isn't it?" With a caustic laugh, Lois tossed the towel into the hamper and started for the exit. "Just you wait until you watch your first patient nearly drown in his own body fluids. Then see if you aren't counting the minutes until you get reassigned."

In the nurses' lounge, Mary heated a kettle of water and then poured them each a cup of tea. They sat across from each other at a small table and sipped in silence for several minutes. A pallor had settled over Lois, her face devoid of any expression beyond utter fatigue. Mary had been nursing long enough to know that letting oneself get run down only increased the chance of succumbing to illness. As long as she worked the isolation ward, she'd have to be even more diligent about taking care of herself.

This meant she couldn't afford another sleepless night like the one she'd just had—all for worrying over the handsome lieutenant.

At long last, Lois stretched out one leg and eased her back. "Guess I haven't thanked you for bringing me to my senses back there. I try not to let it get to me, but in all my years of nursing I've never seen anything like the Spanish influenza."

Staring into her cup, Mary gave her head a sad shake. "And so many still gettin' sick, just when we hoped the epidemic was over."

Lois drained the final few sips of her tea. "Sure doesn't feel like Christmas, does it?"

"Aye, in some ways I must agree." Mary rubbed the swelling along the left side of her face.

Lois's gaze turned sympathetic. She reached across the table and patted Mary's wrist. "Boyfriend lose his temper? You should ditch the creep."

"Oh, no, it's nothing like that." Rising, Mary collected their empty cups and bustled to the sink to wash them.

"Hey, there's nothing to be ashamed of. Some guys just have no class."

"I'm telling you, that isn't what happened." Briefly she explained about yesterday's incident with Lieutenant Ballard. "It was my own fault. I should have called over an orderly instead of trying to quiet him myself."

A knowing smile curled one side of Lois's mouth. "So that's why Mrs. Daley sentenced you to the isolation ward." She braced her hands on her thighs and pushed to her feet with a groan. "Speaking of which, I suppose we'd better get back."

"Yes, I suppose." Mary rinsed and dried their cups and set them on a shelf. "Would you mind if I ran a quick errand first? I . . . well, I'm a wee bit concerned about a former patient."

Lois lifted a brow. "Would it be your handsome lieutenant?"

Mary's only answer was a single-shoulder shrug and the rosy blush burning her cheeks. Without bothering to fetch her warm woolen nurse's cape, she dashed along the connecting breezeway and into the main building. After first making sure Mrs. Daley wasn't on the floor, she donned a mask—as much to hide her features as to avoid the spread of germs—and slipped into Lieutenant Ballard's ward.

But the lieutenant's bed was empty, stripped down to the bare mattress. The chart no longer hung from the footboard, and none of the lieutenant's personal items remained on the bedside table. Standing in the aisle, Mary released a soft moan.

"You looking for the lieutenant?" A rheumatic old soldier in the next bed caught her eye, and she nodded. "They done took him away not an hour ago."

"Took him away?" Mary's chest tightened. "Do you know where?"

"Nobody tells me nothing. All's I know is he had another of them nightmares, woke up yelling and flailing and cursing to beat the band, and the orderlies had him out of here lickety-split."

Bile rose in Mary's throat. They'd gone and done it—had him transferred to an asylum somewhere! Even worse than the thought of never seeing him again was the image of such a fine soldier being locked away, all hope of returning to normal life obliterated with one signature on the commitment papers.

She'd seen it happen with her own Da. Mary was only a wee lass when her father's head was nearly crushed like a melon beneath the hooves of a frightened horse. The wounds healed, but Da was never the same afterward. He'd forget something they'd told him five minutes earlier, lose his temper over trivial upsets, wake screaming from horrid dreams. Mum tended and cared for him with the patience of Job, and Mary had helped as best she could. But when the stress and strain stole Mum's health, she'd had no choice but to commit Da to an institution. He went to be with his Maker only a few months later.

To this day Mary believed her father had died not of old age or sickness but of loneliness. And it was the memory of those years of struggle that prompted Mary to become a nurse.

She trudged from the ward and sank onto the first chair she came to. Sliding the gauze mask from her face, she bowed her head in prayer. *Dear Jesus, wrap Lieutenant Ballard in your gentle arms. Soothe his troubled soul. Restore him to his right mind, and let him bask in Your precious, bounteous peace.*

Annemarie closed the lid on an empty ornament box. "The tree is finished, Mama. If there's nothing else you need me for, I should get to the factory."

Mama turned from arranging greenery along the mantel and surveyed the room. "I believe that's everything. Papa chose quite an exquisite tree this year, didn't he?"

"The best ever, I'm sure." Annemarie coaxed her lips into a faint smile. It had been easy enough to conceal her heartbreak as long as she stayed busy at her tasks, but now, beneath Mama's probing gaze, she felt her mask of reserve slipping.

Mama dusted off her hands and stepped closer, the corners of her eyes crinkling with a concerned frown. "Don't think I haven't noticed how quiet you've been since you came home from your shopping excursion. Did something happen while you were out?"

Something? Where to begin? From the elation of finding all her ceramic pieces had sold to the crushing blow of Gilbert's rejection—all Annemarie could do was choke out a pained laugh as she sank upon the sofa.

"Darling, what on earth?" Arms outstretched, Mama started toward her, only to halt at a rap on the front door. With a regretful shake of her head, she detoured into the entry hall. The front door creaked open. "Chaplain Vickary. How good to see you again."

"Good morning, Mrs. Kendall."

Samuel? Then he must know. Why else would he have come? Annemarie clutched her stomach. She wasn't sure she had the strength to face him yet—not after he'd been so adamant about bringing her and Gilbert together.

Samuel cleared his throat. "I, uh—is Annemarie here, by chance?"

Please, Mama, tell him I'm indisposed.

"In fact, she is. Won't you come in?"

Suppressing a groan, Annemarie rose as her mother led Samuel into the parlor. She tucked a stray curl behind her ear and offered a strained smile, then noticed her coat folded across his arm.

He held it out to her. "You left this at the hospital. I tried to catch you before you got away, but . . ." His words drifted into silence.

Stepping between them, Mama took the coat from Samuel and gave Annemarie a confused stare. "You went to the hospital this morning? Why didn't you say so?"

"I hadn't planned to go." Now, she wished with all her heart she'd never stepped through those doors. She swallowed a sob and spun around, only to be mocked by the benevolently smiling angel atop the Christmas tree.

Behind her, Mama spoke to Samuel, her tone bristling. "Clearly there is more to my daughter's distress than leaving her coat behind after a visit to the hospital she never intended to make. And now, your appearance at my front door, your eyes reflecting no small amount of—what do I see there? Remorse? Guilt?"

"Mama, please." Shoulders drooping, Annemarie turned once more to face them. "It isn't Samuel's fault. He only thought to help."

But she could see her mother was right. Self-reproach did indeed darken Samuel's gray gaze. Doffing his cap and mangling it between clenched fists, he edged forward. "Annemarie, I'm so terribly sorry. I shouldn't have interfered. I should have realized—"

"Realized *what?*" Petite though she was, Mama could roar like a tigress when her child was threatened. "Did something happen with Gilbert?"

The tears Annemarie had fought so hard to suppress now gushed like the Arkansas River at flood stage. "He broke our engagement, Mama! It's over between us."

"Oh dear, oh my dear!" Mama tossed the coat onto a chair and drew Annemarie into a fierce embrace, one hand caressing Annemarie's back with long, firm strokes. "This is what you feared all along, isn't it? Well, it's his loss. And he'll come to regret this foolishness in time, I'm certain."

Annemarie pushed away from her mother's embrace and swiped angrily at her wet cheeks. Oh, how she hated tears, hated giving in to such feminine frailty. Stiffening her spine, she inhaled a quivery breath. "No, Mama, I don't think so. The war has changed Gilbert, changed all of us. There's no going back to the way things were."

Samuel hung his head and whispered out a tired sigh. When he looked up again, understanding showed in his eyes. No, more than understanding, a kind of kinship, as if he'd traveled the same road and lived to tell about it. His voice barely a whisper, he said, "I'm so sorry, Annemarie. I'd hoped—prayed—"

"It's all right, Samuel." She went to him, wrapped her arms around his shoulders, pressed her cheek to his. "Just please keep being Gilbert's friend. And mine. I have a feeling we're both going to need you more than ever in the days to come."

12

$\mathscr{G}$ilbert slumped in his wheelchair as his mother stood over him with knife and fork and sawed a serving of Christmas turkey into bite-size pieces. Bad enough when a nurse or orderly assisted him with his hospital meals. But to sit here helpless while his mother babied him like a two-year-old as his entire family, two house guests, and the servants looked on? Now his humiliation was complete.

His mother rested the silverware upon the edge of his plate. "And how about some gravy on your potatoes and dressing?"

How about you take your seat and leave me alone? "Yes, thank you, Mother." The polite words nearly strangled him.

Marguerite brought the gravy boat from the sideboard. "Let me, Miz Ballard. You sit yourself down and enjoy your dinner."

And thank you, Marguerite. Gilbert stabbed a piece of turkey and tried to ignore the patronizing glances as he chewed.

Uncle Bob Carnahan, Mother's brother from Little Rock, started a basket of rolls around the dining table. "Sure is good to see you up and about, Gil. I was just saying to your Aunt Betty the other day how I still remember the day you climbed the big ol' holly tree in our backyard."

Aunt Betty splayed a hand across her bosom. "Scared us half to death when you came crashing down—must have been a good twenty feet or more! Thank the Lord for your hard head. Why, you were out cold so long we feared the worst."

Gilbert could think of nothing more appealing at the moment than being "out cold." The miserly doctor had doled out barely enough morphine pills to get Gilbert through his forty-eight-hour Christmas pass. His mother and Thomas had brought him home from the hospital yesterday shortly after noon, with instructions to have him back by 1300 hours tomorrow.

At least on Friday they'd finally moved him to a semi-private room in the officers' wing. Now, instead of trying to sleep through the snores and coughs of two dozen ward mates, he only had to listen to one old colonel complain about his gout.

But Friday was a day he'd just as soon forget. Not even those endless hours in a French field hospital and the unremitting torture of having his wounds irrigated and dressed could match the agony of watching Annemarie march silently out of his life.

Somehow, he made it through dinner, despite a clumsy teen-age cousin nearly dumping a bowl of green beans into his lap. Finally, Marguerite served dessert, something he could handle without extra assistance. In addition to the traditional pumpkin, Samuel's mother had contributed two sweet and tangy rhubarb pies made with fresh stalks of rhubarb she'd carried in her satchel all the way on the train from Fort Wayne.

While the ladies retired to the parlor for coffee and conversation, Thomas suggested the men fetch their coats and take advantage of the sun's warmth on the westerly facing front porch. Gilbert suspected the idea had less to do with soaking up a few weak December rays than avoiding Mother's disapproving glare while Thomas smoked one of his Camels.

"I'll pass, thank you. I'm ready for a nap." Gilbert struggled to turn his wheelchair in the direction of the study at the other end of the hall, where Hank, Marguerite's husband and the family's butler, had set up a bed for him. His head ached. His arm ached. His stump ached. And he just wanted to be left alone.

"Here, let me." Samuel gripped the chair handles and rolled Gilbert toward the study. Once inside the room, he kicked the door closed behind them and parked Gilbert near a window where pale sunlight filtered through gauzy curtains.

Gilbert unfastened the top button of his uniform blouse. Mother had insisted he wear the scratchy thing—had to parade her war-hero son for the visiting relatives. "I can handle it from here. Your mother just got to town. Go spend some time with her while you have the chance."

"She'll be here for a week. I'll have plenty of opportunities." Hands folded behind his back, Samuel stared out the window behind Gilbert's head.

The man's stoic silence began to grate on Gilbert's nerves. He slapped the wheelchair arm. "Stop it, will you? I swear, you could give hovering lessons to my mother!"

"Sorry. I'll leave you alone." Samuel turned to go, then paused, chin tucked to his chest. "Really, I'm sorry—"

"Not another word. I'll put up with pity and condescension from anyone but you." Gilbert forced air between his teeth. "And for God's sake stop blaming yourself. It was my choice—mine—to end it with Annemarie. I told you all along that was my intent."

Samuel's shoulders lifted with a shudder. He spun around. "And I've told you all along you didn't have to do it. How can you give her so little credit? Do you think she'd have stayed with you only out of pity or obligation? Can't you see how much she loves you?"

"How many times do I have to say this? She's in love with the man I was before the war. I've changed. Everything's changed." Gilbert gripped the wheel and jerked his chair toward the bed. "Get out, will you? This conversation is over."

Behind him, he heard Samuel's frustrated sigh, and then the quiet click of the closing door. His glance fell on the amber bottle on the bedside table. How many pills were left? Three, maybe four. He'd swallow them all at once if he thought it would put him out of his misery. At best, he'd enjoy a few hours of opiate-induced nirvana. At worst, his mother would find him and panic. He'd be carted back to the hospital and put on suicide watch, if they didn't ship him straight to an asylum.

Pain radiated through his skull while images blistered the backs of his eyeballs—enemy machine guns mowing down wave after wave as his men stormed from the trenches, a blast of artillery fire taking out six infantrymen in one startling burst, German flamethrowers incinerating a whole platoon.

And then the whizzbang with his name on it.

He shoved his mangled left fist against his temple and forced down the howl of angry terror searing his throat. Maybe he *was* crazy—or if not, he soon would be.

He checked the clock and counted the hours—close enough. He downed a pill, maneuvered himself onto the bed, and gave himself over to the arms of Morpheus.

With the Jones Restaurant Supply order complete and out for delivery and the factory partially shut down between Christmas and New Year's, Annemarie welcomed the freedom to devote herself to her own pottery creations. The constant motion of the wheel soothed her, carrying her thoughts away until she lost all track of the passing of time. The smooth, wet clay sliding beneath her fingers was like balm for the burning hole in her heart.

Papa hadn't even said a word when she'd excused herself after their quiet Christmas dinner to spend a few hours in the workshop. After her painful last visit with Gilbert, it had taken nearly the whole weekend before she recovered her senses enough to think of anything else. Then, when she'd finally shown her parents the money Thomas had collected from sales of her ceramic pieces, Mama had clapped her hands in delight, and Papa had nodded thoughtfully.

"I suppose I'll have to get with the times," he'd said, "before Ouachita Pottery runs us clean out of business with their fancy wares."

Even so, it was small consolation.

By early January, Annemarie had two full crates of new pieces to deliver to the Arlington, including the special orders Thomas had given her before Christmas. She rode to the hotel with Papa and a factory worker in one of the Kendall Pottery delivery trucks, and they made short work of unpacking the items and putting them on display.

Thomas stood by to supervise. "Fantastic work, Annemarie. These'll be gone before you know it."

She smiled her thanks, a bubble of pride swelling her chest. "With the extra time to work over the holidays, I'm even closer to perfecting my 'Ouachita sunrise' glaze."

"Definitely a customer favorite." Thomas stuffed his hands into his pants pockets. His voice fell to a murmur. "We missed seeing you over Christmas."

Annemarie took a few steps away from her father. "I hope you and your family had a pleasant day."

"With a houseful of aunts, uncles, and cousins, and a bad-tempered brother who scarcely said three words to anyone the entire time he was home? 'Pleasant' doesn't quite describe it." Thomas's left cheek dimpled in a crooked frown. "Everybody seems to be tiptoeing around the subject, but we all think he's a fool."

"Don't hold it against him, Thomas. I don't."

"Are you kidding? How can you forgive him for dumping you?"

"Do I have a choice?" An aching knot tied itself around Annemarie's throat. "I suppose it was inevitable. We hadn't seen each other for nearly a year—even longer when you count his semesters away at West Point. We fell in love as kids who thought the world was safe. We grew up to find ourselves in a world at war."

"Yeah, yeah, Gil spouts pretty much the same rhetoric. The world's changed. He's changed. We've all changed." Giving a huff, Thomas fumbled through his pockets and pulled out a pack of cigarettes. He tapped one out and lit up, blowing a curl of smoke toward the ceiling. "I need to get back to work. I'll give you a ring in a week or so and let you know how your stuff is selling."

Watching him stride across the lobby, Annemarie felt another tiny piece of her heart tear away. Thomas had his faults, but he was a good son, a loyal brother. He would have made a charming brother-in-law, something Annemarie as an only child had looked forward to.

As it was, now she could look forward to a long and lonely spinsterhood working in her father's factory. At least she had her potter's wheel—and now her father's blessing, grudging as it might be. Perhaps one day she'd fulfill the dream of having her own shop, right here in downtown Hot Springs.

A sudden memory stabbed her—the one and only time she'd dared to put such notions into words, in a letter to Gilbert at West Point. At the time, she thought his reply romantically chivalrous. Now she sensed a touch of his mother's condescension creeping in: *"My darling, once we're married you'll have no need of such pursuits. I intend to keep you far too busy as the beautiful and charming Mrs. Gilbert Ballard."*

Papa dusted off his hands and drew his arm around her. "Ready to go, Annie-girl?"

Swallowing against the twinge beneath her heart, she turned to study the neatly arranged ceramic pieces. "If it's all the same to you, Papa, I'd like to nose around town for a bit, maybe do a little shopping. I won't be long, I promise."

She walked with her father and his helper as far as the truck, then crossed to the other side of Central Avenue and strolled past shops, cafés, and office buildings. Pausing before a vacant storefront, she imagined her ceramic creations filling the display window, her name in crisp gold and black lettering painted on the door. A tiny thrill of hope lifted her heart, and for the first time since Gilbert's rejection—since Wilson declared war on Germany, if she were completely honest—she could look ahead to a future filled with possibilities.

The midmorning sun peeked over Hot Springs Mountain, brightening the bathhouse rooftops and warming the top of Annemarie's head. One ray pierced the dusty glass and illuminated a placard in the display window, partially hidden beneath a strip of crumbling butcher paper. She made out the words FOR LEASE, CALL FOR DETAILS, the name Ralph Patton, and a number.

Ralph Patton. She engraved the name across her mind, determined to place the call at her first opportunity. Probably a bit premature, but how would she know unless she asked?

A streetcar bell clanged behind her. If she hurried, she could catch a ride up Whittington Avenue and get off a block from the factory. Before she could reach the corner, Samuel Vickary exited the trolley, and her heart flip-flopped. She hadn't seen him since his awkward attempt to apologize on that day she'd just as soon forget.

She'd almost decided to forego the streetcar and scurry off in the opposite direction, but then his eyes met hers. He froze for a second, one foot in the street, the other on the curb, until a motorcar horn blasted a warning and propelled him out of harm's way.

With an embarrassed grin, he ambled toward her. As usual, he was without his overcoat, his shoulders hunched against the cold.

Annemarie offered her hand in greeting. "How are you, Samuel? Did you have a good Christmas with your mother?"

"She enjoyed her visit very much. You look well. I hope your holidays were . . ." Dropping his gaze, he toed a crack in the sidewalk.

Annemarie released a flippant laugh. "There's no need to guard your words with me, Sam. We're friends, remember?"

He gave her a sad-eyed smile. "Thank you. Lately, I've been feeling like the ultimate heel. Gil's even banished me from his presence."

Annemarie gave her head a quick shake. "Then he really is a fool." A frosty gust of wind blew a bit of torn newspaper past them, and Samuel shivered. "As are you, Samuel Vickary. Why on earth will you not dress properly when you venture out on a winter's day?"

"I hadn't expected to be lingering on the sidewalk talking to a pre—" He clamped his mouth shut. His cheeks blushed a rosy shade of pink.

An unexpected fluttering began beneath Annemarie's breastbone. His flattery, though interrupted, touched a part of her soul that hadn't stirred in months. She hooked her arm through his and nudged him into a brisk walk. "There's a charming little bakery right up the street. We can warm up with coffee and scones."

☙

Sunlight poured through the bakery window, gilding Annemarie's hair and bringing a glint to her deep brown eyes as they sat sipping coffee at a small, marble-top table. Samuel's breath hitched. He could fall in love so easily if he'd let himself.

But he couldn't, not while the clouds of war still shrouded his soul.

Not while a dying soldier's blood still stained his hands.

Besides, Annemarie loved Gilbert, always would. Surely, it was only a matter of time before they'd reunite. Gilbert was recovering well after his latest surgery. Amazingly, the daily soaks of his shattered arm in the thermal baths seemed to be restoring some strength and mobility. Once his stump fully healed, he could get a prosthesis, and all this nonsense about returning half a man, unable to be the husband Annemarie deserved, would be forgotten.

"Warmer now?" Annemarie nibbled on a buttery scone.

He prodded his errant thoughts back to the present. "Much. Best coffee I've had in ages."

"So where *were* you headed when you got off the trolley?" Her lips curled into a provocative smile. "Am I keeping you from some vitally urgent appointment?"

"Nothing that can't wait. I . . . well, I'm looking to move out of the Ballards' home."

Annemarie fiddled with her napkin. "I thought you were quite comfortable there."

"I was—*am*. I mean, as far as the living arrangements." Samuel inched his chair back and drummed his fingers on the table. How could he explain without sounding uncharitable?

"It's just, seeing so much of Mrs. Ballard and Thomas, I'm finding it hard to uphold the necessary standards of confidentiality."

"I think I understand." Annemarie nodded slowly. "They expect you to share freely about every aspect of Gilbert's recuperation."

"Whether I agree with his reasons or not, as hospital chaplain I'm obligated to respect every patient's privacy."

She shifted, folding her hands upon the edge of the table. "Would it infringe upon his rights too severely if I were to ask you how he's doing?"

"I would be breaking no confidence in replying that, physically, he is mending as well as can be expected."

"But emotionally, spiritually . . ." Annemarie fingered the handle of her coffee cup. "Your silence on those subjects speaks louder than words."

"I cannot say more." Although he wanted to. He wanted to say much more, and not a word of it about Gilbert. He wanted to tell her how beautifully her violet blouse flattered those luminous brown eyes. He wanted to tell her the curve of her mouth when she smiled sent tingles up his spine. He wanted to ask permission to wrap his fingers around the errant curl forever sliding out of her bun, and to caress her ivory cheek.

"Samuel?" She laughed shyly, a curious look bowing her brows. "What on earth is going on in that head of yours?"

Face aflame, he bustled to his feet. "I've been dawdling far longer than I should. I'd offer to see you home—or to your factory—or wherever you're off to—but I've got to get back to the hospital."

Worry etched her forehead. "I shouldn't have kept you."

"On the contrary. This was much more pleasant than traipsing through dreary apartment buildings." He helped her from the chair and into her coat. Outside on the sidewalk he said a hurried good-bye and strode off at a brisk clip toward the hospital.

Arriving at the tiny office he'd been assigned, he flopped into his chair with a groan. For his own sanity he ought to avoid Annemarie at all costs. She made him think thoughts and dream dreams he had no right giving brain space to. Gilbert may have convinced her his feelings had changed, but Annemarie's love for Gilbert had not faded in the least—of that, Samuel was certain.

He gave his head an annoyed shake, as if to clear away his futile notions. A stack of messages lay in the center of his desk, and with a resigned shrug, he sorted through them. The majority were routine requests for prayer. Two patients had asked for spiritual counseling visits at his earliest convenience. Another message was a note from a nurse working the isolation ward, where a soldier severely ill with the Spanish flu feared dying without receiving absolution for his sins and desperately wanted to see the chaplain.

Absolution for sins. The words twisted through Samuel's gut, stirring up images he'd been fighting every moment to suppress for the past five months. How could he convey God's grace to another human being when he struggled so mightily to receive it for himself?

13

For nearly three weeks now, Mary had been working the isolation ward. Saints be praised, the influenza cases had tapered off, and not one death since the worst of the hospital outbreak back in October. Oh, the poor souls suffered gravely, and it was no pleasant task mopping feverish brows and trying to force fluids and nourishment into bodies too weak to respond. But at long last, there appeared light at the end of this dark and dreary tunnel.

She looked up from tending a delirious old gent to see a tall man in mask and gown enter the ward. Ah, yes, the chaplain. "Over here, sir, if you please." Her voice sounded muffled as she pushed the words through her mask.

Though she couldn't see his mouth, his eyes smiled a tentative greeting. "Are you the nurse who sent for me?"

"Mary McClarney, at your service." She pointed toward a curtained-off area at the other end of the ward. "I've got a patient who's certain he's dying of pneumonia. He's not nearly as close to death as he fears, but he's been asking all morning for a priest. I told him on such short notice our nice Protestant chaplain would have to do."

The chaplain's brows drew together. Beneath his mask, Mary could see his jaw muscles flex. "I'll offer what comfort I can."

"I don't have to remind you to keep your mask in place, and to wash up good when you leave the ward." Mary led the way and positioned a chair beside the bed. "Sergeant King, sir," she whispered close to the patient's ear. "I've brought the chaplain."

Rheumy eyes fluttered open. Dry lips parted in a gap-toothed smile before a cough rumbled through the man's chest. He wiggled his fingers, signaling the chaplain to come closer. "Need to . . . confess."

Chaplain Vickary sat on the edge of the chair and cradled the sergeant's hand between his own. "The Lord knows your heart, Sergeant King, and His promise is sure: 'If we confess our sins, he is faithful and righteous to forgive us our sins, and to cleanse us from all unrighteousness.'"

Catholic or Protestant, layman or clergy, truer words were never spoken. Mary smiled beneath her mask and left the chaplain to his duties. A fine man, the chaplain was, so kind and gentle, always ready with a listening ear and a comforting word of Scripture.

A shame he always seemed so lonely, though. Once during the holidays she'd seen him showing his mum around the hospital and grounds, and Mary was glad to know he wasn't spending his Christmas alone. She'd heard he'd taken rooms with the family of handsome Lieutenant Ballard—who, thankfully, hadn't been transferred to an asylum as she'd feared. Mary would admit to no one how often she peeked into the officers' wing, hoping for even a glimpse of the dark-haired lieutenant or at least news of his condition. She had a few sins of her own to confess, mainly for . . . well, for stretching the truth a bit about nonexistent errands taking her past Lieutenant Ballard's room.

"Nurse? Some water, please?"

"Here you go, sir." She held a glass to a grizzled patient's lips. This one was on the upside of his battle with the flu. Another few days without a fever and he'd be disinfected and returned to a regular ward.

A commotion behind her made her whirl around. The chaplain strode past in a blur of white, his face grim, and his breath coming in stuttering gasps. Besides his obvious distress, Mary saw immediately he'd lowered his mask.

Saints above, she'd warned him, hadn't she? She darted after him, catching up as he pushed through the doors. "Chaplain! Do you want to be the next patient in my ward?"

He halted by the hamper, a dazed look in his somber gray eyes. He pulled off his gown and wadded it into a ball. "Sorry, I wasn't thinking."

"Now I know Saint Paul wrote about putting on the whole armor of the Lord, but when it comes to the Spanish influenza, God expects us to use a little common sense." Mary pointed to the sink. "You get yourself washed up right this instant."

Meek as a chastised young schoolboy, the chaplain bent over the sink and soaped his hands. Mary folded her arms and watched, not so much to be sure he didn't miss a knuckle or nail, but because her instincts told her something more than a sick old soldier's confession had happened just now.

"Chaplain, sir, are you all right?"

He shut off the water and dried his hands, then braced his palms on the rim of the sink. Without meeting her gaze, he asked, "Do you believe God forgives every sin?"

"If I know my Scripture, there's only one sin the Bible says won't be forgiven."

"To blaspheme against the Holy Spirit." He turned, lifting weary eyes to meet hers. "What do you think it means?"

"You're asking me?" Her face grew hot behind her mask. Gingerly she lowered it but stayed by the door. "Well, I was always taught it means to reject the truth of Jesus' messiahship, like the Pharisees did. In other words, to deny God is God."

His gaze slid to somewhere beyond her shoulder, and he nodded slowly. "Exactly."

Then, looking as forlorn as if he himself were walking the road to the cross, Chaplain Vickary trudged away.

With the war behind them and the country slowly returning to normal, factory orders had increased significantly since the first of the year. Her days filled with bookkeeping, invoices, and filing, Annemarie was compelled to limit her own pottery making to the evening hours—and keeping busy suited her just fine.

Even so, she'd hinted to Papa that perhaps someday soon they might consider hiring part-time office help. Ever since Monday, the name Ralph Patton had played through her thoughts. Pointless to even make an inquiry when clearly she was in no position to rent shop space. But if she didn't increase production and sales of her ceramic designs, she'd never save up enough to be able to open a shop.

The telephone rang, and Annemarie moved the ledger aside to answer the call. "Kendall Pottery Works."

"Hello, Annemarie. It's Thomas. Will you be there for a few more minutes? I have another nice little wad of cash to bring you."

She drew in a squeaky breath. "Really?"

"Yeah, really." Thomas chuckled. "Why do you always sound so surprised that people are buying your work?"

She had no answer for him and instead replied, "It's almost closing time, but if you're on your way, I'll wait for you."

"Be there in a jiff."

By the time Thomas drove up, Papa had shut down the plant for the day and headed home. Annemarie tucked a receipt into the filing cabinet and then hurried to answer Thomas's tap on the locked front door.

He sauntered into the office and with dramatic flourish pulled an envelope from his inside coat pocket. "For you, Miss Kendall."

Not as plump as last time, but still a sizable amount. Annemarie ran her thumb along the tightly packed bills. "Thank you, Thomas. This is wonderful."

"Oh, and I have three more special orders for you. These folks will be in town for a month or two for spa treatments, so no big rush."

Annemarie glanced over the pages he handed her. "I'll start on these right away."

"I'll be on my way, then. Mother's got big dinner plans for us tonight." He angled a foot toward the door. "Maybe you've heard. Gil was released from the hospital this morning."

A tremor started in Annemarie's abdomen. She swiveled away and laid the envelope and papers on the desk. "No, I hadn't heard. Good news, indeed."

"He'll go back several times a week for outpatient therapy. They're trying to get his arm strong enough so he can handle crutches and won't have to use the wheelchair."

She smiled over her shoulder. "I'm glad for him. For all of you."

"Annemarie." Thomas's voice softened, became pleading. He grazed her elbow with the fingers of one hand. "You should come over this weekend. Let Gil know you still care. He'll come around in time. I know he will."

"I don't think a visit right now would be wise."

"Did it ever occur to you that Mother and I miss you, too?"

"Oh, Thomas." Seeing the forlorn look on his face, she went to him and offered a quick hug. He smelled of spearmint and tobacco smoke. Straightening, she flicked a piece of lint off his lapel and then gave his shoulder a sisterly pat. "You should get home. I need to close up, too, or Papa will be back to drag me home by my ear."

She shooed him out the door and locked it behind him, then fetched her coat and turned off the lights. If not for the scolding she'd get if she skipped supper, she wouldn't even bother going home but would set to work at once on those special orders. Her fingers itched to knead the clay and shape it into something uniquely beautiful upon the wheel, then to fire it in the kiln and add color and drama with paint and glaze.

Soon enough, soon enough. Leaving the steam heat on in the workroom, she exited out the back and started up the street toward home.

The savory aroma of roasting chicken greeted her as she burst through the kitchen door. Her stomach let out a growl, reminding her she was hungrier than she'd thought. "Smells delicious, Mama. Let me hang up my coat and I'll help you get supper on the table."

Mama donned quilted mitts and tugged open the oven door. "Call your papa in from the parlor. He's looking at the mail."

Annemarie paused in the entryway to hang up her coat on the hall tree and then strode into the parlor. Papa sprawled in his favorite chair, a monstrous thing upholstered in plush gray velveteen, and riffled through a small stack of letters and advertisements. She looked over his shoulder. "Anything interesting?"

He glanced up with a shrug. "The light bill. A circular from Stolzenberg's Grocery. And here's a belated Christmas card from your great-aunt Stella, along with a six-page letter. Looks like your mother's already read it. Probably quicker to let her fill you in."

"Probably so." Annemarie couldn't help but chuckle. They usually only heard from this eccentric old aunt at Christmastime, and she was known to ramble on about the events of the past year. "Mama's ready to get supper on the table. She said to . . ."

A motion outside the front window caught Annemarie's eye. She edged behind her father's chair and drew back the curtain for a better look. Across the street, someone tottered back and forth along the sidewalk in front of the Trapps' house. The corner streetlamp didn't provide enough light for her to make out the man's features, but the uniform and fair hair made her think it must be Jack Trapp. "What on earth is he doing?"

"Who?" With a grumble, Papa heaved himself out of the chair. "What are you looking at out there, Annie-girl?"

"Jack Trapp. He looks half drunk."

Joining her at the window, Papa pressed his forehead to the glass. "I don't think it's Jack."

"Then who—" A sudden jolt of recognition made Annemarie suck in her breath. She clutched her father's arm. "Papa, it's Samuel Vickary, the chaplain. Gilbert's friend."

"Are you sure?"

"Positive." Now that he'd moved farther into the lamplight, she couldn't mistake his broad forehead and curly blond hair, nor the fact that—yet again—he walked the wintry streets without his overcoat.

Annemarie hurried to the hall and pulled on her coat, then yanked her father's heavy wool overcoat off the hook. If Samuel Vickary hadn't the good sense to dress for winter weather, she'd have to convince him—or throttle him.

Halfway across the street, she slowed her steps. Samuel saw her. Turned. Smiled. "You're here."

"Well, of course I am, seeing as how we're standing in front of my house." Something clearly was not right. She marched forward. "Samuel, what are *you* doing here?"

His teeth chattered. He tilted his head as if he didn't quite understand the question. "Walking . . . I was walking . . ."

"You idiot. Here, put this on." She draped her father's overcoat around his shoulders. He staggered under the weight, threatening to collapse right there on the sidewalk. "Samuel Vickary, have you been drinking?"

"I walked to your house. I wanted to—" The words slurred. He closed his eyes, shook his head, staggered again.

Annemarie propped him up with an arm around his waist. She didn't detect the least smell of alcohol on his breath. Then in the glow of the streetlight, she saw beads of perspiration across his forehead and temples. She touched the back of her hand to his cheek. "Oh, dear Lord, you're burning up! Papa! Papa, help me!"

Thank goodness, her father had been keeping watch from the front door. He bounded down the porch steps and trotted toward them. "What's wrong with him?"

"He's feverish, confused. I'm not even sure he knows where he is."

"Let's get him into the house." Papa looped one of Samuel's arms across his broad shoulders and wrapped his own arm around Samuel's torso. With Annemarie helping to prod Samuel along, they somehow propelled him across the street, up the porch steps, and through the front door.

By then, Mama had come to see what all the commotion was about. "Put him on the sofa. I'll get some blankets."

"Keep your distance, Annemarie," Papa barked as he deposited Samuel onto the sofa. "If this is the Spanish influenza, you don't need to be exposed—if you haven't been already."

"I didn't catch it when you were sick. I'll be fine." Annemarie took a throw pillow from one of the armchairs and eased it under Samuel's head. Last spring her father had contracted a relatively mild case of the Spanish flu, and Annemarie and her mother both had tended him without becoming ill. Hopefully, they had some immunity.

Mama returned with blankets and tucked them in around Samuel's shivering body. His teeth clacked together in rhythm with his labored breathing. "Cold . . . so cold," he murmured even while shoving off the blankets and clawing at his collar as if he couldn't get enough air.

"Poor man. Joseph, should we call our doctor? Maybe we should drive him straight to the hospital."

"We should call Gilbert. He's at home now." Though Annemarie was loathe to make the call herself, Gilbert seemed likely to know what Samuel would want done on his behalf.

Mama met her gaze with eyes full of empathy. "Get some cloths and a pan of cool water to bathe his face. I'll telephone the Ballards."

14

Gilbert was about to lose his ninth straight game of solitaire when the telephone rang. Learning his mother was arranging an elaborate welcome-home dinner, he'd pleaded fatigue and retired for some peace and quiet before the evening's festivities. It would be a few more weeks before he'd be fitted for a prosthesis and learn how to manage stairs again, so for now his bed remained in the study.

The phone on the desk jangled on and on, until Gilbert thought his head would explode. Surely, Mother or Thomas would pick up one of the extensions? For pity's sake, there had to be at least five telephones in this house. Mother simply hated missing a call from one of her society friends.

Unable to stand it a moment longer, Gilbert snatched the earpiece off the hook. "Hello, Ballard residence."

A pause. "Gilbert? Is that you?"

Mrs. Kendall's voice was almost as familiar to him as his own mother's. He clenched his jaw and swallowed. "I, uh, don't know where everyone else is. Did you want to speak with Mother?"

"Actually, I'm glad you answered." Mrs. Kendall released a shaky breath. "Your friend Chaplain Vickary is here, and he's very sick, probably the influenza. It might not be wise to return him to your house and expose everyone there, but he's delirious with fever, and Annemarie—well, that is, we *all* thought you'd know best what he'd want us to do."

Guilt sucked the moisture from Gilbert's mouth. He drummed his fingers upon the cards strewn across the desk. "Maybe you didn't know—Sam's taken an apartment across town. He moved out yesterday."

"Oh. I see." She paused. "Then would you know if there's a particular doctor we should call, or—"

In the background, Annemarie's voice rang out. "Mama, hurry! We need you!"

"Yes, yes, I'm coming!" Mrs. Kendall stammered an apology and told Gilbert good-bye. The line went dead before he could spit out a hurried demand she report at once about Samuel's condition.

Shouting a curse, he scraped his forearm across the desk and sent fifty-two playing cards flying in all directions. Even with his weak left arm, he somehow got his chair across the room and jerked open the door, only to bang his newly healing stump and yelp in agony. More curses spewed from his lips. "Mother! Thomas! Where are you?"

Footsteps pattered along the upstairs landing. Mother appeared over the railing in robe and slippers, her hair done up in an array of pin curls. "I'm dressing for dinner, Gilbert. What is all the shouting about? And you simply must refrain from foul language. You know I don't abide such talk."

"I don't give a—" He clamped his teeth together and exhaled sharply through his nose. As soon as he found the wherewithal to speak without yelling, he tried again. "Mother, can you please find Zachary for me? I need to get over to the Kendalls' immediately."

"*Now?*" His mother scurried down the stairs. "Oh, darling, I'm delighted you're so anxious to work things out with Annemarie, but Zachary has been dismissed for the day. Besides, dinner will be served in less than an hour, and Marguerite has been cooking all afternoon, and—"

"Samuel is at the Kendalls'. He's taken ill."

She skidded to a halt at the foot of the staircase. "Well, why didn't you say so? I'll phone Dr. Lessman straightaway. I'm sure he'll go right over."

Mother darted off toward the study before Gilbert could reply. He let out a sigh of frustration and stroked the day's growth of stubble along his chin. Dr. Lessman was the crusty old coot who'd been the Ballard family physician since Gilbert was in knickers. What he lacked in bedside manner, he made up for with a keen eye for symptoms and enough medical know-how to fill his own library. It pained Gilbert to admit his mother's bossiness might prove worthwhile in this instance, but asking Dr. Lessman to make a house call at the Kendalls' would probably be quicker than transporting Samuel to the hospital and getting him seen by one of the busy staff physicians.

And if it was influenza, little could be done beyond palliative care. Hearing of so many fellow soldiers admitted to the field hospital after falling victim to the disease—and far too many carried out days later for burial—Gilbert knew firsthand.

His mother returned from the study. "I reached Dr. Lessman. He's on his way as we speak."

Just then, Thomas strode in from the kitchen, his overcoat draped across his arm. "Dr. Lessman? Who's sick?"

Mother explained briefly about Samuel.

"That's awful." Thomas hung his coat in the hall closet. "I just saw Annemarie—" He bit off the word, his face reddening.

Gilbert gave his head an annoyed shake. "Just put your coat back on and hand me mine. You're driving me over to the Kendalls'."

Annemarie stood between her parents in the parlor doorway, wringing her hands as she waited for Dr. Lessman to complete his examination. Samuel was less agitated now but still moaning in delirium. Moments after Mama went to telephone the Ballards, Samuel had nearly flung himself off the sofa, muttering horrible things about guns and bullets and bodies.

Dr. Lessman straightened and closed his medical bag. Still wearing his mask, he said, "Point me to the bathroom so I can wash up. I'll speak with you in a moment."

Mama nodded toward the far end of the hall. "You'll find fresh towels in the cabinet."

Annemarie started toward Samuel, but her father caught her arm. "Best wait until we hear what the doctor has to say. No sense taking any chances."

"It's too late for that, don't you think?" Annemarie pressed one hand to her mouth in a futile effort to hold back tears. She leaned into her mother. "I told him and told him not to go about in this weather without his coat."

"There, there, dearest." Mama slanted a look at Papa. "Just like all men, he's only an overgrown boy who'll do things to suit himself no matter how much mothering he gets."

The doctor returned and stood before them in the entryway. "I understand he's a chaplain at the Army and Navy Hospital. Does he have family in town, anyone he could stay with?"

"His mother is in Indiana," Annemarie said. "He's been living with the Ballards."

Mama squeezed Annemarie's arm. "I didn't get a chance to tell you. Gilbert said Samuel moved into his own apartment yesterday."

"So he's living alone?" Dr. Lessman frowned. "In that case, it's best he stay right here."

"Here?" Papa palmed the back of his neck. "But wouldn't he get better care in the hospital?"

"Not necessarily. In fact, in a hospital setting he's much more likely to contract a secondary infection." The doctor pursed his lips. "No, unless this turns into pneumonia, he'll do better with private care. I can check in on him once or twice a day, and you can always call me if he takes a serious turn for the worse."

Annemarie exchanged a look with her mother. She couldn't miss the worry reflected in Mama's face.

Mama kneaded her hands before offering a tight-lipped smile. "We can move him into the downstairs bedroom."

"Ida, we don't have to." Papa's tone warmed with tender concern. "If he must stay here, we've a spare room upstairs. Between the doctor and me—"

"No, no, it's all right." Mama lifted her shoulders and took a few short steps down the hallway. "Just let me tidy the room a bit. It's been a long time . . ."

Fourteen years, in fact. Mama herself had been the last to occupy the room, where sad memories of a difficult pregnancy and a stillborn child yet lingered. Annemarie hurried after her mother and caught her by the wrist. "I'll see to the room, Mama."

"No, we'll do it together." A resigned sigh escaping her lips, Mama looped her arm around Annemarie's waist. "It's high time I put the past behind me."

Annemarie's parents seldom spoke of their loss, but the haunted look in her mother's eyes a few moments ago suggested a heart that still grieved. Even so, Mama briskly took charge of setting the room in order. Fresh linens for the bed, a quick swipe across the dresser with a feather duster, opening the windows a crack to air out the mustiness.

By the time they finished, Papa and the doctor used a blanket to fashion a litter of sorts. Between the two of them, they carried Samuel into the bedroom. "Best you ladies excuse yourselves while we get him undressed," Papa said. "Ida, fetch a pair of my pajamas. They'll swallow the poor lad but will have to do for now."

Mama had just gone upstairs when a strange clatter sounded outside the front door. A frenzied knock quickly followed.

"What on earth?" Annemarie hurried to the door, but with an influenza patient in the house she hesitated to open it and expose some unwitting visitor. "Who's there?"

"It's Gilbert. Let me in!"

At the sound of his voice, her stomach heaved. She peered through the filmy curtains covering the narrow strip of glass beside the door. Bundled in overcoat and scarf, Gilbert sat in his wheelchair, with Thomas standing next to him. Both looked anxious and impatient.

Striving for a calm she didn't feel, Annemarie eased open the door. "You shouldn't come in. Samuel's very sick."

"That's why we're here," Gilbert snapped, tacking on a curse that burned Annemarie's ears. "What did Dr. Lessman say? Are you taking Sam to the hospital?"

Gilbert's belligerent tone shot bristling indignation up Annemarie's spine. Their engagement may be off, but he had no right to speak to her as if she were a lowly private in his army. "I'll thank you to speak civilly to me—if you speak to me at all, Gilbert Ballard."

"Just tell me—" His jaw trembled as if he fought for control.

Thomas shuffled forward. "What my irascible brother can't seem to ask politely is, is Sam going to be all right? Can we do anything to help?"

"Dr. Lessman thinks it best if we care for Samuel here. We've moved him into our guest room."

"You're not serious?" Gilbert's eyes shot daggers. The fingers of his right hand curled and uncurled around the end of his armrest. "You can't do this, Annemarie. I won't have you getting sick."

She didn't know whether to feel touched by his concern or more indignant than ever. Indignation won out. "First of all, I am not one of your underlings to be ordered about. Second, as we are no longer engaged, you have absolutely no say in what I do or don't do. Now, if you will excuse me, my friend Samuel is ill, and I must see to him at once."

Casting an apologetic glance at Thomas, she closed the door with a thud and rammed the bolt home. Then, before her knees gave way, she stumbled over to the coat tree and sank upon the bench seat.

A pair of pajamas clutched under one arm, Mama hurried downstairs. "Was someone at the door just now? I thought I heard voices."

"Gilbert and Thomas." Annemarie looked up at her mother, a crazy mix of remorse, uncertainty, and stubborn pride twisting through her chest. "I just slammed the door in their faces."

15

$\mathscr{H}$eaven seemed so close . . . close enough to touch. Samuel tried to raise his hand toward the luminous face of the angel hovering over him, but molten chains held him down. Seared his skin. Boiled the breath from his lungs. He was drowning in an ocean of fire.

"It's all right, Sam. Just rest." Cool rain bathed his face.

He slept.

And woke.

And slept.

And dreamed. Smoke and flame. Thundering explosions. The cries of the dying.

He stood on the precipice of a black and bottomless hole, a grave with dragon teeth waiting to chew him up and swallow him. Oh, God, so many graves! Row upon row, death upon death. He read prayers over them, consigned them to Jesus, remembered their names when names were known, remembered their spirits when not a shred of identity remained.

Every one, branded into his memory for eternity. Soldiers who died together and yet utterly alone.

"Yea, though I walk through the valley of the shadow . . ." The words scorched his throat. His lungs spasmed in a racking cough.

An arm moved beneath his head, lifting him. Warm liquid touched his lips. "Here, Sam, try to sip this. It'll help."

He swallowed something lightly salty, gently soothing. Somehow, he found the strength to open his eyes. "Annemarie?"

"Right here." Above a square of white gauze, a tender smile lit her gaze. "Your fever's down a bit. But we've got to get some nourishment into you so you can get your strength back."

He tried to take in his surroundings, but the slightest shift of his eyes sent stabbing pain through his head. Nothing looked familiar—velvet drapes at the window, pale roses vining the wallpaper, a lamp nearby with a pink brocade shade bathing the room in a restful glow.

Not his room at the Ballards', not the hospital. Not the starkly furnished bedroom of the flat he'd just rented. "Where— how long—"

More coughing, until he thought his lungs would tear loose from his chest. Annemarie helped him sit higher, holding an enameled basin near his chin. He was mortified she should see him like this and so graciously attend to such a repugnant task, but he could no more control his body's rebellion than he could hold back a fresh surge of admiration for this kind and gentle woman.

"It's all right, just cough it out." As soon as he'd quieted, she disposed of the basin, then adjusted pillows behind him and bathed his face with a warm cloth. He drifted off again, floated on calm seas, angel's breath whispering in his ear. Surely heaven could be no sweeter than this.

If there is a heaven.

Darkness and doubt crept in to gnaw at his brain like hungry rats in a foxhole. The graves again, bodies everywhere, and all around him the thunder of artillery fire, the *chat-chat-chat* of machine guns, the telltale sting of mustard gas in the air.

"Please, God, make it stop! Make the killing stop!"

"Padre! What are you doing? Get down—"

He forced himself awake, sucked air as if every breath could be his last. *Even though I walk through the valley . . .*

"You sound awful, but Dr. Lessman assures us you're on the mend." Annemarie went to the window and adjusted the drapes, letting in a wider sliver of sunlight. When he winced and rolled his head toward the wall, she gasped an apology. The room darkened once more.

Again, she offered him the salty liquid. "There, that's good. This is Mama's special recipe. Normally she'd simmer it with huge chunks of chicken and a big batch of dumplings—which is what we'll be having for our supper later, but you'll have to settle for just the broth until you're stronger."

Annemarie's prattle nudged away the demons. He swallowed down as much of the broth as his stomach could handle and relished the warm comfort. With his eyes he offered Annemarie his thanks, and then sank into restful sleep.

 ❧

Mid-January and the isolation ward was almost emptied. Praise Jesus, the influenza seemed to be loosing its death grip on the world, and both Mary and her mother had avoided the sickness. She'd heard the poor dear chaplain had succumbed, though, and prayed for him every day. He was being tended at home by friends, so she'd been told, which she took to be a good sign. Serious hemorrhaging or the onset of pneumonia would have landed him in the hospital straightaway.

Mary had even more for which to thank her Lord and Savior when Mrs. Daley finally changed her assignment. Returning to a regular ward, she went back to her usual duties caring for the ailing soldiers most likely to benefit from the unique healing properties Hot Springs offered. Indeed, she'd seen some amazing cures after a course of treatment with the radioactive mineral waters. Thermal baths relieved the pain and inflammation of rheumatism, and drinking the water was said to detoxify the body while stimulating bodily functions.

"And good morning to you, Corporal McDonough." Mary rolled a wheelchair next to the snowy-haired veteran's bed. "Are you ready to go down for your therapy?"

"Been counting the hours. What took you so long, young missy?" A teasing spark lit the corporal's eyes. "Did you have to go all the way to Ireland to fetch that wheelchair?"

"Aye, and don't you wish you were back on the Old Sod? Now get yourself on out of bed, *old man*, before I call for one of them big bruiser orderlies to toss you over his shoulder and haul you out of here." Mary winked and set the brake on the chair, then offered Corporal McDonough her arm as he eased himself off the mattress.

Their banter continued all the way to the therapy wing. The corporal, not much bigger than a leprechaun himself and just as feisty, was a long-term patient with chronic rheumatism and gall bladder problems. As Mary checked him in for his session, a familiar voice behind her sent a quiver up her spine.

"Pick me up in two hours, Thomas, and don't be late this time."

Mary turned as the tall man pushing Lieutenant Ballard's wheelchair looked away with a grimace. In the same moment, the lieutenant's gaze met Mary's, and a shock of recognition made him blanch.

"I, uh . . ." His mouth twisted. His glance darted sideways, then slowly crept upward again. His brows drew together in an embarrassed frown. "I believe I still owe you an apology, Miss—"

"McClarney. Mary McClarney. And it's perfectly all right. No harm done, none at all." She took a step closer and hoped he couldn't hear the pounding of her heart. "May I say, sir, you're looking so much improved. I heard you'd been released."

The man with him cleared his throat and clapped Lieutenant Ballard on the shoulder. "An apology, eh? Someone else you've sliced to ribbons with the razor-sharp tongue you brought home from the war?"

The lieutenant's upper lip curled in the beginnings of a sneer. After a slow, deep breath, he clamped his teeth together and muttered, "Miss McClarney, may I introduce my little brother, Thomas Ballard."

The younger Mr. Ballard's eyes widened in a knowing look. He gave a low chuckle. "Don't tell me. You're the nurse he decked last month."

Mary pursed her lips. "It wasn't as bad as all that, now."

"No need to sugarcoat the facts." Lieutenant Ballard's gaze faltered. "I hit you—no excuses—and I'm humiliated as—"

Mr. Ballard jabbed his brother's good arm. "Now, now, Gil, no swearing in front of the lady."

Mary's face warmed. She offered a shy smile. "Working among soldiers, you can be sure I've heard every kind of curse word known to man—and probably a few only the devil himself might utter."

"I'm sure—"

The lieutenant interrupted his brother with a wave of his hand. "Don't you need to get to the hotel, Thomas?"

With an exaggerated eye roll and mock salute, Thomas Ballard backed away. "Right, right. I'll be back in two hours, on the dot, *sir*."

Lieutenant Ballard massaged his forehead. "Just get out of here, will you?" Then, as if he'd heard the rudeness in his tone, he glanced up at Mary and shrugged. "Apologies again. You don't deserve to have my foul temper inflicted upon you every time we meet."

Just to be standing this close to him—close enough to see the sunlight from the window cast blue streaks through his thick, dark curls—oh, she'd take him in good temper or foul. "You're a fine, brave man who has served his country well. No one on God's green earth can blame you for a little touchiness now and again, considering all you've endured."

"A *little* touchiness?" The lieutenant choked out a harsh laugh. "Miss McClarney, I hit you, and I'll never be able to forgive myself. Please tell me there's some way I can make it up to you."

Mary's heart fluttered. "Well, I—"

A tug on her sleeve drew her attention. One of the hydro-therapy attendants, a burly man with a mustache, stood at her elbow. "Excuse me, Nurse McClarney, but you have a patient ready to return to the ward, and I need to get Lieutenant Ballard started."

Lieutenant Ballard signaled him away with a brisk tilt of his head. "Give us a minute, will you, Lester?" He reached for Mary's hand and pulled her closer.

Suppressing a shiver, Mary hoped it was mutual attraction she detected in his gray-green stare, rather than the mix of guilt and resignation the eyes of her heart could not deny. Oh, she knew full well he'd broken his engagement with the lovely Miss Kendall. Every nurse on the ward was gossiping about it within an hour the day Miss Kendall left in tears. But was he truly over her or only pretending to himself and the world?

Either way, one question remained: could a man like First Lieutenant Gilbert Ballard ever find room in his heart for a common Irish working girl like Mary McClarney?

⚘

Mary McClarney. Quick with a Cupid's-bow smile to cheer a downcast heart or a stern rebuke to shame a stubborn patient into submission. The petite redhead, rounded in all the right places, stood in stark contrast with—

Let it go, Ballard. It's over.

So why shouldn't he be looking elsewhere for a little happiness, a little diversion? He was still a man, after all. Or at least *most* of him was still intact. Although some days he'd gladly amputate his head if it was the only way to be rid of these infernal headaches.

He glanced at the delicately freckled hand cradled in his, and then up into luminous green eyes gazing at him in wonder and surprise. She was attracted to him, he could tell. In fact, as he thought back to his days on the ward—before the infamous morning he'd popped her in the jaw—it sure seemed as if she'd given him more than his share of attention.

What could it hurt? He was lonely, bored, sick of evening cribbage games with Thomas, sicker still of his mother's rigid control over his life, and sickest of all of his own vile company.

"Miss McClarney—Mary." He squeezed her hand. "Would you allow me to take you to dinner one evening soon? It's the least I can do to show you how sorry I am for—well, for everything."

A rosy flush worked its way up her fair cheeks. Her free hand flew to her bosom. "Why, sir, I hardly know what to say!"

"Just say yes." *And quickly, before I lose my nerve or the hopeful gleam in your eye turns to pity.* "We could go tonight if you're free. When does your shift end?"

She tucked a carrot-orange tress under her cap and glanced behind her, then lowered her voice to a nervous whisper. "I shouldn't be fraternizing with the patients, you know. Mrs. Daley doesn't approve."

"I'm not *exactly* a patient any longer, just coming in for physical therapy." Gilbert grinned as he envisioned tugging the cap from her head and letting those lustrous curls shake free. Something stirred inside him, something he hadn't experienced in a long, long time. Something he hadn't dared to even allow himself to feel. But now, it warmed the cold, nearly forgotten place deep within his belly with an intensity he couldn't suppress, and the urgency emboldened him. "Please. It's just dinner. Tell me what time to pick you up."

She looked at him askance, her gaze sliding to his left leg— or lack thereof. "How will—I mean—"

Shaking off a self-conscious twinge, he released an easy laugh. "It's all right. My mother has a driver. Or if he isn't available, there's always Thomas."

Mary's smile softened. Her hand warmed against his palm. "All right, then, I'd love to dine with you. But I'm afraid tonight isn't good. My mum—she's not well, I'm afraid. She'll expect me home to cook for her."

"Then you name the day."

Her eyes narrowed in a thoughtful look, and then her smile beamed once more. "I'm off this Friday. I could get Mum's supper ready early and then be free to join you."

"Friday it is. May I call for you at six?"

"Miss McClarney!" Lester, the mustachioed therapist, wheeled his patient closer, and Mary jerked her hand free of

Gilbert's. "Some of us have a schedule to keep, if you don't mind. Sergeant Weber is waiting to go back to the ward."

Mary gave Gilbert a coy glance, deep dimples cratering her cheeks as she murmured, "Six would be lovely, thank you. I'll leave a note for you at the front desk with my address." Then turning with a swirl of her white pinafore, she nudged Lester aside and seized the handles of the sergeant's wheelchair. "So how was your treatment this morning, Sergeant Weber? Nearly good as new, are we?"

Gilbert watched her go, unable to tear his eyes from the provocative sway of her hips. The ache in the pit of his belly grew stronger. He wanted her. Badly. Or at least what she had to offer. Oh, he'd be a gentleman—or try.

The rest . . . it all depended on Miss Mary McClarney.

16

A pale pink dawn was already creeping through her window shades when Annemarie awoke Friday morning. She sat up with a start and checked the time on her bedside clock—a quarter past seven. For heaven's sake, she never slept this late! Papa would be on his way to the factory by now.

And Sam—Mama should have awakened Annemarie at two this morning to take her turn sitting up with him.

She cinched the sash of her robe, her unruly mass of tangles catching in the collar. Tugging her hair free, she hurried downstairs and found her mother in the kitchen, a pan of poached eggs steaming on the stove. "Mama, were you with Samuel all night long? Why didn't you wake me?"

"It's all right, dear." Mama smiled over her shoulder. "Put some bread in the toaster, please. These eggs are almost ready."

Obediently, Annemarie took two slices from the breadbox, set them on the toaster racks, and plugged the appliance into an electrical outlet. "But Samuel—I told you to wake me—"

"Hush, now, and help me get breakfast ready. The kettle's hot. Fill the tea ball and get some tea steeping." Mama turned down the stove burner and then sprinkled the eggs with a dash of salt and pepper.

Annemarie frowned as she opened the tea canister and scooped black pekoe into her mother's acorn-shaped silver tea strainer. "I should go check on Sam. Did he have a good night? When did you last look in on him?"

"He had a very good night. Which is exactly why I didn't bother to wake you."

"You need your sleep, too, Mama. We agreed to take turns." Donning an oven mitt, Annemarie reached for the burbling kettle. No sooner had she poured the water than the acrid smell of burnt bread stung her nose. "Oh, no, the toast!"

"See what you get for talking when you should be helping?" Mama took a plate from the cupboard and dished out the eggs.

With an annoyed growl, Annemarie unplugged the toaster and used a fork to remove the smoking slices. Once she had two more pieces of bread in place, she started the toaster again, this time standing over it to make sure the bread toasted to a perfect golden brown. "Who's this for, anyway? You hardly ever cook eggs on a weekday."

Mama quirked a grin. "Why, our dear Samuel, of course. He's wide awake and hungry this morning."

Annemarie's heart galloped with giddy delight. "Oh, Mama, is he?"

"The toast, dear, the toast!" Mama laughed as she poured tea into a china cup, stirred in a dash of honey, and set it on the bed tray Annemarie had only just noticed sitting on one end of the kitchen table.

With shaking hands, Annemarie forked the toast onto the plate of eggs. "Do you suppose he wants butter or jam? Or both?"

"Neither." Mama gave her a pointed look. "Dry toast to sop up his eggs is plenty for his stomach to handle for now." She took the plate from Annemarie and set it on the tray next to a folded cloth napkin. "I'd ask you to carry this in to him," she began, the faintest edge to her voice, "but I'm afraid in your state of agitation you'd spill his breakfast in his lap—if you even made it that far!"

"I can manage just fine, thank you." Annemarie cut in front of her mother and wrapped her fingers around the handles of the tray. In a gentler tone she added, "Mama, let me do it. You've spent enough time in his room."

Mama tilted her head to offer a grateful smile. Reaching into a drawer, she withdrew a clean gauze mask. "Here, then. Dr. Lessman said we should wear these at least a few more days, just to be safe."

Annemarie fumbled with the ties, her fingers snarling in her uncombed hair, until her mother finally *tsk-tsk*ed and came to her aid. Then with a steadying breath and no small amount of annoyance with herself, Annemarie hefted the tray. When she started toward the hallway, her mother's low chuckle echoed behind her.

Leave it to Mama to read more into Annemarie's discombobulation than was there. Of course, she was anxious about Samuel's health. His fever had raged, and he'd drifted in and out of consciousness for nearly a week. More than once, they'd been ready to call for an ambulance to take him to the hospital, but Dr. Lessman never failed to come right away to check on his patient and reassure them. Thank the Lord complications had been few and Samuel was expected to recover completely.

Sam, Sam. How attached Annemarie had grown to this dear man in the short time she'd known him. He'd proven to be a steadfast and caring friend, one she'd come to count on even more in the wake of her broken engagement.

Annemarie paused in the hallway. She couldn't even pretend she hadn't seen it coming. Even so, she could scarcely believe how her childhood sweetheart had changed in a year's time. His cool detachment chilled her heart. Worse was the bitterness lurking just below the surface, the anger ready to explode at the least provocation.

Blame the war. Blame the accursed war.

Annemarie's throat closed. She sniffed back the threatening tears and jutted her chin. Hadn't Samuel lived through the same horrors? He may not have carried a rifle or lost a limb, but she'd listened in anguish to his fever-induced rantings about war's death and devastation. He'd lost friends, ministered to the injured and dying, no doubt presided over more burials in a month's time than a hundred clergymen combined would face during the entire course of their careers.

Though she hadn't known Sam before the war, she couldn't imagine he had changed very much from the kind, compassionate, faith-filled man he'd always been. His tender heart, his gentle ways, his loyalty to Gilbert even when Gilbert pushed him away—Chaplain Samuel Vickary defined virtue by his very life.

The bedroom door stood ajar. She nudged it open with her hip and greeted her patient with a cheery smile—one he probably couldn't even appreciate thanks to the mask. "Good morning, Sam! Mama said you were awake and hungry."

He looked tired, but his eyes shone with a clearness she hadn't seen since before he'd taken ill. "The smell of breakfast in the air was just about to drive me insane."

"You probably smelled the toast I burnt." Annemarie set the tray on the dresser. "Will you need help to eat?"

"I don't think so, if you'd rearrange my pillows a bit." Samuel drew a hand along his jaw, nearly a week's growth of beard darkening his cheeks. "Wish I had the strength to shower and shave first. I must reek to high heaven."

"Not to worry. Papa's been seeing to your . . . hygiene." Heat surged in Annemarie's cheeks, and she was thankful he couldn't see her blush behind the mask. She helped him reposition his pillows, then turned to the dresser to retrieve the tray. "Now that you're getting stronger, I'm sure Papa will help you shave soon."

Samuel smoothed the blankets so Annemarie could set the bed tray across his lap. She unfolded his napkin and laid it upon his chest. "There now, all set. Eat before everything gets cold."

He cut off a bite of egg with the side of his fork and lifted it to his mouth. His eyes closed in a look of ecstasy. "Delicious!" After another bite or two he looked up at Annemarie, the corners of his eyes crinkling in a weak smile. "Are you watching to make sure I clean my plate?"

She hadn't realized she was staring and gave a tiny laugh. "Sorry. It's just so good to see you feeling better." She plopped into the bedside chair. "I was—we were *all* so worried about you."

"I'll be forever indebted to you and your parents. I'm practically a stranger, and yet you risked your own health to take care of me." Samuel laid his fork aside. His head fell against the pillows, and he sent Annemarie a worried gaze. "I'll never be able to forgive myself if you get sick."

"Stop such talk right now. We've taken every possible precaution, and besides, the Kendalls are hardy stock." She flicked her hand at his plate. "Your toast is getting cold, and so is your tea. Finish up now, or I shall have to force-feed you again."

With a sigh, Samuel raised his head and bit into a slice of toast. After a few more bites, he took a sip of tea, then licked his lips. "I don't remember much of anything since I took ill. Your mother said you found me wandering up and down the street outside your house."

"You were delirious with fever. I can't imagine how you ever found your way here." The memory of that night brought new waves of confusion. "Or why," she added under her breath.

"*I walked to your house. I wanted to*—"

Samuel's hand shook as he set the teacup into the saucer with a clatter. "Did I—" He covered a cough with the napkin, then rested his head, eyes closed, brow furrowed. "Did I say anything?"

"Nothing made much sense." Annemarie twisted the ends of her sash and mentally replayed some of his ramblings.

"*Never love me . . . always him.*" Someone must have broken his heart, fallen for another.

"*So beautiful . . . not worthy of her.*" But who—and why? No one could possibly be more worthy of love than Sam.

"*Need you . . . please stay.*" Yet only Annemarie had been in the room when he'd murmured those words. He'd groped for her hand. His red-rimmed eyes had bored into hers with a soul-searing intensity she couldn't entirely write off as influenza-induced delirium.

She stole a glance at him and saw he'd drifted off to sleep, his hands lying limp atop the blankets. He'd finished most of his eggs but barely nibbled on the toast. The effort must have exhausted him. As gently as possible, she removed the bed tray and slipped quietly from the room.

When Samuel opened his eyes later, the first thing he noticed was the quiet. The feverish thrumming between his ears had dissipated sometime in the night, along with the rasping rales of chest congestion. All well and good, but the one sound he wanted to hear had also faded—Annemarie's tender voice.

He rolled his head toward the empty chair. Hadn't she been sitting right there while he ate? But now the bed tray was gone, and a brighter sun beat against the window shade between the parted drapes.

Maybe he'd only dreamed she'd brought him breakfast—except those were definitely toast crumbs on the sheet, and the aftertaste of honey-sweetened tea still lingered upon his tongue.

Footsteps sounded outside the door. Samuel's pulse quickened. He shifted higher against the pillows. "Annemarie?"

"Just me." Mask in place, Mrs. Kendall sidled into the room, and Samuel berated himself for the unwarranted stab of disappointment. "Good, you're awake. You were napping so peacefully after your breakfast I hated to disturb you. I thought you might like to know your mother telephoned again."

Samuel eased into a more comfortable position. "I've worried her, haven't I? Has she called often?"

"Every day." Mrs. Kendall's gaze darted about the room for a few seconds before settling on Samuel. "She would have rushed right back to be with you, but we assured her you were being well cared for and wouldn't want her exposed. I was happy I could tell her how much better you're doing today."

"Thank you." The weight of gratitude he owed this family threatened to overwhelm him. "Thank you for everything."

"Not another word. We're so glad we could help." Mrs. Kendall folded her hands at her waist, but the faint tinge of unease hadn't left her eyes.

"Is . . . is everything all right?"

"Oh, don't mind me." With a self-deprecating laugh, she busied herself straightening a doily on the dresser, then adjusted the drapes. "Would you like a little more light in the room? It might cheer you."

Since his head no longer hurt so much, he wouldn't mind at all. "That would be nice."

"I could read to you if you like. Something to help pass the time?"

"Perhaps later. Maybe you could tell me what I've missed these past several days." Samuel gave a low chuckle. "I feel like a grouchy old bear coming out of hibernation after a long winter."

Mrs. Kendall perched on the edge of the chair. "Well, let's see. . . . Things have been in an uproar in Berlin this week. The revolutionist Karl Liebknecht and his Spartacus League have been all over the papers. Then there's a strike going on in Buenos Aires, and they're talking a possible revolution there. Oh, and Attorney General Gregory just tendered his resignation—"

A tired groan vibrated Samuel's throat. "That's the kind of news I can do without. I'm far more interested in what's been happening closer to home."

"Well, then, let me think. . . ." Mrs. Kendall's glance skittered across the walls like a moth looking for a place to alight.

Sudden anxiety knotted Samuel's stomach. He pushed up on one elbow. "Is it Annemarie? Please tell me she's well."

"Annemarie? Of course. She's perfectly fine, off to the factory as usual this morning." Mrs. Kendall leapt to her feet and pressed her palms against Samuel's shoulders until he lay back down. "Just rest now. There's nothing for you to be concerned about."

He didn't go through four years of seminary—much less serve a year in the trenches— without learning to recognize certain signs. His tone low and insistent, he asked, "What is it, Mrs. Kendall?"

With a forced laugh she sank onto the chair. "I'm supposed to be tending to your needs, not the other way around."

"I'm a good listener." He gestured weakly. "And in case you haven't noticed, you have a captive audience."

Mrs. Kendall nodded and withdrew a handkerchief from her pocket. Already a trickle of moisture had slipped from the corner of one eye and into the fabric of her mask. "Both Annemarie and Joseph try to protect me, but the fact is there is nothing they can do. Because in the end, it's between me and the Lord."

She told him then about the weeks spent in this room awaiting the birth of her baby—weeks spent in worry and fear, weeks of pleading for a healthy child, weeks of bargaining with God. And then the grief, the unrelenting anguish when the baby was stillborn. "I blamed God, despised Him, wanted to die myself."

"I'm so sorry." A familiar heaviness settled over Samuel, the same smothering hopelessness he'd carried home from the war—the lives lost, the futility of it all. And, as always, he knew he had to shake it off and be the man of God others expected him to be. But just now, he couldn't think of a single word of comfort to offer the woman who had braved not only the risk of influenza but the specters from her own painful past.

Instead, he blurted out a single question: "How did you survive?"

Mrs. Kendall looked up, surprise lighting her eyes. "Why, Jesus, of course. 'A man of sorrows, and acquainted with grief.' I may have felt alone in my loss, but Jesus was—*is*—always with me. He knows every heartache, every painful step I take."

"*Surely he hath borne our griefs, and carried our sorrows.*" The words from Isaiah sifted through Samuel's thoughts. How many times had he quoted this same passage in letters he'd written to console grieving parents or widows? Cold comfort for a family whose loved one had been blown to smithereens by a grenade, or sliced in two by a blast of machine gun fire, or died a slow, agonizing death from the effects of mustard gas.

His chest ached. It grew harder to breathe again. He eased over onto his side, facing the wall. Rosebuds danced before his eyes. "If you don't mind, I think I'd like to sleep some more."

"Of course." A hand reached across him to adjust the covers. "I'll check on you in a bit."

"Thank you." Before the darkness closed in, before the dragon's mouth gaped, he drew on his last remnants of strength to call to mind the face of hope.

Annemarie.

17

"Well? How was it? Tell me everything!"

Mary offered little more than an annoyed sigh while checking a patient's chart and measuring out the proper dose of medication. "Now, Lois, I'm not the type to kiss and tell."

"Kiss? He *kissed* you on your first date?" The dark-haired nurse wedged herself between Mary and the counter at which she worked, forcing Mary to look her in the eye.

"Careful, now. Can't you see I'm busy here?" Though she tried to sound cross, she couldn't keep a smirk off her face.

"He *did* kiss you!"

Ah, if only. But Lieutenant Ballard—Gilbert, he'd insisted she call him—had been nothing but gentlemanly. Arriving promptly at six last evening, he'd sent his crisply uniformed chauffeur to the door. It rankled Mary's mother that Mary wouldn't allow her to step out to the car so Gilbert could introduce himself properly, but with the chill in the air, Mary had insisted Mum stay inside. They could always meet another time.

And another time there would definitely be! As if dinner at the Arlington weren't enough to assuage the lieutenant's lingering guilt, Mary could scarcely believe he'd asked her out yet again. She had agreed to accompany him next Friday to a dinner club where a popular singer would perform.

Mary gave her head a quick shake. She absolutely *must* keep her mind on her work before she gave her patient a dose of quinine when the order was for aspirin. Bad enough Gilbert had kept her out so late last night, what with today's shift starting at the crack of dawn. Stifling a yawn, she nudged Lois out of the way and verified the label on another medicine bottle.

"Mary McClarney, you're being a brat." Lois stamped her foot. "I want details and I want them *now*."

After dispensing two capsules into a small cup, Mary capped the bottle and turned to Lois with a sigh. "Honestly, there's nothing to tell. We had a lovely dinner at the Arlington, and then he had his driver take us up the mountain to enjoy the view."

Lois harrumphed. "I'll just bet the good-looking lieutenant *enjoyed the view*."

Mary bristled. "I don't like what you're implying."

"Don't play the innocent with me, Mary. I've been around the block a few times." Lois gathered up several used instruments in need of sterilization.

"I am *not* that kind of girl." Mary glared at the other nurse before starting out the door with her tray of medications. "I assure you, all we did was talk."

"All right, if you insist." Lois followed on her heels, adding in a growling whisper, "Just don't let Mrs. Daley find out you're seeing a patient—"

"A *former* patient."

"—or you'll find yourself booted out of the Army Nurse Corps before you can blink twice." Lois marched off in the opposite direction.

Mary didn't doubt what Lois said was true. Mrs. Daley had strict rules about fraternizing with the patients. But even more worrisome was Mary's own mother's opinion of her spending the evening with a handsome, single army officer. Mary had expected Mum to be tucked into bed by the time she arrived home at half past eleven.

But no, there she sat sipping chamomile in the parlor, her Bible splayed open across her lap—open to Proverbs, chapter five, of course, Solomon's advice to his son about loose women.

With a thrust of her hip, she pushed through the door onto the ward, refusing to give another thought to Gilbert Ballard—or to her sainted, if overly vigilant, mother—until she'd distributed medications and seen to her patients' needs.

Even so, and despite what must be suitcase-sized purple smudges under her eyes, more than one patient commented on the secret smile curling her lips and the extra spring in her step this morning.

⚜

Annemarie shut off the engine of her father's Model-T and hurried around to the passenger door to retrieve the box of carefully packaged ceramic pieces. Thomas had promised he'd explained to the people waiting on special orders that she'd been preoccupied nursing a sick friend back to health.

But with Samuel getting stronger every day, Annemarie had finally made time over the weekend to finish up several ceramics projects. Throwing matching candlesticks had proven a challenge—more than once she'd had to pound the clay back into a ball, recenter it on the wheel, and begin again—but the glaze on the lamp base had captured her "Ouachita sunrise" vision like none before.

Thomas met her in the Arlington lobby and relieved her of the crate. "I was hoping you'd be by soon. The display case is looking a little sparse again."

"I'm afraid I didn't bring many new pieces, but I wanted to get those special orders to you as soon as I finished them." Annemarie followed him into his office. "I'll have more time to work now that Sam's improving."

"I heard he's better. Dr. Lessman came by to check Mother's heart the other day." Thomas set the box on his desk and began unwrapping the pottery. "This is exquisite, Annemarie."

The praise warmed her. She peeled away the newsprint cradling one of the candlesticks. "I hope your mother is well. We're so appreciative of her arranging for Dr. Lessman to take over Samuel's care."

"Mother's as healthy as a horse and stubborn as a mule." Thomas quirked a brow as he set the other candlestick in the center of his desk. "You should come by sometime. Mother would love a visit."

"You know I can't do that." Annemarie swallowed over the pinch in her throat. She plucked a scrap of newsprint off the rim of the lamp base.

Thomas crossed his arms and stared at the pottery. A muscle in his jaw twitched. "Listen, Annemarie, you've got to do something, and soon, before it's too late."

She looked at him askance—as if she didn't know to what he referred. "Do what, exactly? Gilbert made his choice. I won't go crawling to him and beg him to take me back."

"I know, I know." Thomas raked stiff fingers through the patch of thinning hair atop his scalp—so unlike Gilbert's thick mass of raven curls. Annemarie shut down the thought at once, while Thomas continued, "The thing is . . . I'm afraid Gilbert's about to do something stupid."

"You mean something even *more* stupid than breaking his engagement with me?" Annemarie narrowed her gaze, one foot tapping out a violent rhythm on the Persian rug. "Believe me, Thomas Ballard, I've imagined every possible act of retribution that wouldn't get me thrown in jail—and a few that would. Gilbert deserves whatever trouble he gets himself into."

She regretted the words as soon as they left her lips. Uttering a gasp, she sagged against the desk and hung her head. "I didn't mean that. Gilbert certainly *doesn't* deserve what he's been through already, and I wish him only the best. It's just—"

"You don't have to apologize to me. You've been a saint through all this. It's Gil who's acting the fool."

Something in Thomas's tone pricked her senses. She tilted her chin. "What exactly is he doing?"

"I probably shouldn't be telling you this, but . . ." Thomas shifted his gaze toward the door, then lowered his voice. "He's going out with someone."

"Going . . . out. You mean with a woman?"

"Yeah, some little Irish girl he met at the hospital. One of the nurses." Thomas examined one of the candlesticks and then carefully rewrapped it.

"One of the nurses." Annemarie started to repack the other candlestick but didn't trust it wouldn't slip through her shaking fingers—or that she wouldn't fling it across the room and shatter it against Thomas's filing cabinet.

"I don't know what he sees in her. I mean, she's cute and friendly and all." Thomas took the candlestick from her and toyed with it, as if his impulses mirrored hers. "Must be the guilt thing."

"Guilt thing?" Annemarie cringed. She was beginning to sound like a parrot. But waging an inner battle between stoic indifference and raging jealousy—which she was quickly losing—she couldn't seem to form a coherent sentence of her own.

"She's the nurse Gil decked that day. The first time he took her out, I think he was trying to ease his conscience. But they have plans again for next weekend. And he's talking like he plans to see a lot more of her."

"Well, if they're compatible . . ." Annemarie turned away, one hand pressed to her abdomen as she calculated the most direct route to the nearest ladies' lounge. This morning's breakfast seemed none too inclined to stay down.

"Compatibility has nothing to do with it. If you ask me, it's all about—" Thomas made a growling sound in his throat. "Well, never mind what I think it's all about. Since when has my big brother ever listened to a thing I said? Now Mother, on the other hand—"

Annemarie glanced at the watch pinned to her bodice. "Goodness, is it half past nine already? I *must* get back to the factory. Our supplier is delivering a large order this morning, and I really need to be there."

Muttering a mild oath, Thomas rubbed his forehead. "I knew I shouldn't have said anything. Now I've gone and upset you."

"No, it's all right." Annemarie stiffened her spine. She would *not* let this news reduce her to a bitter, whining harpy. "All I have ever wanted was Gilbert's happiness, and if this young nurse makes him happy, then I'm glad for them both. I refuse to be otherwise."

Lips quirked, Thomas gave his head a small shake. "This is exactly why you're too good a woman for my brother. He doesn't deserve you."

Snippets of Samuel's feverish rantings crept into Annemarie's thoughts. "Don't be so quick to judge him, Thomas. We weren't there. We have not even the vaguest concept of what those men faced on the front lines."

"And he's not likely to let me forget, either." Thomas stepped behind his desk and opened the center drawer. "Here, don't leave without this," he said, handing her an envelope. "Not as much as last time, but once you start producing again, I'm sure it'll pick up."

Accepting the envelope, Annemarie permitted herself a moment of self-satisfaction. It felt amazingly good to be valued, to have something to call her own.

And since she'd been rejected by the man she'd loved half her life, the honor of being paid for her artistic talents would have to suffice.

✒

"Thank you, Zachary. I'll call for you when I'm ready to leave." Gilbert dismissed his mother's chauffeur with a brisk nod and waited until the car pulled away from the curb before ringing the Kendalls' doorbell.

A few moments later, Mrs. Kendall answered. "Good afternoon Gilbert. Do come in. Samuel has been looking forward to seeing you."

Unlike Mrs. Kendall, judging from the coolness in her tone. At least Annemarie would be at the factory—precisely why Gilbert had scheduled his visit for midafternoon and fully intended to be gone by the time she returned from work.

He wheeled his chair into the entry hall, grateful his left arm had grown strong enough so he wasn't quite as dependent upon others to steer his chair. "I'm deeply appreciative of how good you've been to Sam. I know it can't have been easy, his being so sick and all."

"We were happy we could help." Mrs. Kendall led him past the parlor and staircase, then turned down a hallway toward the far end of the house. "Dr. Lessman says our worries of contagion should be over. Samuel's temperature has been normal for several days now."

"That's good. I take it everyone else has remained in good health?"

"We have, thank you. We took every precaution." Mrs. Kendall paused outside a door at the end of the hall. She tapped lightly. "Samuel? Gilbert is here." Without waiting, she turned brusquely and hurried in the opposite direction.

From the other side of the door came Samuel's weak voice. "Gil? Come in."

He hauled in a quick breath and nudged open the door. "Hey, there, Padre." Wheeling into the room, he found Sam propped up in bed with a book in his lap. Sunken cheeks and a wan complexion were the only outward signs he'd been ill. "Sitting on your fanny, getting waited on hand and foot. I should have you court-martialed for dereliction of duty."

Sam's gaze darkened. He looked away briefly as he laid the book on the bedside table. "I'm a little stronger every day. I don't plan to neglect my work any longer than absolutely necessary."

The thought he'd offended his friend—yet again—tied Gilbert's stomach in knots. He wheeled closer to the bed. "Hey, it was a joke, all right? You've been deathly ill. You deserve all the time you need to get your strength back."

Glancing toward the window, Sam heaved a sigh. "What bothers me is taking advantage of the Kendalls' hospitality for so long. They've been incredibly gracious."

"That's the kind of people they are." Now Gilbert looked away, the weight of what he'd given up pressing upon him like a full marching pack.

"How've you been, Gil? I heard your surgery went well."

"So they tell me." Glad to move the conversation to a less threatening topic, Gilbert described his therapy regimen. "My arm will never be full strength again, but my physical therapist says it'll be good enough for crutches while I get comfortable with my artificial leg."

"How soon will you get your prosthesis?"

"They're already fitting me for one." He slapped the wheels of his chair. "Another couple of weeks and I can finally get out of this thing and on my feet again, in a manner of speaking."

Sam chuckled softly. "I can't tell you how good it is to see you actually looking forward to something."

Gilbert smirked, hoping to disguise the sudden surge of anger. *Look forward to something?* The only thing he looked forward to every day was his pain pills. All he could bring himself to say was, "Sure beats looking backward."

Sam grew quiet for several seconds while he fingered a loose thread on his blanket. He peered up at Gilbert with a furrowed brow. "I know someone who hopes to look forward to a future with you. I wish you'd at least—"

"Don't go there, Sam." Gilbert gave the wheel of his chair a twist and angled himself away. "Anyway, I'm seeing someone else now."

"What? Who?"

"A nurse. We met at the hospital."

Sam leaned toward Gilbert, his hand curling into a fist. "You can't be serious."

Gilbert glared over his shoulder. "Why not? Mary's pretty and kind and she understands me like no one else."

"Mary. Mary McClarney, the nurse you nearly knocked into the next century?" Sam grunted a harsh laugh. "How long has this been going on?"

"We had dinner the other night. I'm taking her out again this Friday." Gilbert gave his jaw a nervous rub. He wished he'd never mentioned Mary's name. Honor wouldn't let him lie to his friend, but pride wouldn't let him back down.

"This is nothing more than a fling. It won't last." Sam sank into his pillows, fatigue stealing the power from his words.

"Why do you fight this, Gil? You know Annemarie loves you. You know you're still in love with her."

The blasted pain started behind Gilbert's eyes again. He clenched his jaw until his teeth ached. "How many times do I have to repeat myself? Annemarie and I are through."

"Why, Gil? Just give me one good reason why."

"Because I *won't* inflict *this* on her." He flung out his arm in a gesture indicating his crippled body. "She deserves so much better. She deserves a man who's whole in every way. She deserves a good man, an honorable man." He shot a pointed stare at Samuel. "She deserves a man like *you*."

18

Friday turned out to be an unusually warm day for January, and Mrs. Kendall thought some fresh air and sunshine would do Samuel good. After lunch, she'd helped him out to the front porch and settled him into a wicker chaise with a blanket tucked snugly around his legs, a couple of magazines on his lap, and a cup of hot tea on a side table.

The afternoon sun on Samuel's face lulled him into a pleasant lethargy. He'd finished the tea awhile ago and found nothing of particular interest in the magazines, so now, left with his own thoughts, he found his mind drifting to places he had no business going.

A white steepled church. Samuel at the pulpit, Annemarie at the organ. Smiling at him, always smiling. A cozy parsonage next door filled with the laughter of children—their children. A raven-haired girl with bows in her hair, a towheaded boy with snails in his pockets . . .

The rumble of an automobile jarred him out of the daydream. He gave himself a mental shake and then had to laugh at his own foolishness. For heaven's sake, he'd never heard Annemarie play an organ, didn't know if she even knew how.

The car, a wood-sided depot hack, stopped in front of the Kendalls' house. The driver bustled around to the rear door and hefted a suitcase while a woman in a gray coat and flat-brimmed hat climbed out onto the sidewalk.

Samuel sat forward. "Mother?"

She looked up with a mile-wide smile. "Oh, Sam, my boy Sam!" Seconds later she plopped onto the chaise next to him and wrapped him in a bear hug.

Samuel breathed in the sweet rosewater scent of her and relished the reminder of home. When she finally released him, he asked, "Why didn't you let me know you were coming?"

His mother smacked his cheek with a noisy kiss. "I wanted to surprise you."

The hack driver waited at the bottom of the porch steps. "Ma'am, your luggage?"

"Just set it by the door, if you please." She reached into her purse for some change and pressed it into the driver's hand. "Thanks so much for your trouble."

As the driver nodded and left, the front door flew open. Mrs. Kendall gave a delighted gasp. "Ursula, you're here! I promise, I didn't say a word to spoil the surprise."

"Ida! At last we meet. Thanks so much for inviting me to your home—and especially for all you've done for my son."

The two women embraced like old friends, and Samuel could only sit there under his blanket and shake his head. They seemed to have momentarily forgotten about him anyway. Mrs. Kendall pressed for details about the journey from Fort Wayne, and Samuel's mother pattered on about how lovely the weather was compared to January in Indiana.

"Well. Let's get you settled into the guest room." Mrs. Kendall lifted one of the smaller pieces of luggage. "Joseph will be home from the factory soon. He'll get the rest. You'll be stay-ing upstairs. I hope it's all right."

"Perfectly fine. My, what a lovely home . . ."

Their voices trailed off as the front door closed behind them. Samuel contemplated what to do with himself until either his mother or Mrs. Kendall remembered they'd abandoned him on the porch. He might still be deplorably weak, but he wasn't completely bedridden anymore. It wouldn't hurt to move around a bit and try to regain some strength.

A train case sat next to his mother's large suitcase. He could surely carry it as far as the foot of the stairs. Tossing the blanket aside, he swung his legs off the side of the chaise and stood. Just a little lightheaded, but not so bad. After tugging at his flannel robe to make sure he wasn't exposing the neighbors to anything unseemly, he bent to retrieve the train case and then carried it inside.

He started across the entry hall, the train case growing heavier with each step. From somewhere upstairs came the ladies' laughter. The sound echoed like a gong inside Samuel's skull, seeming to come from everywhere at once. The edges of his vision yellowed, then darkened. Something crashed to the floor next to him, and suddenly the floor rose up to meet his face.

"Sam!" Cool hands touched his cheek, then gently rolled him onto his back. "Oh, Sam, are you all right? Can you hear me?"

He opened his eyes to see Annemarie kneeling over him, a stray curl looping across her left eye. He watched his hand rise up—all on its own, as if he had not one shred of control—and twine that curl around one finger. The tress was as soft as he'd always imagined it, sliding through his fingers like fine silk.

When his hand brushed her face, she gave a small gasp. His arm thudded to his chest. He tried to swallow, to breathe, but his throat felt paralyzed. He squeezed his eyes shut. *Stop it. Stop this at once, you idiot!*

"Annemarie! What happened?" Mrs. Kendall's voice, the creak of footsteps on the staircase.

"He doesn't seem to be hurt, Mama. I think he must have fainted."

Fainted. Quite the manly thing to do. Collecting himself, Samuel tried to sit up.

"Easy, now." Annemarie helped him lean against the coat tree bench. "What on earth were you doing, Sam?"

"I was just coming in from the porch with . . ." His glance fell upon his mother's train case. The latch had popped open, spilling underclothing and toiletries across the floor.

"Samuel Vickary!"

He'd recognize that tone anywhere. His mother bustled down the stairs and began scooping her things into the train case, muttering the whole time. "Why, if you weren't still so feeble, I'd have half a mind to tan your backside, young man. What were you thinking, trying to tote luggage in your condition?"

"Now, Ursula, don't be so hard on the lad. He only thought to help." Mrs. Kendall looped an arm beneath Samuel's. "Here, Annemarie, take his other side and let's get him to the sofa."

Before he could protest, the two women had hoisted him to his feet. Retrieving his dignity, he shook himself free. "I'm *not* a sack of potatoes. I can get there under my own power, if you don't mind."

At least he hoped he could. The parlor seemed a thousand miles away just now. He fixed his gaze on the sofa and willed one foot in front of the other until he finally plopped down on the cushions. He tugged the robe around him and drew several breaths while listening to Mrs. Kendall introduce Annemarie to his mother.

No doubt they'd find plenty to talk about. He could just imagine his mother glibly relating embarrassing stories from

Samuel's childhood. Like the time when he was five and the clothesline collapsed on him and he ran blindly around the backyard with his mother's bloomers flapping in the breeze. Or his thirteenth birthday, when his mother insisted he should invite not only the boys but also the girls from his Sunday school class. When it was time for the party, she found him locked in his room because out of nowhere a gargantuan pimple had erupted on his chin and he was mortified for the girls to see him.

"A penny for your thoughts." Annemarie stood in the doorway, a curious smile dimpling her cheeks. She crossed the room and handed him a glass of water, then sat on the other end of the sofa, one leg demurely tucked beneath her. "You looked a million miles away. Thinking of anyone special?"

"Only my own ineptitude." True enough. How could he admit what he was thinking—the secret pleasure it gave him to imagine Annemarie knowing every little thing about him, the secret wish to know everything there was to know about her?

He swept the thoughts aside while he took several sips of water. "It seems early for you to be home. Or are you in on my mother's surprise visit, too?"

"I did know she'd be arriving this afternoon, but Mama swore me to secrecy." Annemarie drew a throw pillow into her lap and toyed with the fringe. "The reason I'm home early, though, is because I'm going out this evening."

"Out?" Samuel nearly choked on the word. A sudden spate of envy brought a boulder-sized lump to his throat.

"One of my girlfriends invited me to a dinner club. There's an up-and-coming jazz singer in town for one night only. Carla Steiner—maybe you've heard of her?"

Samuel well remembered the vivacious platinum blonde. Shortly after he'd shipped over to France, Carla Steiner had put on a show to entertain the troops. "I'm glad you're getting out. You've spent entirely too much time looking after me the past couple of weeks."

"Not another word. The only thing needed to make this evening better would be if you were well enough to go along." Annemarie's gaze turned thoughtful. She put the cushion aside. "You're right, though. I do need to get out more. The war is over, and I have friends and family and good health. It's time to take myself off the shelf and start living again."

"Annemarie, dear." Mrs. Kendall appeared in the doorway with Samuel's mother. "Come help me with supper and let Ursula visit with her son for a bit."

With a quick squeeze of his hand, Annemarie rose so Samuel's mother could sit beside him on the sofa. He tucked the hand she'd touched into the pocket of his robe and savored the memory. And only a memory it would remain, because he had no right to anything more than friendship from the woman who'd claimed his heart.

❦

Horns, strings, and drums pulsed an up-tempo beat Annemarie could feel all the way to her toes as she and her friend Dorothy stepped through the doors of the Emerald Club. Several parties already milled about waiting to be seated, but Dorothy grabbed Annemarie's hand and bypassed them all.

"Good evening, Rodolpho." Resting a bejeweled wrist upon the maître d's desk, Dorothy gave the mustachioed man a beguiling smile. "I'm Dorothy Webb, the owner's niece. You should have a front-table reservation for my friend and me."

"Ah, Miss Webb, of course!" Rodolpho snapped his fingers at a young man in a starched white shirt and black bow tie. "Miguel, table two for these lovely ladies. Mr. Webb has requested a complimentary bottle of champagne for their table, so bring it right out."

Dorothy caught Annemarie's eye and winked. "Nice to have relatives in high places, isn't it?"

"Yes, but *champagne?*" Annemarie couldn't suppress a giggle. "I've never tasted anything stronger than root beer in my life!"

"Then it's about time, don't you think?"

Arriving at their table, the waiter pulled out Dorothy's chair, and she seated herself with a swirl of chiffon. When the waiter did the same for Annemarie, she thanked him with a reserved smile and pretended she regularly enjoyed such deferential attention. Her attire may not be as stylish as Dorothy's, but she felt quite dressed up in the magenta tea gown she'd resurrected from the back of her closet. The bright color simply hadn't seemed appropriate while the war eroded everyone's spirits and so many wore the somber shades of mourning.

She opened the oversized menu and browsed the entrées, many of which she couldn't even pronounce. "Um, Dorothy, there are no prices."

Dorothy rolled her eyes. "Honey, if you have to ask the price, it means you can't afford it. But don't worry. Dinner's on my uncle. I'm his favorite niece, you know."

"Lucky us!" Annemarie tried again to decipher the menu but couldn't begin to decide what to order. "I'm completely at a loss. What are you having, Dot?"

"I'm going with the house specialty, beef bourguignon."

"*That* I've at least heard of. Sounds perfect."

Miguel returned shortly with two crystal glasses and a bottle of champagne in a silver ice bucket. With an expert flourish, he popped the cap and then filled the champagne glasses. Pale golden liquid bubbled enticingly, a delicate fruity aroma filling the air.

Lifting her glass, Dorothy chimed, "To the end of the war and our boys coming home!"

"Hear, hear!" Annemarie toasted with her friend, then took the tiniest sip of champagne. Between the bubbles tickling her nose and the tartly sweet taste, she had to stifle a sneeze.

While she plucked a handkerchief from her satin evening bag, Dorothy gave the waiter their orders. By then, a tuxedoed master of ceremonies appeared onstage. As the musicians played the final notes of "St. Louis Blues," he stepped up to the microphone.

"Ladies and gentlemen, the Emerald Club is proud to host an exclusive one-night engagement for the lovely and talented Carla Steiner. Let's show Carla our appreciation with a huge Hot Springs welcome!"

Applause broke out, and the orchestra began a fanfare that brought goose bumps to Annemarie's arms. The gorgeous blond singer sauntered onto the stage, her teal gown shimmering with rhinestones. A white fur boa draped low across her shoulders, the tails brushing the floor behind her.

The master of ceremonies graced her hand with a gallant kiss, then backed offstage as the orchestra segued into "I Ain't Got Nobody." For the first few bars Annemarie was swept away by Carla's rich contralto. But then the lyrics filtered into her consciousness, and a wistful melancholy settled into her heart. Fingering the stem of her champagne glass, she sank into the plush velveteen chair cushion and sighed.

"Hey, now." Dorothy nudged her arm, a sad smile creasing rose-red lips. "This evening's supposed to cheer you up. Forget about that cad who dumped you. You'll meet someone new, and then he'll be sorry."

The song ended to deafening applause and a few wolf whistles that Miss Steiner acknowledged with a sultry smile and a wave of her white-gloved hand. With a nod to the orchestra leader, she began her next number. The livelier piece helped Annemarie shake off the mantle of gloom. She came to have fun, after all. Gilbert Ballard could just—

A commotion to her left drew her attention. Two waiters bustled to create a wider aisle, dishes and glasses clattering as diners rose to move their chairs aside and shift tables farther apart. An attractive young woman with flame-red hair strode through the opening, and behind her a man in a wheelchair.

Gilbert!

Annemarie's heart hammered like a cadre of snare drums before it sank to her toes and stopped—utterly stopped. She could die right there on the spot.

"Annie? Are you okay?" Dorothy leaned forward, blocking Annemarie's view. "The champagne's not bad, is it? I know you're not used to it, but—"

"It's him—*him!*" Her voice came out in a coarse whisper. She gave a brusque nod in Gilbert's direction.

By the time Dorothy caught her meaning and followed her gaze, a waiter was assisting the redhead into her chair while the maître d' guided Gilbert's wheelchair up to their table. "Oh my. You want to get out of here, honey?"

Stretching tall, she inhaled long and slowly through her nose. "Absolutely not." She tucked a loose curl behind her ear and pasted on her most serene smile. "We came to hear Carla Steiner. Not to mention I'm starving, so I'm not leaving until I've eaten every last bite of my beef bourguignon. *And* dessert. Didn't I see Black Forest cake on the menu?"

"The best in town." Dorothy smirked, leaning close to Annemarie's ear. "Good for you, honey. I'm proud of you."

Gilbert had arranged to have Mary seated at his right so he'd have his good arm available for . . . wherever the evening led. "Enjoying the show?"

"Oh, yes!" A shivery sigh escaped Mary's lips. "Mercy me, but this is an elegant place! If I'd known, I'd have found something more glamorous to wear."

"You look fine." Truth be told, he doubted she owned anything nicer than the dusky brown frock she wore. But the simple lines imbued an understated sophistication, and the cream-colored lace collar did something wonderful to her lightly freckled complexion. His fingers itched to stroke the curve of her cheek, to touch the soft, pink ripeness of her pouty lower lip.

Fumbling with the huge menu, Mary glanced his way with a self-conscious giggle. "You're staring."

"Sorry, can't stop myself." He let his hand graze the tender skin on the back of her wrist. His belly throbbed with longing.

But was she the type of girl who'd give him what he wanted—what he *needed*? All these years he'd saved himself, kept himself pure for Annemarie. Not even those French femme fatales with their butchered-English come-ons had turned his eye. Instead, he'd fantasized about his wedding night, taking Annemarie to his bed and finally releasing the pent-up passion he'd suppressed for so long out of respect for her and obedience to God.

Well, God hadn't done him any good lately, and Annemarie was out of the picture. Now all he cared about was finding relief from the loneliness, from the depression, from the constant raging headaches that made him half-blind with agony.

Mary closed the menu and cast him a demure smile. "I'd best let you order for me. I can't make heads nor tails of these fancy names."

"My pleasure." He'd been eying the steak au poivre but decided with his weak arm he'd probably make a fool of himself trying to slice through the beef. "Let's go with the duck à l'orange. I'll order some wine as well."

"None for me, thank you. I'm a teetotaler."

And why was he not surprised? So much for getting her a little tipsy and then sending Zachary off for a smoke later while the two of them nuzzled in the backseat of the car.

Their server returned to take their orders, then left them to enjoy Carla Steiner's performance while they waited for dinner. She'd moved into a plaintive rendition of "After You've Gone," and the words stabbed Gilbert's soul. A jilted lover pouring guilt upon the man who'd left her crying and alone—as if he didn't feel guilty enough already. When the singer turned her gaze toward their side of the room, he looked away.

And straight into Annemarie's cool brown stare.

She arched one brow and offered a semblance of a smile before returning her attention to the stage. She certainly wasn't crying over him now, and her indifference cut deeper than the surgeon's knife.

Pain throbbed behind his eyes until he wanted to gouge them out. His arm ached. His stump felt like he'd set it on fire. He had to get out of there—*now!*

19

*M*ore than a week had passed, but every time Annemarie thought about seeing Gilbert enter the Emerald Club with the little red-haired nurse parading along beside him, a stinging coldness swept through her. How he could so easily cast her aside, then take up with someone new so quickly—

Or maybe it hadn't been all that quickly. What if going to war had become a convenient opportunity to put some distance between them? He might have started seeing other women as soon as he landed on foreign shores. How many had there been? How long had he been playing her for the fool?

Of course Dorothy had sympathized, but Gilbert and his date left the club almost immediately after he'd caught Annemarie's eye—and just as well. She hoped he was duly embarrassed to be seen in public with another woman so soon after their breakup.

God forgive her, she didn't wish him ill. But he'd hurt her, hurt her terribly! At least Sam understood. Other than Dorothy, he was the only person she'd confided in about that horrid night. All week he'd tried to convince her Gilbert was only putting up a front, that his feelings for Annemarie were as strong as ever, and someday he'd realize it. Although Annemarie didn't share Samuel's confidence, his reassurance meant more than she could say.

By the following Monday, Samuel insisted he was fit to return to his hospital duties. With Papa driving and Samuel in the backseat of her father's Model T, Annemarie twisted to study Samuel's face for any telltale signs of fatigue. "Are you sure you're ready to go back to work? A few more days to get your strength back wouldn't hurt, you know."

"I promise I'll take it easy. I've been away from the hospital long enough." Samuel gave her hand a pat and then pushed open the rear door.

"Well, all right, but I wish you weren't set on returning to that lonely apartment afterward. You and your mother are welcome to stay with us as long as you want."

"Annemarie's right, son." Papa smiled over his shoulder. "We have plenty of room, and Ida's enjoying the chance to get to know your mother."

"I'm sure Mother will be over to visit often. She's planning to stay at least another week or two." Samuel laughed. "Who knows? Now that she's retired from dressmaking, she may decide to stay in Hot Springs as long as I'm stationed here just so she can keep an eye on me."

An unexpected pang squeezed Annemarie's stomach. "You don't anticipate being reassigned any time soon?"

"Not that I know of, but . . ." Samuel dipped his chin, his gaze shifting sideways. "With the army you never know."

"But surely—"

Papa tapped the steering wheel. "Let the poor man get on to work, Annie-girl, so you and I can do the same."

She cast Samuel a parting glare. "Just you take it slow today, Sam, do you hear me?"

"Yes, ma'am!" Grinning, he gave a crisp salute before climbing out of the car.

Annemarie waved through the window as they drove away, unable to clamp down on the niggling fear that she was losing her friend.

Honestly! He'd still be in town, for goodness' sake, living and working only a few blocks away. Still, they'd spent so much time together over the past three weeks that his absence from her home, her everyday comings and goings, would be tangible. Just knowing he was there, a friend to talk to and share with, someone to confide in when she seesawed between the pain of heartbreak over Gilbert and the blistering desire to wring her ex-fiancé's neck—

Admit it, Annemarie. You've grown attached to Sam Vickary, and you'll miss having him underfoot.

"Stop your frettin', young lady. The lad's the picture of health now. He'll be just fine." Papa turned off Central Avenue and headed up the road to the factory.

She crossed her arms and stared straight ahead. "He's just stubborn enough to push himself beyond his limits. I should probably go over on my lunch hour and check on him."

Papa guffawed. "I'm beginning to think there's more to your concern for Samuel Vickary than you're letting on."

Annemarie flung a disbelieving gaze at her father. "And what's *that* supposed to mean?"

"No need to get all hoity-toity with me. I'm only stating the obvious." Papa swerved to pass a double-parked milk truck and then glanced at Annemarie with a crooked grin. "Listen, dear one, I know Gilbert has broken your heart and you're still getting over the dastardly scoundrel. But seems to me our nice young chaplain could be more than a little interested in seeing what might develop between you two."

"You can't be serious! Sam's a good friend, nothing more."

"Your mother and I were 'good friends' before we married. Friendship's not a bad way to begin."

Annemarie harrumphed and glared out the window. "You forget Gilbert and I were friends before we became engaged."

"Yes, but childhood friendships don't always grow into lasting relationships. Now, with you and Samuel—"

"Papa!"

They'd arrived in the parking lot behind the factory. Annemarie exploded from the car and marched across the lot while furiously digging through her purse for the back door key. Once inside the workroom she yanked off her coat and tossed it over a hook, then stood there and seethed. The idea there could ever be anything between her and Sam! Papa had to be mistaken, because every word out of Sam's mouth was about never losing hope Gilbert would soon come crawling back to her and begging her forgiveness.

Her father quietly closed the door and hung his overcoat beside hers. "Don't you think it's about time you stop denying the obvious? You're attracted to Sam. He's attracted to you. What harm can it do to see where things lead? I doubt you'd find a better man if you searched the whole world over."

Annemarie slid a glance toward her father, but in her mind's eye she pictured Sam, his mouth quirking into that silly, off-center smile that made him so endearing.

She gave herself a mental shake. Surely, Papa was reading much more into their friendship than could possibly be true.

But one thing he was *not* mistaken about: Annemarie could search the rest of her days and never find a man as true and loyal and honorable as Army Chaplain Samuel Vickary.

❦

"You're a good man, Padre. Glad to see you back on duty." The old soldier—the same one from the isolation ward who one month ago had been convinced he was at death's door—gripped Samuel's hand and gave it a firm shake.

"Thanks, Sergeant King. It's good to be back." Samuel extracted his nearly bloodless hand and unobtrusively flexed his fingers a few times while moving a chair closer to the sergeant's bedside. "It's especially good to see you alive and kicking. Clearly the Lord has more use for you here than in heaven."

"Your prayers made the difference, no doubt about it. Up to now I've been pretty useless just about anywhere the Lord chose to put me. But your promise of the Lord's forgiveness gave me something to hold onto, a reason to live so's maybe I could yet become a better man."

Samuel could only nod as his thoughts returned to that day. The same overpowering sense of shame churned his belly—guilt over sins he'd long since repented of but could never forget. Would—*could*—God truly forgive him?

Would he ever be able to forgive himself?

"Just sorry you had to catch the danged influenza, Padre. Tears me up to think you may have got it from me." The sergeant, a long-term rheumatism patient, drew up one leg and massaged his knee. "Took a lot of guts for you to visit all us sick folks every day like you did."

Bravery had nothing to do with it, and Samuel wished they could change the subject. "The worst is over, so they tell me. How can I pray for you today?"

While Sergeant King shared recent news about a troublesome teenage grandson over in Tulsa, Samuel looked across the ward to see the young Irish nurse Mary McClarney approaching. The instant their eyes met, she quickly glanced away, her freckled cheeks reddening. She couldn't be unaware of Samuel's friendship with Annemarie. She couldn't even presume he wouldn't know she'd been seeing Gilbert.

Forcing his mind back to the sergeant, Samuel offered a few scriptural assurances about prodigal sons and promised to keep Sergeant King's grandson in his prayers. He excused himself and strode toward the exit, hoping he could escape the ward without being drawn into a conversation with Mary McClarney.

No such luck.

"Chaplain, a word if you don't mind?" Mary finished administering a patient's injection, then gathered her supplies onto a small metal tray and covered them with a cloth. She nodded toward the door, and Samuel followed her out. After depositing the tray in the work area behind the nurses' station, Mary suggested they talk in an unoccupied waiting room nearby.

"I have a feeling I know what this is about, Miss McClarney." Samuel strode to the window and laced his fingers behind his back. "And I'm not at all sure we should be having this conversation."

"But I've no one else I can confide in. Not even my dear mum would understand." She came up beside him and wrung her hands. "I know you're friends with Gilbert—Lieutenant Ballard—and I just want you to know I didn't pursue him. A girl of my station—why, if he hadn't first approached me, I'd never in my life have been so bold."

Samuel could hear the sincerity in her voice. He chewed the inside of his lip as he turned to face her. "What are you asking for, Mary? My blessing? That isn't mine to offer."

"I know, sir, but to know you understand would surely ease my mind." She rested her forehead against the windowpane, her warm breath misting the glass. "Do you think I don't know he's still in love with *her*? Do you think I don't realize he's only using me for a time?"

"And you're all right with that?" Samuel touched her shoulder, and she looked up at him with red-rimmed eyes. "Mary, you're a fine and caring nurse, a Christian woman with a good heart. You've no reason to settle for anything less than a man completely devoted to you. And that man *isn't* Gilbert Ballard."

Her lower lip trembled. Tears spilled down her cheeks. "But he could be, if only he'd let himself. We're good together. I know his needs, his fears, his pain. I can love him like no one else."

Looking into her eyes, Samuel saw the truth behind her words, and a great sadness filled him. Sadness for Mary, for Gilbert. Sadness for Annemarie. "Yes," he said, sweeping away a teardrop with the side of his thumb, "but can he ever really love you?"

"But can he ever really love you?"

The chaplain's question wove a tapestry of confusion through Mary's thoughts. Was it so wrong to believe Gilbert saw her as more than a momentary diversion? Did she hope in vain his feelings for her might someday deepen into something real and lasting?

She couldn't forget the awkwardness of the night at the Emerald Club, the shock of knowing Miss Kendall had seen them together. Gilbert had hurried them out before they'd even had a chance to order dinner, and with his headache raging, she'd expected to be taken home straightaway, her lovely evening with the man of her dreams cut miserably short.

But it hadn't been that way at all. Gilbert had ordered his chauffeur to take a slow drive around town and then asked if he could rest his head in Mary's lap until the pain subsided. She'd massaged his temples, his neck, his shoulders, until he'd groaned in blessed relief and drifted into peaceful slumber.

Nearly two hours later, with her legs buzzing from the weight of his head and her back stiff from sitting so still, he'd finally stirred—and the look of gratitude shining from his eyes warmed her head to toe. If such a gaze didn't speak love, Mary didn't know what did.

Except . . . since then Gilbert had barely spoken ten words to her. She'd seen him only briefly when he happened to arrive for a treatment at the same time she was escorting a patient to or from the physical therapy floor. Oh, he'd smiled rightly enough but always seemed preoccupied or in a hurry.

Or was it embarrassment over his unseemly dalliance with an unsophisticated Irish nurse?

In any case, she certainly wouldn't risk hospital gossip by making any overtures of her own. No, she must maintain her dignity, remain hopeful, and strive for patience.

And pray. If the Lord meant for the two of them to be together, He'd bring it about in His own good time.

And then Wednesday afternoon it happened.

"Mary?"

At the sound of his voice, she whirled around, nearly dropping the stack of fresh linens in her arms. She cast a quick glance right and left, but except for Gilbert, the corridor was empty.

A lazy grin tugged at one corner of his mouth. "Hope I didn't startle you."

"Heavens, no." *And lying's a sin, Mary McClarney.* She swallowed the nervous prickles climbing up her throat. A pillowcase slid to the floor, and she stared at it as if it might sprout wings and fly back to her. Anything to keep from looking into the eyes of the man who could slice her anxious heart to shreds or send it soaring heavenward with just one word.

He wheeled closer. "I've missed you, Mary."

"Have you, now?" Mary drew her shoulders back and forced her eyes to meet his. No matter how sweet his words, his tone, his pleading gaze, she wasn't without pride. "I'm not hard to find, should anyone care to come looking."

"I care, Mary. Honestly I do." A regretful frown deepened the dimple in his right cheek. "Truth is I worried you might be put out with me for ruining our date the other night. I did promise you dinner, after all, and then had the nerve to fall asleep in your lap."

"You needn't apologize. I could tell you were upset by—" She drew her lower lip between her teeth. Bringing Miss Kendall into the conversation would only amplify his discomfort—and Mary's. "I mean, it was clear how much pain you were suffering. My father had headaches like that, too."

"I knew you understood." Gilbert's hand sought hers, and she nearly dropped the sheets again. "Will you give me another chance? Dinner this weekend? You name the time and place."

"Well, I . . . " Between the hopeful look in his eyes and the smooth warmth of his palm cradling her hand, she could hardly think a coherent thought. To her left, a storage room door stood ajar. With another hurried glance in both directions, she nodded toward the door. "Perhaps we should . . ."

He took the hint, and she followed him into the storage room. As she nudged the door closed behind them, he turned his chair to face her. His gaze slanting downward, he murmured, "I've been a cad, Mary. Please let me make it up to you."

Monday's conversation with the chaplain swirled through Mary's brain, bringing with it a measure of the good sense she seemed to lack whenever in the presence of Lieutenant Gilbert Ballard. Taking a step backward, she speared him with an accusing stare. "Seems like you're always needin' to make something up to me. But I'm not someone to be pitied. Nor am I a woman to be toyed with whilst your own heart is mending. Ask me out because you want to be with me, or we'll not be seeing each other again."

Gilbert flinched, and for a long, painful minute she expected him to wheel himself out the door and vanish from her life as quickly as he'd come into it. Then slowly he lifted his gaze to meet hers, and the tortured look beneath those dark and twisted brows bored a hole straight through her soul. His voice low and ragged, he said, "I don't deserve you, Mary McClarney. But I need you. I need you like the air I breathe."

Her hand flew to her heart, as if she could stifle the ferocious pounding behind her sternum. Need wasn't the same as love . . . but couldn't it become love . . . someday?

Gilbert lifted an imploring hand. "Please, Mary."

The linens cascaded to the floor. Slowly, slowly, she sank to her knees in front of his chair, her whole body atremble as he leaned forward to draw her against his chest. His breath scalded her cheek as his lips sought hers. Her fingers crept upward to twine themselves through his thick black curls, and she claimed them in a way she'd only dreamed of that night in the backseat of his car.

Now Gilbert's hungry kiss claimed her, until the urgency of his need made her tear herself from his arms with a whispered cry. She huddled amongst the scattered linens, her heart threatening to explode from her chest. The air in the tiny room pulsed with the sounds of their gasping breaths.

Footsteps sounded in the corridor, and Mary leapt to her feet. "Lord have mercy! What are we doing?" Frantically she gathered up sheets and pillowcases, now wrinkled and soiled, and prayed whoever approached didn't stop at the storage room.

When the steps continued on, she braved a glance at Gilbert. Would he now think her a shameless harlot? He said he needed her. Did he only mean in *that* way?

He ran a hand across his upper lip and gave her a shaky smile. "I know what you're thinking, Mary, and you're wrong. But I won't apologize for kissing you, and I'd do it again—I will do it again, every chance I get, if you'll let me." Again, he reached for her hand, tugging her knuckles to his lips for a searing kiss. "Say you'll let me, Mary. Say it."

She closed her eyes and savored the memory of his mouth on hers, and now the sweet, gentle fire of his lips as they grazed each finger. "I will. Lord help me, I will."

20

*B*alancing a serving bowl in each hand, Annemarie followed her mother into the dining room. "I'm certain we only set two extra places, but you've enough food here to feed everyone in our congregation."

Mama's laughter bubbled as she set a platter of roasted chicken in the center of the table. "No one should walk away hungry after Sunday dinner." She took the bowls from Annemarie and set them on either side of the platter, then tapped her index finger against her lips. "Peas, potatoes, chicken, rolls . . . What have we forgotten?"

"Butter and jam? And don't forget the gravy's simmering."

"The gravy—oh, dear! We'll have lumps for sure!" Mama nearly trampled Annemarie in her rush to return to the kitchen.

While Annemarie adjusted a place setting, the doorbell chimed. Sam! Her heart fluttered at the thought of seeing him again, and immediately she chided herself for such a girlish response. For perhaps the hundredth time that week, she recalled her father's not-so-subtle hints about the friendship between her and Sam growing into something more.

Nonsense. Utter nonsense. She scraped damp palms along the sides of her skirt and marched to the entry hall. Through the sheer curtains beside the front door she glimpsed Sam and his mother waiting on the porch. With a quick intake of breath and praying her voice would hold steady, she opened the door. "Good morning—or is it afternoon already? Do come in!"

Mrs. Vickary slipped off her gloves before taking Annemarie's hand. "So kind of your mother to invite us." She gave Samuel a meaningful smile. "There were too many Sundays this past year when I dined with no one's company but my own."

"Ursula!" Mama bustled in from the dining room and gave the small blond woman a sisterly embrace. "Come to the kitchen with me. I need your help repairing the gravy. I got distracted and let it simmer too long unattended."

With a hitch in her throat, Annemarie turned to Sam. He stood in the open doorway, a crooked little smile bowing his lips. She motioned him inside and closed the door. "You look well, more color to your cheeks since I saw you last. And praise God you're wearing your coat!"

Laughing, he shrugged his arms out of the sleeves and tucked his wool scarf into a pocket. He looked dapper in a starched blue shirt and gray sweater vest. "Thank my mother. She's been doting on me as if I were a helpless schoolboy."

"Good for her." Taking his coat, Annemarie caught the woodsy scent of his aftershave. A sudden impulse to press the garment to her face nearly melted her knees like hot butter. Resisting with every ounce of willpower, she spun away before Sam could read anything into her expression, but her hands still trembled as she draped the coat over a hook on the hall tree.

Honestly, such foolishness!

Annemarie gathered her wits enough to show Sam into the dining room and then hurried down the hall to call her father from the study. She found him poring over the Sunday papers, a halo of pipe smoke encircling his head. "Dinner's on the table, and the Vickarys are here."

Papa gave a wink as he laid the newspaper aside and rose. "Now perhaps you'll satisfy your concerns about Samuel's health and stop mooning about the office instead of tending to business."

"Mooning about? Please!" Annemarie linked her arm through her father's as they started toward the dining room. "I've never *mooned* a day in my life."

"What would you call it then? I plumb lost track of how many times I came in from the factory floor last week to find you staring off at nothing and a blob of ink smeared across a ledger page."

"I was . . . calculating."

"Mm-hmm. Calculating when you could next lay eyes on your Sam, no doubt."

Annemarie slapped her father's hand. "He isn't *my Sam*. We're only friends, Papa. How many ways must I say it?"

They rounded the corner into the front hall, the dining room now only a few steps away. Time to end this line of conversation once and for all. With a silent but fervent prayer her father wouldn't so much as hint at such ridiculous ideas during dinner, Annemarie took her seat across from Sam and his mother. The Lord willing, she'd get through this meal with her runaway feelings in check and her dignity intact.

After dessert had been served and the dishes cleared, Papa pushed back his chair and gave his belly a satisfied rub. Turning to Samuel, he said, "I like a good long walk around the neighborhood after Sunday dinner. Good for digestion, you know. Care to join me while the ladies chat?"

Samuel shook his head. "Ordinarily I'd enjoy the exercise, but it's been a long week, and I'm afraid I haven't the energy quite yet." He cast his Cupid's-bow smile toward Annemarie's mother. "However, if the ladies would rather converse without a gentleman present, I'll gladly occupy myself with a book or magazine."

"Fiddlesticks." Mama flicked Samuel's arm with the corner of her napkin. "Women's conversation can become quite tedious. We'd welcome the male point of view, wouldn't we, ladies?"

Annemarie's eyebrows shot up. "Of course."

Although she couldn't help wondering why, after missing Sam's company all week—very well, so Papa hadn't misread *that* aspect of their relationship—she should feel so awkward about spending an afternoon with him now. Only one thing explained it: Papa's teasing had made her overly self-conscious, all but ruining the casual candor of their friendship.

She only hoped Papa would drop his teasing long enough for her to feel comfortable around Sam again.

"Coming, dear?" Mama rested a hand on her shoulder. "Samuel and Ursula are already settled in the parlor."

Annemarie gave herself a mental shake. She *must* be going daft if she hadn't even noticed when everyone else left the table. She rose with a sigh. "Perhaps I should start on the dishes."

"They'll keep." With a dismissive wave, Mama started across the hall.

When Annemarie reached the parlor, she found Mama and Mrs. Vickary had claimed the two matching chairs closest to the fireplace. That left Annemarie to choose between her father's oversized gray easy chair—which would swallow her whole—or else sit with Samuel on the sofa. No matter she'd perched beside him there many times before and thought nothing of it. Today, however, everything was different.

Samuel stood as Annemarie entered the room, his smoky eyes lighting up for the briefest moment before he tipped his gaze toward the floor. His hesitant smile only heightened Annemarie's uncertainty. As deep as their friendship had grown—and she continued to tell herself it was *only* friendship—she couldn't shake the feeling he intentionally kept parts of himself locked away.

Maybe it was so with everyone who returned from war. Maybe there were things that didn't bear remembering, much less to be spoken of.

Her thoughts returned to Gilbert and all the changes the war had wrought in him, and a different kind of melancholy settled over her. She longed to ask Sam what more he knew about Gilbert and the red-haired nurse. Was it a one-time thing, or had Gilbert truly moved on?

Not a conversation for a Sunday afternoon, especially with Mama and Mrs. Vickary in the room.

Although the two ladies seemed quite caught up in their animated chat, hands gesturing as rapidly as their tongues flew, and feminine laughter trilling.

Annemarie motioned for Sam to take his seat and then settled on the far end of the sofa. "Our mothers have certainly become fast friends."

"Your mother has been a lifeline for mine. She's been at loose ends for the past couple of years, first retiring from her dressmaking business, then my going off to Europe."

"She's such a personable woman. Doesn't she have friends back in Fort Wayne?"

"Oh, yes. But among her closest friends she's the only widow, so . . ." Samuel lifted one shoulder in a weak shrug.

Annemarie smiled her understanding. "I can only imagine how difficult it's been for her. I'm glad she could come and stay with you for a while."

But one thing she didn't understand, and now hesitated to ask: why Sam chose not to retire from the chaplaincy after the war ended and return to his hometown. Perhaps the answers were wrapped up in the darkness she sometimes sensed in him.

Noticing a lag in the conversation across the room, Annemarie looked up to see Mrs. Vickary striding toward her. The small woman edged onto the sofa between Annemarie and Samuel and then patted Annemarie's knee.

"My dear," Mrs. Vickary said, "I've just been telling your mother about my dressmaking business. I had my own shop, you know, right in downtown Fort Wayne. A rather successful enterprise, if I do say so, myself."

And a rather curious statement, coming out of the blue. Annemarie inclined her head. "Yes, I believe Sam's mentioned it."

Sam pushed off the sofa and came to stand near Annemarie's other side. "I've been telling Mother what a gifted ceramic artist you are, and she's admired several of your pieces on display at the Arlington."

"Oh." Annemarie blinked, her gaze flitting between Sam and his mother. "That's so nice. Thank you."

Mrs. Vickary scooted closer. "Have you looked seriously yet into opening your own shop—a place to exhibit and sell your wares?"

A tiny gasp escaped Annemarie's throat. She pictured the vacant building on Central Avenue, recalling the owner's name—Ralph Patton—and the telephone number she had never called. She glanced up at Sam, her brows drawn together. Had she ever once voiced this dream aloud to him—or to anyone since Gilbert's tactfully worded disparagement?

Samuel shoved his hands into his pants pockets, one corner of his mouth curling upward. "Here's a woman who could help you, if you'll let her."

But how? How did he know?

Then Annemarie remembered those long days and nights while she sat at his bedside. She'd rambled on about all kinds of things, partly to fill the silence, partly to keep from going insane with worry, never imagining for a moment that in his feverish sleep he'd hear or remember a word of it.

Now Mama stood next to Samuel, a curious smile lighting her face. "Is it true, dear? Have you given thought to having a ceramics shop?"

Annemarie pursed her lips. "It's just a dream, Mama. And not a realistic one."

"And why not, dear?" Mrs. Vickary clasped Annemarie's hands. "I ran my shop for nearly twenty-five years, the last seven as a widow. I'd be pleased to share whatever knowledge I gained from the experience."

Tugging her hands free, Annemarie stood and paced across the room, then swung around to face the trio. "Really, it's impossible. Besides, Papa needs me at the factory, and there's the matter of startup costs—rent, furnishings, equipment, supplies. Not to mention the possibility I'd never sell enough to cover expenses."

Samuel laughed out loud. "Selling your creations should be the least of your worries. I've seen how quickly your work disappears over at the Arlington. And isn't Thomas still supplying you with special orders?"

"Sometimes more than I can keep up with, but—"

"And as for the factory," Mama put in, "with the war over, there are plenty of veterans looking for work. Your father should have no trouble hiring a capable replacement."

The front door banged shut, and Papa burst into the room. "Replacement? For whom?"

Casting Annemarie a pointed look, Mama gave her head a tiny shake and then strode across the parlor to seize her husband's elbow. "Joseph, dear, you look thirsty from your walk. Come to the kitchen and I'll pour you a tall glass of water."

Annemarie waited until her parents left the room before turning an I-told-you-so frown upon Sam and his mother. "There you have it. Even if every other objection could be countered, Papa would never agree to my leaving the factory."

"Oh, don't sell your mother short." Mrs. Vickary gave a wry laugh. "Your father may wear the pants in this family, but it's a wise man who heeds his wife's good sense."

"Good sense?" Annemarie crossed her arms and sank into the nearest chair. "Forgive me, but what is sensible about starting a business venture with no capital and no guarantee of success?"

A look crossed between Samuel and his mother, and the sudden fire in their eyes brought a chill to Annemarie's spine. Sam slid his arm around his mother's shoulders as they marched over to Annemarie's chair.

"Miss Kendall," Sam began with mock formality, "may I introduce you to your first two investors."

⬟

It took Samuel and his mother a full week to convince Annemarie they were serious about their offer, and still another three days before Samuel persuaded Annemarie to telephone Mr. Patton, the owner of the shop space she'd become interested in.

The balding gentleman agreed to meet them at the building on a Thursday noon. Giving his handlebar mustache a tweak, he combed Samuel with an appraising glance. "Army chaplain, are you? My son served in France. Dreadful war. Simply dreadful. Glad to help out a returning soldier and his bride."

Samuel's neck flamed. He flicked an embarrassed glance at Annemarie. "Miss Kendall and I are just friends."

"My mistake." Mr. Patton chuckled and consulted some jottings in a small black notebook. "Ah, yes. I see it was *Miss* Kendall who telephoned." This time he turned his thoughtful gaze upon Annemarie. "You're inquiring about leasing the shop for yourself?"

"That's correct." Annemarie seemed to grow another inch as she lifted her chin. "I'm a ceramicist. I'm interested in this location for my studio and salesroom."

The man inched backward and narrowed one eye. "Well, now, I don't see how—"

Samuel shouldered closer and pushed his chest out, trying to appear a little more imposing himself. "If you're concerned about Miss Kendall's business acumen—"

"I can speak for myself, Samuel." The confident tone in Annemarie's voice might fool Mr. Patton, but Samuel sensed her nervousness in the way she clutched her handbag in a death grip. With a polite nod in Samuel's direction, she returned her attention to Mr. Patton. "Perhaps I didn't mention I'm the daughter of Joseph Kendall? Our family has operated Kendall Pottery in Hot Springs for three generations. I grew up learning the business and have managed the factory office for the past six years."

Mr. Patton tugged at the lapels of his overcoat. "Managing an office for an already thriving operation is one thing. But before I could lease the space to a sing—" At Samuel's ominous glare, he cleared his throat and swallowed. "What I mean is, I require my tenants to sign at least a six-month lease, with two months' rent paid up front."

Samuel caught Annemarie's doubtful glance and reassured her with a discreet nod. He and his mother had already discussed how they would help Annemarie with the initial costs of establishing her shop, agreeing that with Annemarie's proven talent the investment would be money well spent. Mother had made a tidy profit on the sale of her dressmaking business, and with Samuel her only child and no grandchildren in the foreseeable future, she was more than glad to assist another woman with entrepreneurial aspirations.

As for Samuel, what else did he have to spend his money on? Most of his pay while overseas had gone straight into savings, and beyond food and shelter his current needs were few. Let Annemarie believe his interest in seeing her dream fulfilled was born only of friendship. She need never suspect his motivations ran much deeper—so deep, in fact, that he could scarcely admit them to himself.

Within an hour the papers were signed, and Samuel handed Mr. Patton his personal check, drawn on his recently opened Hot Springs bank account, for the first two months' rent. Annemarie could take occupancy the following weekend, and with Samuel promising he and his mother would both pitch in for cleaning and setup, Annemarie hoped to open for business by early March.

"Oh, Sam!" Annemarie hugged his arm as they exited Mr. Patton's office down the street. "I can hardly believe this is happening! You've become such a dear, dear friend, and I'll never be able to thank you enough."

His heart tripped. If only he could halt right here on the sidewalk, take her into his arms, and show her plainly how much he cared for her. Instead, he simply patted her hand and tucked it closer to his side. "This calls for a celebration. Must you rush back to the factory, or may I take you to lunch?"

Her smile fairly glowed. "I think Papa can spare me for a bit longer. They serve a delicious lunch menu at the Arlington. It would give me a chance to tell Thomas I'll soon be displaying my wares in my own showroom."

So off to the Arlington they went, Samuel nearly bursting his uniform buttons with the secret joy of strolling along Central Avenue with Annemarie Kendall on his arm.

Until, entering the Arlington Hotel lobby, he came face to face with the one man who could turn his fantasies to dust.

Gilbert.

21

*P*adre. Fancy meeting you here." Gilbert adjusted his grip on the crutches he'd barely learned how to maneuver. His artificial leg still chafed—more adjustments to made, obviously—and his stump ached from the pressure.

"It's good to see you, Gil." As Samuel's gaze swept Gilbert from head to toe, his nervous smile broadened with a sincerity not even a man of the cloth could fake. "And especially good to see you out of that chair."

"Still practicing, but it's a start." Gilbert relished a moment of self-satisfaction before forcing himself to meet Annemarie's gaze. "You're both looking well. Out for an afternoon stroll?"

"Sam has graciously invited me to lunch." Annemarie hiked her chin. "We're celebrating."

Gilbert's glance slipped to where Annemarie's fingertips peeked out from beneath Sam's arm. They stood so close that not even the tiniest glimmer of daylight shone between them, and the sight ripped through Gilbert like machine gun fire. Celebrating, eh? So much for Sam's denials. The padre had apparently moved in fast.

Gilbert's jaw muscles bunched. He tried to keep his voice steady. "Well, then, don't let me keep you."

Samuel bent close to Annemarie's ear. "Why don't you get us a table? I'd like a moment with Gilbert."

A glimmer of concern danced behind her eyes, but she nodded and slipped her hand free. With what could only be taken as a warning glance over her shoulder—directed straight at Gilbert—she marched toward the restaurant.

Samuel stepped closer, his gaze calm and steady. "You have nothing to be jealous of, Gil. There's nothing more than friendship between Annemarie and me."

A guttural laugh scraped loose from Gilbert's throat. "Jealous? Whatever gave you that idea? I told you in the hospital you two had my blessing."

"I didn't believe you then, and I don't believe you now." Samuel exhaled sharply and drew a hand down his face. His tone became imploring. "Look at you—standing on two legs again, your strength returning. You and Annemarie can pick up where you left off. You can have the life together you'd always planned on."

If only . . . *if only.* Gilbert's fingers tightened around the crutches, his left arm throbbing. He searched his heart, his soul, for even the faintest remnants of the man Annemarie had once loved.

But that man no longer existed. He lay dead and buried in a shell hole on the Western Front. This Gilbert—the man now standing, however shakily, before his rival—struggled to feel anything these days beyond simmering rage and the constant ache of his war wounds.

He feigned an indifferent smile, the effort making his cheeks twitch. With a nod toward the restaurant he said, "It's rude to keep a lady waiting." Then, mustering his remaining pride, he swiveled, recovered his balance, and prepared to limp away. "Nice seeing you, Sam. Glad you're over the flu."

Before he'd taken three steps, Samuel caught his arm. Those piercing gray eyes snapped with determination. "Look me up next time you're at the hospital. We should talk again."

"Why? So you can pray over my misguided soul? Sorry, Padre, too late for that."

"Gil—"

He jerked his arm free and stumbled across the lobby before he drove his fist straight through Sam's face.

Reaching the door to his brother's office, he banged it with the tip of his crutch. "Tom. Thomas!"

Thomas jerked the door open. "I hear you, for crying out loud. And so does half the hotel, I imagine. What are you doing here, anyway?"

"Zachary dropped me off after my therapy appointment." Gilbert pushed past his brother and headed for the nearest chair. Flopping into it, he tossed his crutches to the floor. "We need to talk."

Thomas circled his desk and sat down, hands folded across his abdomen. "At home you do nothing but sit in the study and sulk. You rarely even take meals with Mother and me. And now you want to *talk*?"

"Don't give me your guff. I haven't the patience for it."

"Or for little else, if you ask me." Thomas's mouth twisted in a sneer. "Let's have it, then. What's on your mind, oh brother mine?"

Gilbert swallowed. It galled him to no end that he needed Tom's help—needed *anyone's* help. The words nearly choked him: "I need a job."

Thomas's mouth fell open. He stared for a full three seconds. "A job. You're asking *me* for a job? I thought you were a career army officer."

The envelope in Gilbert's breast pocket felt like a lead weight. *Honorable Discharge from The United States Army.* The papers had arrived three days ago, another dream up in smoke—quite literally. Sometimes he could still smell the stench of gunpowder and his own burning flesh. He fingered the brass button at the base of his throat. Why he still wore his uniform he had no idea. Habit, mostly.

Or possibly to convince himself he was still a soldier.

Gritting his teeth, he lifted his eyes to meet his brother's. "Obviously I'm not much use to the army anymore, or at least that's how they see it. So I was hoping there might be a job for me here at the hotel." He grimaced and rubbed his aching stump. "Preferably a desk job."

Thomas had the decency not to laugh. "I can see you're serious. I'm not currently aware of any openings, but let me look into it." He laced his fingers atop his desk. "Are you . . . I mean, monetarily speaking . . ."

"Am I broke? Not yet." He thought of the wad of cash he'd traded this morning for the morphine pills now tucked away in an inside pocket. "But I . . . have expenses. Things I can't expect Mother to pay for."

This time Thomas couldn't suppress a snort. "I guess so, the way you're wining and dining the little redhead from the hospital. Not exactly the class of woman Mother would approve of."

"Leave Mary out of this." Gilbert gripped the chair arms, a surge of protectiveness tightening his gut. He could use one of those morphine tablets right now to take the edge off his guilt—not to mention his impulse to flatten his brother against the far wall. But he needed Thomas on his side. He needed that job.

Inhaling a slow breath, he forced himself to speak calmly. "I'm just trying to make a go of civilian life, Thomas. Anything you can do to help will be appreciated."

"Apple pie á la mode—delicious!" Annemarie dabbed her mouth with the corner of her napkin. After complying with the Save On Sugar campaign during the war, enjoying a sweet dessert felt like a guilty indulgence. "Thank you for lunch, Sam. Although I should be treating you. It's the least I can do to show my appreciation."

Samuel stirred cream into his coffee. "You can thank me by proving your ceramics shop a raging success."

A shiver raced up Annemarie's spine. Could she really make and sell enough of her creations to turn a profit? Papa certainly had his reservations despite the returns she'd shown him from her sales through Thomas at the Arlington. And even though she'd promised to continue working half-days at the factory for the next couple of months, Papa had been even less thrilled about having to hire her replacement.

It could turn out to be a good thing all around, however. Their neighbor Jack Trapp had done bookkeeping in the army, and now, home from the war, he needed work to help support his mother and younger sister. Annemarie had already suggested her father interview him. Perhaps she could begin teaching Jack the office routine as early as next Monday, and then get busy on a slew of new ceramic pieces to stock the display shelves she needed to install—

Staring at Sam, she pressed two fingers to her temple and gasped a jittery laugh. "It's only just dawning on me how much work lies ahead!"

His lips bowed in an enticing smile as he reached across the table to touch her hand. "And you'll have plenty of help."

Her skin tingled beneath his fingertips, her carefully guarded feelings betraying her. She resisted the impulse to tuck her hand into her lap.

"What is it, Annemarie?" The tender look in Sam's eyes spoke more than mere friendship. "We've been sitting here for nearly an hour, and you've said nothing at all about seeing Gilbert again. It must have affected you."

"Of course it affected me. I doubt there'll ever come a day when seeing him doesn't stir regrets over what might have been." She moved her hand until it rested in Samuel's palm. His warmth both soothed and exhilarated, blotting out all thoughts of Gilbert.

Dear Lord, was Papa right?

Samuel quickly pulled away and busied himself crumpling his napkin beside his dessert plate. "I nearly forgot. I have an appointment back at the hospital. We should go." He signaled their waiter, who hurried over with the check. Laying some bills in the waiter's hand, Sam edged his chair away from the table. "I'd offer to wait at the trolley stop with you, but—"

"No, no, it's fine." Annemarie's heart dipped. She allowed Samuel to pull out her chair and help her on with her coat. "Will I see you this weekend?"

"Just let me know when you want to get started at the shop, and Mother and I will both be there ready to work."

Mother and I. For the first time since Mrs. Vickary arrived in town, Annemarie wished she'd go back to Indiana.

She walked with Sam as far as the front desk. After thanking him again for lunch—for *everything*—she veered down the corridor to see if Thomas could spare a moment. Now was as good a time as any to let him know her plans for the shop. She found his door ajar and peeked inside to see him riffling through a desktop card file, his forehead furrowed deeper than a freshly plowed field.

Tapping on the doorframe, she peeked inside. "Thomas? Is this a bad time to speak with you?"

He looked up with a start. "Never a bad time for you, Annemarie. Come in and have a seat."

"It's just you looked so deep in thought." She dropped into the chair across from him and laced her fingers atop her handbag. "Is everything all right?"

"Yes—no." A sharp sigh sliced the air. "You'll hear this sooner or later, so might as well be from me. Gilbert was just here asking me for a job. The army's discharged him."

"Oh, no." She squeezed her eyes shut to think how Gilbert must be dealing with yet another setback. As long as she'd known him, military life was all he'd lived, breathed, eaten, or slept. Peering expectantly at Thomas, she asked, "And are you able to help him?"

"I'm going through staff positions right now, looking for any possibility of a vacancy—or rather, anything he'd be suited for." One side of Thomas's face skewed into a grimace. "Not easy to place a man whose sole work experience involves battle strategy, giving orders, and blasting holes through enemy lines."

Annemarie cast him a pensive smile. "Not much different from a business manager's job, wouldn't you say?"

"Hadn't thought of it like that." Giving a tired smirk, Thomas set the card file aside. "Still, everyone's scrambling for work these days. Several of our hometown doughboys have applied here already, looking to do anything from scrubbing floors to busing tables. We've hired as many as we can afford. Managerial positions, on the other hand, are few and far between."

"Well, I'm sure you'll do your best for Gilbert." Annemarie pulled her lips between her teeth. She cared about Gilbert's struggles, prayed he'd find his way again. But he'd made it clear he was out of her life, and there wasn't much she could do— that he'd *allow* her to do—to help. Instead, she needed to focus on her own future.

Inching toward the edge of her chair, Annemarie cleared her throat. "Actually, the reason I stopped in is to tell you I'll soon be taking my ceramics off display here."

Thomas jerked his chin up. "What? Why?"

"Because I've decided it's time to open my own showroom. I've just leased space in a vacant building down the street."

"Have you?" Looking stunned and yet full of admiration, Thomas rose and circled his desk to give Annemarie a kiss on the cheek. "Well, congratulations. If anyone can make a go of it, you certainly can. But the lobby won't be the same without your lovely pieces on display."

"I was thinking about that. Perhaps you wouldn't mind if I kept a few things here with a placard directing interested parties to my new shop?" Annemarie stood, her handbag clutched at her waist. "And, naturally, I'd encourage my customers to patronize the Arlington."

"Sounds like a fair exchange to me." Thomas tugged on his earlobe. "You, uh, wouldn't be in the market for a savvy business manager, would you? Because I could recommend someone . . . someone with a vested interest in your success."

"It'll certainly be awhile before I could afford to hire—" Understanding dawned, and Annemarie's stomach clenched. She held up one hand. "No, Thomas. Absolutely not. How could you even suggest such a thing?"

He seized her outstretched hand and pressed it between his own. "He needs you, Annemarie. Yeah, he's being hardheaded and stupid, but he'll come around in time. He just needs a reason to believe you're still there for him."

"*I* haven't gone *anywhere*. Gilbert broke it off with *me*, remember?" Shock and anger choked her until she could barely speak. She took two steps backward, nearly tripping over the chair leg. "If you'll excuse me, I must get back to the factory."

"Wait. I'm sorry." Thomas blocked the door. "Don't leave mad, Annemarie. I'm just trying to help." Pain creased the corners of his eyes. "This is my big brother we're talking about—the guy I always looked up to. To see him return from the war a broken man—broken in spirit, broken in body—it hurts like you can't even imagine."

Annemarie's gaze softened. She gripped Thomas's wrist. "I know exactly how much it hurts. I hurt for Gilbert as much as for myself. But I can't fix him. *You* can't fix him. The best we can do is love him and pray."

"Then . . . you do still love him?"

"I never stopped." Tears caught in Annemarie's throat. Unable to say more, she gave her head a tiny shake and hurried from the office.

Mary stood barefoot at the kitchen sink, the cool linoleum like balm to her aching feet. She'd just come off a seven-day shift and was more than ready to have another Sunday free so she and Mum could attend Mass tomorrow. She rinsed and wiped the last plate, set it in the cupboard, and then limped across the floor to collapse into a chair.

Her mother padded into the kitchen. She'd already changed into her gown, robe, and slippers. "I told you I'd do up the dishes right after my bath. Why didn't you wait?"

"I don't mind, Mum." Mary offered a tired smile.

"Poor lassie, working such long hours and then rushing home to see to the chores and fix our meals." She pushed aside a stray lock of Mary's hair before planting a kiss on her forehead. "I'm sorry as can be I can't do more around here."

Mary listened with concern to the phlegm rattling in her mother's chest and thanked the Lord yet again that they'd been spared the Spanish flu. Drawing on her last bit of energy, she rose to fill the kettle. "I'm for a cup of tea before bed. How about you?"

"It would help my cough, sure enough. But you sit down and let me. I've strength enough to do that much." Mary's mother set out cups and then measured tea leaves into a strainer. "And while the kettle boils, perhaps you'll tell me more about this young man of yours. All's I've seen of him is a peek in the rear window of his automobile."

A guilty twinge squeezed Mary's heart. She'd done everything possible to evade her mother's questions about Gilbert. But as he pressed to see her more and more frequently, she knew she'd eventually have to own up to her feelings . . . and her fears.

"He's got a job now, part-time anyway. The army's discharged him because of his disability." And she only knew that much because he'd seemed unusually keyed up yesterday during another tryst in the hospital storage room—one of many they'd enjoyed of late. Normally he insisted on talking little and kissing often, but this time he'd poured out his anger over the loss of his military career in one breath, and in the next stated his brother had found him a part-time position managing schedules for the Arlington housekeeping staff.

"I feel for all those poor lads trying to make their way in the world now the fighting's done." Mum leaned against the counter as she waited for the water to boil. "Still, I'd like to get to know the man who's claimed my only daughter's heart."

A shiver ran through Mary's chest. She shot her mother a wide-eyed stare. "Oh, Mum, he has indeed! I'm falling in love for sure, but I'm scared witless it can't last."

"Now why on earth would you think such a thing?" Mary's mother strode across the room to cup Mary's chin in her bony hands. "It's the Ballard boy who's the lucky one. You're as fine a girl as any man could ever want."

Mary couldn't meet her mother's gaze. If Mum knew how Mary had given herself to Gilbert time and again in that cramped little room—how she'd let him run his hands along her curves, devour her mouth with kisses, press his body against hers so tightly she could feel his aching need—

"Mary, what's wrong? Don't lie to me, child. Has he taken advantage?"

"No!" She ducked around her mother and made a pretense of checking the teakettle. Truth be told, she wondered who was taking advantage of whom. In a relationship with Gilbert—handsome and charming, a man of status and privilege, a decorated soldier—Mary had nothing to offer and everything to gain, because the one thing Gilbert wanted most from her she refused to give. Up to now she'd been able to forestall his passion with tender words and promises. Besides, more often than not, their stolen moments dissolved when Gilbert's headaches raged and nothing would soothe him but her practiced touch.

Her mother's arm slipped around her shoulders. "Then what is it? Why can you not believe the man's feelings are true?"

Sighing, Mary swiveled into her mother's embrace. "Because his heart belongs to another, and he'll never be fully mine until he finally lets her go."

22

$\mathcal{S}$amuel's visits didn't usually take him to this section of the hospital, but after winding through hallways to find the room of a naval officer who'd requested pastoral counseling, he'd gotten turned around and found himself in a service corridor.

As he approached the end of the hallway, a door clicked shut behind him. Glancing over his shoulder, he saw Nurse McClarney scurrying toward him. She moved with her head down, her hands busily working loose curls back under her cap. Then seconds later the door opened again and Gilbert hobbled out, his crutches click-clicking on the tile floor.

Nausea curdled Samuel's stomach. Before either of them noticed him he ducked around the corner and into a window alcove. Judging from differing sounds of their footsteps, he guessed Mary had veered left at the corner but Gilbert had turned right—the same direction Samuel had taken. Any second now, Gilbert would pass, and Samuel held his breath in hopes Gilbert would keep right on going.

Never mind what he'd told Gilbert that day at the Arlington: "*Look me up next time you're at the hospital.*"

But two weeks had elapsed, and even coming in for physical therapy appointments several times a week, Gilbert had never once darkened Samuel's office door. Then as the days passed, with Samuel spending evenings and weekends helping Annemarie ready her shop and his nights dreaming about her, he'd ceased caring if he ever saw Gilbert again. Let the louse ruin his life chasing a skirt, stealing forbidden kisses in a storage room. Samuel decided he'd held back long enough. He would gladly pick up the pieces of Annemarie's shattered heart if she'd let him.

And lately she'd given him every indication she would.

I love her. God help me, I do.

Then why did he feel so guilty?

"Hey, Padre. Long time no see."

He looked up to see Gilbert staring at him, a sleepy smile skewing his mouth. For a blinding moment Samuel couldn't think of a thing to say. Then he blurted out, "I didn't know they were holding therapy sessions in closets these days."

Balancing on his crutches, Gilbert combed splayed fingers through his tousled hair and chuckled. "You should try it sometime. Works wonders."

"I could put a stop to your rendezvous with one word to Mrs. Daley."

"Sure you could." Gilbert's words slurred. His eyes glazed momentarily before he nailed Samuel with his glare. "But I know you better than that, *Padre*. You're too good a man to risk getting Mary fired just to get back at me."

Samuel took a step forward, fists clenched at his sides. "Why are you doing this, Gil? To yourself? To Mary?"

"I'm not doing anything *to* anyone. Mary and I are good together. She makes me . . ." Gilbert wavered and glanced aside. Then with a stuttering sigh he muttered, "Actually, it's none of your business. Excuse me."

Watching Gilbert limp off on his crutches, Samuel felt hollow inside. He'd already lost too many friends. Some he'd buried in graves marked with little more than a makeshift cross or a helmet propped against a rifle stock. Others he'd bade good-bye to as the war ended, and they went their separate ways. But getting to know Gilbert aboard the *Comfort*, then requesting this assignment here in Hot Springs, Samuel had hoped he'd finally found the "friend who sticks closer than a brother" spoken of in the Book of Proverbs.

He'd never dreamed in a million years how one woman— one beautiful, desirable, incomparable woman—would rip their friendship to shreds.

Trudging to his office, Samuel decided he hadn't the strength to finish out the day. It would be easy enough to excuse his early departure with lingering fatigue from the flu, so he tacked a note on his door saying he'd return first thing in the morning. Then, instead of catching the trolley to his apartment, he opted for a walk. Maybe the fresh air would help clear his head.

The next thing he knew, he was standing outside Annemarie's shop. The fresh butcher paper he'd helped Annemarie tack up last weekend now blocked his view of the interior, but rustling sounds and the indistinct glow of light bulbs told him someone was inside.

Picturing Annemarie beyond the door, he felt the last vestiges of exhaustion float away on the March breeze. He tried the latch, but wisely she'd kept it locked. "Annemarie? It's Samuel."

Her happy voice carried through the glass. "Hello, Sam! Be right there. I just—"

A thunderous crash shook the windows. Propelled to a state of instant panic, Samuel yanked on the door handle, but the lock held fast. "Annemarie! Are you all right?"

Her only response was a muffled groan. Agonizing seconds crept by as he waited for anything more, all the while trying to figure some way into the building. Precious time would be lost if he had to circle the block and find the alley entrance—and the rear door would more than likely be locked as well.

Then, just as he'd made up his mind to ram his boot heel through the door, it swung open. Annemarie stood before him, her dark hair a disheveled mass and blood seeping through a tear on her sleeve. His hurried glance took in the toppled stepladder next to an upended bucket. Brown, sudsy water seeped across the floor.

Annemarie's mouth twisted into something between a grimace and an apologetic smile. "It isn't as bad as it looks—or sounded."

He reached out, longing to crush her against him in relief. Then sanity prevailed. He ushered her over to a chair and peeled back the torn fabric covering her forearm. "Here, let me see how bad it is. Does it hurt much?"

"I told you, I'm—" Annemarie's back arched. She sucked air between her teeth.

"Don't dare tell me you're fine when I can see otherwise." Samuel glanced about for anything he could use to stanch the bleeding but saw nothing more useful than a pile of grimy cleaning cloths. Then noticing the muslin apron Annemarie wore, he grabbed the corner, folded it to a clean spot, and pressed it against the gash on her arm. "This may need stitches. I should get you to a doctor."

A moan escaped Annemarie's lips. Her usually rosy complexion had turned ashen. "It's just a scratch."

"Yes, and scratches can become infected." Assisting medics on the battlefield, Samuel would have reached for hydrogen peroxide or carbolic acid. He'd flushed out more bullet and shrapnel wounds than he cared to remember. He tugged Annemarie to her feet, praying she wouldn't faint. "Let's get you to the sink and run some water over your arm. Then I can get a better look."

In the lavatory at the rear of the shop, Samuel held Annemarie's arm under the faucet and watched the last trickles of blood disappear down the drain. She smiled up at him. "See? I told you it was nothing."

At least her color had returned. And now Samuel felt lightheaded. He took a towel from the rack and wrapped it around Annemarie's wound, then cradled her arm to his chest. "Do you have any idea how badly you frightened me?"

"My dear, dear Sam. Such a worrier you are." With her other hand she reached up to stroke his cheek. Her dewy-eyed gaze, her lips so alluring, her touch gentle as an angel's kiss . . .

His heart hammered, and he prayed the Lord would forgive him for what he was about to do—but then perhaps he was already beyond forgiveness. Either way, it mattered little, because nothing—*nothing*—would satisfy him now until he claimed Annemarie as his own.

Still sheltering her injured arm between them, he moved his other arm slowly, gently, around her shoulders and pulled her to him. His fingers twined in the remnants of her bun until the last of the pins fell free and her mass of black curls tumbled loose down her back.

Surprise brightened her eyes, and then sweet realization. She tilted her chin. Her lips parted. "Yes, Sam. Yes."

Her murmured invitation was all the permission he needed. His mouth found hers with a tender fury, and he drank in the sweet fullness of her lips like an elixir of life.

Lightness invaded Annemarie's body, as if a whole galaxy had coalesced into one immense, incredible, unquenchable star. She'd never felt so alive, so replete, so unbearably . . . happy.

The kiss melted into placid release. "Oh, Sam, Sam . . ."

He nudged a stray curl off her cheek, his gray eyes shining with unshed tears. His lips curled into the boyish smile she'd come to adore, and he shook his head as if in utter disbelief. "I have wanted to kiss you for such a long time."

Leaning into his chest, she grazed his cheek with another kiss and cherished the subtle rasp of his day's growth of whiskers against her lips. One hand caressing his nape, she moved her mouth near his ear and whispered, "Then why didn't you?"

With a sigh, he eased away, his Adam's apple bobbing. Tenderly he parted the towel covering her arm and examined the injury she'd all but forgotten. "The bleeding has stopped. I don't think you'll need stitches after all."

"Sam. You're changing the subject."

His glance darted around the lavatory as if he saw it for the first time, and then he fixed her with a stern stare. "What *were* you doing on that ladder—and with no one here to help you? Why, if you'd been hurt any worse, if you hadn't been able to get to the door—"

"But I wasn't. I did. And I'm *fine*." Annemarie gave a hopeless chuckle. "Honestly, Samuel Vickary, you are worse than a mother hen."

Flouncing out of the lavatory, she seized the mop she'd left by the rear door and marched back to the showroom. True, she may have been a *wee* bit foolish climbing the stepladder to clean the top of a display shelf by herself. But if it took her foolishness to finally break through Sam's reserve and convince him to kiss her, then the risk had been well worth it.

Annemarie's lips tingled with the memory of that kiss, and her stomach did a tiny flip-flop. Partly in ecstasy . . . and partly from guilt, for she couldn't remember Gilbert's kisses ever evoking such a thrill of emotion. As she set the bucket aright, she glimpsed Sam pacing to the front window, one hand behind his back, the other stroking his chin. A thoughtful expression drew his mouth into a frown.

He felt it, too—the fear they'd crossed an invisible line with no going back, no return to the easy, bantering friendship they'd forged over the past several weeks. But after that kiss— a kiss she must now admit she'd secretly dreamed about since Sam's recovery from the Spanish flu—would she even want to?

She busied herself with the mop in hopes Sam wouldn't notice the flush heating her cheeks. What if Papa was right? What if God had intended all along that Sam, not Gilbert, would be the one she'd share her life with?

"Let me." His hand covered hers on the mop handle, and she trembled.

"Really, it's—"

"I insist." Samuel wrested the mop from her grip and began sopping up the spilled water with a fervor to match the set of his jaw. "You realize one word to your father about your fall and he'll put his foot down once and for all about your opening this shop. And I wouldn't blame him, not in the least."

"Sam." She stepped in front of him, arms locked across her chest—as if her false bravado could still the flutter beneath her breastbone. "Don't think for an instant you can use threats or busyness to brush aside what just happened between us. You kissed me. You *wanted* to kiss me." Her voice fell to a breathless murmur. "And I wanted your kiss."

He rested his hands atop the mop handle. His eyes found hers, and in them she read longing, uncertainty, foreboding . . . until his lids closed like a curtain shutting her out. "It was wrong. I tried to convince myself otherwise. I wanted to believe I had every right to kiss you . . . to *love* you . . . but I don't."

Love her? Annemarie's heart caught in her throat. When Samuel started to turn away, she clutched his arm, forcing him to face her. "But of course you have a right—*every* right! Why would you say such a—"

Instantly she knew: *Gilbert.* Sam had pledged loyalty to his friend, promised both Gilbert and Annemarie countless times he'd find a way to bring them back together.

"No," she said, now gripping both his arms. The mop bounced off the fallen stepladder and clattered to the floor. "I will not let you thrust aside your feelings for me—my feelings for *you*—because of a man who has turned against us both."

His gaze searched hers with a desperation that tore at her soul. "If only I could believe—if I could be certain—"

"Certain of what? That six months or a year from now Gilbert won't come to his senses and decide he still loves me? That I won't someday regret today, our kiss, this moment?" Her hand crept up his arm until she rested it at the base of his neck. Warmth seeped into her palm, and she could feel the beat of his pulse. With a sad smile she stretched upward to brush his lips with the tenderest of kisses. "How can I ever"—she kissed him again—"regret"—and again—"this?"

She knew the moment he surrendered. A tremor shot through his body and his arms encircled her, drawing her against him until she feared he'd crush the breath from her. His mouth found hers with a hunger equal to her own.

At the sound of a loud *a-hem*, Annemarie jerked out of Samuel's arms. With startled gasps, they both swung around to face the intruder.

"Thomas!" Annemarie tugged at her bodice with one hand and shoved her unkempt hair off her shoulder with the other.

"Obviously I'm interrupting something." Wearing a contemptuous frown, Thomas glanced from Annemarie to Samuel and back again. "I thought you were opening a shop, not making time with the local chaplain."

Indignation shot up Annemarie's spine. "I resent your suggestion of anything improper."

"Oh, do you?" Thomas gave a harsh laugh. "Seems it was only yesterday you were engaged to my brother. Didn't take you long to move on."

Samuel stepped forward. "Gilbert had every chance to set things right with Annemarie. He made his choice."

Thomas doffed his bowler and slapped it against his leg. "I know . . . I know." With a pained exhalation, he strode across the room to examine a display cabinet where Annemarie had already set out some of her ceramic creations. "It's just hard to watch my brother throwing his life away, you know? Wasting it on self-pity and redheaded nurses."

Despite every promise to herself that Gilbert would no longer hurt her, the memory of seeing him with Mary McClarney at the Emerald Club that night jolted Annemarie like a jab to her midsection.

Jealousy? No. She truly believed she'd moved beyond such raw emotion where Gilbert was concerned. But, like Thomas, she hated seeing the man she once loved—the friend she'd grown up with—forego the life he'd worked so hard for. She carried no ill will toward the young nurse. Miss McClarney was probably an innocent victim in this sad turn of affairs, little more than a plaything, a distraction for Gilbert as he coped with war's ravages on both his body and his spirit.

She felt Samuel's hand upon her shoulder, and he cast her a concerned half-smile. She wanted to reassure him but questioned whether her feelings toward him weren't her own way of dealing with Gilbert's rejection.

Thomas spoke again, interrupting her thoughts. "I didn't stop by looking to pass judgment. I saw the door open and thought I'd see how the shop was coming along." He paused to peruse his surroundings, then gave a brisk nod. "Looks like you'll be opening soon. I'd be happy to bring over your pieces from the Arlington anytime you're ready."

"Thank you, Thomas." Annemarie walked behind the counter and retrieved the small sign she'd ordered from the printer:

ORIGINAL CERAMIC DESIGNS
BY ANNEMARIE KENDALL
STUDIO AND SALESROOM LOCATED ON
CENTRAL AVENUE
ACROSS FROM FORDYCE BATHHOUSE

She handed the placard to Thomas. "You'd offered to keep a few pieces on display. Choose any you'd like."

"My pleasure." Thomas heaved a groan and pulled Annemarie into his chest for a hug. "Still love you like a sister. You know I wish you every happiness, don't you?"

"I do." Annemarie kissed his cheek. "And I wish the same for you *and* your brother."

With a tip of his hat to Samuel, Thomas marched out the door.

Annemarie turned toward Samuel, and the look on his face nearly ripped her heart in two. He shoved his hands into his pockets with a tired shrug. "What have we done, Annemarie? What have we done?"

What have I done?

Gilbert rolled onto his side, the silver-framed portrait of Annemarie cradled in shaking hands. Darkness shrouded the room—his own bedroom at long last, now that he could manage the stairs. Not expertly by any means, but at least he no longer felt like *quite* such an invalid.

Still a cripple, though. Still impaired. Still . . . *less*.

A knock sounded outside his door. "Gilbert, darling?"

He groaned and slid the picture frame beneath his pillow. "What do you want, Mother?"

She nudged open the door. "Aren't you feeling well, son? I thought you were going out again." Disapproval crept into her tone. "It's so rare these days to find you at home on a Friday evening."

"Slight change of plans." Could she detect the slur in his voice?

"Not another headache? Oh, darling . . ." Sweetness and sympathy once again, his mother strode to his bedside. She hovered over him to stroke his temple. Her thick, bejeweled fingers felt cold against his skin, and he longed for Mary's soothing touch.

Mary, Mary. He would think only of his sweet, giving Mary.

Except he wouldn't be seeing her tonight after all, thanks to that witch Mrs. Daley changing Mary's schedule at the last minute.

"Shall I have Marguerite bring dinner to your room?"

"Not hungry." He wanted to slap his mother's hand away, beg her to leave him in his misery.

"I am quite concerned for you, Gilbert." Pouting, she settled her bulk onto the edge of the mattress. "You cannot disguise the fact that you have been drinking more heavily since returning home."

"What of it?"

"Besides the fact that overimbibing is unhealthy, it is unbecoming for a man of your station." She sniffed. "As are certain other activities in which you have indulged of late."

Gilbert clenched his jaw. Of course, she referred to his relationship with Mary. He should have known neither Thomas nor their inscrutable driver, Zachary, would be able to keep his secret for long.

Although Mother would be even more displeased to know the spunky Irish nurse was the most virtuous of her son's indulgences. Pure as new-fallen snow, Mary remained the one shining light in this dark valley through which he traveled. Though he'd pressed for more—*begged* for more—she granted him only her kisses, her caresses, her inexhaustible trove of empathy and understanding.

And if he couldn't be with Mary tonight . . .

"Get up, Mother." He elbowed her in the spine until she rose, then swung his legs off the side of the bed and reached for his prosthesis.

"You're coming down to dinner then?" She fluttered her hands in a vain attempt help.

"No. I'm going out after all." He tugged at his trouser leg until it slid down to cover the infernal contraption attached to his thigh. Though the artificial leg gave him a semblance of normalcy, it remained a source of perpetual discomfort. "Hand me my crutches, will you?"

His mother complied but with no small amount of disdain. "Are you seeing her again?"

"No, Mother dear. I'm safe from her wickedness for tonight." Casting his mother a withering glance over his shoulder, he snatched up his tweed jacket and hobbled to the door, every footfall shooting pain through his skull.

At the landing he paused to work his arms into his jacket sleeves, then checked the inside pocket for his vial of morphine pills. Almost empty, thanks to yet another killer headache. He reminded himself to contact his supplier first thing in the morning. In the meantime, he'd have to settle for a night of poker, cheap cigars, and free-flowing booze. Although if he kept this up, his income from the part-time job Thomas had finagled for him wouldn't suffice.

Why are you doing this to yourself, Gilbert?

The question caught him up short, nearly pitching him headfirst down the staircase. He wasn't sure whose voice echoed through his head—Samuel's, Mary's, Annemarie's?

God's?

As if God cared. Where was God when the artillery shell exploded? Where was God when Gilbert's blood poured from his severed thigh? Where was God the day Gilbert looked down from a hospital window to see his sweetheart walking away on the arm of his best friend?

Why was he doing this to himself? Because if he were bad enough, vile enough, contemptible enough, maybe he'd convince Annemarie and everyone else that she truly was better off without him.

And maybe, in the process, he'd convince himself.

23

"Why you thought you needed me to check your work, Jack, I'll never know." Annemarie tapped the ledger page with her pencil. "And I daresay your handwriting is oceans more legible than mine!"

Jack Trapp looked sharp in his crisply starched shirt, paisley tie, and gray pinstriped vest. He nudged his chair back and shot Annemarie a self-satisfied grin. "Army life's good for something, I suppose. Clerking for army muckety-mucks taught me plenty about bookkeeping, filing, and the like."

"And if it kept you away from the front lines and safe from harm, all the better." Annemarie returned his smile with a twinge of sadness for all the men who weren't as fortunate.

Like Sam. Like Gilbert.

Shaking off such melancholy thoughts, she retrieved another invoice from the stack they'd been working through. "What do you hear from your sister Joanna? Is she still in Paris?"

"We had a letter just yesterday. The Army Signal Corps is keeping her busy while the bigwigs iron out the peace treaty. Hopefully she'll be home by summer."

"She's so brave to have volunteered." If not for Papa needing her at the factory—and the fact that Annemarie's French was atrocious—she might have joined her neighbor for an overseas adventure. Serving her country as a Hello Girl, as the wartime telephone operators were called, would have been so much more exciting than filing invoices and inventorying supplies.

And maybe in France she could have made her way to Gilbert when he needed her.

Why, oh why, couldn't she let such thoughts go? He'd made his choice. And she'd made hers. Every moment she spent with Samuel, she found herself falling ever more deeply in love. At least she prayed it was love. She only knew she hadn't felt so happy and alive since those halcyon days before Wilson declared war on Germany and Gilbert sailed away on a troop ship.

She handed Jack the next invoice. "I've explained before about the Mountain Valley Water account, haven't I?"

"Yes, a standing order for ceramic jugs to be filled monthly." Jack flipped to another page in the ledger and made an entry. "I've been making myself a list of reminders—which orders are due when, payroll schedules, customer contact names . . ."

"You are the picture of efficiency." Annemarie checked the time—nearly noon—and bounced up from her chair. "And I am about to be late meeting Sam for lunch."

Jack stood and helped her on with her light spring coat. "Last-minute planning for the grand opening of your shop?"

A shiver raced up Annemarie's spine. "I can hardly believe it's only a few days away. Next Monday will be here before I know it!" She found her hat and handbag and hurried to the door. "Remind my father he promised to bring the car for me at my shop this evening. I've told him a thousand times already, but he still won't remember."

"You bet. Thanks again for your help this morning."

"As if you needed it. Why, I'm already ancient history in this office." With a jaunty nod, she scurried out.

Putting all thoughts of the factory behind her, she made it to the corner just as the trolley arrived. She climbed aboard and found a seat only seconds before the car lurched forward with a clang. The March breeze carried a whisper of early-spring blossoms as it toyed with the curl she could never keep in place. She dearly loved springtime—the palest shades of green peeking out through the trees, poking up through the lawns. Tulips and jonquils nosing through fragrant mulch, dogwoods and redbuds dotting the mountainsides with hints of color . . .

The most splendorous season of all, a time for new beginnings.

"Central and Reserve," the conductor called, and the trolley ground to a stop.

Annemarie stepped to the pavement and marched up the hill toward the imposing array of red brick and Swiss chalet-style buildings comprising the Army and Navy Hospital. Hurrying up the steep flight of steps from Reserve Avenue, she glimpsed Sam waving to her from the administration building veranda. Her throat clenched, and she waved back with ferocity.

He met her on the pathway in front of the building, where he swept her into his arms and kissed her soundly—a kiss for all the world to see, and she didn't care. Releasing her, he offered a smile tinged with concern. "You're late. I was worried."

"Jack had some questions about the factory accounts, and the time slipped away." She wished she could soothe away the doubt she constantly read in Sam's expression, in the hesitant tone of his voice.

She wished for freedom from her own doubts and misgivings and prayed springtime would be a time of new beginnings for them both. Hooking her arm through Sam's, she leaned into his shoulder. "I'm starved. Where are we going for lunch?"

Sam kissed her temple. "How does a picnic sound?"

"Delightful! The weather is perfect for a picnic."

"Wait here," he said, leaving her on the path. "I'll be right back with the hamper."

Annemarie couldn't help but laugh at the picture Sam made as he bounded up the hospital steps like a schoolboy. On the veranda, he retrieved a picnic basket covered with a red ging-ham cloth—and by the looks of it, he'd brought enough for half the county. Nearly bent double by the weight, he was huffing and puffing like a freight train by the time he rejoined her on the path.

Annemarie wrapped her hands around the basket handle to help carry the burden. "I hope we're not going far. What on earth have you packed for us?"

"Oh, just a few sandwiches and salads, some fruit and cheese, bottled spring water. The hospital kitchen was most obliging." Samuel nodded toward a grassy area south of the building. "There, how about under that tree?"

"Perfect. Because I don't think we can carry this thing another inch." She groaned with relief when they deposited the hamper in the lacy shade of an elm tree just leafing out.

Folding aside the cloth, Samuel reached into the basket and brought out a fuzzy plaid blanket, which he spread at the base of the tree. He turned to Annemarie and bowed from the waist. "Your table, miss. May I seat you?"

"Why, thank you." With a coy smile, she offered Samuel her hand as she gracefully lowered herself to the ground. "I do hope you'll join me, kind sir."

"I was hoping you'd ask." Samuel plopped onto the blanket next to her, and the light of laughter shining in his eyes made her heart soar.

If only it could always be like this—the past locked securely away, the war but a distant memory, their only thought the joy of being together. She reached for Samuel's hand, and he pulled her toward him for a tender kiss.

Sometime later, the remnants of their lunch scattered across the blanket, Annemarie leaned against the tree trunk and wrapped her arms around her bent knees. Contentment seeped through her limbs like rich cream, and the world seemed softer somehow.

Samuel ran a finger along the back of her hand, his touch featherlight and dreamy. "What are you thinking?"

She turned a smile his way. "That I'd like to stay right here under this tree for the rest of my life."

"Hmm. What if it rains?"

"It won't. Rain is strictly forbidden."

Samuel scooted against the trunk and rested his head near hers. "I hear summers can get mighty hot around here."

"Nope. Not under this tree."

"Hail? Sleet? Snow? I suppose you're having none of those either."

"Absolutely not." She tucked her head into the crook of his shoulder, and he enfolded her under his arm. With a long, sad sigh, she asked, "Tell me why, Sam. Why can't we make this moment last forever?"

"If I could make it so, I would." His warm lips brushed her forehead, and she felt her growing sadness creep into him. He held her in silence for a long time, his chest rising and falling in rhythm with her own, until finally he nudged her to her knees and then stood to help her to her feet.

"Must we go?" She tucked her arms beneath his and studied his gaze, now dark and brooding.

"I have hospital calls to make, and you have a grand opening to prepare for." He laughed gently. "Or have you forgotten?"

Somehow she had, for though their lunch plans had included going over last-minute details, not one word had been spoken about the shop. "Blame yourself for distracting me with this marvelous picnic. How could I think of anything else in such an idyllic setting?"

His languorous smile suggested her studio opening had been the furthest thing from his mind as well. He drew a teasing finger down the length of her nose before bending to gather up the picnic supplies. "I'll meet you at the shop immediately after my last appointment this afternoon. I expect it'll be shortly after four—five at the latest."

Annemarie helped him fold the blanket. "I couldn't do this without you, you know. You've made a lifelong dream come true."

Their hands meshed as they drew the ends of the blanket together, and she was loathe to let him go. He looked ready to voice a reply but then swallowed and turned away to finish folding the blanket.

Always, always the specter of guilt rising between them—his, her own.

Dear Lord, You who make all things new, set us free from the past once and for all.

Pausing at the top of the hospital steps, Gilbert closed his fist around the railing until his arm shook. The curse he'd barely managed to suppress scalded his throat. He wished he were crushing Sam's pious little neck.

"You coming, Gil?" Thomas looked up from a lower step. "You're on the clock this afternoon, remember?" Then his gaze followed Gilbert's to where Annemarie and Samuel were packing up the remains of a picnic. "Might as well accept it. Annemarie has moved on."

Now Gilbert turned his rage upon Thomas. He shook the end of his crutch in Thomas's face. "I don't need your sass, *little brother*. Bad enough I have to work for you."

"And you won't be for long if you keep up that attitude." Thomas glared. "So, are you coming with me, or are you going to stand there wallowing in self-pity over something you brought on yourself?"

Seething, Gilbert cast a final glance toward the couple striding along the path. Though it galled him to admit it, he knew Thomas was right. Gilbert's first mistake was showing Annemarie's photograph to Samuel aboard the *Comfort*. He'd seen the attraction in Sam's eyes . . . the longing . . . even then. And having already determined he could never burden Annemarie with his disabilities, Gilbert had decided to take full advantage. He'd even told Samuel point-blank he had Gilbert's blessing to pursue Annemarie's affection.

Then why—*why*—did seeing them together make him want to rip both their hearts out and cast their writhing bodies off the nearest cliff?

He looked up to see Thomas striding toward the car without him. Well, good riddance. Gilbert had better things to do than sit at a cluttered desk in a cramped office poring over house-keeping staff schedules. Besides, Thomas would never fire his own brother, or their mother would never let him hear the end of it.

On the other hand, Gilbert didn't look forward to another confrontation with Samuel and Annemarie. Before they noticed him, he sidled back inside the hospital and made his way to the wing where Mary would be working. If anyone could take the edge off his anger, it was she.

He skidded to a halt at the entrance to the ward. The eagle-eyed chief nurse Mrs. Daley *would* be making rounds at this hour.

"Lieutenant Ballard." The woman with the steel-gray top-knot pressed her knuckles against her narrow hipbones. "A word, if you please."

"Ma'am." He pulled in a long breath through his nose, then released it noisily as he followed the nurse to a more private corner.

Hands folded at her waist, Mrs. Daley shot him a one-eyed glare. "The hospital rumor mill is running rampant. Be warned, I will not have you sullying the reputation of one of my nurses."

Gilbert's chest rose, ready to explode. "Don't—" He reined in his temper along with his tongue, then lowered his voice and tried again. "Don't take this out on Mary. Please. She's done nothing wrong."

"Be that as it may, this hospital has standards that must be adhered to. I have already instructed Miss McClarney any further . . . *visits* . . . with you on hospital property will result in her immediate expulsion from the Army Nurse Corps."

Jaw trembling, Gilbert nodded. "I understand. You have my word."

$\mathscr{L}\!\blacktriangledown$

By Saturday afternoon, with both their mothers assisting with the finishing touches, Samuel decided little remained to prepare Annemarie's shop for Monday's grand opening. While Annemarie and Mrs. Kendall returned some cleaning supplies to the back room, Samuel surveyed the arrangement of pottery to be displayed in the front window.

"What do you think, Mother? Should this taller piece be moved farther back?"

"Not too far, or the light won't be right." Samuel's mother edged the rose-colored vase a fraction of an inch to the left. "Annemarie does such exquisite work. I'd purchase this for myself if I thought I could carry it safely home on the train. It would go so well with the wallpaper in the dining room."

"I'm sure we could wrap it securely." Although Samuel suspected transporting the vase was the least of his mother's concerns. Between ensuring Samuel had fully recovered from the influenza, and then helping Annemarie with her plans for the shop, she'd stayed on much longer than originally planned. He squeezed her shoulder. "You're homesick, aren't you?"

"A wee bit." She swiveled to face him and smiled into his eyes. "It would be much easier to go home if I weren't so worried about my only son."

"I'm fine, Mother. Feeling fitter than ever, in fact."

Arching a brow, she brushed a speck of dust from the placket of his Oxford shirt. "Physically, yes. But what about here?" She patted his chest. "It's your heart I'm most concerned about."

He tried to laugh off her remark while pretending to notice a smudge on a display cabinet door. "Annemarie makes me happy. I believe I make her happy, too."

"I've no doubt either way." She stilled his hand as he busily polished the imaginary smudge. "But I'm your mother, and it's been clear since I first arrived there's something troubling you, something you refuse to talk about, perhaps even admit to yourself."

Samuel straightened. Was he that transparent? "It's the war, that's all."

"*All?* My darling boy, though I never set foot on a battlefield, I listened to every news report, read every word printed in the paper. What you endured was an ordeal beyond imagining."

Samuel strode across to the sales counter in search of something else with which to distract himself. "Stop, Mother. Please. I don't want to talk about it."

"I know you don't, and that's the problem." His mother linked her arm through his, effectively stopping his meaningless activity. "You listen to everyone else's stories—all those troubled soldiers who come to you seeking counsel and prayer—but you hold your own story inside. And it's eating you alive."

Annemarie's lilting laughter preceded her return from the back room. "No, Mama, I am *not* shopping for a new dress for the opening. My mauve watered silk will do just fine."

"But it's such a special occasion. You deserve something new." Mrs. Kendall waggled a lace-edged handkerchief toward Samuel's mother, who silently released her hold on Samuel's arm. "Help me convince her, Ursula. I know a lovely little dress shop. The three of us could— Oh, dear, why such long faces? Is something wrong?"

"Sam?" Annemarie marched to his side, her gaze probing.

With a forced smile, he took her hand and pressed it to his lips. "It's nothing. Mother was just talking about needing to return home soon."

Her furrowed brow said she didn't quite believe him, but she turned to his mother and said, "It must be hard to think of being apart again, especially after Sam was away for so long. I'm glad you've been able to stay as long as you have."

"And I've enjoyed every minute of it." Samuel's mother perused the showroom with a satisfied sigh. "Well, it appears there is not a thing more to be done here—*except* to shop for a dress," she added with a wink.

"Oh, no, you can't take Mama's side!" Annemarie raised both hands in protest. "Please, Sam, convince them I don't need to go shopping."

"I'm afraid that's beyond my powers of persuasion." Samuel retrieved their coats and handbags, then ushered all three ladies toward the door. "Go forth and shop. I'll lock up behind you."

He'd anticipated spending the rest of the afternoon in Annemarie's company, but one look in her eyes just now and he knew the moment they were alone she'd plead for honesty about what he and his mother had really been talking about.

His own story. Oh, God, would she still love him if she knew?

The memories crashed in upon him like an artillery barrage, and he sank to his knees in the middle of the shop.

"Please, God, make it stop! Make the killing stop!"

"Padre! What are you doing? Get down!"

"Give me your rifle, Private—now!"

"No, Padre, you can't!"

"God's deserted us. I'll kill them all myself, every last one of them!" While enemy fire raged around them, Samuel grappled for control of the skinny kid's weapon.

The boy jerked backward then slammed against Samuel's chest, his mouth open in surprise. He coughed once, twice, and blood gushed from his throat. The boy's weight pulled them both down, down, down, into the blood-soaked earth.

On his knees in the stubbly field, while bullets chewed up the trunks of trees already stripped bare, Samuel lifted his eyes to a heaven gone mute. Cradling the private's limp body, he raised a bloody fist toward the sky and cursed the God who had betrayed them all.

24

"Bless me, Father, for I have sinned."

"And what is your sin, my child?"

The priest appeared little more than a shadowy form through the latticework of the confessional. Mary swallowed the tears threatening to choke her. "I've been free with my affections toward a man."

In the momentary silence, she pictured Father Francis's grim expression. He'd been a friend to Mary's family since they came to Hot Springs nearly twenty years ago. He'd taught Mary the catechism, presided over her First Communion. After Mary's father was injured, Father Francis had provided both comfort and aid, seeing them through those difficult years with utmost patience and kindness.

And now she'd let him down. "Father?"

"I heard you, my child." Father Francis cleared his throat. "Have you . . . committed adultery with this man?"

"No! I mean, not in the way— Oh, Father, I'm so confused! Is it adultery if I have desired in my heart to—to—" Mary's pulse throbbed at the mere thought of Gilbert's touch, his kiss, his passionate embrace.

The priest's profile shifted slightly, his chin raised. "But you have not acted on these desires? You have remained sexually pure?"

"Yes, Father."

His voice softened. "And are you in love with this man?"

"Yes, Father." Her reply came out on a moaning sigh.

The priest's shoulders shook with a soft chuckle. "My dear child, such desire is only normal when a man and a woman fall in love. And temptation does not become sin unless acted upon."

Both hands flew to her mouth to stifle a sob. She lifted her gaze to the mahogany ceiling of the small chamber. "Saints help me, if I could only be sure he returned my feelings!"

An edge returned to the priest's tone. "He has not said as much?"

"Not in words, no, but I believe he does feel a special affection for me. And I'm so deliriously happy when we're together." She knotted the damp handkerchief she clutched into a twisted mass. "But afterward I feel so . . ." *Ashamed. Dirty. Used.*

Father Francis heaved a groan. "It seems to me it isn't penance and forgiveness you need so much as the wise counsel of Scripture. Meditate on Saint Paul's letter to Timothy, where he instructed his young protégé to shun youthful passions, live a life of faith, and call upon the Lord with a pure heart. If you're walking with the Lord, He will keep you on the straight and narrow path."

"I'm trying, Father, truly I am."

"Then go in peace, my child, in full assurance of our Savior's love."

Mary bowed her head as Father Francis made the sign of the cross, but before she exited the confessional, he added sternly, "And one last thing, Mary Elisabeth Assumpta McClarney—talk to your mother."

She'd tried. Oh, she'd tried. But Mary feared shaming her mother even more than the good Father Francis. *"You can't play with fire and expect not to be burnt,"* Mum had told her time and again whenever temptation led her astray. Whether as small a transgression as teasing the neighbor's cat (Mary still bore the scar on her inner arm) or as foolish as wearing her frilly spring frock to Easter Mass during a late-season blizzard (she'd suffered the worst cold of her life afterward), Mary had to admit her mother's admonitions were usually well-founded.

But if Mum knew how close Mary had come to giving Gilbert everything—*everything*—he asked for, she'd lock Mary in her room for eternity and throw away the key.

And giving up Gilbert wasn't something Mary was prepared to do.

Please, Jesus, she prayed as she hurried out to join her mother in the pew, *grant Gilbert the strength to rein in his passions. And if he can't, Lord, grant me the strength to keep saying no.*

✒

Sitting in church with her parents Sunday morning, Annemarie barely heard the pastor's message. Her thoughts raced ahead to tomorrow's grand opening, only to spiral backward to yesterday afternoon. After seeing her mother and Ursula onto the trolley with their purchases—including the tiered day dress of lavender crêpe de Chine Annemarie had finally settled on—she'd returned to the shop for a final inspection.

When she'd found Samuel still there, looking as surprised to see her as she to see him, her skin prickled with worry. He claimed he'd only stayed to do some last-minute tidying up—but for nearly three hours? Though he laughed it off as absent-mindedness, he'd seemed unusually tired, distracted, even anxious. Something clearly wasn't right.

Well, she'd invited him to come for Sunday dinner after he concluded worship services in the hospital chapel. Perhaps by then she could pry an explanation from him.

Then, while her parents stopped to greet Jack Trapp and his mother following the service, Annemarie found herself face-to-face with the daunting Mrs. Ballard. Though their families had belonged to the same congregation for years, Annemarie couldn't shake the impression Gilbert's mother used the church more as a social venue than for spiritual enrichment. When she attended worship at all, afterward she flitted from conversation to conversation with her socialite cronies.

But today the woman had made a beeline straight for Annemarie. She pulled herself up to her full imposing stature. "You've been avoiding me."

Annemarie tried her best not to recoil, as much from the cloying scent of expensive perfume as from Mrs. Ballard's accusing stare. "Of course not. I've just been preoccupied."

"With your ceramics shop. I understand." Mrs. Ballard's expression turned patronizing. She rested a gloved hand on Annemarie's arm. "Such a . . . *courageous* endeavor for a young woman such as yourself. I admire you, dear heart, truly I do."

Annemarie heard the *but* coming. *But a shop is so plebeian. As Gilbert's wife, you would have enjoyed a life of affluent elegance.*

And utter boredom.

The sudden realization stabbed Annemarie through the heart, reminding her again how Gilbert had brushed off any suggestion of her continuing to work after they married. No matter that Scripture directed a man to leave his mother and father and cleave only to his wife. Any wife of Gilbert Ballard would also "marry" his mother—because Evelyn Ballard would have it no other way. Gilbert's wife would be expected to participate fully in Hot Springs society, from decorating her husband's arm at prestigious social events to serving on the boards of any number of reputable charities—and strictly at the direction of her would-be mother-in-law. Annemarie realized long ago Mrs. Ballard served only in capacities where her generosity would be acknowledged—as in the quarter-page newspaper article covering her "selfless contribution to America's wounded soldiers" in the form of twenty-five hand-sewn flannel pajama sets.

Gathering her thoughts, Annemarie graced Gilbert's mother with her most disarming smile. "Why, thank you so much. I do hope you'll drop by for my grand opening. I'll be displaying several new pieces featuring my 'Ouachita sunrise' motif."

Mrs. Ballard sniffed. "I do have a full calendar, but if I have time . . ."

Thomas came up beside his mother, rolling his eyes in disdain. "She has time, I assure you. In fact, I shall personally escort Mother to your opening."

With an arched brow and a polite nod, Mrs. Ballard excused herself.

Thomas toed the carpet. "Sorry about that. But you know Mother."

Indeed. "Do you suppose you'll convince her to come tomorrow?"

"If I have to hogtie her to the hood of the car."

They both laughed as they stepped through the doors into the midday sunshine, and Annemarie couldn't stop herself from murmuring, "I do pity the woman who eventually marries you or Gil—" Heat climbed into her face. "That was utterly thoughtless. Please forgive me."

"Nothing to forgive when you're merely stating the obvious." Shaking his head, Thomas halted on the church lawn beneath the fringed shade of a pine tree. "Why do you think I've worked so hard at avoiding relationships?"

"Oh, Thomas, you're going to make some girl a wonderful husband someday."

"Provided we move to Timbuktu immediately after the wedding—and *that's* contingent upon actually making it to the altar before Mother can scare her off." He grinned at Annemarie. "If I could find a girl like you, I'd have it made. You never let my mother intimidate you for long."

Annemarie shivered. If he only knew! She clasped his hand, studying the neatly manicured nails, the faintest ink smudge on the finger where his fountain pen would rest. His were strong hands, caring hands, hands of a man who'd be gentle with his beloved's heart. She prayed someday Thomas would know true love . . . the kind Annemarie was only just discovering in Samuel.

She tilted her chin to meet Thomas's troubled gaze. "You do understand it wasn't your mother who came between Gilbert and me. If our love had been strong enough, nothing would have kept us apart."

"I know." Thomas filled his lungs with air and then released it in a gusty sigh. "I just hope he isn't setting up another unsuspecting girl for a broken heart."

Before Annemarie could reply, her parents caught up with her, reminding her they needed to get home to finish dinner preparations. As she bounced along in the backseat of the Model T, she lifted a prayer heavenward for Nurse Mary McClarney.

✐❤

"Go in peace, serve the Lord with gladness." Head bowed, Samuel folded his hands as patients and visitors filed out of the chapel.

With each day that passed, his hypocrisy grew. How could he stand here Sunday after Sunday—how could he proclaim Christ's blessing and forgiveness on his daily hospital rounds—while he felt himself falling farther and farther away from the God he had pledged his life to serve?

Father, forgive—

"Fine sermon, Padre."

He looked up to see Sergeant King standing before him. Clad in a frayed green robe over striped pajamas, the grizzled soldier leaned heavily on a cane.

At a loss for words, Samuel only smiled. He wouldn't admit the message today was one he'd pulled from his files—a sermon written back when faith came easy and war remained a distant rumble on the horizon. He stepped off the dais and offered his arm to the sergeant. "May I walk you back to the ward?"

"Be my pleasure." Sergeant King shuffled alongside Samuel as they made their way along hospital corridors smelling of floor polish, disinfectant, and the competing aromas from the meal trays. "You met the new doc yet?" the sergeant asked. "Came onboard this weekend."

"I took some time off yesterday. Hadn't heard someone new had come on staff." They reached the sergeant's ward, and Samuel held the door for him.

"Nice enough guy, just transferred here from Walter Reed. Before then, he served in one of them field hospitals over in France."

The man had seen the worst the war could offer. Samuel felt for him. "What's his name?"

"Russ. Dave Russ, I think he said. You two could probably trade war stories."

"Russ?" Samuel swallowed. The name was similar, but the likelihood this was the same man . . .

Sergeant King rubbed his forehead. "Nope, it's Donald. Dr. *Donald* Russ." He pointed across the ward. "There he is now. I can introduce you."

Recognition corkscrewed through Samuel's belly. Though the doctor now sported a neatly trimmed beard, his tall, lanky frame and characteristic slouch were unmistakable. Hard to forget the man who'd practically carried Samuel through the final weeks of the war. If not for Dr. Russ's staunch support and unfailing compassion, with one stroke of a pen he could have permanently ended Samuel's career as a military chaplain.

Maybe it would have been better if he had.

In any case, he couldn't face Dr. Russ. Not now. Not today. Haste sharpened his tone as he said, "I'll have to meet him another time. It's later than I realized, and I'm expected for dinner with friends."

Handing off Sergeant King to a nurse, Samuel hurried out, never slowing his pace until he exited the hospital and reached the promenade. His heart slammed against his ribs. One hand holding his side, he collapsed onto a park bench.

Why was the past catching up to him now, just when he'd convinced himself he could put it all behind him and begin anew?

Just when he'd finally allowed himself to fall in love again?

Fool! He should have spoken with Dr. Russ at once, explained his need to keep the past in the past. The doctor, of all people, would understand. He knew exactly what Samuel had endured, the secret shame entombed in the darkest depths of memory.

Breathing easier, Samuel made up his mind to meet with Dr. Russ privately first thing tomorrow. The man had helped Samuel before. Surely he would again. Head in his hands, Samuel tried once more to pray. *Father, forgive me. Father, forgive me—*

He could get no further than those three words. It was one thing to trust that God heard and answered, helped and healed, when he prayed on behalf of others. But for himself, when his sin chafed like filthy rags beneath the façade of his chaplain's uniform, would he ever know God's peace again?

⚜

"Where is Samuel?" Annemarie fussed with a place setting on the dining room table, her gaze drifting to the front door.

Ursula Vickary set a basket of rolls on the table. "Someone probably caught him after services with a need to talk. You know Sam. He can never turn a hurting soul away."

Annemarie thought she detected the merest hint of displeasure—or was it concern?—in Mrs. Vickary's expression. Dare she mention how she'd found Sam yesterday afternoon? She forced nonchalance into her tone. "He's spent so much time helping me at the shop these past several days. I hope he hasn't overtired himself. Did he seem all right when he left for the hospital this morning?"

The hesitation before Mrs. Vickary answered spoke volumes. She moved to the window, her shoulders heaving with a worried sigh. "Samuel hasn't seemed *all right* since his first letters home from France."

Annemarie joined Mrs. Vickary at the window. Clouds had drifted in, obscuring the sun and bringing a chill to the afternoon. "It's horrible, isn't it—how the war has changed the people we love."

"And our love will carry them through." With another sigh, Mrs. Vickary patted Annemarie's arm. "I'm going to help your mother finish in the kitchen. Stay here and watch for Samuel. He'll be here soon, I'm certain."

Mrs. Vickary must have sensed Annemarie needed a few minutes alone. Best to use the time for prayer—for Samuel, for Gilbert, for all of them. She donned a thick wool sweater from the hall tree before stepping onto the front porch, where the March wind tugged at her skirt and blew wisps of hair across her eyes. She had a feeling Sam would be walking today—his usual mode of transportation whenever he needed to gather his thoughts. And he'd done a lot of walking since arriving in Hot Springs. She knew for a fact he'd taken his shoes in to be resoled at least once already if not twice.

"I never knew how much I appreciated a good pair of shoes," Sam had told her once. She hated the thought of his tramping all over France with blisters on his feet, wet socks, and boots either worn completely through or so caked with mud he could hardly lift his legs.

Halfway down the block, she spotted him—arms swinging, eyes to the ground, walking with purpose. A sunbeam broke through the clouds just then, shining directly upon his golden head, and the sight made her heart lift with pure joy.

"Sam. Sam!"

He stopped in the middle of the sidewalk, his chest heaving from the climb up the sloping street. When his eyes met hers, his face exploded into a smile that nearly split his face in two—the look of someone who'd been away a long, long time and had finally come home. A look she hoped to see again and again and again, every day for the rest of her life.

A look that convinced her beyond all doubt that she had fallen deeply, inexorably in love with Samuel Vickary.

She broke into a run, the urgency to lose herself in his arms banishing all sense of decorum. She crashed into him, spinning them both in a dizzying dance. Before they toppled over, she found her footing and paused to catch her breath. "I worried when you were so late."

"I stayed to walk Sergeant King back to the ward." He pulled her beneath his arm and kissed her temple. His glance slid sideways for an instant, tension lines flattening his lips.

"Is he well?" she asked, though she suspected the elderly sergeant was the least of his concerns.

"Yes, yes, fine." Samuel looped his arm through Annemarie's and they continued up the walk. "I've kept your mother holding dinner long enough. She'll think I'm the worst of dinner guests and never invite me back."

Annemarie laughed with him, but several steps later, she tugged him to a halt. He faced her with a furrowed brow, one corner of his mouth curled upward, and she couldn't keep the worry out of her tone. "You can't fool me, Sam. I know you're troubled about something. Is it Gilbert? The war? If you think I wouldn't understand—"

"I don't want to talk about any of that right now." His gaze caressed every inch of her face, as if he wanted to memorize each curve and angle. His hand found the base of her throat, his touch like a tender flame upon her skin. The lines around his mouth softened, and he drew her closer, closer. With his lips mere inches from hers, he whispered, "All I want—all I *need*—is to know you care for me."

"I do, Sam. I care for you more than words can express— more than I ever thought possible." She melted against him, not caring if neighbors or passersby witnessed her brazenness, and sought his lips. He tasted of spearmint and coffee, his mouth softening against hers with a tenderness both sweet and urgent.

He finally pulled away, but slowly, reluctantly, like a stubborn child told to pack up his toys and go home. Though she would happily forego dinner entirely to stay here locked in his arms, drinking up his kisses, she couldn't shake the sense that he would never be fully *present* with her until he dealt once and for all with the demons from his past.

25

There, that should be a lot more comfortable." The prosthetist helped Gilbert to his feet, then passed him his crutches.

Gilbert tested his weight upon the newly refitted artificial leg. "I don't feel the pressure points like before." He took a few tentative steps. "Yes, definitely better."

"Good. As your stability improves, you can try using a cane and get rid of those cumbersome crutches."

Gilbert nodded across the room toward a rack of canes. "Mind if I give it a try now?"

"Sure, see how it goes." The prosthetist selected one and exchanged it for Gilbert's crutches. "You'll use it on your right side, opposite your prosthesis."

"That'll help, since my left arm is the weak one." Gilbert steadied himself as the prosthetist explained the proper sequence for forward movement. His first few steps were wobbly, but he quickly caught on.

Once he felt secure on a flat surface, they moved to an area where he could practice on a short flight of stairs. By the time Gilbert's appointment ended, he felt renewed confidence. Since he now looked less like a cripple and more like a whole man, maybe the pitying stares would end.

Maybe Annemarie—

White-hot pain blazed through his skull. Rage, jealousy, hate—it all mixed together in an emotional tornado that sucked the breath from his lungs. Forgetting everything he'd just been told about which leg to move with the cane, he stumbled and pitched forward.

The prosthetist grabbed his arm. "Easy, there. Gotta take it slow, okay?"

Just as suddenly the maelstrom subsided, leaving in its wake only shame and self-loathing. Gilbert found his balance and averted his face before the man could notice the wetness sliding down his cheeks. He shook off the beefy hand supporting him. "I'm fine . . . fine."

Or he would be, once he replenished his morphine supply.

Before his emotional state collapsed further, he exited the clinic and found his way to the hospital administration building. From the lobby he telephoned Thomas at the Arlington to say his appointment was over. As usual, Mother had Zachary otherwise occupied for the day.

"It'll be another ten minutes or so. I'm in the middle of something." A sneer crept into Thomas's tone. "But I'm certain you can find something—or should I say *someone*—with whom to occupy yourself."

Gilbert bit back a snide reply. "Just get here when you can. I'll be watching for you."

There'd be no rendezvous with Mary this morning. At a quiet dinner last night, she'd made it clear she could no longer compromise her position at the hospital—nor her reputation. If Gilbert wanted to court her properly, he could call at her home, meet her mother, and treat her with deference instead of stealing kisses in dark closets and pressing for more than she was willing to give.

So he'd been a cad. He admitted it. But he'd made up his mind to honor Mary's request as best he could. She was all he had now, and he needed her. Needed her under whatever terms she named.

Using the cane had tired him more than anticipated. On the veranda outside the hospital entrance, he limped to the far end and then rested against the railing while he waited for Thomas. It was quiet here, a peaceful calm settling over the spring morning. After yesterday's chilly gloom, the sun had ventured out again, and it was turning out to be a grand St. Patrick's Day, perfect for Annemarie's opening—

He slammed the lid on such thoughts and turned his focus to Mary. She would surely know how to celebrate the Irish holiday. With her gorgeous red hair, she'd look divine in a frock of emerald green. If he behaved himself, called on her like a gentleman, maybe she'd—

An unmistakable voice drifted down from the veranda one floor above him. ". . . happier than I've been since before the war. Annemarie's the best thing to ever happen to me. When I'm with her, I can forget for a while, pretend I'm . . . normal. Human. Alive."

"But if you love her, Samuel, then you owe her complete honesty." Another man's voice, also vaguely familiar. "Don't let this haunt you for the rest of your life. Let Annemarie know your struggles. Let her help you come to terms with what happened so you can accept forgiveness and put the past behind you."

So the pious chaplain had a secret, did he? Gilbert's nerves sang. He slunk deeper into the shadows.

The echo of an open palm slapping wood cut through the morning stillness. "Because of my weakness, my reckless stupidity, a man is dead. Do you suppose Private Braswell's parents would forgive me if they knew I was responsible?"

"It was war, Sam. *War.* You weren't the first man to snap under pressure, and you sure won't be the last."

A face to go with the voice began to emerge in Gilbert's mind—Dr. Russ, his attending physician aboard the *Comfort.* When had Dr. Russ come to Hot Springs? And what did he know about Samuel that Samuel was trying to hide . . . or hide *from?* If it could hurt Annemarie—

"Gil. You ready to go or not?" Thomas strode toward him, impatience firming his jaw.

"Didn't see you drive up." Gilbert shot a quick glance overhead. The voices had faded, as if the men had taken their conversation farther along the veranda.

"Well, get a move on, will you? I don't want to be late for Annemarie's grand opening."

An event for which Gilbert needed no reminders. Thomas had tried to convince him to tag along, but the awkwardness would have been unbearable. "You have time to drop me off at the hotel first, right?"

Thomas smirked. "As you wish, milord."

"I can do without your sarcasm, thank you." Gripping his new cane, Gilbert did a quick mental review of the prosthetist's instructions, then stepped out. It felt amazingly good to stand erect again, to walk with restored confidence.

"A cane, eh? Looks like you're making progress." Thomas fell in step beside him, surprise lighting his eyes . . . and perhaps a touch of admiration?

"Progress. Right." How long had it been since Gilbert could honestly say his little brother looked up to him? Hard to garner respect from others when he had so little for himself.

Was it too late? Too late to reclaim the honor he craved from his family, from his peers?

From Annemarie?

An idea slithered into his brain, coiled around his heart, sank its fangs deep into his wounded pride. Thomas, his mother, Samuel, even Annemarie had called him a fool for giving her up. Annemarie still loved him, he'd swear to it. She'd only turned to Samuel because Gilbert had pushed her away.

Because she believed Samuel to be the honorable man Gilbert was not.

If she were to learn otherwise . . . if Gilbert could unearth the details of this wartime secret Samuel so desperately wanted to keep buried . . .

Annemarie had been Gilbert's once. If he had his way, she would be his again.

When a door opened and a nurse wheeled a patient onto the veranda, the doctor motioned Samuel around the corner. "I mean it, Sam. You've spent as much time with shell-shocked doughboys as I have, maybe more. It happens to officers, enlisted men, ambulance drivers—doesn't matter how much training we've had." A hunted look crept into Dr. Russ's eyes. "Everybody's got a breaking point, and in this war, way too many of us found ours."

Samuel studied the doctor's face. "You? When?"

Dr. Russ replied with a harsh laugh. "Why do you think I transferred here from Walter Reed? Once we left France and I wasn't triaging more patients in a single hour than stateside doctors handle in a month, I thought I'd be fine. Then a couple weeks ago I cracked, couldn't deal with fixing one more botched amputation, couldn't explain to one more wife or mother why her soldier gets the shakes every time a door slams or a car backfires."

"I'm sorry. I didn't know."

Dr. Russ sighed. "I didn't tell you my sob story to belittle yours. I just want you to know you're not alone in this. And you don't have to be."

"If we were only talking about a bad case of shell-shock, maybe I could believe you. But what I did—" Samuel's gut cramped. Images exploded behind his eyes. "The men depended on me to keep up their morale, to be an example of steadfast faith through the horrors of war, and I failed them. I failed God."

"The unforgivable sin. Yeah, you've talked about it plenty." Stepping closer, Dr. Russ slid his hands into the pockets of his white coat. "You may think you deserted God, but I guarantee God has never left you. He'll see you through this if you'll let Him, and your faith will be all the stronger for it."

With all his heart, Samuel wanted to believe Dr. Russ's words. He'd heard them before, during the long, dark nights immediately following Private Braswell's death. When the nightmares rocketed Samuel out of his hospital bed in a clammy, guilt-induced sweat, Dr. Russ would sit reading Scripture to him until the panic abated. *Yea, though I walk through the valley of the shadow of death, I will fear no evil; for thou art with me . . .*

But even when Samuel had recovered enough to resume his duties, he'd watch yet another ambulance disgorge its gory cargo and have to bite down on the inside of his lip until it bled to keep from screaming curses at God all over again. If not for Dr. Russ's calm assurance, if not for his constant reminders of how much these soldiers needed Samuel to be strong for them, to pray with them, to speak God's blessing upon them in their final hours, he might have taken the easy way out. A pistol wouldn't have been hard to come by. One shot to the temple and his troubles would be over. After all, it should have been Samuel who died, not the innocent young private.

"I know what you're thinking, Sam." Dr. Russ stiff-armed him, jolting him out of the past. "Don't go there. Promise me."

Samuel's vision cleared. He offered a weak smile. "Don't worry. I've long since realized suicide isn't going to solve anything, just speed me on my way to eternal judgment. And I have too much to atone for before I meet my Maker."

Dr. Russ flashed a doubtful smirk. "Not by my reckoning. Or God's either, if I know my Bible. How does the verse go? 'There is therefore now no condemnation to them that are in Christ Jesus.'"

"Romans 8, verse 1." Samuel braced his forearms on the railing and heaved a pained sigh. "But how do I dare believe I'm *in* Christ Jesus after denying Him as I did?"

Leaning in beside Samuel, the doctor grinned beneath his whiskers. "Seems to me denying Jesus puts you in real good company. And just look what the Lord did with Peter and Paul after His forgiveness restored them."

Samuel stared at his clasped hands. If he closed his eyes, he could still imagine them drenched in Private Braswell's blood. But hadn't Saint Paul's hands been stained with blood as he'd gone about persecuting anyone who spoke in the name of Christ? And what about King David, who lusted after Bathsheba and then schemed to have her husband, Uriah the Hittite, killed in battle? The Lord still called these men, forgave them, used them mightily.

"Trust me, Sam. This burden of guilt is Satan's doing, not God's." Dr. Russ clapped him on the shoulder. "You're a good man. God's man. Don't let Satan—or anyone else—convince you otherwise."

"A part of me knows you're right. And I'm trying to keep the faith." Samuel stood erect and faced the doctor. "It's just . . . when the past breaks into the present, as it seems to do with such alarming regularity . . . it's all I can do to hold myself together and keep my eyes on the Lord."

"It'll get easier with time, I promise."

Samuel couldn't suppress a sardonic laugh. "Exactly the words I've used to counsel others."

"Then heed your own counsel and believe it." Dr. Russ glanced at his watch, then looked up with a sly grin. "Say, don't you have somewhere else to be this morning?"

Annemarie's grand opening! Samuel checked his own watch—five minutes to ten. He'd planned to be at the shop in plenty of time for the ribbon-cutting ceremony, which meant he'd have to race like the wind if he didn't want to miss it entirely.

Adrenaline surging, he glanced around for the quickest way down to Central Avenue. Then, pausing, he seized the doctor's hand. "Thanks for the talk. You've helped more than you know."

"Anytime, Padre. Now get a move on. You wouldn't want to keep your sweetheart waiting."

❧

Annemarie hated to keep Mayor McClendon waiting, but she couldn't bear to start the ribbon-cutting ceremony until Samuel arrived. He had as big a stake in her shop as she did—perhaps more, since he and his mother were her primary investors.

Pacing on the sidewalk outside the shop, she peered down the street in the direction of the hospital. "Do you see him yet, Mama?"

"Your young eyes are better than mine, dear. Give him another minute or two."

"Excuse me, Miss Kendall." A middle-aged man tipped his bowler hat. "I'm afraid the mayor has other appointments this morning. Unless we begin immediately . . ."

"Of course, of course." Worry collided with disappointment as Annemarie returned her attention to the small crowd gathered in front of her shop. She should be delighted so many friends and members of the local business community had come out to support her, but without Sam here, her enthusiasm waned.

Then, as she strode to the shop entrance to stand beside Mayor McClendon, she heard a commotion behind her. The crowd parted, and Samuel burst through. He made his way to her side, his eyes speaking apology.

"I worried you wouldn't arrive in time." Annemarie entwined her hand in his and squeezed. "But you're here now, and that's all that matters."

The man in the bowler hat coughed discreetly. "Are we ready now, Miss Kendall?"

"Yes, indeed." Annemarie squared her shoulders and turned to face the gathered friends, business owners, and dignitaries. She'd prepared a brief speech and introductions, but all rational thought vanished, and at first she could only laugh in happy amazement.

One hand still locked in Sam's, the other resting at the base of her throat, she finally regained her composure and prayed her voice wouldn't crack. "Forgive me, but I still can hardly believe this day has arrived. I have so many people to thank. My father, Joseph Kendall, for teaching me everything he knows about the pottery business."

Looking sharp in his Sunday-best suit, Papa winked at her, his gaze filled with pride.

"My mother, Ida Kendall, for her patience and understanding when my pottery skills far outpaced my aptitude for domesticity."

Mama gave an exaggerated nod of agreement, and laughter rippled through the crowd.

"My good friend Thomas Ballard, who provided my first public venue by displaying my creations in the Arlington Hotel lobby."

Thomas tipped his hat. "Our loss, your gain."

"And last but certainly not least, Army Chaplain Samuel Vickary and his mother, Mrs. Ursula Vickary. This venture has become a reality thanks to their encouragement and generous financial backing, and I will be forever indebted to them—or at least until the shop turns a profit," she added with a laugh.

Samuel's grip tightened, and he cast her a meaningful smile. Next to him, his mother beamed.

An alderman handed the mayor a huge pair of gold-plated scissors. The mayor held them out to Annemarie. "Shall we?"

"Let's."

They turned toward the shop door, where a broad pink ribbon had been draped across the entrance. Annemarie placed her hands next to the mayor's on the scissors, and together they snipped the ribbon. As it parted, the crowd burst into applause and cheers.

Proudly, Annemarie opened her shop door to admit her first patrons. Mayor McClendon and his entourage stayed only long enough to partake of cookies and cider while touting the current city hall agenda to anyone who would listen. Annemarie doubted they gave her ceramic works much notice. Her visitors from the Central Avenue business district lingered a bit longer, but after congratulating her and perusing the displays, they gradually filtered out.

Soon everyone had gone except Annemarie's parents, Sam, Mrs. Vickary, and Thomas. Sagging with exhaustion, Annemarie whistled out a noisy breath. She felt as if her face would split in two from smiling so much, and her right hand had endured so many crushing handshakes it had almost gone numb.

Mama wrapped her in a hug and then released her with a delighted sigh. "What an absolutely perfect day!"

"Only one thing could make it better." Annemarie set her hands on her hips, her gaze combing the display shelves. "Unfortunately, not one of this morning's visitors is yet a paying customer."

Papa sidled over and slid his arm around Annemarie's waist. "Oh, they will be soon, I'm certain." He planted a kiss on her temple. "Congratulations again, Annie-girl. I may have balked at your artsy ideas at first, but I'm not too proud to admit I was wrong. Those uppity Ouachita potters are probably quaking in their clay-stained aprons as we speak."

Papa left then to return to the factory, but not without some playful grousing about how much he missed having Annemarie in the front office. Mama and Mrs. Vickary left a few minutes later, and though the shop seemed too quiet, Annemarie didn't mind one bit being alone with Samuel.

She approached him with a deferential nod. "Good day, kind sir. Are you shopping for anything special? Perhaps a gift for your mother, or your . . . sweetheart?"

His teasing smile lit up the room. "I'm afraid the gift I'd like to give my sweetheart must be purchased elsewhere."

"Is that so?" Annemarie waltzed around him, letting her fingers glide up his coat sleeve. "Does she prefer roses? I can refer you to an excellent florist."

"Roses aren't quite what I had in mind."

"Then perhaps a shawl, or a dainty pair of lace gloves. There's a lovely little boutique down the street."

"I wouldn't dream of covering my sweetheart's hands with anything but this." Samuel trapped her hand in his and drew it to his lips, eliciting a shiver. "Unless it would be . . ."

Annemarie's stomach fluttered. She could scarcely breathe. "Yes?"

Every trace of playfulness vanished. "I think I was already falling in love with you the first time Gilbert showed me your photograph. But you were his then, and I had no hope." He swallowed, the cords of his neck tightening. "I never thought— never dreamed—"

She hushed him with two fingers upon his lips. "When will you accept that Gilbert and I were never meant to be? I've given my heart to you now, Samuel Vickary, and it's yours to keep . . . forever."

His hooded gray eyes turned darkly serious as he searched her face. "Are you sure? Absolutely certain? Because if there's even the slightest chance—"

"For Gilbert and me?" Annemarie gave her head a firm shake. "If you don't believe anything else, believe this: Gilbert Ballard is out of my life and out of my—"

The front door burst open. Annemarie spun around to see Evelyn Ballard sweep into the shop, the tails of a fox-fur boa riding in her wake. "My dear, dear girl, can you ever forgive me? I had *every* intention of arriving in time for the ceremonies, but Marguerite *would* accidentally drop an entire jar of peach preserves on my new peau de soie pumps the moment I started out the door."

Still dealing with Mrs. Ballard's unexpected—not to mention untimely—arrival, Annemarie struggled not to laugh. She suspected Marguerite's "accident" was no accident at all, because the perceptive servant would know Evelyn Ballad was the last person Annemarie cared to see at her grand opening.

But just as she opened her mouth to reply, another visitor appeared on the threshold. Annemarie looked past Mrs. Ballard's boa-bedecked shoulder and realized she'd been wrong. The *very* last person she'd hoped to see this morning now stood before her.

The air whooshed from her lungs as she uttered his name: "Gilbert."

26

*G*ood morning, Annemarie . . . Samuel." Gilbert's tone was polite yet chilling, not unlike his catlike stare. His glance shifted between the two of them, and he grinned knowingly.

Annemarie stiffened. "I'm sorry you both missed the festivities. I believe there are still a few cookies left. May I serve you a cup of cider?" She turned toward the refreshment table and hoped they wouldn't notice how their arrival had unsettled her.

More than that, she hoped Samuel didn't notice. He struggled hard enough to trust in her affection only to be waylaid with doubts every time her former fiancé appeared.

Dear God, will Gilbert always hold such power over our feelings?

Mrs. Ballard joined her at the table and helped herself to a plate of cookies. She bit into a crispy gingersnap, crumbs dribbling onto her bosom before she could catch them. "Mmm, delicious. Your mother baked these, didn't she?" Brushing away the crumbs with a napkin, she glanced around the shop. "Charming, simply charming. I'll be sure to tell all my friends to patronize your establishment."

Patronize being the key word, naturally. Annemarie read disdain in every pore of the woman's smugly smiling face. Why had Mrs. Ballard *really* come this morning? Certainly not to admire Annemarie's ceramics. More than likely, she coerced Gilbert into coming along for the sole purpose of reminding Annemarie of everything she'd given up by not marrying Mrs. Ballard's son.

If Gilbert weren't standing right there—and looking more handsome and self-assured than Annemarie had seen him since before the war—she'd explain to Mrs. Ballard yet again it was her son, not Annemarie, who called off the engagement.

And that Annemarie was now completely and consummately in love with Samuel Vickary.

Gilbert strode farther into the shop, then nudged the door closed with his elbow. Only then did Annemarie notice he used a cane now. He stood tall again, and proud, an arrogance about him that set Annemarie's nerves on edge. He lifted an eyebrow in Samuel's direction. "You're certainly quiet this morning, Sam. Not even a friendly hello for an old friend?"

Samuel dipped his chin, but his smile never found his eyes. "How are you, Gilbert?"

"Fit as a fiddle, as you can plainly see." Gilbert clenched his left hand and rapped on the top of his artificial leg. "If you don't count the missing parts. But all I've lost is a limb. When I think of all the poor souls who've lost their minds, if not their souls . . ."

An unreadable look passed between Gilbert and Samuel—a look that sparked a sudden protective urge in Annemarie. She filled two cups with cider, offering one to Gilbert and one to Samuel. "Please, gentlemen, no talk of the war on this fine day. I won't have it."

"I agree, dear." Mrs. Ballard sipped cider while strolling about the shop. "I must say, Annemarie, you do have quite a talent. Your work is so much more decorative than those pedestrian pieces your father turns out in his factory."

Now Annemarie's hackles rose in defense of her father. "Kendall Pottery Works is a highly respected business in this community—all across Arkansas, in fact. If not for our *pedestrian* ceramics, local restaurants, hotels, schools, and wholesalers would be forced to take their business farther afield, along with a sizable chunk of the area's economic foundation."

Gilbert's mouth curled in an admiring smile. "I had no idea you were so civic-minded, Annemarie."

"Of course she is, dear. She's a business entrepreneur, after all." Completing her circuit, Mrs. Ballard set her plate and cup on the end of a display case. "Come, Gilbert. We must be on our way. So nice to see you again, Samuel. All the best with your shop, Annemarie."

Holding the door for his mother, Gilbert paused and cast a backward glance toward Annemarie. For a fraction of a second, the disdainful look he'd arrived with mellowed into something between contrition and yearning. Then, as his gaze slid to Samuel, his eyes hardened again. With a brisk nod, he shuffled out the door and was gone.

Annemarie turned to Samuel, ready to apologize for both Mrs. Ballard's pomposity and Gilbert's baffling attitude, but the words froze on her tongue when she caught the troubled look on his face. She went to him and looped her arm through his. "Don't, Sam. He isn't worth it."

He tried to laugh, but the sound was hollow. "He still wants you. Can't you see?"

"I don't care what Gilbert wants. You shouldn't either."

"But—"

"I said, *don't.*" Annemarie moved closer, until she could feel the warmth of Samuel's breath against her face. She cupped his cheek and slanted her lips against his, while her other hand crept behind his head so he couldn't pull away.

She needn't have worried. He drew in a long, trembling breath through his nose as he enfolded her in his arms, and their lips fused in a kiss like a white-hot flame. When Samuel's lips turned salty and wet, Annemarie realized she tasted his tears.

Gently she broke the kiss and smoothed away the wetness with her thumb. "Sam, Sam, my darling, what's wrong?"

"Wrong? Nothing!" Hands at her waist, he rested his forehead against hers. "Nothing in my life has ever felt so *right*."

How could I have been so wrong?

Gilbert tore his gaze from the shop window and gripped the handle of his cane until his fingers throbbed. The headache he'd staved off earlier after a hastily arranged meeting with his morphine supplier now pummeled his brain with a vengeance.

Why had he let his mother coerce him into accompanying her to Annemarie's shop?

Even more idiotic, why hadn't he resisted the urge for one last glance? If he'd only kept walking, he'd have spared himself the torment of seeing Annemarie in Samuel's arms. Their kiss, so passionate, so tender, so—

"Gilbert. The car is waiting." His mother summoned him with an impatient wave. "Thomas will be expecting you to return to your hotel duties."

Yes, indeed, he'd have been much better off sitting at his cramped little desk in a back room of the Arlington, tweaking cleaning staff schedules while trying to ignore the conglomeration of kitchen aromas competing with the smells of furniture polish and floor cleaner.

This was not the life he'd planned, not by a long shot.

Before his mother could embarrass him in front of every shopper and business patron along Central Avenue, he limped down the sidewalk to where Zachary waited at the curb. The tall, ebony-complexioned driver opened the rear door of the Peerless and assisted Gilbert's mother inside, then turned to help Gilbert.

He hesitated, chewing the inside of his lip. "Never mind, Zachary. I'll walk."

"You sure, sir?" Zachary cast him a worried frown, his gaze flicking toward Gilbert's bad leg.

His mother leaned sideways on the seat, craning her neck until she caught Gilbert's eye. "Don't be foolish, son. Get in the car now."

That clinched it. "I'll see you at home this evening, Mother. Have a lovely afternoon."

With a jaunty wave, Gilbert began his march down Central Avenue—in the opposite direction from the Arlington Hotel. Let his mother stew and fret. Let Stanley deal with his own staff scheduling problems for the day. Gilbert had people to see. Secrets to uncover.

A sweetheart to win back.

Over a week now, and not so much as a glimpse of Gilbert in a hospital corridor, much less a proper call at Mary's home.

And he'd promised!

Momentarily blinded by welling tears, Mary fumbled as she reached for a medicine vial. It slipped through her shaking fingers and shattered on the tile floor.

"For goodness' sake, Mary McClarney!" Lois jumped back, nearly spilling the tray of instruments ready to be sterilized.

Mary swiped at her damp cheeks with the corner of her apron. "Now I've done it. Mrs. Daley will be taking this out of my wages." Sniffling, she scurried to the closet for a broom and dustpan.

"Here, let me." Lois set down her tray and then wrested the broom from Mary's hands. "Get a towel to soak up this mess. Then we'll toss it all in the waste bin and Mrs. Daley will never be the wiser."

"Until the next inventory." Mary bit her lip. "No, I'll tell the truth and pay the consequences. Better that than what happened to the orderly who was caught pilfering morphine tablets from the dispensary."

Lois barked out a grim laugh as she swept up fragments of broken glass. "Can't believe he'd be so bold. Or stupid. This is a military hospital, for heaven's sake. Did he think they wouldn't notice? And you know who I really feel sorry for? The poor souls he's gotten addicted to morphine, and now here they are without a supplier. The situation will only get worse, you'll see."

Lois's tirade stirred something in Mary's memory—something she realized she'd been avoiding all these weeks. She dropped the towel she'd just taken from the cupboard and clutched her stomach.

Gilbert, an addict?

Dear Father, no!

But she was a nurse. How could she deny the obvious? The slurred speech, drowsiness, glassy-eyed stares. Sweating, chills. Euphoria plummeting into despondency in the blink of an eye.

And what of those vague "appointments" that, to the best of Mary's knowledge, had nothing to do with his physical therapy?

"Mary?" Lois touched her arm. "Are you coming down with something? You're whiter than your apron."

"No—yes—" Mary swallowed, tried to think.

Lois guided her to a chair. "If you need to go home for the day, I can cover for you. Mrs. Daley will understand."

Mrs. Daley, understand? Not likely. But Mary decided she must see Gilbert immediately. If her suspicions proved true, he needed her more than ever—or so she dared to believe.

She glanced up at Lois with a weak smile. "Actually, I'm not feeling well at all. Perhaps it'd be best if I left early. Would you make my excuses to Mrs. Daley?"

"Sure, honey. You bet." Lois helped her to her feet. "Can you make it home on your own?"

"I'll be fine. I'm just a little . . . nauseated." Which certainly she was.

Lois arched a brow. "Nauseated? Mary, you aren't—"

"No. Heavens, no!" Mary's cheeks flamed. "It's probably something I ate, that's all. A little rest and some fresh air and I'll be right as rain." She gave Lois a grateful hug and hurried out before her friend could ply her with other questions she wasn't prepared to answer.

Once she'd traipsed far enough up Central Avenue to be certain Mrs. Daley wouldn't glance out a hospital window and glimpse an "ailing" young nurse who looked much too vigorous to be claiming stomach distress, she quickened her pace. It was just past two, so she hoped to find Gilbert at the Arlington. If she confronted him there, in the privacy of his office, perhaps she could convince him to be honest with her about his addiction.

And about his feelings.

⟡

Leaving the officers' wing after sharing a prayer with an ailing colonel, Samuel headed across the hospital. The highlight of his days had become his visits with Sergeant King, whose unassuming nature reminded Samuel of his own father.

Dad had been so proud to know his only son would get a college education. And while it saddened Samuel to think his father died without seeing him graduate or knowing of his call to the ministry, Samuel couldn't help but feel relief Dad hadn't lived to see his son go off to war.

When he reached the nurses' station outside Sergeant King's ward, he paused to give his uniform blouse a tug and straighten the cross pin on his collar. It had been a good week. Not as many nightmares, if that were any measure. He began to wonder if Donald Russ's reappearance in his life might possibly be God's doing, because during their conversations over the past several days Samuel found himself closer and closer to believing he could put the past behind him.

Closer to believing God could—and did—forgive this hopeless sinner.

"Hey, Sam." Donald breezed through the swinging doors from the ward, his white coattails flapping. "Just the man I want to see. You have time for a cup of coffee?"

"It'll have to be quick. I still have a number of patients to see."

"You and me both. But this is important." The doctor clapped him on the shoulder and propelled him in the direction of the staff lounge.

Samuel shot him a questioning frown. "You talk like a man with an agenda."

Donald's easy smile turned serious. He slanted a nod toward the lounge door, indicating he wouldn't say more until they could talk in private.

Once inside, and after Donald made sure they were alone, Samuel leaned against the counter while the doctor poured coffee. "Well? Are you going to fill me in or not?"

The doctor took a tentative sip from his mug. "I need a favor, Sam."

"Anything. Just ask."

"I visited a church yesterday, and afterward during coffee hour the pastor invited me to attend a small dinner party he's hosting next Friday."

Samuel looked askance at his friend, who didn't look at all pleased about this invitation. "And?"

"And, since I happened to mention I'm single, I think the pastor's looking to pair me up with his marriageable spinster daughter."

Suppressing a laugh, Samuel swallowed a mouthful of hot coffee to keep from spewing it across the space between them. He gasped in pain and shock as he plopped his mug onto the counter and fumbled in his pocket for a handkerchief. Dabbing his lips, he said, "Excuse me, Donald, but may I ask how you arrived at this conclusion?"

"Well, it just seemed odd he'd randomly invite a complete stranger to a dinner party, so I casually asked if I might know anyone else on the guest list. He said there'd be one other army veteran from the congregation, along with his lady friend."

Samuel scratched beneath his ear. "Sorry, I still don't get the connection. Where does the spinster daughter come in?"

Donald heaved an annoyed sigh. "As I was leaving, an elderly lady who happened to overhear the conversation couldn't wait to inform me how glad the pastor was when the war ended, because it meant the 'boys' would be returning to Hot Springs and he could finally marry off the last of his daughters."

"Ah, I see." This time Samuel couldn't suppress the chuckle he'd been holding in. "I assume you are now going to explain what this has to do with the favor you're asking of me?"

"I'm getting to it." The good doctor glared but then had the decency to lower his gaze in apology. "See, I mentioned to the pastor I've got an army buddy who's also new in town . . . sort of . . . so I asked if you could join the party."

"Now hold on! If you're thinking to add me into the 'eligible bachelor' mix—"

"Wouldn't think of it. I know how you feel about Annemarie, so I told the pastor you'd probably want to bring your girlfriend."

Samuel liked thinking of Annemarie as his girlfriend. Grinning, he wadded the coffee-stained handkerchief into a ball and stuffed it into his pocket. "It all becomes clear now. You want an ally on hand to run interference in case this 'marriageable spinster daughter' turns out to be . . . shall we say . . . not your cup of tea."

"Exactly. I mean, look at me, Sam. I'm nearly forty years old and rather the worse for wear. If this girl's father is thinking of marrying her off to a wizened old geezer like me, then I can't help but wonder . . ." Donald pursed his lips. "How can I put this delicately?"

Samuel waved a hand. "I get the picture. I can't promise Annemarie will be free, but I'll certainly tag along if you think my presence will help." He sighed. "I owe you that much, and a whole lot more."

The doctor's eyes lit with gratitude, but he hurriedly replied, "You don't *owe* me a thing. We're just two pals helping each other out. It's what friends do."

The statement touched a chord in Samuel's heart, making him even more grateful Donald Russ had transferred to Hot Springs. All over again, he suffered the aching disappointment of his failed friendship with Gilbert. Was it completely beyond repair?

With a promise to extend the dinner invitation to Annemarie, Samuel excused himself to continue his hospital visits. As soon as he finished for the day, he locked his office door and marched up Central Avenue in hopes of arriving at Annemarie's shop in time to walk her to the trolley stop.

She was just setting the *closed* sign in the window when he stepped inside the showroom. Her smile flashed welcome and a different kind of invitation, this one unspoken but so much more enticing than accompanying Donald Russ to a stuffy dinner party.

Samuel kicked the door shut behind him and swept Annemarie into his arms. After a quick but oh-so-delightful kiss, he set her on her feet. "How was your day? Lots of customers, I hope?"

Annemarie groaned. "I'm afraid the bloom is off the rose."

She looked so forlorn that Samuel immediately pulled her into his arms again. "You've only been open a week. It takes time to build a business."

"But there was so much more interest immediately after the grand opening. I sold several pieces last week and even took a handful of special orders. Today I counted exactly three customers, and two of them only stopped in to ask directions."

Samuel kissed the top of her head. Her hair smelled like lilacs and vanilla with a hint of potter's clay, and the scent drove him mad with longing. He looped a loose curl around his finger and savored the satiny feel.

Scowling, she tilted her head to look into his eyes. "Are you listening to me?"

He dare not admit that pottery sales were the last thing on his mind just now. "It's far too soon for you to be discouraged. Business will pick up, I'm sure of it."

"I hope you're right." She sagged against his chest. "Because if it doesn't, I'll never be able to repay you and your mother."

"Not another word." After another lingering kiss that left him hungry for more, Samuel decided he'd better help Annemarie finish her end-of-the-day chores before passion got the best of them both. While she gathered up her things, he switched off lights and made sure the back door was locked, then waited on the sidewalk while she latched the front door behind them.

She looped her arm through his and leaned close as they started up the street. "A girl could get used to having a gentleman escort her to the trolley after work every evening."

"And a guy could get used to having a lovely lady on his arm for all the world to see. Speaking of which . . ." He told her about Donald Russ's dinner engagement. "Would you mind accompanying me?"

"Mind? It'll be fun!" They reached the corner and settled onto a bench to wait for the trolley. "I'm just glad you have a friend in town. Even with your mother here, you've seemed so lonely."

Looking into her dusky brown eyes, warm with affection and concern, Samuel felt a different kind of loneliness. He didn't want to see her onto the trolley only to wave good-bye until tomorrow. He wanted to take her home with him—to *their* home. He wanted it to be just the two of them, husband and wife, "till death us do part."

"Sam?" She touched his cheek. "You have that look in your eyes again."

He captured her hand but couldn't meet her gaze. She read him far too easily, and he didn't want to spoil the moment. "If you mean the look that says it's nearly suppertime and I'm starved, you're right. I can almost smell Mother's roasted rosemary chicken from here."

"Don't, Sam. You don't have to pretend with me." Her eyebrows drew together. With a sniff, she faced forward, both hands locked primly atop her handbag. "One day soon I hope you'll trust me enough to share *all* of who you are with me."

The clang and rumble of the approaching trolley saved him from plying her with yet another excuse and apology. He would tell her someday—he knew he must—but there remained three other people he must find the courage to make peace with first: Private Braswell's grieving parents . . .

And himself.

27

*B*y midweek, Annemarie felt somewhat heartened about her business prospects, especially after selling several smaller items along with a uniquely designed sixteen-piece dinnerware set. The warmer spring weather had brought out the casual tourists along with the serious spa-goers, so Annemarie hoped the onset of summer would mean even more visitors to her shop.

Her primary concern lately involved how to juggle both the creative and the merchandising side of her business once Samuel's mother returned to Indiana. Mrs. Vickary had been giving several hours each day to overseeing the showroom, thus allowing Annemarie uninterrupted time to work at the wheel, shape a hand-thrown design, or apply glaze to the greenware she'd fired in her father's kiln. Yesterday Mrs. Vickary stated she must go home by week's end, at least temporarily, while she decided whether to pull up stakes and join Samuel here in Hot Springs.

The best part about such a possibility was the implication that Sam must be expecting to stay awhile. Military assignments were subject to change with little notice, and ever since Annemarie had begun to acknowledge her feelings for Sam, she'd dreaded news of his transfer. How could she bear to choose between the uncertainty of a romance newly born and everything she cherished right here in this bustling Arkansas resort town—family, friends, and now her own pottery studio and shop?

That thought brought her mind full circle and back to the problem at hand. As both shop clerk and artist, she wouldn't find it as easy to simply disappear into the back room as she had at her father's factory when office work was caught up. Without Mrs. Vickary on hand, it would mean leaving the showroom unattended.

Unfortunately, hiring a paid assistant wasn't in the budget. If Annemarie wanted to maintain her inventory, she'd have to start work earlier or stay later—or both.

While she sat behind the counter studying the abysmal figures in her sales ledger, the shop door opened and Samuel's mother stepped inside. Annemarie looked up and smiled. "Did you have a nice lunch with Sam?"

"Samuel treated me to a delightful meal at the Arlington." Mrs. Vickary removed her hat and gloves and tucked them in a cubbyhole behind the front counter. "I told you, you should have come with us."

"You deserved the time alone with Sam. I know how much you're both going to miss each other."

Mrs. Vickary laughed as she snatched up the feather duster and whisked it lightly across a pottery display. "Oh, I'm certain Samuel won't miss me any longer than it takes him to walk from the train depot to a certain shop on the avenue."

Warmth crept up Annemarie's neck and into her cheeks. She dropped her gaze to the ledger page and tried to focus on the figures, but she might as well be reading Greek.

"You should spend some time in the workshop while I'm here. I peeked at the lovely lamp base you brought over from the kiln yesterday. It's going to be striking."

"Do you think so? I'm experimenting with glazes again. Perhaps you'd give me your opinion—"

The front door creaked open, and Mrs. Vickary went to greet the patron. "Good afternoon. May I help you?"

Mrs. Vickary blocked Annemarie's view of the visitor, revealing only a glimpse of plain olive-green skirts and a halo of red hair. Then a shy voice replied, "Beg pardon, ma'am, but I'm looking for Miss Kendall."

The speaker's delicate Irish brogue made Annemarie's stomach curl in upon itself—only to plummet to her toes when Mrs. Vickary stepped out of the way. Annemarie's gaze landed on the face of Mary McClarney, the nurse from the Army and Navy Hospital.

Annemarie rose and stood ramrod-straight at the end of the counter. *Awkward* couldn't begin to describe this moment. How exactly was she expected to respond to the new woman in Gilbert's life? It certainly wasn't jealousy she felt. But though Annemarie no longer doubted the depth of her feelings for Samuel, the pain of Gilbert's rejection wasn't easily forgotten.

Somehow Annemarie finagled some semblance of a smile. "Miss McClarney. Welcome to my shop."

"Sorry to bother you, Miss Kendall—"

"Annemarie, please."

"Thank you kindly. I wonder if I might speak with you"— Mary's gaze darted sideways—"alone."

With a deferential nod, Mrs. Vickary excused herself and disappeared into the workroom.

Annemarie took a cautious step closer. "How can I help you?"

"Truth be told, I don't quite know where to start." Mary wandered over to a table where several pottery pieces sat atop a pristine white cloth. "You made all these? They're beyond lovely. And expensive, too, no doubt."

Those last words were uttered with a tinge of envy, if Annemarie were any judge. "I try to price my merchandise fairly. Is there something particular you're interested in? Perhaps we could negotiate—"

"Negotiate. Now there's a fancy word for you." Mary spun around to face Annemarie, her green eyes ablaze. Whatever timidity she'd arrived with seemed to have evaporated. "Fact o' the matter is, I am here to negotiate. But not for the likes of gewgaws like this." She waved a dismissive hand in the direction of the display.

Annemarie locked her arms across her ribcage. "If you're here to determine whether I still have any hold upon Gilbert's heart, then you've wasted a trip."

"Nothing of the kind. Because I already know the answer to that question. You've more hold on his heart than you want to admit."

"How can you say that, when—"

Mary raised her palm. "When he's the one who spurned you? But the fact means nothing when it comes to his true feelings. You and I both know he broke your engagement because, coming home from the war all shot up and crippled, he didn't want to be a burden or an embarrassment to you."

"He wouldn't have been. I love Gilbert."

"See there, I knew it." Mary practically pounced, one finger pointing accusingly.

"No, Mary, you misunderstand." With a steadying breath Annemarie continued, "I will always care for Gilbert, but now only as a friend. It's over between us. Gilbert has moved on with you. I have moved on with—"

"The kindly chaplain. So you'd like to believe." Mary's defiant façade crumpled. Her tone became ragged, her mouth a grimace. "I love Gilbert, too, you see. But the love he still harbors for you is killing him inch by inch, and I'll never have his heart as long as he thinks there's a chance this side of heaven he can win you back."

Silence enveloped the shop as Annemarie let Mary's words sink in. A few weeks ago, she may have leapt upon that glimmer of hope and determined to fight for Gilbert's love with everything in her. But today those words were meaningless.

She lifted her chin to fix Mary with a serene but confident stare. "My heart belongs to one man only, and it is *not* Gilbert Ballard." Then her gaze softened, and she reached across the space between them to seize Mary's hand. "I wish I knew how to reassure you, Mary. I wish I knew how to help Gilbert. But what else can either of us do now except pray?"

Mary's eyes darkened, and she glanced toward the window with a sigh. "I'm fearing it will take a heap of prayer and then some before Gilbert's broken parts are healed." Then, brushing wetness from beneath her eye, she murmured. "Forgive me for troubling you, but I had to know for certain where you stood."

"And now you do."

"Aye, for all the good it'll do me."

Mary left then, and standing at the window Annemarie watched her trudge up Central Avenue like a tired old woman, as if her last remnants of hope were fading. Annemarie ached for the girl while a quiet anger simmered in the pit of her belly—anger at the war, anger at Gilbert, anger at her own powerlessness to set things right.

Only one thing would assuage such churning emotions. Shoulders rigid, she marched to the workroom and donned her clay-stained smock. With a polite nod at Samuel's mother, who tried her best to look busy straightening supply shelves that didn't need straightening, she said, "If you don't mind watching the front, I'll work for a while."

"Of course, dear." Mrs. Vickary started for the door, then paused to rest a hand on Annemarie's arm. "Is everything all right? Who was that young woman?"

"Just a nurse I know from the hospital. Everything's fine." She slammed a brick of clay onto her work surface and began kneading with ferocity. Things certainly were *not* fine, but she wouldn't burden Samuel's mother with her worries only days before the woman planned to leave.

No, somehow God would work things out—for Gilbert and Mary, for Annemarie and Sam. The Great War couldn't stretch its long, hideous shadow over their lives forever.

Or at least she prayed as much.

⚘

Gilbert rapped on Thomas's office door and then stepped inside without awaiting an invitation. "Here's the weekend cleaning staff schedule. I'm taking off early."

Thomas looked up with a start. He drew his right eyebrow into a downward slant. "Just like that? Not 'May I leave early this afternoon if it's all right with you'?"

"Would you feel better if I groveled at your feet, O Great One?" Gilbert slapped the schedule in the center of his brother's desk, upsetting a neat stack of envelopes.

Grabbing up the envelopes, Thomas patted them into some semblance of order and set them out of Gilbert's reach. "I hired you, big brother, and I can just as easily fire you."

"Enjoying the power, aren't you?" Gilbert tried to ignore the sudden twist in his gut. He couldn't lose this job, not after he'd gotten himself so deeply in debt. Between the gambling, the booze, and the—

Gilbert's grip tightened on his cane. He was *not* an addict, no matter what Mary might believe. She didn't understand what he'd been through. She wasn't there when the grenades were going off, when machine gun fire chewed through whole forests like so much kindling.

She wasn't there when he came to in a crater and saw his own leg sticking up out of the rubble six feet away.

Sweat burst out on his upper lip, his forehead. A tremor worked its way from his spine to his fingertips. He sank into a chair before he collapsed.

"Gil, you okay?" The annoyance left Thomas's expression. He hurried around the desk.

"Phantom leg pain, that's all." A lie, but not much of one. He rubbed his thigh and then released the catch to allow his artificial knee to bend.

Thomas propped a hip against the front of the desk. "Believe me, Gil, I take no pleasure in being your boss."

Gilbert uttered a hollow laugh. "Thanks."

"You know what I mean." Groaning, Thomas massaged the bridge of his nose. "Let's start over, okay? You want to take off early. I get it. It's Friday night, and you've got plans. With the sweet Miss McClarney, I presume?"

"Naturally." Shame gnawed at Gilbert's belly. Ever since Mary had cornered him in his dumpy little office last Monday, he'd worked to convince her she was wrong—about his addictions, about his unwillingness to commit to her, about his obsession with Annemarie. He hoped his invitation to tonight's little dinner party would be enough to convince her.

But the truth was he wanted her along for one reason only: to assure his host he was once again romantically involved and therefore unavailable. Otherwise, Pastor Yarborough would be pushing his spinster daughter upon him from the moment he walked through the door.

And tonight Gilbert had a much more pressing agenda than fending off the Wellesley-educated but oh-so-homely Patrice.

He did care for Mary . . . in his way. She was good for him, no denying it. All right, so he drank a bit too much, relied a bit too heavily on the morphine to take the edge off his pain, both physical and emotional. He didn't need her lectures, though. Didn't need her questioning his feelings, not when he'd made up his mind to win back Annemarie.

With a tired shrug, Thomas reached behind him to retrieve the staff schedule. Lips skewed, he gave it a cursory glance. "Looks fine, all bases covered. Okay, then, get out of here. Enjoy your date."

Gilbert nodded his thanks as he pushed to his feet and locked the artificial knee. Date? Hardly! Tonight was all about learning everything he could about Samuel Vickary's wartime record. The man harbored a secret, one he clearly didn't want revealed.

But the persuasive Pastor Yarborough and his loquacious wife could pry conversation out of a rock. A relaxing dinner, a few drinks, perhaps a cigar or two on the front porch, and surely the good Dr. Russ would open up. Before he knew what hit him, he and Gilbert would be just a couple of army pals regaling each other with war stories while the ladies sipped tea in the parlor.

After calling for Zachary to pick him up, Gilbert made his way down to street level to soak up a little March sunshine while he waited. Eyes watering, head already pounding, he squinted against the glare but refused to move into the shade. He'd had enough of clouds and gloom—France had been cold, wet, dark, and miserable. If things went according to plan, he'd soon be basking again in the sunshine of Annemarie's smile.

Sorry, Mary, but tonight you're just a means to an end.

Samuel had decided on civilian attire for the evening. Even though these days, thankfully, his uniform remained clean and dry, nine or ten hours a day in stiff, scratchy wool was plenty. Earlier in the week, his mother had insisted they visit a haberdashery, where she helped him choose a handsome pair of gabardine slacks and a natty tweed blazer. She made sure the tailor altered them for a perfect fit.

"You're filling out again since you got over the flu." His mother finished adjusting his tie and then patted his chest. "Looks good on you."

"Mom's home cooking certainly helps. I'll probably waste away to skin and bones again after you leave." Samuel's lips twitched into a shaky smile. His mother would board the train for Fort Wayne in the morning, and he'd only begun to realize how empty his little apartment would seem without her.

A rap on the door announced Donald Russ's arrival. Stepping into the small foyer, the doctor eyed Samuel up and down. "Aren't you the dapper one? Good thing you're bringing Annemarie along, or Pastor Yarborough would be setting his sights on you for his future son-in-law."

"Yarborough?" Samuel didn't remember Donald mentioning the name of their host before now—or had he simply been too preoccupied to take note? "That wouldn't be Pastor Irvin Yarborough of Ouachita Fellowship?"

"One and the same." They started down the outer stairs. "You know him?"

"We've . . . met." Samuel gnawed the inside of his cheek. Both the Kendalls and the Ballards attended Ouachita Fellowship. Samuel's duties conducting services in the hospital chapel had precluded him from attending worship elsewhere, but Pastor and Mrs. Yarborough had been occasional dinner guests in the Ballard home while he lived there.

The possibility Gilbert might be among tonight's invitees didn't bear thinking about. Besides, Samuel had a hard time believing Gilbert had bothered to grace the inside of a church since his release from the hospital. He'd openly declared he'd given up on God—or rather, that God had failed him. And Gilbert's actions of late certainly were anything but godly.

Who are you to judge?

The familiar voice of condemnation made him draw up short as they reached the curb. Long hours spent in prayer and meditation upon Scripture these past several days assured him the voice belonged not to the Holy Spirit but to Satan, the "ancient serpent" referred to in the Book of Revelation, the "accuser" thrown down by the power of God and the authority of Christ.

Even so, faulty thought patterns were hard to break. He had no choice but to lean hard into Jesus until the voice was permanently silenced.

"She's a beauty, isn't she?"

Samuel blinked and stared. It took him a full second to realize Donald referred to the slightly used motorcar he'd purchased a few days ago, a 1916 Saxon Roadster. Pulling himself into the present, Samuel stroked the glossy black finish. "A fine set of wheels you have there, Dr. Russ."

"Purrs like a kitten, runs like a dream. Hop in." Donald motioned Samuel into the passenger seat and then settled himself behind the wheel. "Can't believe you're still hoofing it around town. When are you going to get yourself an automobile?"

"I enjoy walking. Clears my head." Heaven knew he needed plenty of head-clearing these days.

As Donald pulled away from the curb, he glanced over at Samuel. "You're looking pensive again. Not allowed. You're supposed to be watching out for me tonight, so I need you on full alert."

"Have no fear. If I notice the young lady in question moving into attack formation, I shall employ my extensive arsenal of charm and wit to divert her aim."

Samuel spoke lightheartedly, but the military allusions too easily darkened his thoughts, rekindling his growing urgency to contact Private Braswell's family, express his remorse, and beg their forgiveness. They needed to know their son died a hero.

He died saving Samuel's life.

Adrift in such thoughts until Donald parked the Roadster in front of Annemarie's house, Samuel gave himself a mental shake. He refused to dampen anyone's good spirits this evening— least of all Annemarie's.

Then, as he reached for the handle to open the car door, he looked at Donald and Donald looked at him. The same realization must have hit them both simultaneously, and they grinned at each other like schoolboys who'd just gotten away with skipping class.

Yes, Samuel's evening was about to get even better. Donald's car was only a two-seater, which meant the only place for Annemarie was on Samuel's lap.

"Are you sure you're not too uncomfortable?" Annemarie sat as lightly as she could upon Samuel's thighs, but every time Dr. Russ swerved around a corner, it threw her off balance and either pressed her against the door or more snugly into Sam's chest.

She didn't mind in the least. Just not necessarily while another gentleman kept glancing their way with a knowing grin that shot flames up Annemarie's neck.

Finally, they arrived at a modest Victorian house on Prospect Avenue, a house Annemarie recognized immediately—her pastor's.

Dr. Russ came around to get their door and assist her out of the car. As she found her footing on the sidewalk, she cast Sam a questioning glance. "You didn't tell me we were dining with the Yarboroughs."

"Didn't realize it myself until this evening." Samuel shoved the car door closed. His uneasy smile suggested he'd read her thoughts.

The fine hairs on the back of Annemarie's neck prickled. She scanned the street for any sign of either the Ballard family car or Thomas's automobile. When she didn't see either one, she whispered out a relieved breath. Ouachita Fellowship was a large congregation, after all. Why suspect the worst? The other guest Sam mentioned could be any one of a number of returning servicemen.

Besides, Pastor and Mrs. Yarborough both knew about the broken engagement. They'd never be so inconsiderate as to purposely throw Gilbert and Annemarie together.

Sam tucked her hand in the crook of his arm as they followed Dr. Russ to the Yarboroughs' front door. While they waited beneath the porch light, Annemarie ran her fingers down Sam's lapel, worries forgotten, her love for him bubbling up within her like clear spring water. She smiled coyly. "You're looking especially handsome tonight, Chaplain Vickary."

The tension lines around his eyes melted into a look of love to match her own. She wished they were alone on the porch, because the sudden longing to taste his mouth upon hers made her knees go weak. She loved him heart and soul—she knew it from the depths of her being. Perhaps they could steal one quick kiss before—

The front door swung open, and Pastor Yarborough shot out his long, bony hand. "Welcome, welcome! So glad you could come, Dr. Russ."

"Thanks. Call me Donald." He pumped the pastor's hand. "Let me introduce Chaplain Samuel Vickary and his lady friend—"

"Annemarie?" Salt-and-pepper brows stretched toward Pastor Yarborough's rapidly receding hairline. "Dear me, what a surprise!"

She accepted the pastor's outstretched hand, her edginess returning. "You weren't expecting me?"

Dr. Russ gestured toward Samuel. "Meet my friend Chaplain Vickary, Pastor. I mentioned he'd be bringing a date."

"Of course. But we had no idea—" The pastor cleared his throat. "Chaplain Vickary, I'm honored to make the acquaintance of another man of the cloth." His confused glance darted between Annemarie and Samuel. "So . . . the two of you . . ."

"Yes, Pastor, we're together now." Lifting her chin, Annemarie tightened her grip on Sam's arm. "Sam makes me happier than I've been in years."

Pastor Yarborough gave a bemused nod. "Then I'm . . . I'm glad for you. It's just—"

Mrs. Yarborough appeared at her husband's elbow. Dressed in bright coral, she looked as round and plump as an overripe peach. "Goodness, Irvin, don't leave our guests languishing on the porch." She gave a startled gasp. "Dear me, is that our own Annemarie Kendall?"

"I hope it's all right," Annemarie began, stepping through the door. Was her unannounced arrival *that* unnerving to her hosts?

Pastor Yarborough leaned toward his wife and spoke out of the corner of his mouth. "She came with the chaplain, dear."

"So I see." Mrs. Yarborough shot her husband an oddly curious grimace, her brows quirked like two flattened question marks. "My, my, if this isn't an interesting turn of events. Should we—"

"I think we must."

When both the Yarboroughs turned sympathetic glances her way, Annemarie's stomach heaved. "Don't tell me," she said, reaching for Samuel's hand and gripping it for dear life. "You've invited Gilbert."

28

*H*igh time you called upon my daughter like a proper gentleman, Lieutenant Ballard."

Standing at Gilbert's side in the McClarneys' tiny parlor, Mary cringed. "Now, Mum, you know—"

"What I *know*, dear girl, is that you've been making time with this randy fellow for weeks now—"

Mary's creeping blush flamed like a raging fever. "Mum!"

"—and the most I've seen of his face is a glimpse through the window. He's here and gone without so much as a fare-thee-well."

"Mrs. McClarney, you have my deepest apologies." Gilbert's easy smile oozed charm. He lifted his cane fractionally off the floor and tipped his head. "As you can see, I've been rather incapacitated since the war. I've only recently been able to move about with any semblance of freedom."

Mum crossed her arms, while her slippered toe beat out a staccato rhythm on the carpet. "Yes, so Mary's told me. And I feel for ya, truly I do." She reached for Mary's hand and drew her close. Her gaze softened. "But this girl's my only daughter, the light of my life." Turning back to Gilbert with a glare, she added, "And I insist you treat her like the lady she is."

"Yes, ma'am, by all means." Gilbert dipped his chin, his dark eyes clouding.

"Mum." Pressing her mother's hand, Mary lowered her voice. "Gilbert has done as you asked, and now you've embarrassed us both. May we go now, please?"

For an unbearably long moment, Mary's mother stood in silence while Gilbert endured her scrutiny. Then the fragile hand gripping Mary's began to tremble. She turned to her daughter with a frantic, barely audible whisper. "I don't trust this man. His eyes—there's something not right about him."

Mary shoved down the lump of worry constricting her chest. If she gave voice to her own simmering doubts, Mum would forbid her to leave with Gilbert—forbid her ever seeing him again. "It's all right, Mum. If you don't trust him, at least trust me. You know how it was with Da. We loved him in spite of . . . everything."

"Then you're sayin' . . . ?"

"Yes, Mum." Blinking back a tear, Mary averted her face from Gilbert's view and murmured, "I love Gilbert Ballard, and I'm daring to believe he loves me, too. In spite of everything."

Her mother slowly wagged her head back and forth, resignation turning down the corners of her lips. "Mary, Mary, such a way you have with broken things. Be careful this one doesn't break your heart as well."

Behind them, Gilbert cleared his throat. "Mary? It's getting late."

"Yes, yes, coming." She tugged her mother into a quick hug, then snatched up her shawl and handbag.

On the way out to Gilbert's car she sent up a prayer to the Lord of Lords that falling in love with Gilbert wouldn't turn out to be the biggest mistake of her life.

It took several minutes of diligent protests before Annemarie convinced Sam, Dr. Russ, the Yarboroughs, and—most importantly—herself that they had no need to shield her from Gilbert's presence. They were bound to meet at church and in other social situations during the course of their lives, and Annemarie might as well get used to it.

Mrs. Yarborough wrung her pink, pudgy hands. "Just so you understand, this evening was entirely at Gilbert's suggestion. Apparently he was Dr. Russ's patient aboard the hospital ship that brought him home from the war, and when Gilbert happened to notice Dr. Russ in church last Sunday, he asked if we'd invite them both for dinner so they could catch up."

"Unfortunately," Pastor Yarborough cut in, "Gilbert was also adamant about our not mentioning his name. He wanted the reunion with Dr. Russ to be a surprise."

"I'm sure he did." The doctor shared an exasperated look with Samuel before turning to Annemarie. "I'm sorry for dragging you into this. If I'd had any idea—"

"You don't have to apologize," Annemarie insisted. "We're all adults. It'll be fine." At least she hoped it would. "Besides, I'm looking forward to catching up with Patrice. I haven't seen her in ages."

Mrs. Yarborough practically shimmied with relief. "She's waiting in the parlor." Taking Annemarie's arm, she looped her other arm through Dr. Russ's, and something akin to greed flashed in her eyes. "Dear Dr. Russ—may I call you Donald?— our daughter will be simply thrilled to make your acquaintance, I'm sure."

Shoving her concerns aside, Annemarie winked at Sam over her shoulder, and he answered with a crooked grin. Obviously, the doctor's suspicions were correct. He'd become their latest target in the quest for a husband for Patrice.

The young lady in question stood with hands folded at her waist, her lips bowed into a prim, almost ethereal smile. By now, Patrice must be sick to death of her parents' ceaseless matchmaking efforts. They'd certainly tried and failed with every other single gentleman of marrying age in their circle of friends—Thomas included.

But Annemarie had always suspected Patrice couldn't care less about marriage. A woman with higher aspirations, not the least of which was political office, Patrice was a staunch member of Arkansas' Political Equality League. She spoke out loudly and often in favor of women's suffrage, much to the embarrassment of her conservative parents—which was probably why they remained so anxious to marry her off.

"Dinner will be served shortly," Mrs. Yarborough announced. "We're just waiting on our two other guests."

Two other guests? Tensing again, Annemarie angled a raised-eyebrow glance at Sam. He squeezed her hand, and she squeezed back, while praying with every ounce of her faith that Gilbert would be accompanied by his mother or Thomas. If there was anyone else on this earth with whom Annemarie was unprepared to spend an evening socializing, it was Nurse Mary McClarney.

The grandfather clock in the Yarboroughs' front hall chimed half past the hour. Seven-thirty already? No wonder Annemarie's stomach was rumbling. She was surprised she could even think about eating, considering the circumstances. Probably nerves as much as anything. At least the lively conversation between Dr. Russ and the Yarboroughs' daughter dominated everyone's attention so completely that no one seemed to notice Annemarie's edginess, not to mention the squeaks and gurgles she tried desperately to suppress.

"I assure you I'm entirely in favor of women's suffrage," Dr. Russ was saying. "I only meant I have reservations about where this will all lead. Will women then insist on positions of authority in churches, in government, in the armed forces—"

Patrice jutted her chin. "Are you implying women are incapable of responsible leadership?"

"Not at all. But if women turn their backs on home and family—"

"You show your ignorance, Doctor." Patrice harrumphed. "Or perhaps you espouse a double standard. Why is it perfectly all right for men—decent family men whom you'd never accuse of neglecting their wives and children—to hold down jobs or serve their country, but unacceptable for women to do the same?"

Samuel leaned near Annemarie's ear and whispered, "Somehow I don't think Donald needed us along at all. He's doing just fine repelling Miss Yarborough's advances."

Annemarie couldn't suppress a titter. "Advances? Looks to me like an all-out frontal attack—and *not* with any intention of courtship!"

"I have to say, though, she's not nearly as unattractive as rumor would have it." Samuel raised a brow. "In fact, I have to wonder if Donald is engaging her so argumentatively *because* he finds her enchanting."

"Argument as a form of flirtation? A fascinating concept." With a sardonic smile, Annemarie sipped sparkling cider from a dainty cut-glass cup, a useless assault on her intensifying hunger pangs.

Mrs. Yarborough entered from the dining room with a tray of canapés. She handed tiny linen cocktail napkins to Samuel and Annemarie. "My apologies for making you wait for dinner. Perhaps these will—"

At the clack of a brass door knocker, the plump pastor's wife heaved an immense sigh and set the tray and napkins on a side table before following after her husband to greet the late arrivals.

Annemarie's stomach suddenly gave a roar that was partly hunger, mostly nerves. With a muttered, "Excuse me" she marched over to the table and scooped up three toast points spread with pale yellow cheese. Some kind of insane logic convinced her if she had a mouthful of canapés, she could delay speaking to Gilbert a few minutes longer.

Pastor Yarborough's baritone echoed in the front hallway as he greeted his guests. "No, no, not too late at all. Come in and say hello before we sit down to dinner." Then a meaningful throat clearing, and Annemarie didn't catch his next words. No doubt he was explaining Annemarie's attendance.

Well, let Gilbert sweat a bit, too. He deserved it.

More murmuring from the hall before Pastor and Mrs. Yarborough led their guests into the parlor. Then Annemarie glimpsed Mary McClarney on Gilbert's arm, and sudden chagrin made her choke on her canapé. Seized by a fit of coughing, she turned away, napkin and toast points tumbling to the floor as she fought to catch her breath.

Instantly, both Samuel and Dr. Russ came to her aid. A solid slap to her upper back dislodged the bit of toast, and while the doctor helped her into a chair, Samuel called for a glass of water.

"I'm—fine." Annemarie gasped out the words. She pressed a hand to her chest as she sipped from the water glass Mrs. Yarborough handed her, hardly daring to glance across the room where Gilbert and Mary stood at a polite distance. *Why, Lord?* Why did Gilbert have to bring Mary? How would any of them ever survive the discomfiture of this ill-planned evening?

Mrs. Yarborough patted Annemarie's shoulder and offered a fresh napkin. "I'm so sorry, my dear. Are you sure you're all right?"

Nodding, Annemarie coughed gently into her napkin but kept her eyes averted. *Lord, let me disappear right now!*

Samuel sank on one knee beside her chair. "Do you want to go home? We don't have to stay."

"No," she whispered—the exact opposite of her true desires. But she must show herself the better person or she'd never be able to hold her head high in Hot Springs society. "No, it'll be fine. Let's not spoil the evening for Dr. Russ."

Now the doctor edged closer. Samuel stood, and they exchanged words Annemarie couldn't make out. Eyes narrowed in a look of sympathetic understanding, Dr. Russ gave Samuel's shoulder a squeeze and then crossed the room to offer his hand to Gilbert. "I must say, Lieutenant Ballard, you're looking a hundred times better than the last time I saw you."

"Dr. Russ, a pleasure to see you again. I didn't intend on making such a dramatic entrance, however." Gilbert nodded toward Annemarie. "My apologies to Miss Kendall."

Rising, Annemarie hoped she could find her voice. "Think nothing of it." A bit raspy, but another slow breath restored a measure of control. "You do look exceedingly well, Gilbert. Hello, Mary. What a lovely dress. Green is your color."

"Thank you." Mary's glance skittered to the floor and up again. "I'd no idea you'd be here, or—"

"Nonsense. There's no reason we can't all be friends." Well, there were plenty of reasons, but she wouldn't think about them right now. She linked arms with Samuel. "Imagine, here you gentlemen are, all together again after your journey home on the *Comfort*. Small world, isn't it?"

"Indeed." Pastor Yarborough rubbed his hands together as he edged over to his wife. "Fiona, dear, let's not make our guests wait for dinner a moment longer. All this excitement has honed my appetite to razor sharpness."

And taken what was left of Annemarie's clean away.

Blast it all, why did Dr. Russ have to bring Samuel and Annemarie along? Not that Gilbert should be surprised. He'd surmised during their days aboard the *U.S.S. Comfort* that during the war the doctor and the chaplain had developed a deep and personal bond. Now he knew the bond included the keeping of certain secrets—the reason Gilbert had arranged this interesting little gathering in the first place.

Except Samuel was *not* supposed to be here.

Although . . . maybe the situation might turn out in Gilbert's favor after all. Kill two birds with one stone, so to speak. Uncover Sam's secret *and* expose it in one dramatic coup d'état.

"More roast beef, Gilbert?" Mrs. Yarborough offered him the platter.

"Don't mind if I do. Delicious as always, Mrs. Y." Out of habit, he grasped the serving plate with both hands, forgetting his left arm still lacked strength. The platter tipped, and slabs of tender, juicy roast nearly slid off the edge before Mary rescued him.

Setting the platter on the table between them, she shot him a green-eyed smile filled with empathy . . . and more. It was clear she'd fallen in love with him. And soon, he would break her heart. A pang of regret stabbed like a bayonet. Mary was a good girl, deserving so much better than he'd offered, and he'd taken advantage at every opportunity. Only her Christian morals and firm resolve had prevented him from giving his desires free rein.

But the discovery that Sam hid a dark and shameful secret had awakened him to his true desires, and now not even Mary's tender caresses and selfless devotion were enough to deter him from battling for Annemarie's love with every weapon at his disposal.

Even if it meant destroying the man he once called friend.

Cherry pie and piping hot coffee concluded the awkwardly quiet meal, and as Mrs. Yarborough and Patrice cleared the table, the pastor invited the guests to return to the parlor. Samuel and Annemarie went straight to the far end of the sofa, obviously putting as much distance between themselves and Gilbert as possible.

Fine. Gilbert intended on prying the desired information from Dr. Russ anyway, so he deliberately chose the chair next to the doctor's. Noticing Mary glancing around for where she should sit, he cast her an apologetic frown. "We'll be telling war stories, Mary. You'd much rather visit with the ladies, wouldn't you?"

"I'd love to hear a good war story." Her features hardened into a steely smile as she set one hand firmly upon Gilbert's shoulder.

Pastor Yarborough brought over a spindly, straight-backed chair and placed it next to Gilbert's. "Here you are, Miss McClarney. And I'll make sure these fine gentlemen mind their words for the ladies' delicate sensitivities."

Mary uttered a dismissive laugh. "No need to guard your words on my account. I'm a nurse at the Army and Navy Hospital, don't forget. There's little on God's green earth I haven't heard already."

"All the more reason we should be considerate." Samuel drew Annemarie's hand into his lap and cradled it tenderly. "I suggest we spare the ladies—and ourselves."

Gilbert's jaw ached with the effort required to keep his expression impassive when all he wanted to do was grab Samuel Vickary by the lapels and beat his face to a pulp. But no, he wouldn't win any points with Annemarie that way. She'd have to see for herself Samuel wasn't the honorable man she believed him to be—and Gilbert was every bit the man she remembered and once loved.

"You make a good point, Sam." Gilbert stretched out his good leg and rested his hand atop his cane. "Why ruin an otherwise pleasant evening reminiscing about a time we'd all rather forget?"

"I agree." Dr. Russ fingered one of the doilies covering the chair arms. "I, for one, have had all the war talk I can stomach for a lifetime."

"I'm sure you have, Doctor." With a casual chuckle, Gilbert added, "Pastor, this might be a good time to break out that bottle of brandy I brought. Nothing like a good cognac to top off a delicious dinner and smooth the way for relaxing conversation."

The pastor made a few noises about why, as a man of the cloth, he *really* shouldn't imbibe, but how could he refuse to partake of Gilbert's generous contribution to the evening? He hurried to the hallway to fetch the bottle, and shortly afterward Mrs. Yarborough carried in a tray of crystal brandy snifters. Even if Gilbert hadn't witnessed firsthand the pastor's penchant for a glass of fine wine with a sumptuous meal, the fact the Yarboroughs even owned a set of snifters spoke volumes. Gilbert wasn't at all surprised when the pastor poured himself a generous splash.

He wasn't surprised, either, when Samuel stoically refused, as did the ladies. Dr. Russ accepted a glass, however—definitely part of the plan—and sipped it slowly as Gilbert asked how he enjoyed life in Hot Springs.

"It's a charming city, a lot to offer." Dr. Russ swirled his snifter. "But, of course, I've visited here several times. I was born and raised near Fort Smith, if you recall."

"Yes, a fellow Arkansan." Gilbert raised his glass. "Finest state in the U.S. of A. And we Arkansas boys sure proved our worth in France, didn't we?"

Annemarie stiffened. "I thought we'd agreed not to discuss the Great War."

"Great. That certainly describes it." Gilbert rubbed his left thigh as he sipped his brandy. "Most every country in the Northern Hemisphere, plus Australia, New Zealand, parts of Africa and South America—"

"Humph." Patrice, seated next to her mother across the room, lifted her nose in the air. "War is what happens when you leave the government of nations to men."

"Now, dearest . . ." Mrs. Yarborough cast her daughter a warning glance.

Mary sat forward. "Hasn't it been a lovely spring? Do you garden, Mrs. Yarborough? My mum always has me plant pansies in the window boxes so we'll have plenty of blooms to brighten the house come springtime. I think this year's batch is—"

"Mary, be a dear and fetch the brandy." Groaning inwardly, Gilbert handed her his glass. He didn't need a meddling Irish nurse derailing his agenda.

Mary started to rise, but as she cut a sharp glance his way, Mrs. Yarborough leapt from her chair. "Keep your seat, Miss McClarney. I *am* the hostess, after all." She retrieved the bottle from a side table and topped off Gilbert's glass. "Anyone else?"

"I'll take a bit more." Dr. Russ drained his snifter and then extended it for a refill. "Excellent vintage, Gilbert. A fine Rémy Martin, with hints of jasmine and hazelnut, if I know my cognac."

"And you do!" Dr. Russ, a brandy connoisseur? Maybe Gilbert's luck was on the upswing. He could certainly use a bit of good fortune after his disastrous losses at Oaklawn this week. Should have put his money on St. Allan as his tipster advised. The two-year-old colt had set a new track record. "So there. Something to talk about besides war. Although I doubt the ladies would enjoy a discussion of the finer qualities of cognac any better. What about horse racing, Dr. Russ? Do you bet on the ponies?"

"Most definitely not. Might just as well light a match to a twenty-dollar bill as take a chance at the track."

Mrs. Yarborough cleared her throat. "I daresay, ladies, perhaps we should adjourn to the dining room and allow the gentlemen to discuss whatever amuses them." She set the bottle of brandy on the table between Gilbert and Dr. Russ and then signaled the ladies to follow her. "Miss McClarney, perhaps you'd share your cultivation tips. My pansies never quite seem to thrive."

Yes, indeed, Gilbert's luck was turning. Without Mary standing sentinel or the distraction of watching Samuel fawn over Annemarie, maybe he could finally get down to business.

29

*G*ilbert was up to something. Annemarie felt certain. The look in his eyes, the smirk that curled his lip for the briefest of moments when Mrs. Yarborough suggested the ladies retire to the dining room—no word described it other than *smug*.

Mary sensed it, too, if Annemarie wasn't mistaken. The girl stood, her steps faltering. "We won't be staying too late, now, will we? Mum will worry."

Gilbert waved her away with the tip of his cane. "Go along, Mary. Have a nice chat with the ladies."

Annemarie shifted on the sofa, giving Gilbert her back. She entwined her fingers with Sam's and cast him a pleading gaze as she whispered, "Maybe we should go now. Gilbert's determined to get himself drunk, and Donald along with him, from the looks of things. This will only end badly."

Samuel offered a none-too-confident smile of reassurance. "I'll keep an eye on things, make sure neither of them gets out of hand." He brought her fingertips to his lips for a gentle kiss and then gave a weak laugh as he nodded in Dr. Russ's direction. "Besides, I'm afraid Donald's already beyond the point of needing me to drive us all home."

"Samuel Vickary." Dr. Russ slurred his words. "Are you referring to my love affair with brandy?"

Gilbert's harsh chuckle pierced the air. "I do believe we're kindred spirits, Donald, my man. What else besides brandy so soothingly warms a gentleman's insides with so little risk to his heart? Certainly not any woman I've ever met."

Annemarie glanced over her shoulder in time to see Mary wince. Again, she turned to Sam. "I don't like where this is headed. Let's make our excuses and leave. *Please.*"

Worry crept into Sam's eyes. He pushed off the sofa and helped Annemarie to her feet, then kept her hand tucked firmly against his side as he addressed Dr. Russ. "Donald, perhaps we ought to call it an evening. Don't you have an early surgery in the morning?"

"Rescheduled for eleven-thirty." The doctor slanted a knowing look toward Samuel, his gaze darting meaningfully toward Gilbert and then to his brandy snifter.

Their exchanged glances set Annemarie's teeth on edge. Exactly how many of them here tonight had ulterior motives?

Patrice sidled over to where Mary now stood. "Honestly, Annemarie, I should think you'd have discovered by now it's useless arguing with a man. They'll have things their way, right or wrong—and it's usually wrong."

"Patrice! *Must* you insult our guests?" Despite a simpering smile, Mrs. Yarborough hissed the words like an exasperated mother cat. Her gaze finally settled on Annemarie, and she extended a beckoning hand. "Come now, dear. No reason to rush off, is there? We ladies will have a cozy chat in the other room."

Outnumbered, Annemarie had no choice but to concede. But even if she could put aside her concerns about leaving Gilbert and Samuel in the same room together, the thought of whiling away an hour or more in idle conversation with the prim Patrice Yarborough, her obsequious mother, and the plucky young nurse who only had eyes for Gilbert—

Lord, help! Her fingers ached with the need to escape to her pottery wheel.

Samuel shifted his stance uneasily as he watched the ladies retreat to the dining room. Before Mrs. Yarborough whisked the French doors shut behind them, Annemarie shot him one last desperate glance. The look in her huge brown eyes reminded him of the confused and terrified deer he'd cornered in a ravine long ago on a boyhood hunting trip.

Cornered. Exactly how he felt just now. He yearned to leave as badly as Annemarie, but the tingling tightness in his gut told him to bide his time while the evening played out.

"Sit down and pour yourself some cognac, Sam." Gilbert gestured with his own glass. "Good for what ails you."

"Thanks, but at least one of us should stay sober." He glanced toward the pastor, who had somehow managed to fall asleep amidst all the commotion. The softly snoring cleric's empty brandy snifter dangled from his fingertips. Samuel relieved him of the glass and set it on an end table.

Donald chuckled. "Should we help the poor fellow up to his bed?"

"Leave him," Gilbert replied. "The old man never could hold his liquor. One drink and he's out like a snuffed candle."

"Convenient, isn't it? The pastor out cold, the ladies in the other room . . ." Donald's tone no longer held even the suggestion of inebriation. He set down his glass with a *thunk*, crossed one leg over the opposite knee, and folded his hands. "Okay, Gilbert, you have us where you want us. Time to pay the piper. What 'tune' would you have us dance to tonight?"

Gilbert's nostrils flared. He blinked several times and then gulped his brandy. "I have no idea what you're talking about."

Picking up on Donald's cues, Samuel entered the fray. "Don't pretend, Gilbert. If I didn't realize it before, I do now. You orchestrated this whole evening for a purpose." He backed off slightly and gave his ear a thoughtful tug. "With one possible exception, of course. You were as taken aback to find me here with Annemarie as we were to learn the Yarboroughs were awaiting your arrival."

"You've got me there, Sam." A nervous laugh vibrated Gilbert's chest. "Part of what you say is true. Mother finally coerced her prodigal son into attending church last Sunday, and when I happened to glimpse Donald across the way, I thought it would be nice to get reacquainted. And knowing what charming hosts the Yarboroughs are, not to mention Patrice would be at home . . ." He spread his hands as if the other men couldn't possibly deny the logic in his reasoning.

Donald snorted. "I'm at the hospital fifty hours or more a week. You couldn't pop in there to say hello? Or invite me to meet you at a restaurant or coffeehouse? Why bring Miss Yarborough and her parents into this at all, when clearly they have no idea what your real intentions are?"

"You keep hinting about my *real intentions*." Gilbert's chin jerked. "What would those be, dare I ask?"

Samuel jammed his hands into his pockets to keep from throttling the man. "Answer the question, Gilbert."

"Which one? I heard two. Or was it three?"

Frustration clawed at Samuel's nerves. He sank onto the sofa, elbows braced on his knees. "Stop playing us for fools and give us a straight answer."

Sweat popping out on his upper lip, Gilbert massaged his left thigh until Samuel wondered how he kept from rubbing a hole through his trousers. Finally, he pinned Donald with an icy stare. "Admit it, Doc. You know there's bad blood between Sam and me. Since your loyalty is obviously to him—and seeing as how you've already determined I have ulterior motives—why would I assume you'd give me the time of day?"

Donald heaved a frustrated sigh. "Why wouldn't I, Gil? You were my patient. I cared about you then, and I care what happens to you now."

"Right. And I've got a surefire insider tip for you at the races this weekend."

Samuel and Donald exchanged looks. Gambling, drinking . . . and, judging from the sweating, dilated pupils, and increasingly noticeable muscle tics, most likely morphine addiction. Signs Samuel should have picked up on long ago. He'd certainly had plenty of experience talking and praying wounded doughboys through their dependence on painkillers.

He rose and went to stand in front of Gilbert's chair. Unceremoniously he relieved Gilbert of his brandy snifter. "You've had enough for one night. Why don't you go home? I can call Zachary for you. We'll see to Mary."

"Some nerve you've got, *Chaplain* Vickary." Gilbert spat the words, his mouth curling into an ugly snarl. "So faithful and pious, with your butter-wouldn't-melt-in-your-mouth charm. How can Annemarie not see right through your posturing?"

Now Donald stood, inserting himself between them—and probably saving Samuel from doing something he'd regret. His fists ached with the need to wipe that smug smile off his former friend's face.

"Sam's right," Donald said. "You need to leave before you disgrace yourself more than you already have."

Gilbert laughed out loud. "I'm willing to bet my army pension that I'm not the only one in this room who's disgraced himself." He gripped his cane with both hands, drew it to his shoulder, and pretended to fire it like a rifle—straight at Samuel's chest. "Gotcha."

Samuel recoiled with a shudder. For the space of half a second his vision clouded, and he was back in a bloody field in France.

"Sam." Donald's grip bit into his upper arms. "Sam, sit down. *Now.* Let me—"

"No—I'm—" Samuel's pulse thrummed in his ears. He sensed the darkness creeping closer, but he fought it. *The Lord is my shepherd . . . Yea, though I walk through the valley . . .*

"Confession is good for the soul, Sam." Gilbert's taunting voice echoed as if it came from deep inside a tomb, bouncing off the sides, slamming into Samuel's brain. "Who'd you kill, Sam? Braswell, wasn't it? Doesn't sound German to me."

The ringing in Samuel's ears intensified until it became one continuous barrage of machine-gun fire. Black and yellow and red—so much red—zigzagged across his vision. A part of his brain registered Donald's angry shout, "Who told you?"

"I overheard the two of you talking at the hospital. So what's the story, Doc? And why are you covering for this *honorable* man here?"

The room, the voices, the whole world receded, leaving Samuel at the gaping precipice of yet another hastily dug mass grave.

Sixty-seven dead after the latest skirmish. At least that was how many dog tags Samuel had gathered. Hundreds more, hammered and bloodied, would never lift another rifle or march into another battle. After slogging through the blood-soaked battlefield, sifting through remains that often no longer even resembled a human being, Samuel tasted the bile rising in his throat. Arms, legs, hands, feet—bits and pieces of human flesh scattered across endless acres like some macabre jigsaw puzzle.

Invisible giant pincers squeezed the air from Samuel's lungs and threatened to crush whatever life remained in his stammering, struggling heart. How many more would have to suffer and die before humanity—before God Himself—had had enough?

Sixty-seven dead. Sixty-seven bodies, or what was left of them, carried with as much grace and dignity as expedience would allow and laid to rest in one massive, anonymous grave. But Samuel knew their names, had made himself repeat and memorize each one as he turned their dog tags over to the battalion commander. Prayers had to be said, letters had to be written, families had to be comforted . . . when there was no comfort to be had.

Daylight faded as the last shovelfuls of dirt were scraped onto the funereal mound, when more shots rang out. Officers shouted commands. Return fire concussed the night air. Artillery from both sides arced overhead like shrieking red demons and blasted new craters into the already blackened, pockmarked earth.

Then the screams. The wretched, disbelieving screams of the wounded and dying.

Unbridled fury seared Samuel's throat. Still standing at the graveside, he stumbled in the soft dirt, went to his knees, pushed up again. Foxholes and gun emplacements lay between him and the enemy, but he wouldn't be deterred. "Please, God, make it stop! Make the killing stop!"

As he charged toward the battlefront, someone shouted his name. A doughboy clambered out of a foxhole and seized Samuel by the arm, nearly yanking him off his feet. "Padre! What are you doing? Get down!"

"Give me your rifle, Private—now!" Heaven be hanged, he'd fight like a real soldier if that's what it took to end this bloody war.

"No, Padre, you can't!"

"God's deserted us. I'll kill them all myself, every last one of them!" While enemy fire raged around them, Samuel grappled for control of the skinny kid's weapon, but the boy held firm. "Your sidearm, then. Give me something I can fight with. I won't—"

A shot. One single shot, close enough it rang in Samuel's ears. He felt the recoil against his chest. His hand stung. And then he was cradling Private Braswell's bleeding body, his own uniform soaked in Private Braswell's blood.

"I killed him." He sank to his knees—not in a stubbly field in France but on a plush Persian carpet in someone's dimly lit parlor. "God forgive me, I killed him."

"Crushed eggshells and coffee grounds, that's what my grandmum always used in her gardens."

"How interesting. I shall begin saving mine with tomorrow's breakfast."

The women's conversation had grown continually louder as voices rose in the parlor, but Annemarie barely comprehended the tedious discussion of gardening tips. She'd positioned her chair near the closed doors, all the while straining to hear what the men were saying in the other room. She caught only a few words here and there, something about killing and honor and . . .

A sudden and ominous silence descended beyond the French doors. Instinct drew Annemarie to her feet. She clutched the back of her chair, only vaguely aware the other women had ceased their prattle and now eyed her with confused stares.

Patrice touched her elbow. "Annemarie? Are you ill?"

Ears attuned to any further sounds from the parlor, Annemarie waved a dismissive hand.

Behind her, Mrs. Yarborough whispered, "Perhaps she needs to use the lavatory. Patrice, why don't you—"

"*Please*," Annemarie hissed. She edged toward the door, reached for the knob—

"Sam. Sam, can you hear me?" The urgency in Dr. Russ's tone sent an icy tremor up Annemarie's spine.

She pushed through the double doors and flew across the hall, only to draw up short at the parlor entrance at the sight of Sam crouched on the floor. He pressed his head into the carpet, his whole body convulsing with muted sobs.

Dr. Russ knelt beside him, his long, thin arms enfolding Samuel as if by sheer physical strength he could silence the demons. "It was an accident, Sam. It's over now. Just let it go."

For a long, crazed moment Annemarie could do nothing but stare, her mind screaming for answers. What had happened here? Who could do this to her Samuel?

She swung her gaze to Gilbert, her chest heaving on a wave of anger. "What did you say to him? *What have you done?*"

"I did it for us, Annemarie." Gilbert gripped the chair arms and pushed himself upright.

"For us?" she repeated. "There is no *us*."

"But there can be again." Gilbert fumbled for his cane, then wavered, his left leg buckling. While she simply stared in stark confusion, he reached down to adjust something on his artificial limb. Then he took two hesitant steps toward her, his free hand outstretched. "I should never have pushed you away like I did. I still love you, Annemarie. And you still love me. We can start over, like none of this ever happened."

She shook her head. "No. No, we can't."

Numb with shock and bewilderment, she turned to see Dr. Russ and a disheveled Pastor Yarborough lifting Samuel to his feet.

"Sorry for dozing off," the pastor muttered. "What happened? Did he take sick all of a sudden?"

"Never mind." Annoyance laced Dr. Russ's words. "Just help me get him to my car. I'm driving him to the hospital."

His words spurred Annemarie into motion. She darted to the doctor's side. "I'm going with you."

Dr. Russ paused only long enough to offer a regretful smile. "There's not room for you both this time. Leave him to me. I'll take good care of him."

Shaking with fear, aching with love, she could do nothing but watch Dr. Russ and Pastor Yarborough walk a stumbling, unseeing Sam out the front door and help him into the doctor's Roadster.

As she stood in the doorway watching the doctor drive away, Annemarie felt a gentle tug and turned to see Patrice at her side. "I'm sure he's in good hands," Patrice murmured. "Are you all right?"

The weight of the entire evening sank upon Annemarie's shoulders like a boulder. She hugged herself and waited for tears that refused to fall. Finally, she murmured, "I just want to go home."

30

$\mathscr{M}$ary stood in the shadows beside the staircase, one hand shoved against her roiling stomach, the other covering her mouth. Oh, mercy, she should have surmised from the start that Gilbert had more on his mind this evening than a friendly reunion with an army buddy. Hadn't he been a wee bit *too* contrite when she'd confronted him about his addictions? Promising to shape up, pleading for her forgiveness, assuring her he'd come calling and meet her mum like a proper gentleman.

And all for this—to win back the love of Miss Annemarie Kendall.

Except his grand plan appeared to have backfired. Well, fine and dandy for him.

While the Yarboroughs hovered around the poor Miss Kendall, fetching her wrap, the pastor offering to drive her home, Mary edged into the parlor. She spied Gilbert slumped in a chair, his artificial leg poking out stiff and straight, and all she wanted to do was pummel some sense into that curly black head of his.

Slowly, tiredly, he lifted his gaze to meet hers, his pupils like black, bottomless pits. A sheen of perspiration across his face reflected the lamplight. A dazed smile coaxed up the corners of his mouth. "My head hurts, Mary. Could you . . ."

Any other time she'd have welcomed him into her arms, happy to massage away the pain, thankful he needed her. She'd dared to hope need could grow into love.

She'd been wrong.

Arms folded, she stood before him. A coldness had settled in her bones. "Out of pills, are you? Out of friends as well, so it appears."

Squeezing his temples between his palms, he leaned forward and sucked air through his nostrils. "Help me, Mary. Help me."

"And why would I be helping you after you've gone and made a first-class fool of yourself—and of me?"

Glancing up, he extended his hand toward her. His whole arm trembled, whether from desperation or morphine withdrawal or both, she wouldn't hazard a guess. His eyes cleared for a moment, and in their depths she saw straight through to his tortured soul. "Why?" he said. "Because you love me."

"Indeed I do. And far better than you love yourself, Gilbert Ballard." Lips pressed flat, she went about realigning chairs and straightening throw pillows. Next, she found Mrs. Yarborough's tray, gathered up all the brandy snifters, and carried them to the kitchen. Never let anyone say Mary McClarney didn't know how to be a considerate guest.

And perhaps while she attended to such duties, Gilbert would use the time to pull his sorry self together enough to explain to her exactly what had transpired. In her service as an army nurse she'd cared for plenty of ill or wounded soldiers, but never in her life had she seen such stark and unholy torment as she'd read in Chaplain Vickary's eyes before Dr. Russ took him away—all brought on by Gilbert, she had no doubt.

Patrice met her as she returned from the kitchen. "Forgive me, Miss McClarney. I'm afraid with all the excitement we've completely neglected you."

Mary dipped her chin. "Think nothing of it. I'm more concerned about the poor chaplain."

"Quite staggering, isn't it? I can't imagine what came over him. He seemed fine at dinner." Patrice clucked her tongue. "A dreadful end to the evening, I'm afraid. And so sad for Annemarie."

"Yes. Annemarie."

Always Annemarie.

"Father has just left to drive her home." Patrice slid a disapproving glance toward the parlor. "I daresay we should have asked him to take you as well. Perhaps when Father returns—"

"Don't trouble yourself. I'll just be fetching my wrap, and Gilbert and I will be on our way."

Not that she had a clue as to how she'd maneuver a near-stuporous Gilbert out the door and into the driver's seat of his car. She could only hope the fresh air would revive him enough so he wouldn't steer them into a gully or off the side of a mountain before he got her safely home.

What he did to himself afterward, she didn't much care.

Or so she tried to convince herself. They'd driven only a block or two—thankfully doing no worse damage than running the left front tire through the Yarboroughs' flowerbed as they left—when she insisted Gilbert pull over.

"Now, Gilbert Ballard, you'll be telling me what in heaven's name you said to Chaplain Vickary that left him in such a state."

He kept his hands on the steering wheel, his eyes forward. He appeared more clearheaded now, his chest rising and falling with slow, purposeful breaths. "You don't want to know, Mary. You really don't want to know."

"I think I deserve to know, considering how I let you use me as one of your pawns in whatever malicious game you were playing."

Muttering a curse, Gilbert pounded a fist against the steering wheel and then broke down in tears. "I didn't know. . . . How could I have known?" He shot her a look of desperation. "God help me, Mary, I've destroyed him!"

❦

Annemarie held herself rigid as she stood before the hospital reception desk. "I'm here to see Chaplain Vickary."

The elderly nurse on duty offered a tight-lipped smile. "The chaplain is unavailable until further notice. Is there someone else—"

"He's a patient here. I know." Annemarie balled her hands into fists. "Just tell me how to find his room."

A pause. "Are you a relative?"

"No, but I'm—" *I'm the woman he loves, the woman who adores him more than life itself. The woman who can't wait even a moment longer to be with him, to hold him in my arms and kiss away the nightmares.* She blinked back a tear, fighting to control the tremor in her voice. "I'm Annemarie Kendall. Please, I must see him."

The nurse's eyes softened. "Ah, yes, Miss Kendall. Let me check with the charge nurse."

Nodding her thanks, Annemarie stepped away while the woman rang someone on the hospital telephone. Moments later she signaled Annemarie over. "I'm told you may go up. Dr. Russ will meet you at the nurses' station."

Annemarie waited barely long enough for the nurse to direct her to Samuel's floor before she raced up the nearest flight of stairs. By the time she skidded around a corner and spotted Dr. Russ at the desk, her pulse thundered in her ears.

Dr. Russ looked up from the chart he was studying. "Annemarie. I'm so sorry I didn't call you before now."

"Never mind. Just tell me how Sam's doing. I've been so sick with worry I didn't even go to bed last night." The scent of potter's clay still clung to her hands, but she doubted any of the pieces she'd thrown in those tense, toilsome hours would even be worth firing.

Dr. Russ motioned toward the waiting area. The last thing Annemarie felt like doing was sitting quietly and listening to a long medical explanation of Sam's condition, but she could see from the doctor's expression he was as worried about Sam as she.

She sat stiffly on the edge of a worn tweed armchair. "Just tell me. Is he going to be all right?"

"In time." Pacing in front of her, Dr. Russ massaged the back of his neck. "Last night was . . . well, frankly, it was inevitable. I'd just hoped Sam's memories would return under much more controlled—and far less hostile—circumstances."

"Memories? From the war?" Annemarie clutched her abdomen. "Are you saying he'd intentionally blocked things out?"

A tortured look deepened the doctor's frown. He pulled a wooden chair closer to Annemarie and sat down, hands clasped between his knees. With quiet deliberation, he told of the first time he'd met Sam, the day an ambulance had brought him to the field hospital where Dr. Russ was assigned. At first he'd thought the chaplain had been wounded—there was an incredible amount of blood soaking his uniform—but after a thorough physical examination the doctor determined it was only a severe case of shell-shock.

"*Only.*" Dr. Russ uttered a cynical laugh. "I say it like it was nothing serious. No more serious than the thousands of other soldiers who'd had all the war they could stomach." His neck arched. A vile, sickening sound came from his throat. "No one—*no one* with an ounce of humanity in his bones—can go through what these men did and come through it unchanged."

Samuel, Gilbert . . . Annemarie's heart broke for both of them. For all the soldiers America had sent to war. "Please," she murmured, gently touching the doctor's arm. "Tell me about Sam."

Dr. Russ sighed and sat straighter, looking off to the side as if reliving the events he described. "All I knew at first was a chaplain had lost it on the battlefield when a doughboy died in his arms. But the things Sam said in his sleep . . . I knew there had to be more to the story. When they brought in a wounded soldier from his unit a couple of weeks later, I finally talked the guy into telling me what happened—but only after he made me promise I'd never betray his padre."

The doctor then described how Samuel had just presided over a mass burial for nearly seventy dead soldiers. Exhausted both emotionally and physically, when the next round of fighting broke out he'd gone berserk. As he grappled with a private over control of his weapons, the private's own pistol discharged, killing him instantly.

Annemarie thrust a hand to her mouth to stifle a sob. *Oh, dear Jesus, help my poor Sam!*

"It was pretty clear Sam didn't remember all the details, and I wasn't going to be the one to tell him. Bad enough he blamed himself for Private Braswell's death. Until last night, he believed what was logged in the official report, that the boy was killed by enemy fire, not his own gun."

As Annemarie let the doctor's words sink in, a tremor began deep in her belly. Her clenched fists shook as she raised her eyes to meet Dr. Russ's. "Gilbert—he knew all this?"

"Not all of it. Apparently he overheard part of a conversation between Sam and me, just enough to give him the ammunition he was looking for." The doctor pushed to his feet and resumed his pacing. "Why he felt he had to bring down a good man like Sam, though, I'll never understand."

Annemarie understood—far too well. That the charming boy she'd grown up with, the brave and honorable man she had once loved, could stoop to such a dishonorable act of revenge— the thought made her sick with anger and disillusionment.

Slowly she stood. "Please take me to see Sam now."

Dr. Russ skewed his lips. "I have him heavily sedated. He needs to rest. He's not alone, though. His mother's with him. She cancelled her train ticket home."

Annemarie's heart broke all over again at the thought of what Sam's mother must be going through. "Poor Ursula. Does she need anything? Can I—"

"I think she just dozed off, actually. It's been a long night."

The longest night of Annemarie's life! Torn between consideration for Sam's mother and the yearning to rush to his side, she prayed for patience. "Then I won't disturb her. Is it all right if I wait here? Will you send for me—"

"Of course." Dr. Russ draped an arm around her shoulder in a brotherly hug. "He'll pull through this. He's suffered a huge setback, but his faith will carry him through."

Annemarie would have to rely on faith as well, and though it took every ounce of willpower she possessed, on her way out of the hospital she paused to pray for the man responsible for this tragic turn of events.

Then she marched up Central Avenue, through the front doors of the Arlington Hotel, and straight to the front desk. "Gilbert Ballard—is he in?"

The startled desk clerk withered beneath her searing gaze. "Well, ma'am, I don't rightly know—".

"Just direct me to his office, then."

"Down the hall, take a right at the first corner, then the third door on your left."

With a crisp "Thank you," Annemarie pivoted on her heel and strode away.

Minutes later she arrived at the doorway to a closet-sized, windowless office. The room was so crammed with furniture and filing cabinets she could barely squeeze in edgewise. Fortunately—or perhaps *un*fortunately—the object of her wrath was indeed at his desk, and looking as haggard as she'd ever seen him.

Gilbert glanced up, his glassy eyes widening at the sight of her. He fumbled around, straightening his shirt collar and tie, running a nervous hand along his stubbly jaw. "If you came to inform me what a shameless heel I am—"

"Shameless about sums it up." Annemarie's chest lifted. She stepped closer, shoving an annoying strand of hair off her face. "I don't even know you anymore, Gilbert Ballard. And I cannot begin to fathom what your father would have to say if he could see you now. *Disappointed* would barely cover it. He would be heartbroken, disgraced, disgusted."

Gilbert braced an elbow on the desk and planted his forehead in the palm of his hand. Trembling fingers wove through his black tangle of hair. "Call me every name in the book. I deserve it."

Seeing him so weak and broken brought back memories of the day he'd returned from the war, and it wrenched Annemarie's heart. She moved a stack of files from a chair and then sat down, one hand reaching across the desk. "Why?" she murmured. "Just tell me why."

He sniffed. "Because I never stopped loving you."

"You think I don't know that?" She closed her eyes briefly. "You lie so terribly, you know. You always have."

A wry laugh rattled his throat. "Guess it's why I'm so lousy at poker."

"Oh, Gilbert, Gilbert . . ." Annemarie tugged his hand away from his face and held it tightly in her own. Tears slid down her cheeks. "I wish I could erase everything that happened to you in France. I wish the war had never happened at all, to any of us. I wish—"

"If wishes were horses, beggars would ride." Sitting a little straighter, Gilbert examined her clay-stained fingertips. "Bet I know where you spent last night. I'm sorry, Annemarie." He lifted his gaze to hers, his voice breaking. "I'm so terribly, terribly sorry."

"I believe you." Slowly, hesitantly, she withdrew her hands and folded them in her lap. "But an apology alone can't undo the destruction you've caused. Because of you, Samuel is now living a nightmare he may never awaken from, battling demons I'm not certain he has enough faith to defeat."

"I didn't know what I was doing." Gilbert shuddered. "I honestly didn't mean for it to go this far. I just wanted—"

"I know exactly what you wanted. But it's too late. You can't play God with people's hearts."

He splayed his hands across the desk, his head lowered. "Can you forgive me . . . or at least not hate me?"

"I am praying fervently for the strength to forgive you. Perhaps in time, when Sam is better and this is all behind us . . ." Annemarie stood with a tired sigh. She ached to reach out and run her fingers once more through those raven curls. But as a concerned friend, nothing more.

As she turned to leave, she added softly, "I do still love you, Gilbert. I always will. But I've given my heart to Sam."

". . . more unrest in Germany and Poland. How disturbing."
A rustle of newspaper accompanied the softly spoken words.

Samuel recognized his mother's voice and slid his eyes open.
She sat silhouetted in a sunbeam pouring through the window,
and for a moment the brightness dazzled him.

"Look, he's waking up." Donald's voice came from somewhere near Samuel's feet.

Confused, Samuel shifted his gaze to take in his surroundings. "What's this—the hospital?" His tongue stuck to the roof
of his mouth like a thick wad of cotton. He tried to raise himself
on one elbow, but his limbs felt as if they belonged to someone
else. "What happened to me?"

"There, there, son." His mother came to his side and pressed
him back against the pillow. "You've been asleep for a long
while, that's all."

"Let's sit you up some." Donald came around to the other side
of the bed and cranked the head up several degrees. "Thirsty,
I'll bet." He offered Samuel a glass of water.

Drinking gratefully, Sam fumbled around his brain for some
memory of what had landed him in a hospital bed.

Then he remembered, and the water he'd just swallowed
surged back into his throat on a wave of bile. He shoved the
glass into Donald's hand and then pressed his palms into his
eye sockets. His whole body shook. "No . . . no . . . please,
God, no!"

Arms wrapped around him, cradled him, soothed him. Tears
mingled with his own. "Let it go, son. It was an accident. You
can't keep blaming yourself."

A needle pricked his arm, and the room faded to velvet
blackness.

When he roused again, night enveloped him. The only illu-
mination was a sliver of light from the corridor. Gradually he

became aware of someone's hand wrapped around his. A dark form slumped upon the edge of the mattress.

The figure stirred, sighed, stretched. Then, "Sam? Are you awake?"

Annemarie! Her nearness brought such sweet agony he couldn't make his throat work to form a reply. He pulled her hand to his chest and held it there while he tried to make sense of the past few hours . . . days . . . or had it been weeks?

"Oh, my dear Sam!" She sat on the bed next to him and laid her head in the crook of his shoulder. Her soft, warm lips grazed his neck. "It's all right, Sam. Everything's going to be all right."

He wanted to believe her. With every fiber of his being, he wanted to believe her.

But then once more the memories crowded in. He'd killed a man. *He* had killed Private Braswell. Not a bullet from a German rifle but from Braswell's own sidearm. And Samuel's finger had been on the trigger.

God, forgive me. Oh Lord, forgive me!

For taking a soldier's life, for blaming God, for running from the truth all these months instead of resting in God's mercy and goodness.

He trembled, and Annemarie nestled closer, her love so pure, so powerful, Samuel could scarcely take it in. He didn't deserve such love.

"As much as she loves you, I love you even more, My son." The words resonated in his spirit as clearly as if God had spoken them aloud. *"Be strong and of good courage . . . for it is the Lord your God who goes with you; he will not fail you or forsake you."*

Newfound peace burrowed deep into Samuel's heart. He shifted his head until he could peer into Annemarie's eyes— two shimmering pools of liquid satin reflecting the light from the corridor. He swept aside the silky strand she could never keep out of her eyes and then kissed her forehead. "I'll be all right now," he said, meaning it, believing it as never before. "You should go home, get some rest."

"I don't want to leave you." Her breath warmed his cheek with whispered urgency.

Gently he eased her off his chest, nudging her until she stood beside the bed. He sat up slowly, his brain still foggy from whatever drugs they'd given him, and then pulled her into his arms. He kissed the back of her hand, inhaling the earthy smells of clay she could never quite wash away. "I mean it. Go home—and *not* to your pottery wheel."

The door edged open, admitting a wider shaft of light. Donald Russ's tall, thin frame filled the opening. "Thought I heard voices in here."

Samuel winced. "If you've brought another needle . . ."

"Do you need one? Or are you ready to rejoin the living?"

"Beyond ready. How long has it been, anyway?"

"Just a couple of days, actually. Today's . . ." Donald checked his watch. "Well, I suppose it's already tomorrow. It's ten past twelve on Monday, the last day of March."

Two days lost. It was enough. Samuel returned his gaze to Annemarie. Now that he could see her more clearly, he realized how haggard she looked—her dress rumpled, her hair coming unpinned, dark smudges beneath her eyes. The thought that he'd put her through such torment only added to his remorse.

But he could still make things right. With God's help he would.

"Donald, would you please see that this lady gets home safely?" He squeezed Annemarie's hand. "I'd like to get some sleep now—some *real* sleep, without the help of your infernal drugs—and tomorrow I'll be going away for a while."

"Sam?" The anxiety in Annemarie's voice ripped holes in his heart.

"There's something I have to do. Something I should have had the courage to do a long time ago."

"But you'll be back?"

Would he—*could* he return? He bowed his head and sighed. "The future is out of my hands. I can't promise anything except that I will always love you."

31

Stupid, stupid girl. Mary blinked until her eyes cleared and tried once more to focus on the patient's chart she held. If she'd claimed a wink of sleep all week, it was by God's grace alone. Since Gilbert had finally gotten sober enough to take her home last Friday, she'd made herself half-crazy between fretting over the brainless, besotted idiot, who hadn't so much as called since then, and berating herself for still—*still!*—holding out hope he'd come crawling back to her.

"Mary?" Lois nudged her with an elbow. "Not crying over that heel again, are you?"

"Had something in my eye, that's all."

"Sure you did." Giving a snort, Lois thumbed through a stack of medical orders. "Believe me, honey, he's not worth it. Forget the creep. Find yourself a guy who'll treat you right."

"Don't lecture me. I've not the patience for it." Mary swiveled away from the desk before Lois gave her another earful of endless yet utterly useless advice for the lovelorn.

Lois gave a tiny gasp. "Um, Mary . . ."

She turned, ready to launch into her own lecture about minding one's own business, especially on hospital time, when she found herself riveted by Gilbert's beseeching stare.

He edged up to the desk. "I need to talk to you, Mary."

A quavering began deep inside her belly, whether from anger or panic or unrequited love, she couldn't honestly say. She strove to keep her voice level. "I'm working, as you can plainly see. This isn't a good—"

"*Please.*" Gilbert brought his clenched fist down upon the desk with quiet insistence, then repeated more gently, "Please." His gaze shifted nervously in Lois's direction, and he lowered his voice even more. "I'm sober now. I've had time to think."

One look in those desperate hazel eyes and Mary was done for. She handed her chart to Lois. "Lieutenant Zipp has a physical therapy session in ten minutes. Can you wheel him over for me?"

Lois lifted one eyebrow as she took the chart. "Are you sure?"

Firming her mouth, Mary gave a single nod. Lois reluctantly left on the errand, and Mary motioned Gilbert toward a nearby waiting room. Once inside, she closed the door and then leaned against it, afraid her legs wouldn't hold her.

Gilbert stared out the window for what seemed like an eternity before he sighed and pivoted to face her. "Here I go, apologizing again." His attempt at a chuckle sounded more like a tired, pathetic moan.

Mary crossed her arms but didn't budge from the door. "If you weren't so good at getting yourself into trouble, you wouldn't have to apologize so often."

She expected his usual sarcasm, or at least a rakish curl of his lips, but instead he closed his eyes and lowered his head. "I deserved that." Looking up, he took a step toward her, and she couldn't stop herself from cringing. If he touched her now, she'd crumble. Fall right back into his arms as if nothing had changed. *Dear Jesus, give me strength!*

She hiked her chin and forced herself to stand erect but kept one hand on the doorknob, as if it could save her from her own treacherous emotions. "Just speak your piece and be done with it. I've work to do."

Gilbert ran a hand across his eyes as he hauled in a shaky breath. "Like I said, I came to apologize, not that it's worth anything after what I've put you through. But I wanted to tell you face-to-face you were right. Right about everything."

Mary narrowed her gaze. "Everything?"

"The morphine. My feelings for Annemarie . . ." He glanced away, then back again, his voice faltering. "The fact that I was just using you."

The words sliced through Mary like a scalpel, and she cried out before she could stop herself.

"I never meant to hurt you, Mary." He took two strides closer, reached out, and grazed her cheek with the ball of his thumb. "I care for you. Please believe me."

She drew away from his touch. Her lips trembled. "You've a fine way of showing it."

Both hands locked upon his cane, he straightened, his eyes as clear as she'd ever seen them. "Give me a chance and I will. I'm going to fix things, Mary. You have my word."

He left moments later, without so much as stealing a kiss or even pretending to offer his typical empty promises. Instead, he simply said, "Wait for me."

As the door closed behind him, she stumbled across the room and sank upon a tattered sofa, hands clasped until her knuckles whitened. "Let his words be true, Father. Don't let me hope in vain!"

*

"I hope you enjoy the vases, Mrs. Fox. Thank you for coming in." Annemarie handed the petite, silver-haired woman her wrapped purchases along with a receipt. "And bring your grandson by one day soon and we'll talk about pottery-making lessons."

As the door closed upon the brisk April afternoon, Ursula Vickary came up beside Annemarie. "Sharing your talents with the next generation of potters? What a lovely thing to do."

"More necessity than altruism." She reached for the apron she'd draped across the back of a chair. "I decided giving lessons might be one way my studio could generate a little more income."

Ursula clucked her tongue. "I sincerely hope you aren't still fretting about repaying Samuel and me for our investment. Why, I expect in the near future, it won't matter one whit."

Annemarie's stomach clenched. "Have you heard from Sam? Is he coming home soon?"

"No word yet. I just meant . . ." Shrugging, Ursula offered a sympathetic smile before reaching for the feather duster beneath the counter. "Don't you need to get back to your workshop? I'm excited to see how the new glaze you've been experimenting with will turn out."

As always, work remained Annemarie's sole distraction from the concerns she couldn't shake. Samuel had left shortly after noon on Monday saying only that he needed to lay some old ghosts to rest. He wouldn't even permit Annemarie to see him off at the train station but insisted on saying their good-byes at the shop. Not even a flood of tears had swayed him to offer assurance of his prompt return. All he would do was repeat, "It's out of my hands."

It was Thursday already, and Annemarie felt she'd go mad if she didn't hear from him soon. Ursula's decision to extend her stay in Hot Springs brought a measure of comfort, not only for her continued help in the studio but also because the woman's presence gave Annemarie hope Samuel would eventually return to them. She had to believe that when he did, he'd be all the stronger for having taken this time to put the past behind him.

If only it wasn't taking so long!

Hours later, Ursula called to Annemarie from the workroom door. "It's closing time, dear. Are you going to stay and work awhile longer?"

"I think I will." Annemarie studied the depth of color on the decorative urn she'd been working with. More green, less blue . . . and perhaps a touch of amber. "Any more customers this afternoon?"

"Two, in fact. I sold a pair of candlesticks and a ewer-and-bowl set. Oh, and one of the ladies placed an order for a dessert service."

Annemarie smiled her satisfaction. Maybe she'd yet make a go of this enterprise. She dipped her brush in a pot of glaze.

Ursula cleared her throat meaningfully. "You *will* stop soon and go home to supper, won't you?"

"As soon as I finish here." Smirking, Annemarie raised one hand. "I promise."

She vaguely heard the click of the lock as Ursula left through the front door. Then moments later someone rapped on the glass. Surely, Ursula had set the *closed* sign in the window—or perhaps she'd forgotten something and couldn't get her key to work.

Laying aside her paintbrush, Annemarie wiped her hands on a stained rag as she marched to the front of the studio. "Coming, coming . . ."

When she saw who waited on the other side of the door, her stomach heaved.

Gilbert.

No, Lord, I can't, not today—

"Annemarie, please let me in. Please."

Her hand shook as she reached for the latch. She pulled open the door. "You shouldn't have come, Gilbert. There's nothing more to be said between us."

His forlorn expression almost made her regret her dismissive tone. He took one step into the shop and glanced around. "I thought maybe Samuel would be here. The hospital would only say he's no longer a patient Dr. Russ won't even talk to me."

Annemarie crossed her arms. "Can you blame him?"

"Not in the least." He cast a sheepish frown toward the floor before lifting pleading eyes to Annemarie. "Please, just tell me where I can find Sam. I need to make things right with him or I won't be able to live with myself."

"I'm sorry, but *I* don't even know where Sam has gone off to." The truth of her words brought a quaver to her voice.

"What are you saying? He's left town?" Gilbert reached out as if to grasp her arm, but when she flinched, he drew back.

"Yes, he's gone, thanks to you!" Whatever measure of forgiveness she'd accrued over the past few days evaporated—along with the fragile remnants of hope she'd ever see Sam again.

Beads of perspiration dotted Gilbert's ashen face. He gripped the doorframe. "I swear I'll make this up to you and Sam if it's the last thing I do."

Then, before she could reply, he swiveled on his heel and marched out of the shop. Hugging herself in the doorway, Annemarie watched as he strode up Central Avenue and climbed into the backseat of the Ballards' sleek Peerless. Seconds later, the car sped away.

She could only pray Gilbert wouldn't try anything more impulsively stupid than he'd done already.

Two long days and nights on the train, and now two sleepless nights in a shabby Denver hotel room while Samuel contemplated what exactly he'd say to Mr. and Mrs. Braswell.

Provided they'd even agree to talk with him.

Upon arriving in Denver, he'd made discreet inquiries about the family based on what he remembered about Private Eddie Braswell. The son of a schoolteacher, Eddie was the eldest of five children. Friends said the boy was a mediocre student but a hard worker—always diligent, always dependable, always dutiful. After Wilson declared war, Eddie had been the first among his peers to enlist in the army.

"Yessiree, he's sorely missed around here," an elderly neighbor told Samuel as they stood on the man's front lawn late Friday afternoon. "You knew him? Served over yonder in France, did you?"

"I did." Samuel ran a thumb along the worn edge of his Bible and gazed up the street toward the Braswell home. "Do you know what time Mr. Braswell gets home from school?"

The neighbor checked his watch. "Anytime now. Five o'clock at the latest. But his wife'll be home. I'm sure she'd be mighty pleased to chat with someone who knew Eddie from the war."

Samuel seriously doubted it.

"Eddie's buried somewhere on the front lines, his folks say. Hear tell they can't even find many of the graves, so those boys'll never make it home for a proper burial." The man's gaze drifted to Samuel's chaplaincy insignia. "But I reckon you'd know all about that."

Samuel gave a solemn nod. A motion caught his eye, and he looked up to see a slump-shouldered man in a brown suit trudging along the sidewalk.

"There's Ed Braswell now," the neighbor said. He clucked his tongue. "Hasn't been the same since Eddie Junior was killed. Just drifts along like a tumbleweed most days."

The man turned in at a picket gate. Steeling himself, Samuel thanked the elderly gentleman for his time and then strode up the street.

"Mr. Braswell," he called as the man reached a weathered front door with peeling gray paint.

Pausing with his hand on the knob, Mr. Braswell turned with a smile that quickly changed to a look of confusion. "A little late for the army to be sending a chaplain by, isn't it?"

"The army didn't send me." Standing outside the fence, Samuel brushed aside a drooping, unkempt vine. "May I come in, Mr. Braswell? I knew Eddie. I . . . I was with him when he died."

An hour later, the truth laid bare before Private Braswell's parents, Samuel sat with his hands locked around his Bible. He hadn't opened it once, but simply holding it served to remind him that no matter what happened next, God was with him.

Slowly he raised his head. "Words will never suffice to express my profound remorse for causing the death of your son. I want you to know that when I leave here, I'm turning myself in to the military authorities."

"Is that necessary, Chaplain? We know it was an accident." Mr. Braswell drew his wife's hand into his lap. "There's been plenty of pain to go around. No need adding to it."

"Ed's right," Mrs. Braswell said through her tears. "Eddie would hate to think of you being punished for his death. He looked up to you—wrote letters talking about how brave you were, how you encouraged all the soldiers with your faith in Jesus. Why, he even wrote that maybe after the war he'd like to become a pastor and serve the Lord just like you."

Samuel's throat closed. He'd come here dreading condemnation at worst, praying for forgiveness at best. He never expected to be blessed so extravagantly through a fallen soldier's letters home.

Even so, by morning he'd boarded a train headed for Camp Dix, New Jersey, where he intended to seek out his former battalion commander, set the record straight, and accept whatever disciplinary action a military court deemed appropriate.

Staring out across fields and forests greening up from spring rains, Samuel fingered the cross pinned to his collar and wondered how much longer he'd be wearing the uniform of an army chaplain.

32

*H*ead throbbing from morphine withdrawal, Gilbert reined in his impatience while Colonel Nelson Peters perused a file. The grizzled officer, one side of his face scarred with burns, deftly flipped pages with his left hand. The stump of his right arm was tucked away inside a folded coat sleeve.

Colonel Peters sat back. "The report says Private Braswell was shot while trying to get his company chaplain out of harm's way. You're saying this is incorrect?"

"No, sir." Gilbert repressed a growl. "I'm saying Chaplain Vickary may try to submit a different account, and I want to make certain the facts aren't distorted."

Clearly confused, the colonel tapped the pages with his stubby fingers. "But you just told me you weren't there. Private Braswell's commanding officer, who cites accounts from actual witnesses, signed off on this report. Exactly which facts are in question here?"

Gilbert rubbed his jaw. It hadn't taken much imagination to guess Samuel's intentions. Honorable to a fault, what else would the man do after regaining his memory but confess his guilt? So Gilbert had made the journey all the way to Camp

Dix hoping against hope to arrive in time to keep Sam from possibly ruining the rest of his life. But apparently Sam hadn't shown up yet, and now Gilbert had talked himself into a corner with no way to backpedal.

"Excuse me, Colonel." The adjutant sidled into the office. "Sorry for the interruption, sir, but there's a Chaplain Samuel Vickary here, and he insists upon seeing you immediately."

Colonel Peters arched a brow. "Hmm, as Lewis Carroll's Alice would say, 'Curiouser and curiouser.' Then let's not keep the chaplain waiting. Send him in."

"Wait." Seizing his cane, Gilbert snapped to his feet, locking his artificial knee before he tumbled face down upon the colonel's desk. "Please, sir, if I could speak with Chaplain Vickary first—"

"Gilbert?" Cap in hand, Samuel entered the room. A wary look clouded his eyes. "I . . . don't understand. Why are you here?"

The colonel pushed his chair back and propped one ankle across the opposite knee. "I've been trying to determine that for myself. Chaplain, it seems the lieutenant is concerned you're going to dispute a battlefield report, and for some reason he thinks he knows more than either you or your company commander."

Swiveling to confront Sam, Gilbert lowered his voice to a rasping plea. "Don't, Sam. Let the report stand."

Samuel edged forward. "Why are you doing this?"

"Because I'm a cursed fool." Sweat soaked Gilbert's armpits. He clenched both fists around the handle of his cane in an effort to still the muscle spasms. "Because I've hurt the two friends I value most in this world, and I want to make things right."

Forgiveness shone in Samuel's eyes, but he gave his head a sad shake. "Scripture says, 'You shall know the truth, and the truth shall make you free.' I'm here to make things right, too."

"Sam, I'm begging you. Go back to Annemarie and live your life."

The colonel stood and strode around his desk. "All right, gentlemen, let's have some answers. Somebody better explain right now, or I'll have you both thrown in the brig for wasting my time."

✐

Over a week had gone by with not so much as a word from Samuel. Annemarie hefted the misshapen vase she'd removed from the kiln earlier and flung it against the workroom wall. Shards of pottery rained down in a sickly satisfying torrent.

A deep-throated chuckle sounded behind her. "Perhaps I should come back another time."

Cheeks flaming, Annemarie whirled around to face her father. "It was ruined anyway."

"Well, it certainly is now." Papa scanned the room and then marched over to the corner where Annemarie kept a broom and dustpan. He began sweeping up the broken pottery. "I daresay this is no way to run a business, young lady. Producing shoddy inventory? I thought I taught you better."

Annemarie might argue with her father if the vase were her only failed attempt. Unfortunately, since Samuel had left town, she'd produced a whole boxful of irregular pieces not worth the clay she'd used.

She flounced over and yanked the broom from her father's hands. "I can clean up my own messes, thank you very much."

Papa planted his fists against his hips. "Are you sure about that, lassie?" His voice softened. "Because it seems to me you've gotten yourself into quite a mess with those two young men in your life."

"Don't lecture me, Papa."

"I'm merely stating a fact." He snatched back the broom and continued sweeping.

Groaning, Annemarie sank onto the stool at her worktable. "If you're not here to lecture me, then why *are* you here in the middle of a workday? Aren't you needed at the factory?"

Papa emptied the dustpan into a waste bin and then brushed off his hands. "Truth be told, I've been missing my girl. Bad enough your pretty face isn't gracing the front office anymore. But to make matters worse, you're rarely home in time for dinner, and you worked so long and hard last weekend you didn't even go to church with us on Sunday."

"I should have, I know. But the thought of facing everyone . . ."

"By 'everyone,' you mean the Ballards, I take it . . . or just one of them in particular?"

"I can't help it. After what Gilbert did to Sam—" Even more worrisome was the thought of what he might do next, if he hadn't already. Annemarie folded her elbows on the table, tears pooling in her eyes.

"There, now, don't cry, Annie-girl." Her father came to her side and enfolded her against his warm, solid chest.

She snuggled close, taking comfort in the manly potpourri of aromas—smoke and clay and bay rum aftershave. "What if Sam doesn't come back, Papa? How can I live without him?"

The rough hand patting her back stilled. Her father straightened. "I don't believe it's a question you'll ever need answered."

"What?" Annemarie lifted her head. "Why would you—"

From the corner of her eye, she glimpsed a shadow in the workroom doorway. Twisting out of her father's embrace, she gave a shriek and leapt to her feet. "Sam! Oh, Sam!"

Then she was in his arms, holding him, kissing him, running frantic hands along the stubbly growth of whiskers on his cheeks as if to convince herself she wasn't dreaming. He looked tired and travel-worn, and smelled faintly of tobacco, but an immutable spark lit his eyes. He cradled her face in his palms before claiming her lips in a passionate kiss that left no doubt her Sam had finally come home.

✐❧

Home. Samuel could no longer remember a time when he hadn't thought of Hot Springs, Arkansas, as home. From the moment he first admitted his love for Annemarie, he'd somehow known home would always mean anywhere she was.

Loathe as he was to end the kiss, he needed even more to see her face, to look into her eyes and see the love shining there. He swept the tears from her cheeks with his thumbs. "My darling, my darling, don't cry."

"I was afraid . . . so afraid I'd never see you again." Sobs choked her. She kept her arms locked around him as if she'd never let him go again. "What were you doing all this time? Why didn't you call or write?"

Samuel cast a glance toward Annemarie's father, who stood a few paces away. "Sir, may I take your daughter for a walk? I have some explaining to do."

"I'm sure you do, lad." Mr. Kendall motioned them toward the rear door. "Not to worry, Annie-girl. I'll keep an eye on the shop."

Annemarie looked none too comfortable leaving the showroom in her father's care. With a quick glance over her shoulder, she slid her hand into Samuel's as he closed the door behind them. They walked in silence to the end of the alley and then turned up a long, climbing lane off Central Avenue. West Mountain loomed behind the houses on their right, the trees green and lush with April freshness, the scent of pine heavy in the air.

"Well? I'm waiting." Annemarie slowed her pace, while her grip on Samuel's hand tightened.

He told her then how he'd searched out Private Braswell's parents and confessed his responsibility for their son's death. He told about their incredible kindness, their understanding, and forgiveness. He told how he'd traveled from Denver to Fort Dix to correct the report and turn himself in, only to find Gilbert waiting for him in the colonel's office.

"Gilbert was there?" Alarm filled Annemarie's eyes. "Why?"

"He wanted to stop me."

"Stop you from telling the truth?"

"I couldn't let him. I couldn't have lived with myself otherwise." Samuel smoothed the worry lines from Annemarie's forehead. "But it's all right. Everything's all right now."

It still brought a catch to his throat to realize how the men in his company had tried to protect their chaplain. Colonel Peters had shown him the report, in which everyone questioned swore Braswell had been hit by enemy fire. "Even after I confessed what really happened," Samuel told Annemarie, "the colonel refused to amend the report. He said as far as he was concerned, 'enemy fire' was accurate, because Satan was surely running rampant that day."

"Oh, Sam, Sam . . ." Beneath a spreading oak, Annemarie cradled his face in her hand.

He kissed her fingertips, the earthy taste of clay lingering upon his lips. "On the train ride home I spent more time in my Bible than I had in months. And the Lord kept sending me back to a particular passage again and again—the verses from Jeremiah 18, where he goes down to the potter's house."

Annemarie smiled. "I know the one you mean. 'And when the vessel that he made of the clay was marred in the hand of the potter, he made it again another vessel, as seemed good to the potter to make it. ' I've pondered the verse many times as I've worked at the wheel."

"I feel as though I've been pounded down and reworked quite a bit this past year." Samuel drew Annemarie into his arms. "I don't know yet what God is making me into, but I do know His ways are good."

"Yes, God *is* good, and so are you." Annemarie tilted her head to gaze into his eyes. "You're a good man, Samuel Vickary. An honorable man. A man I'm proud to know and to love."

Samuel swallowed over the lump in his throat. He pressed her hand to his thudding heart. "A man you'd take as your husband?"

Annemarie's breath hitched. "Are you proposing?"

He grinned. "I am."

She snuggled closer, her eyes shining. "Then I'm accepting!"

Epilogue

It was a perfect June afternoon with not a cloud in the sky, the sun blazing across the Ouachitas in all their forested splendor—a perfect day for a wedding if ever there was one. Only a few short hours ago, Samuel's bride had promised before God, their families, and half the city of Hot Springs, if the overflowing church pews were any indication, to love, honor, and cherish him as long as they both should live.

Never had she looked more beautiful.

Never had he felt more alive and whole.

"Well?" Annemarie poked him in the ribs. "Are you going to stand there all day with a silly grin on your face, or will you perform the required husbandly duty and carry me over the threshold?"

He laughed. "Is it a requirement? What if I injure my back? Trip and fall? Drop you on your—"

"You wouldn't dare!"

"Oh, wouldn't I?" With a provocative grin, Samuel scooped Annemarie into his arms, crushing yards of white satin and lace between them.

Annemarie gasped. "Sam! What are you—"

Silencing his bride with a kiss, Samuel carried her through the front door of his newly purchased two-bedroom bungalow and then plopped her onto her feet in the middle of the parlor. "Welcome home, Mrs. Vickary."

She sighed and nestled against his chest, and the sweet scent of jasmine filled his nostrils. "Oh, Sam, I've never been happier."

For a moment the old worries crept in. "Do you mean it? No regrets?"

Annemarie leaned back to cup his cheeks with her palms. Her gaze grew dark and stern. "Samuel Vickary, don't you ever ask me such a thing again. If I regret anything, it's that it took me so long to realize God had been shaping us for this day all along."

"I suppose He was." Samuel pulled her close again, still hardly able to believe he held the love of his life in his arms. "When I consider I might never have met you if not for the war, if not for befriending Gilbert onboard the *Comfort*, if not for coming to Hot Springs—"

"I would now be a miserable spinster still keeping the books for my father's pottery factory instead of married to the kindest, handsomest, most wonderful man in the world."

Samuel cast her a doubtful frown. "You're certain you and Gilbert—"

"Yes, Sam, absolutely certain." Her eyes softened. "I've told you before, there will always be a tender place in my heart for Gilbert. I was in love with the man I *imagined* my childhood friend would grow up to become. Neither of us could have predicted how life would change us."

"You mean the war." Memories Samuel would never be entirely free of brought a tightness to his throat.

"Darling, darling . . ." Cupping his cheek, Annemarie stretched up to press warm lips against his cheek. "Not today. Promise me."

Barring the door of his mind against the darkness, Samuel kissed her forehead. His glance shifted to the open doorway, where a blue, blue sky shone bright overhead. A lightness invaded him, buoyed him, swelled until he thought his chest would burst. As long as he had Annemarie by his side, as long as he walked in the light of God's love and forgiveness, the clouds of war would remain but a distant memory.

Discussion Questions

1. As the story opens, Annemarie is happy and relieved to learn the war is over, but she can't help fearing the war has severely changed the man she loves. Has a traumatic life event affected you or someone you care about? What changes did you notice? What support was offered?

2. Annemarie is at odds with her father over her desire to create more artistic ceramic pieces than what her father manufactures. How do you see human creativity and artistry in the light of God as Creator? How do you express your own creativity?

3. During their journey home, Samuel and Gilbert form a deep bond of friendship. What do they have in common? How are they different? Do you have a "friend who sticks closer than a brother"?

4. When Annemarie is troubled, she finds escape at the pottery wheel. What activities do you find comforting when you wrestle with a difficult issue? Do you ever find that distracting activity allows you to focus more fully on God?

5. Gilbert's war wounds make him feel less than a man, and he fears Annemarie's pity more than anything. Have you experienced a time when pride or self-doubt kept you from sharing your struggles with others? What was the result?

6. Though Samuel is attracted to Annemarie, he is determined to keep her and Gilbert together. What do you think of his motives? Can you recall a situation where you sacrificed your own desires in order to protect the interests of someone you cared about?

7. In the early twentieth century, a woman's place was thought to be in the home, but when American men

left to serve in the Great War, the role of women in the workplace began to change. Compare Annemarie, Mrs. Ballard, and Mary McClarney, three very different women.

8. Gilbert's addictions cause increasing problems in his life. What can his struggles teach us about where to turn in times of pain and disappointment?

9. Samuel's faith was shaken badly by what happened on the battlefield, and after lashing out at God, he feared he'd committed the unforgivable sin. What do you think God does with our anger and doubts? Is anyone truly beyond redemption?

10. World War I ushered in the term *shell shock*, and soldiers diagnosed with the problem were considered "weak." Today the military calls it *combat and operational stress reaction* (COSR), defined as "expected and predictable emotional, intellectual, physical, and/or behavioral reactions from exposure to stressful event(s)." How have attitudes and treatments evolved over the past century in regard to war's effects on the human psyche?

11. As Samuel's memories return, he feels he must make amends for the death of Private Braswell and accept whatever consequences the military deems right. If we believe Jesus died for our sins and God has forgiven us, is it still important or necessary to make atonement to people we have wronged? Why or why not?

12. "Happily ever after" only happens in fairy tales. What kind of future do you imagine for Samuel and Annemarie? For Gilbert and Mary? What kinds of problems and struggles should they anticipate? Based on all they have already been through, how do you think they would cope?

We hope you enjoyed *When the Clouds Roll By* and that you will continue to read Myra's Till We Meet Again series. Here's an excerpt from the next book of the series, *Whisper Goodbye*.

Whisper Goodbye

1

Hot Springs, Arkansas
Saturday, June 14, 1919

Searing sunlight assaulted Gilbert Ballard's burning eyes. He rubbed them furiously, cursing both the brightness and his battered heart for the wetness sliding down his face. Stupid to have stayed this long. Stupid to have come at all.

But no. He *had* to see for himself, had to be convinced beyond question the girl he'd once pledged his heart to—the girl whose heart he'd broken—was utterly beyond reach.

Annemarie Kendall. Now Mrs. Samuel Vickary. And all because of Gilbert's own pride. His foolishness. His arrogant, self-serving, pain-induced idiocy.

Groaning, he drew his gaze away from the happy couple beaming from the steps of Ouachita Fellowship Church and concealed himself behind the glossy leaves of a magnolia tree. A physical craving rolled through him, every nerve screaming for the deliverance one morphine tablet could bring. Not an option, though. He'd sworn off the stuff after promising Mary he'd kick the vile addiction.

He'd gladly settle for a stiff drink instead. Although how much longer he could count on alcohol's availability remained to be seen. With hard liquor already in short supply thanks to wartime bans on production and sales, on July 1 the Wartime Prohibition Act would shut down all bars and saloons, denying him even the solace of a frothy mug of beer.

"Drinkin' yourself into oblivion's no less a sin than losin' your soul to drugs, Gilbert Ballard." Sweet Mary McClarney's chiding tone sang through his brain like the voice of reason it was.

And he would listen. With God's help, at least this once, he would listen.

He climbed into his blue Cole Eight Roadster and drove away before anyone at the church across the street could notice him. Somehow, some way, he had to purge Annemarie Kendall— Annemarie *Vickary*—from his heart once and for all.

He sped through town, dust flying as he left the paved streets for rougher roads. If he could drive far enough, fast enough, he might outpace the unrelenting emptiness that had haunted him since the war. Those weeks lying in a French field hospital, then the voyage home on the *U.S.S. Comfort*, had given him plenty of time to think. Plenty of time to conclude he'd never be the husband Annemarie deserved, to vow he would not consign the woman he loved to marriage to a cripple.

As if to spite him, the stump of his left leg began to throb. Slowing the car, he reached down to massage his thigh. The fit of his newest prosthesis had eliminated the worst of the discomfort, but it didn't stop the recurring phantom leg pain. Sometimes invisible flames tortured his nonexistent foot. Other times he imagined a thousand needles stabbing his calf. Today, it felt as though giant pincers were squeezing the entire length of his leg.

He swung the steering wheel hard to the right and jammed his foot on the brake pedal. The roadster lurched to a stop at the side of the road, while the grit raised by his skidding tires swirled through the open windows, nearly choking him. Stifling a spate of coughs, he patted his shirtfront, fumbled through his trouser pockets, felt along the underside of the automobile seat. *Just one pill . . . one pill . . .*

Sweat broke out on his forehead. He lifted trembling fists to his temples. How many weeks had he been off the morphine now, and yet his body *still* betrayed him!

Mary. He needed Mary.

By force of will, he steadied himself enough to get the automobile turned around and aimed back toward Hot Springs. Mary would be at the hospital now. He pictured his dimpled Irish lass's flame-red riot of curls spilling from her nurse's cap as she made her rounds. If he could wheedle a few minutes alone with her, lose himself to her tender touch, she'd drive the demons away.

She was the only one who could.

✐

"Time for your medication, Corporal Donovan." Mary McClarney filled a water glass and handed it to the frail young soldier in the bed. As he swallowed the pills, she frowned to herself at his sallow complexion. Possible liver involvement? Something the doctor should follow up on.

With a thankful nod, the corporal handed her the empty glass. "You're an angel of mercy, Nurse McClarney."

"Aye, and don't be forgettin' it." Mary winked as she made a notation on the corporal's chart.

"Will Dr. Russ be making rounds soon?" The soldier shifted, one hand pressed to his abdomen. "I wanted to ask him why I've still got this pain in my side."

"Postsurgical soreness is to be expected." She lifted his pajama top and gently peeled back the dressing where a bowel obstruction had been repaired earlier in the week. "Your incision looks good, though—healing nicely."

"Yeah, but . . . I don't feel so well. Kinda nauseous, you know?"

"I'll see what we can find to calm your stomach." With a sympathetic smile, Mary glanced at the watch pinned to her smock. "However, I fear the good doctor may be a tad late this afternoon."

"Nearly forgot—Chaplain Vickary's wedding." Corporal Donovan gave a weak chuckle. "The padre's sure been floating on air lately."

"Indeed. Everyone on staff is happy for him." Perhaps Mary most of all—if only she dared hope the chaplain's marriage to Annemarie Kendall meant the end of Gilbert's obsession with his former fiancée.

Mary sent an orderly to fetch warm tea and soda crackers for the corporal, then gave him a reassuring pat on the arm before continuing her rounds. Best to keep busy. Best not to think about Gilbert or wonder how this day affected him.

As if she could keep from wondering! Even as she went about her nursing duties with all the necessary attention to detail, an invisible force tugged at her spirit, dividing her will, drawing away pieces of her heart in an unrelenting search for Gilbert, always Gilbert.

"Miss McClarney." The snapping tone of Mrs. Daley, chief nurse at the Hot Springs Army and Navy Hospital, glued Mary's shoes to the floor.

"Yes, ma'am?" Gripping the medicine tray she carried, Mary inhaled slowly between pursed lips and turned to face the gray-haired tyrant. What now? Had Mary failed to properly dispose of a soiled bandage? Left a syringe uncapped? Overlooked a vital notation on a patient's chart?

Mrs. Daley dropped a folded sheet of paper on Mary's tray. "A message for you from Reception. Please don't make me remind you to keep your personal affairs separate from hospital work."

"Yes, ma'am." Mary curtsied before she could stop herself, although it seemed only fitting, considering Mrs. Daley's imperious nature.

The woman gave Mary an odd look before pivoting on her heel and marching away.

Anxious to learn who'd sent the message, Mary hurried into the work area behind the nurses' station and deposited her tray. *Please, Lord, don't let it be about Mum.* Mary's mother's chronic bronchitis often left her weak and short of breath. If she'd taken a turn for the worse . . .

Fingers trembling, Mary unfolded the slip of paper.

Meet me at the oak tree. Please.

No signature. Not so much as the sender's initials. Only seven simple words rendered in the manly scrawl that never failed to set her insides aquiver.

Her limbs thrummed with the compulsion to rush from the hospital and straight to Gilbert's side. In every stroke of the pen, she sensed his need, his longing, his pain. She should have expected today, of all days, he'd need her most of all. She should be glad of anything that drove him into her arms.

If only it were anything but his despair over losing Annemarie.

Well. With more than an hour left on her shift, she couldn't exactly march out of the ward and hope to escape the wrath of Mrs. Daley. She certainly wasn't of a mind to risk her career— her livelihood—at the whim of a dark-eyed rogue who'd drop her in a moment if there were a ghost of a chance he could reclaim his lost love. Let Gilbert Ballard stew in his own juices for a while longer, and maybe one of these days he'd realize Mary McClarney was not a woman to be trifled with.

She'd just convinced herself to ignore Gilbert's pull on her heart and go on about her work when footsteps sounded behind her. Certain it was Mrs. Daley come to chide her for shirking her duties, she tried to look busy sorting medicine vials and hypodermics.

"Ah, Miss McClarney. Just the person I was looking for."

She recognized the familiar baritone of the kindly Dr. Russ, and relief swept through her. Turning, she stifled a surprised gasp to see the doctor was now beardless—and, dare she say, even more handsome than before. She offered the tall man a shy smile. "Back from the wedding festivities already, sir?"

"Duty calls. I stayed long enough to see the happy couple off in style." The doctor laid a chart on the counter between them and ran his finger down the page. His breath smelled faintly of strawberries. "You were the last to check on Corporal Donovan, I see."

"Yes, I gave him his three o'clock pills on schedule." Mary bit her lip. "Is there a problem, Doctor?"

"I hope not." Dr. Russ stroked his chin, looking almost surprised to find no facial hair beneath his fingers. He must have shaved only this morning, no doubt a concession to his best man duties. "You noted he's still having abdominal pain. Did you check his surgical incision?"

"Perfectly fine and healing nicely."

The doctor glanced again at the chart. "Your notes also say he looks jaundiced. When did you first make that observation?"

Mary flicked her gaze sideways as she weighed her answer. "I'd have to say it's been a gradual thing, sir. Yesterday I thought it might only be the light, but this afternoon the yellow tinge to his skin and eyes seemed more pronounced. I knew you'd want to be informed."

"Good work, Miss McClarney." Dr. Russ's eyes twinkled with an approving smile. "Your sharp eye might well have saved Corporal Donovan's life."

"Really, sir?" Mary's face warmed. She stood a little taller. "What do you suspect?"

"Not sure yet, but if his liver is failing, the sooner we start appropriate treatment, the better his chances." The doctor's jaw flexed as he perused the chart. He glanced at Mary. "Are you in the middle of anything pressing?"

"Well, I . . ." Mary looked away, guilt tightening her chest as she crumpled Gilbert's note and stuffed it into her pocket. Hadn't she already made up her mind on that score? She cleared her throat. "Sir, if you'd give me five minutes to finish putting away these supplies—"

"Perfect. While you do that, I'll make a list of medical conditions I'd like you to research for me."

"Research? You want *me* to . . ."

The doctor was already scribbling on the back of a wrinkled envelope—by the looks of it, from a wedding invitation. "Go to my office and look through my medical reference books. You'll find pen and paper in the desk."

A thrill of anticipation sped Mary's movements as she emptied her supply tray. Taking Dr. Russ's list, she marched past the nurses' station, barely acknowledging her friend Lois's confused stare.

But she couldn't ignore Mrs. Daley's stern glare when the wiry chief nurse blocked her path. "Exactly where are you off to in such a hurry, Miss McClarney? I certainly hope that cryptic message you received wasn't your lover summoning you to another tryst."

She should have known Mrs. Daley couldn't resist peeking at Gilbert's note. Still, the woman's accusation cut deep—and far too close to the truth. Mary squeezed her eyes shut briefly while she formed a careful reply. "Lieutenant Ballard is *not* my lover." And certainly not in the tawdry sense Mrs. Daley's tone implied. "I assure you, ma'am, I've the utmost respect for hospital policy and would never jeopardize my position in the Army Nurse Corps."

"I sincerely hope that is true, young lady." The woman hiked her chin. "Now, hadn't you best get back to work? I'm sure you have plenty to do right here on the ward."

Mary couldn't resist a haughty look of her own. "As a matter of fact, I'm off on an urgent errand for Dr. Russ. A patient's life could be at stake."

That silenced the old biddy. Lightness returning to her step, Mary brushed past Mrs. Daley and strode to the exit. She marched along the connecting breezeway and into the elegant, Swiss chalet–style administration building, where she finally reached Dr. Russ's office on an upper floor.

Sometime later she was grateful to realize during the time she spent researching diseases of the liver, thoughts of Gilbert hadn't interrupted even once.

☙❦

Traffic sounds and exhaust fumes wafted up the hill between the bathhouses lining Central Avenue. Propped against a spreading oak tree within sight of the Army and Navy Hospital wing where Mary worked, Gilbert mopped his brow with a handkerchief already damp enough to wring out. He checked his watch. Again. Five minutes more, and he'd have waited a full hour. Did Mary purposely keep him cooling his heels, or couldn't she escape the old hag of a chief nurse?

Obviously, Mary wasn't coming. If he had a lick of sense, he'd march—make that *limp*—to his car and go home.

Someone called his name just as he reached the long flight of steps leading to where he'd parked his roadster on Reserve Avenue. Leaning on his cane, he turned.

A young, dark-haired nurse waved from the path as she hurried toward him. "Wait, Lieutenant, please!"

She looked familiar . . . a colleague of Mary's, perhaps? He racked his brain for a name but came up empty. Which wouldn't surprise him, even if he'd known her for ages. Ever since the whizzbang found him at the Marne, he did well to remember his own name.

White skirts billowing, the nurse nearly mowed him down in her rush to catch up. She caught his wrist and clambered for breath. "I'm . . . sorry . . . didn't want you to . . . get away."

"Not likely, considering the death grip you have on my arm." He stared pointedly at her white-knuckled hand.

With an embarrassed gasp she released him. "You must think I'm crazy." Tucking strands of nut-brown hair into her bun, she gave a nervous chuckle. "See, I was just getting off work when I noticed you under the tree. I figured you must be waiting for Mary."

Gilbert hesitated, his jaw shifting to one side. This woman could very well be one of Mrs. Daley's spies.

"You don't remember me, do you?" The young nurse smiled coyly. "I'm Lois Underwood. Mary's friend."

"Lois. Of course." He only wished he could honestly say he remembered her.

"Anyway, when I saw you out here, waiting just forever on this hot summer day, I felt awful for you." Lois dropped her voice. "I guess Mary didn't tell you she's doing special research work for Dr. Russ."

Gilbert bristled at the name. Army surgeon Donald Russ had been Gilbert's physician aboard the *Comfort*, then was later transferred to the Hot Springs Army and Navy Hospital.

Rather too conveniently for Gilbert's taste, considering the role the man had played in keeping Gilbert and Annemarie apart.

With a silent groan, he edged sideways, forehead pressed into his palm. When would he get it through his thick skull? The *only* person responsible for losing Annemarie to Samuel was Gilbert himself.

"Are you all right, Lieutenant?"

He lowered his hand to see Lois Underwood staring up at him with a worried frown. "I'm fine. And you can drop the 'Lieutenant.' The Army mustered me out months ago."

"Honorable discharge. I know. You're a hero, Lieuten—"

"Stop, will you?" With an apologetic sigh, he added, "Just call me Gilbert. Please."

"Really? Well, thanks!" Lois beamed as if he'd just presented her with the Medal of Honor. "I guess that means we're friends, right?"

"Certainly. Any friend of Mary's . . ." An automobile horn tooted at the intersection below, reminding Gilbert he just wanted to go home. Except now, he had this image in his head of Mary and Dr. Russ, the two of them ensconced in his cozy little office—doing *research*.

He hammered down the surge of jealousy threatening to blow the top of his head off. The green-eyed monster had destroyed his life once before. He wouldn't let it win twice. "Look, Miss . . ." Blanking again. Not good.

"Lois. Lois Underwood. Like the typewriter. No relation, of course." Her laugh jangled like a tin can filled with marbles.

"Lois. Yes. Thanks for your concern. I'm just on my way home, if you don't mind." Once again, he started for the steps.

And once again, Lois Underwood's strident call drew him up short. "Hey, you wouldn't want to give a girl a ride, would you? I need to pick up some things downtown, and it's an awful hot day for walking."

Gilbert drove the tip of his cane into the top step. Shooting her a rakish grin that belied his annoyance, he motioned for Lois to join him. "Where can I drop you, Miss Underwood?"

"Oh, thanks! Thanks loads!" She scurried to his side and linked her arm through his as they proceeded down the steps. "And you can call me Lois. I mean, since we're friends now."

Reaching the street, he held the passenger door of his roadster while she climbed in, tucking the skirt of her nurse's uniform around her legs. "What a fancy automobile! Must have cost you an arm and a le—" She clamped a hand to her mouth. "I'm sorry. I didn't mean—"

"What's an arm and a leg between friends?" Gilbert winked and clinked the end of his cane against his prosthesis before circling around to the driver's side.

Truth be told, if Mary wouldn't deign to interrupt her *research* to respond to his urgent plea, then delivering the vivacious, if rather cloying, Miss Underwood to her destination might distract him just as effectively from the day's events.

As long as the route didn't take them past Ouachita Fellowship Church.